GRAND *love*

GRAND LOVE

JC HAWKE

IVY ROSE PUBLISHING LTD

Dedication

To love,
For your persistence, understanding, and lessons.
Mason & Nina took us both on a journey, one that many would've
probably given up on.
Thank you for never giving up and for sharing this story with me.

P.S. You'll always win.

PROLOGUE

Mase

THE SMELL OF STALE SMOKE WAKES ME.

My eyes peel open, and I wince at the lights that temporarily blind me. I close them again and swallow. My mouth is scratchy and dry, and as I push myself up into a seated position, my body gets pelted by a wave of pain. I feel battered, and that smell, it's disgusting.

Looking around the room, I notice I'm not at home. I'm in a hotel room, and not one I'm familiar with. It's small and dated, with curtains that hang half off the runners. The window is thrown open and I get another hit of the cigarette smoke that wafts in with the breeze.

How the fuck did I get here? I was at the club with Charlie... "Fuck!"

My palms connect with the carpeted floor, and I pull myself up and to my feet, setting the room spinning.

Patting my pockets, I find my phone and see that I have a

ton of missed calls. Hundreds of missed calls. "What the fuck?"

Scarlet is at the top, and I call her first, hoping she can come to get me. I move to the door while checking I have my wallet and keys in my pockets.

"Mason! What the fuck?" she whisper-shouts down the phone.

"Scar, I'm on my way home. Is Nina pissed? I don't know what happened."

"Are you kidding me?"

I jog down the steps and towards the exit, waiting until I'm clear of the building before telling her, "No, I just woke up in some dingy hotel. The boys must have left me."

"Elliot said—Fuck, Mason, we're at the hospital. It's Nina."

I pause on the sidewalk, my heart in my throat as my world comes to a screeching halt. "What?"

"She's at Rosemadden, I can't tell you why, but you need to get here. Now."

"She's at the hospital?" I frown, my head pounding.

"Yes! Where are you, I will send Vinny?"

WE PUSH through the double doors to the ward Vinny led me to and I'm instantly jolted back three steps. Elliot's hand flattens on my shoulder and forces me into the corridor.

"The fuck, Montgomery!" I roar.

His chest heaves as he stands, hands on his hips, shaking his head. "You stupid fucking" —his palms connect with my chest sending me to the floor when I lose my footing—"prick!"

I tilt my head to the side as I look up at him, my eyes wild. "What the hell are you doing?"

I know he wouldn't get this wound up over nothing, and that only makes my stomach twist tighter. Something's wrong.

"You've fucked it," he spits.

"What?" I pull myself up, looking down the corridor at the few people who are staring. "Where's Nina?"

He grabs two handfuls of my shirt in his fists and crowds me. My annoyance at him snaps, and I shrug him off. "Stop goddamn doing that!"

"You're not seeing her," he tells me, adamant, making me frown. "Go home."

"Don't be so ridiculous." I go to step past him, and he blocks me. "Elliot, get out of the way."

He shakes his head, his eyes full of something heated that burns a lifetime of understanding in seconds.

"Ell, get out of my way. Now," I bite out, my body bristling with anger. I just need to get to her.

"Fuck you."

I rear my fist back and swipe it through his jaw, knocking him back and through the double doors.

"Jesus Christ!" someone gasps.

"Mason!" Scarlet shouts. She rushes to me while Charlie stalks past me and over to Elliot. I look down at him as he rises to his feet, stretching out his neck.

I stand, body trembling as I fight to keep the scraps of my control.

"Somebody tell me what the fuck is going on?" I snap, panic taking over.

No one says a word, they just look between one another.

"Where is she?!" I demand, my voice untamed.

"I don't think you should go in right now, Mason," Megan tells me, and I eye the door at her back.

"What on earth is going on?" a woman asks, stepping out of a small office. "You were warned about the noise."

"Where is she?" I ask, barely recognising my own voice. "My girlfriend. Nina Anderson, she's here. Where?"

She turns to face me, looking at the side of my forehead before narrowing her eyes. "She isn't taking visitors right now."

Why are they doing this? What is wrong with her? "Please!" I beg.

She shakes her head. "You all need to go home now, you've been here all night and—"

I barge past Megan, and she grabs my arm. "Mase!"

"Get off!" I push her from me and push open the door, falling through and into the room. Nina is sat up in bed, the sheets clutched tight in her hands.

I breathe a sigh of relief, my eyes burning as I look at her. She's okay. "Nina."

"You cannot be in here; she needs to rest," the nurse calls from my back.

I frown and bring my eyes back to Nina but she dips her head, hiding from me.

It cuts me in two.

"He can stay," she says after a beat.

The nurse moves toward her, lifting her arm and quickly taking her blood pressure.

I step forward—

"You!" My head snaps around to Lucy, she stalks towards me until she is stood before me, her hand connects with my face before I can even see it coming.

"What the fuck!" I roar, grasping my face as I stare incredulously at her.

"Out! All of you. How dare you." The nurse points at the door in pure frustration.

"You will never! Never! Hurt her again," Lucy grinds out, wiping her tears and stepping in front of Nina.

"What the hell is going on?" I ask, trying to look past her at Nina.

"Can you give us a minute?" Nina says. "I promise I will keep calm."

I struggle to hear her, and my brows drop low as I catch her sad face.

The nurse gives me a death stare. "You have a minute. If I can hear you from out there, you are out. The lot of you. Never in my forty-four years have I seen anything like it!" She leaves the room and Lucy follows her, not looking at me as she passes.

I rush to Nina's side. "What happened? Scar wouldn't tell me, she said she couldn't." I grasp her hand and she rips it away. "Baby, I'm sorry. I woke up in a hotel. I cut my head. I think I fell. I don't know what happened last night."

Her lip trembles, then she pulls something from under her blanket, placing it between us on the bed. She turns her head away from me.

I lift the photo, not believing my eyes. A baby, outlined in the small image. "You're pregnant?" I ask in disbelief before a smile splits my face. "I... fuck. I'm the dad? We are pregnant?"

"No, I am pregnant. And of course, it's yours."

"Oh my god." I laugh, staring at the image in wonder. She's pregnant. "And you're okay?" I go to take her hand again, but she pulls it away. It has my heart hammering in my chest. Something is wrong. "The baby?"

"Healthy."

Leaning over, she pulls a bag from the end of the bed, reaching in and pulling out an envelope. She thrusts it into my chest. "Here. Congratulations."

I pull out the contents and find four images. Bile rises in my throat as I take in the woman, legs spread and dancing on my lap, her lips mere inches from mine. "What? I don't understand. This isn't me."

"Don't!" she screams, making my entire body flinch and my body run hot. "Don't you fucking dare lie to me!"

"I'm not. Nina, this isn't me." I shake the images in my hand.

What the fuck!

"Get out," she says, barely audible.

Panic floors me, threatening to take me *all* the way down. "No!"

"Get out! Get out of my life and stay the hell away from me. I hate you! I hate you so much it hurts because you have me now. You have me trapped for life, and I can't leave. I hate you, Mason Lowell, with everything inside me."

My throat burns with her words. She doesn't mean that. "Don't say that. Let me fix this. This isn't real."

"Yes, it fucking is, Mason! It's real. She is real. That *is* you."

I shake my head, confused. What happened last night? "I don't understand. Give me a chance to figure this out, and I can explain."

"Explain what? How you fucked a prostitute?" My chest cracks. "Because if the picture wasn't clear enough, the fact you never came home last night is explanation enough. Done! I am done!" Tears line her face and I feel my own start to fall. "A stripper? You might as well have fucked my mother."

"No." I shake my head vehemently. "I didn't sleep with anyone. I woke alone." I try to hold her, but she shoves me off. "Stop! Please, I don't want to upset you. Nina. You can't leave me again."

She lifts her eyes to look at me, confusion and hurt washing out her beautiful face. "Nina, we are having a baby. Let me figure this out," I beg.

"No." She holds my eyes, defiant. Her tears flow and all I want to do is reach out and rid them. "Believe me when I tell you, this is it. I can't do this anymore." She tears two scan photos free and slaps them to my chest again. "Get out."

No. "I didn't do this. I didn't do anything."

"Leave!" she sobs, and it has me snapping. She can't do this. Why is she doing this?

"Walk away from me now, Nina, without giving me a chance to explain, and I won't ever forgive you for it. I won't keep begging on my knees to keep you."

My nostrils flare as I fight to keep my chin from trembling.

"You think this is me leaving you? You ended this the minute her lips touched yours. Now, leave." I watch as she swallows, her brows dipping low. "Please, just go."

"That's it. We're done?" I wipe at my face, feeling utterly hopeless.

"Yes."

And angry. So fucking angry.

My entire body shakes as my world crumbles around me.

She's hurting. I know how much this will hurt her.

I attentively lean in, keeping my focus on her tear-lined cheek which is forced away from me. I kiss her forehead. "You were everything I wanted and more. I promise you were enough."

You were enough, Pix.

I leave the room and every single set of eyes in the corridor fall on me. Silence. Not one word, as I walk past them and through the double doors.

"Lowell!" Elliot eventually calls.

I snigger and face him. He stands in the doorway, chewing at his bottom lip as he contemplates what to say.

I turn and keep on walking.

1

Nina

One Year Later

"Da Da Da."

Small hands grip my cheek, pinching tight until my eyes snap open. A grin spreads wide across my baby boy's chubby cheeks and he begins bouncing his bottom on the mattress excitedly. I smile wide along with him.

My beautiful boy sleeps in his cot most nights—I try to keep a routine. But sometimes, just before the day gives way to the dawn and sleep hasn't come, I find myself reaching for him.

"Mummy isn't ready to get up yet, baby."

"Da Da Da Da."

"Mum Mum Mum Mum. Learn it already." I smile, laying him alongside me, letting him nestle into my chest.

"There's nothing left, my precious boy."

He couldn't take to breastfeeding as a newborn, which

made the first month hell on earth. Some days, he would scream the house down until we'd get the right position, and it was never the same from one feed to the next. It made me feel like a failure. Like I wasn't doing it right. We're now seven months in and my milk has all but dried up.

My hand smooths through his dark brown hair, and he lifts his still sleepy eyes to me, peeping through his long lashes. "Good morning, baby." I plant a soft kiss on his head and close my eyes, enjoying the peace and contentment he brings me.

"Mummy has work today," I whisper softly into his hair. "You get to spend the day with Daddy." My lip tips up as my words settle around us. I'm happy that he will get to see Mason today. If there is anything my boy loves more than me, it's his dad.

And maybe my boobs.

Co-parenting with a person you hold so much resentment for should probably be difficult, but it's been easier than I expected. At first it was hard. The sleepless nights and my hormones being up and down from one day to the next made things tough, and no one tells you about the days that follow after having a baby or the initial haze that is so easily forgotten. I think it was day three when it hit, the tears I'd hide from everyone because if they asked, I wouldn't have a reason for them. I had no idea what was wrong but I felt completely lost. I thought I was crazy. I thought I was a bad mum for feeling the way I did.

The support from our families is what makes everything possible. I know that, and I'm forever indebted to them for the time they give up for us. I know they wouldn't have it any other way, though. The little monkey has them all wrapped around his finger.

His breathing evens out into soft puffs against my chest and I know he's dropped off to sleep. It's our thing. Every morning he wakes and snuggles into me, and every morning he drifts straight back off to sleep not five minutes later. You wouldn't think he had just slept for ten hours straight.

Sliding my arm out from under him, I stand and stretch, watching as he lies on the comforter, completely sated. He's the most precious thing on earth to me. I still can't believe I made him.

Reluctantly, I lift him from the bed, careful not to wake him as I place him in his cot. I need a quick shower before I leave for work.

I haven't danced since I fell pregnant, and I'm unsure why because I miss it terribly. It's who I always was, but it's not who I am right now. Dancing was all I had growing up and then I had my beautiful baby boy, and he became the centre of my world. Maybe one day I will go back to it, but right now it doesn't feel like something I can dedicate my time to wholeheartedly.

Dance is so much more than just dancing, it's an expression of the soul and sometimes that can be draining.

Lucy is in the kitchen when I finish in the shower. She comes over most days to help me where she can. Especially on the two days I work. Getting a baby up, bathed, dressed, and fed all before seven thirty isn't an impossible task, but another pair of hands always helps.

"Good morning, sunshine," she sings, her hands deep in the sink as she washes the baby bottle from last night.

We had to alternate between the bottle and breast a lot

because of our situation, and although it bothered me that I couldn't feed exclusively and that now I can't get a supply at all, I know this is the only way.

"You're extra chirpy this morning." I scrunch my nose at her as I move to the island, taking the steaming mug of coffee she has laid out for me. She is dressed in a black skirt and white blouse. She looks sexy. She looks sexed. "Ugh, you got laid."

"Uh-huh." She points the baby bottle brush at me, soap suds dripping to the floor. "You should try it sometime."

"I don't think anyone will want this train wreck. I have extra... bits now."

"You make that sound truly awful."

"You know what I mean."

She smiles over her shoulder at me. "My boy must be sleeping?"

Friends who love your children as much as you do, unconditionally, not because they should or want to, just because they do—that's special.

"Yep, out like a light... Ted or Miller?" I ask, smirking behind my coffee cup.

"Miller," she says after a beat.

I knew it! "Hmmm, that's what? Your fifth date?"

"I wouldn't call it a date."

"No?"

"Nope, more like... like..."

"Sex," I finish for her.

"Yeah." She chuckles. "Just really great sex."

"Good for you, Luce."

It shouldn't surprise me that she has already slept with Miller, but it does. She's different these days—more relaxed.

"You heading out in a minute? You're going to be late," she says.

But still a control freak.

"Yes, if I must. What time are you meeting Mason?" I ask.

"Ten. He needs to pop into the office first. I told him I would meet him there."

"Perfect, the bag is packed and in the bedroom," I tell her, pulling on my cardigan and picking up my things.

She gives me a tight smile, and I know she wants to say something. "He asked about Joey again on Friday."

"Right?" I roll my eyes and turn to walk towards the door.

"Nina—"

"Luce. Don't. Just leave it, please."

She flicks her wrist, waving me off, and I know she isn't mad at me. "El will be dropping off tonight. I have to help Jean down in the Mayfair shop." She turns and starts walking towards my lounge.

"Luce." She turns to face me. "Thank you."

She nods her head once; she knows how much I appreciate her. "Get out of here, wench."

I started working at The Earl Marks Hotel a little over a month ago. So far, I have managed to fly under the manager's radar. Pretty impressive for someone who has no idea what they are doing. I had training—they showed me everything I needed to know to man the main desk. Yet for the life of me, I cannot figure it out. Luckily, I'm never on my own, and when I can, I volunteer to help behind the scenes. It's only two days a week, but it's enough to contribute towards my apartment and bills.

I have support from Mason, and he chose from a list of apartments that Charlie and Vinny picked out for us. I had to put my pride aside and allow it, and in hindsight, I'm glad I did. I never would have managed in my one-bedroom apartment with a newborn baby. You couldn't swing a cat in that place.

We live in an apartment in Pimlico. It's compact and has two bedrooms but the lounge and kitchen are spacious and allow a safe living space for us both. It wasn't what I wanted. I always thought I'd have a more homely place away from the busy city when I eventually had children, but that wasn't an option with the number of people helping us on a daily basis. It worked for me to live close to the city centre, and if that meant swallowing my pride and accepting a little help, then I knew I had to do it. Not just for me, but for my son.

I can cover the majority of my rent with the money I make from my monthly wage which is a relief, but the bills and food, reluctantly, I have to take from the money Mason gives me.

We live frugally, but comfortably.

Vinny is waiting at the curb when I get to the bottom of my building's steps. He always picks me up to take me to and from work. I start early and finish late. By the time I hit month eight of my pregnancy, I gave up being the hero and just got in the car. It was the easier option.

As much as I know Vinny cares, I also know ferrying me around London isn't his doing. But to complain and draw attention to it means I have to face *him,* and I've done just fine avoiding him this far.

"'Morning, Vin!" I smile, sliding into the front seat and kissing him on the cheek.

"You're going to be late." He scoffs, pulling out into traffic.

The sun is just coming up, peeking through the skyscrapers and beaming in through the windscreen, temporarily blinding me.

I flip down my visor. "You wouldn't let me be late," I tell him.

"Put your belt on, love," he says, a small smile tugging at his top lip. "How is the little man this morning? He seemed fussy on Sunday. His teeth seem to be bothering him."

"He slept right through. But I think you're right, his bottom two are cutting through. I just hope they don't take too much longer. For his sake."

"Me too. I was hoping to take him out for the day on Thursday; you're working, and Mason has a meeting. He said it was fine, but I thought I'd ask first."

"You never need to ask permission to spend time with my son, Vinny," I tell him, watching as his features warm at my words.

"Well, that's settled then." He jigs in his seat, almost as if he's excited, and I turn to look out the window to save him the embarrassment of catching him.

WORK IS SLOW. We are so high-end that everyone moves at a snail's pace. You wouldn't catch someone bolting around the corridors at The Earl Marks. Nope. It's caviar and suit jackets at breakfast. Well, maybe not caviar for breakfast, but it's all very well-to-do business people here on conferences or work trips. That being said, I am paid extremely well here. Especially as my CV didn't have a lot going for me. The pay and the extravagant tips make it worth my while. I learned to smile extra wide when I got my first fifty-pound tip for holding open a door.

Ridiculous.

Ashley, my work colleague, is processing a guest's invoice and I am sitting waiting to call the valet for the guest. It's a talent to get it here right on time, and so far, I have failed miserably. My hands sweat as I grip the phone tight, my eyes glued on his credit card in his hand, waiting for the perfect moment to strike.

He pauses on the way to the card machine, and I lift my eyes to meet his. His dark brows are pulled in as he watches me watch him.

I plaster a smile on my face and relax the phone in my hand. "Hi."

"Nina, could you check the delivery in the back office for me?" Ashley asks me, looking at me with a smirk.

"Sure." I roll back my chair and smooth down my skirt, then make my way to the office, glad to be off the front desk. I can't make a fool of myself back here.

Ashley strolls in a few minutes later.

"Why do you have to be such a creeper?" She chuckles, looking over at me from the door. "Leave that. I just needed you away from the guests."

"I'm not that bad!"

"You were staring all wide-eyed at him." She laughs. "He asked if you were okay when you left."

"Great, they think I'm crazy."

"Come on, we have a shit ton of emails to get through this morning."

By CHOICE, I made my shifts long. I work twenty-four hours over two days. It's hard work and I miss my boy so much, but I know he will appreciate it one day and it gives me adult conversation. I need it for my sanity just as much as the money.

Elliot is fast asleep on my sofa when I push through my apartment door. Toys surround his feet and *Mr Tumble* is on the TV.

"El? El." I place a hand on his shoulder, and he jolts awake, snorting.

"Huh."

I smile down at him. "Sorry, you were asleep."

He sits up, running his hand through his blond hair. "Shit, I was going to clean all this up. Sorry."

He begins tidying up the toys, but I stop him with my hand on his arm. "It's fine, I'll do it. Did he go down okay?"

He considers lying to me. I can tell by the way he pauses. "He didn't want to leave Mase. He cried until he had his bottle and dropped off at about seven. I think he was just exhausted from all the crying."

Shit. I drop my head.

"It's not your fault, Nina, it's just his age. He's becoming more aware."

"Yeah, I suppose. I feel like I'm keeping him from Mason. Maybe I need to let him put him to bed at home here when he isn't keeping him overnight."

Elliot stares at me wide eyed. "Yeah. Yeah, I actually think that would be amazing. For all of you," he adds.

They must think I am a complete bitch. I know I've been reluctant to see Mason, but I would never put my child through unnecessary pain for the sake of myself. I hope they know that.

"I always knew there would come a time that *this* wouldn't be enough."

"You're an incredible mother, Nina, don't beat yourself up over it." He leans in and kisses my head. "I'll see you in the week, okay?"

"El."

"Yup?" He spins on his heel to face me.

"Could you not mention this to Mason? Give me a couple days to get my head around it. See how I can make it work around our routine."

His jaw flexes and I see his Adam's apple bob in his throat. I shouldn't ask him to keep things from his best friend. "Sure," he says, before turning and leaving.

I clean the lounge and wash up the few dishes in the sink, then go to my bedroom where I drop into the rocking chair and watch my beautiful baby boy sleep, pushing all thoughts of his father back into the tiny compartment that's buried deep in the depths of my heart.

Mase

"ALL I'M SAYING IS that maybe things could be different now. It's been a year, Lowell."

I shake my head as Elliot continues his pointless attempt to get me to reach out to Nina. It's been seven months and apart from a handful of texts, there has been no communication.

I haven't seen her in seven months.

The mother of my child.

Nina.

At first, I didn't deal with her demands well. I'm not proud of the months that followed after she left me.

I became destructive and cold, sleeping with women like I did when I was in college—with no emotion or regard for them. Anything to fill the emptiness that came with being in the penthouse alone.

A hoard of voids that never got filled.

"Let it go already. It works for now," I tell him, eyeing the sheet in my hand. We have a board meeting this afternoon which Elliot is presenting. It used to be my job, however, when I turned up to work half cut and calling out the people who ride our asses in the company last Christmas, the decision was unanimous that Elliot take the reins.

I lost my way for a little while.

"She brought it up. It was her idea," he continues, and I roll my eyes.

I don't believe that for a second. "Well, then she can ask me about it herself, can't she?"

"You're both too stubborn for your own good."

"She is," I defend.

She did this.

He mumbles something under his breath that I don't catch.

"Here." I hand him the forecast for the next four months,

glad I don't have to deal with it anymore. "Don't miss the figures on Rosehill. Hector will only ask if you forget it."

He snatches the piece of paper from my hand, frowning as he reads through the figures.

"You good?" I smirk.

He ignores me, letting the sheet of paper fall to the table and then he turns to face me.

He's relentless.

"Just give her a text? Ask to drop off or pick up from hers?"

"You're wasting your time," Charlie says from the door. "She's too stubborn to let you back in so easily."

"Aldridge is right. Let her go, Montgomery. I have." I pat his back as I walk past him and towards Charlie at the door.

"You've let her go, my arse! Where are you fuckers going anyway?"

"Golfing," Charlie replies, grinning wide.

I watch as Elliot's frown only gets deeper.

"Elliot." He snaps his eyes to me. "Don't fuck it up." I nod to the paper on the desk and leave. Years of being in the office alone while Elliot did whatever the hell he wanted is finally paying off.

Rounding the reception area, I eye George. "Get Vinny for me and—"

"Already here." He points to my office.

"What?"

"He's in your office, right now. Came in like a flapping fairy." He pinches the bridge of his nose as if it's all too much. "I told him you were in Elliot's office and that I would help him, but he refused. Silly stubborn man."

Charlie looks just as perplexed as I'm sure I do.

Walking into my office, I see him sat at my desk, reading glasses on and focused on a file in front of him.

"Vin?"

He looks at me over the top of his glasses, looking older than his fifty years. It takes me back to my father sitting behind the very same desk. It seems like a lifetime ago now.

"I found her, Mase. The woman from that night. I finally found her."

My body goes rigid, unsure if I've heard him right.

"She ran out of money, by the looks of it. Scott found her in Stratford."

I snigger, completely shocked and lost for words. Fucking months of searching for the hooker who ruined my life, and she was under our nose this whole time?

"You have eyes on her?" I ask.

"Yeah. That's not all though." His face is grim as he rises to his feet. He removes his glasses, chucking them to the table in defeat as he brings me the piece of paper. "You should see this."

"Jerry Lockwood," I read aloud, studying the piece of paper.

Nina's biological father.

"*Her* dad."

I jerk my head up, confused. "Whose fucking dad?" I snap.

"Jasmine Lockwood." He pauses, his own anger evident as he swallows the lump in his throat. "She's Nina's half sister, Mason."

2

———————

Mase

"He has another kid?" I ask, dumbfounded.

"I looked deeper when I found Jasmine. He wasn't on her birth certificate, but she carried his name. I was curious as to why."

"And?" I ask.

"I couldn't find anything, just the same money trail back to him from the monthly payments. Just like Nina. I don't think there has ever been contact, at least not in the years I can trace. I looked into his child support payments and found four different accounts, one being Sarah Anderson and Jasmine's mother Veronica Mayer."

"Nina has more than one sibling?" I frown.

"Three, and they all get the same standard payment from Jerry's account."

"Hush money?" Fucking prick. "I want everything on him. Go deeper."

"Scott's already on it," he confirms, nodding his head at

me as I search the sheet of paper for Jasmine's address.

"What are you doing?" Charlie snaps. "You can't approach her without speaking to Nina first."

"The fuck I can't! She's the reason I share my child; I don't give a fuck who she is. I want answers."

"And if you ever want to get Nina back—which I presume you do, seeing as you're so hell-bent on finding out who 'set you up'."

"I don't want Nina back."

He ignores me, carrying on. "Then do you not think you should speak to her first, find out if she wants this dug up? This doesn't just affect you, Lowell."

"Charlie's right, Mason," Vinny agrees.

My face screws up in annoyance. "When did you pricks turn so soft? This woman fucked me over. I don't owe a damn thing to anyone."

"No, but you have a child now, mate, and we don't need another Marcus," Charlie states.

"I'm not going to fucking kill her, Charles! Jesus Christ! I just want to know who paid her." And take the bastard down. "Give me the address."

"I'll come with you," Charlie tells me.

"You sure? I don't want my hotshot lawyer having to cover my ass." I shake my head and snatch up the file from the desk, hoping the address will be in there.

He follows me to the door, giving me a shove in the back.

"Mason," Vinny calls and I turn, already knowing what he is going to say. "Don't do anything stupid."

"Yeah," I huff, slipping out the door.

As fucking if.

Nina

I'M FINISHING a feed when the doorbell rings. The click of the lock sounding a couple seconds later. "Joey?" I call out.

"Yeah, just me." He smiles as he comes into view, looking around the apartment briefly before his eyes come back to me. "Little man sleeping?"

"Yeah, just. Thank you for coming over, saves lugging the pram onto the overground."

"Anytime. You know that."

"I can't believe he's outgrown it so soon, I didn't think I'd need to upgrade until he was at least two."

"The boy sure can eat." Joey chuckles, pushing his dark hair back from his face. "Want me to get his seat?" he asks, nodding to my full arms.

"Yeah, please. It's in the cupboard."

Joey disappears around the corner, and I sit and smile to myself. "We are so lucky, baby boy," I coo.

"I had four paintings sell this week, all off the wall," Joey tells me excitedly as he walks back into the room with the car seat.

"That's incredible, Joey. I told you!" I whisper-shout, smoothing a hand over the soft hair that tickles my chest as I try to move without waking him.

Joey's photography has really started to take off. He has one year left at university and his placement has already offered him a job at the gallery when he finishes.

"Yeah, you did." He grins, placing the seat on the sofa. "Where's the bag?"

"In my room, can you grab it?"

"Sure thing." He heads off in the direction of the bedroom, and I smile. At first, I found him intrusive, borderline too much, and it is probably why I pushed him away when I first met him. But once you get to know Joey, you see that he only cares. Joey gives a shit. And you can't hate someone for caring too much.

"Here, I picked up the blue bunny too. Just in case. That everything?"

"Yep, think so."

AFTER FINDING a stroller in the first shop we went into, we decided to grab some lunch. Joey hasn't got much of a budget after his bills, so we settle for The Elm, both of us ordering a sandwich.

"How's your assignment coming along? Did you get the shots you wanted over the weekend?"

"Yeah, I did, actually. Thank you for the inspiration."

"Of course, any way I can help!" I smile, glad I could do something for him for a change.

"Did you get the email I sent last night? The studio listing."

My face drops and I lean in, fiddling with the blankets that drape over the car seat. If anyone has pushed my dancing (or lack of) since I stopped, it's Joey.

"Nina, you'll do what you want, I know that, but you should at least go look. It's cheap as chips on rent." He pauses, not wanting to annoy me with what comes out of his mouth next. "You have the money in the bank."

I shake my head, sitting back in my seat and crossing my arms over my chest. He's referring to the money Mason gives me, which I don't see as my own. Yes, I use a small percentage of the monthly payments for living expenses, but the rest is set aside for our son. It's not my money, and I don't want it. "Where would I find the time, Joe? I have a baby and I work now."

He gives me a look, tilting his head to the side, looking all boyish. "Come on, you suck at your job." He laughs.

"Piss off," I hiss quietly. "It pays the bills."

"So would your dancing," he tells me over the rim of his coffee cup. "You forget I've seen you dance. You're good."

"Have you heard from your brother?" I throw at him, getting more personal than I should.

"That's a low blow." He rolls his eyes, letting out a breath.

"Keep your nose out then."

He glares at me, his eyes pinched tight as he says, "Christmas."

"What?"

"I'm going home to see Jasper at Christmas. He wants to know more about Mum, and I know I need to face my shit and sort my life out." He pops a brow and I roll my eyes.

"Touché, asshole."

"I can come with you. If you decide to have a look," he says, referring to the studio.

"I'll think about it."

He smirks at me. "Good."

"Do you know what you're going to say to Jasper?" I ask, giving him a pitiful look.

"Nope. He wants to know more about Mum. His therapist thinks it would help." He runs his tongue over the front of his teeth. "I think being the oldest and having to take care of her, deal with the medicines and hospital crap, it made me desensitised to it all by the time it took her. He only remembers a screaming woman; he's older now and needs the closure."

Joey's mum suffered from the same mental illness as Joey does. Schizophrenia. Unfortunately, when Joey was only young, she took her own life. It isn't something he speaks about often, but when he does open up, I know I have to be careful with what I say.

"That makes sense." I give him a sad smile. "She would be proud of you, from what you have told me. That I'm certain of."

He throws his head back, laughing, but I sense it's not sincere. I know going home will be tough. I feel bad for even bringing his brother up. "You're too nice, Nina." He continues to laugh. "Oh, to have your innocence."

"What?" I frown, shaking my head as a smile tugs at my lip.

"Nothing." He shakes his head, draining the rest of his coffee. "Come on, let's get you two home."

THE GIRLS ARE SPREAD around my lounge when I finish putting the little man to bed. One thing I have always stuck to is a bedtime routine. Bath, bottle, book, and bed.

"Please tell me you've ordered already!" I tell them, rubbing my stomach as it grumbles.

"It's on the way." Scarlet smiles.

"Thank God, I barely ate today. What was so funny just

now? I was halfway out the door and you idiots woke him up."

"Luce went official," Megan tells me, waggling her brows at Lucy across the room.

"Really?!"

"No! Well, yes. I need to speak to him. The conversation was all kinds of fucked up." She holds a hand up, shaking her head.

"In what way?"

"He—" The girls both burst out laughing. "He wanted to go bareback. I said I don't do that with people I'm not in a relationship with and he just asked me, right there and then as he hovered at my..." She gestures down there.

"And you said yes?"

"What would it have looked like if I said no? I'd look like a slut."

Lucy doesn't do casual dating, or she didn't. Something changed last year and honestly, I think it's for the best. Her 'relationships' (with complete assholes like Hugh) used to kill her for weeks before, she was always too emotionally invested and always too willing to give 'one more chance'.

"Lucy, it doesn't make you a slut. It's very normal to have sex and not be in a relationship. And if you want to use protection, you should."

"We did." She nods, tight-lipped. "I told him I had a friend who got knocked up after the first time and she was on the pill." She raises her brows as she sips her wine.

"Corrr, what a whore bag," Megan jokes.

I launch a pillow at her head. "Fuck off."

"What about you, little miss innocent over there. Is Dr Hottie still fucking with you?" I eye Scarlet knowing her silence is to keep the talk off of her. We haven't discussed anything but her for the past couple 'girls' nights'. She started her medical degree at the end of last year and met a very, very handsome surgeon. Shame he is also very married.

"Ugh, don't. Nothing has changed over here. Apart from my panties, I tend to take a couple pairs for the day now."

"Oh, wow." I chuckle.

"I don't get it." She shrugs. "The guy is a jerk, if he was my husband I'd be pissed."

"Has he made a move?" Lucy sits forward.

"No! God, I've made it very clear I'd never go there with a married man. He's just... intense, the way he looks at me."

Lucy cringes. "Slimeball."

"Hottest slimeball I've ever seen," Megan adds.

"What are we all like, in our prime and none of us can find a man," I tut.

"Umm, I'm more than happy on my own, thanks," Scarlet scoffs.

"I don't know how you live out at the house by yourself, Scar. The place gives me the creeps." Lucy shivers. "Anyway, I'm taken. Happily fucking. Condom and all." We chuckle.

"I have everything, bar the man," I groan.

"You could have the man too... Sorry. Just saying," Scarlet says on a shrug.

"That ship sailed, Scar, as much as I love your enthusiasm." I smile over at her. She took it hard when me and Mason split up. Luckily, I didn't lose her as a friend. "I actually wanted your opinion." I shuffle up the sofa and bring my legs up under me. "I think I'm going to let Mason come here to drop off and pick up. I'm hoping it will make things smoother. For everyone."

"What?" Luce mutters.

"Bad idea?" I wince.

"Not at all," she says. "Just surprising. It's been a while."

"Yeah, I can't even imagine what it would be like to see him again. It scares me a little," I tell them.

"As long as you don't kill him," Megan says, giving me a soft wink.

"I just feel like it will rip open the wound all over again, making myself vulnerable when I'm only now finding my feet."

They go quiet, all lost in thought. It's been a crazy year for us all. They have been there for me every step of the way and I know it hasn't always been easy. In fact, it's been a nightmare at times. Juggling full-time jobs and then dealing with me and my issues after dark.

"I can't rely on you guys forever." I sip my wine.

"Yeah, you can." Lucy gives me a reassuring look, one that leaves no room for question. "But I do think this is the next step and the right one."

"Do you ever wonder about him? Like..." Scarlet looks at me, trying to think of the right words.

I give her a tight smile. "All the time, Scar."

All the damn time.

Mase

I PUT the Bentley into park and stare up through the windscreen at the tower flats in front of me. Clothes hang from the balconies, along with flags and football shirts. The place is a dive. "She lives here?" I ask Charlie as he continues to read the file.

"You need to read this before you go barrelling in there, Mase. She has kids."

"What?" I frown, flicking my eyes to the paperwork. "How many?"

"Two. Both in care." He shakes his head as he reads. "She was arrested for being in possession of class A drugs. You need to get more details before you do this. Come back another time."

"When was this?" *Who the fuck is this girl?*

When he doesn't answer, I throw open my door. "Lowell, just give me a fucking second," he snaps.

I climb from the car and button my suit jacket, lifting my eyes to find two men standing on a balcony three floors up. Cigarette smoke rises between them as their eyes find focus on me. I nod my head to them and round the car.

"You coming, princess?" I ask through Charlie's window.

He climbs from the car and removes his tie and jacket, then runs his hand through his hair, messing up his styled waves. "Let me do the talking."

"Fuck off."

"Trust me. Let me do the talking," he warns, walking past me and into the building's entrance.

The cold concrete floor is littered with bottles and plastic waste, haphazardly swept off to the sides to create a walkway. The walls have a musty smell, mould lining the cold concrete. The place is filthy.

We take the stairs to the ninth floor and come to a stop outside flat 36. I stand to the left of the door whilst Charlie steps up and knocks.

"She might be at work," he tells me when she doesn't answer after a minute, but I give him a look that says, 'at this time of day'.

She's probably sleeping off last night's shift.

The door rattles then opens. "Who are you?" she asks in a strong east London accent.

I can't see her from my concealed spot, but I can see Charlie, and his reaction has me craning my neck around the door to get a look at her.

Her eyes are scanning Charlie up and down as she pulls on the hem of her jumper. Her eyes meet mine and realisation quickly sets in.

"You," she panics.

"Lowell!" Charlie warns as I wedge myself between the door and the doorframe, stopping her from shutting it.

I look up and into her face, only inches away from my own.

Those eyes.

I'd remember them anywhere. They still haunt me in my dreams.

She has bleached hair, which throws me off, because if it was dark, you'd think she was the girl I fell in love with once upon a time.

This is Nina's sister alright.

"Get out or I'll call the police," she yells, her voice shaking.

"Good idea. Although, I'd open a couple windows first."

She scoffs. "No one ever got arrested for smoking a bit of weed, rich boy," she taunts, stepping back. And I get the sense her words lack the confidence she probably intended.

"No, maybe not, but my friend here. He is one of the best lawyers in the city. I've seen the pull he has in a court of law."

"You don't scare me," she says, flicking her eyes to Charlie.

My hand snaps out, grasping her jaw tight enough to show I'm serious but loose enough to not leave a mark. "Who paid you?"

"What? Get off me." She struggles, trying to snatch her head away from my grip.

"You'll fucking tell me! You—"

"Lowell!" Charlie steps between us as she pushes my hand from her face. "You were paid to pose in photos with this man, yes?" he asks.

I put my hands on my hips as my nostrils flare.

"I want you to leave." She looks at the clock on the wall. "You need to leave."

"Not until you tell me who paid you!" I snap, completely losing my cool.

"Lowell," Charlie repeats.

"We leave now, and she'll never let us through the door again!" I turn back to face her. "Tell me!"

"I don't know, okay? I just did what I was told to do."

I can feel my face heating as I step towards her. I go to run my hand through my hair, and she flinches, making me pause and question *why*.

I tilt my head, glaring as I search her bloodshot eyes.

She walks to the window and peeks out, her hand shaking on the curtain. "You need to leave. Please!"

"Are you safe here, Jasmine?" Charlie asks, picking up on the same feeling I am.

She frowns, smoothing the yellow strands of hair behind her ears. "Yes. Who the hell do you think you are?"

"You need to tell me who paid you! I won't hesitate to have you arrested and thrown in prison."

Threatening her is probably the last thing I should be doing right now.

"What for?" She frowns.

I can see Charlie's eyes burning into the side of my head, but I don't face him. "For being a fucking whore!" I yell, the last of my control clearly gone.

She frowns, shrinking back, her face awash with sorrow.

This woman isn't a prostitute.

She hasn't got it in her.

"What's that noise?" Charlie asks, but I can hear nothing past the drumming in my chest.

She's not going to tell me.

She doesn't know.

Jasmine's eyes dart to the door between the kitchen and the sofa, and I still as the noise registers.

"Is that—"

Stepping forward, I push open the door with the palm of my hand, which gives me the perfect view of the room behind it.

The blood that was boiling on the surface of my skin seems to drain from my body, leaving me staring wide-eyed at the baby standing up in the cot.

Jasmine moves quickly, bending and scooping the little girl up in her arms, clinging on tight.

She didn't want us to see this.

Shit.

"What the fu—"

"Lowell, shut up," Charlie warns, his voice noticeably

softer. "You have two boys, both in care?" he asks Jasmine, taking a step towards her.

Her eyes close and when they open tears brim them.

"Not from my doing. I'm getting them back."

"I've read your file, Jasmine, please don't lie," Charlie states.

"I'm not lying. I took the blame, but it wasn't me."

I snort, making Charlie turn. He pins me with a glare. "And this little one. She's yours?"

"Yes." A tear runs down her cheek and I turn, running my hands through my hair. I don't want to feel sorry for this girl —she ruined my life.

"You have no record for this baby. Why?" I ask.

"She'd be taken away; I can't lose any more of my babies, I can't," she cries.

"Fuck!"

"Lowell!"

I walk to the kitchen, shaking my head as I take in the baby bottles amongst the dishes. How didn't I notice them before?

My eyes catch something in the sink, and I lean over to get a better look.

A used syringe lies in the bottom of the sink.

I see red.

"Show me your arms," I demand, taking quick strides to her.

Lifting her arm, I search for track marks but don't find any, just bruises on her bicep. Four fingers and a thumb wrap around her small muscle in a purple and black marking.

I close my eyes, running my tongue over my teeth, my head fucked.

What now?

How do I leave her here? How do I leave a baby here?

This woman wrecked everything.

She's Nina's sister.

Nina.

"You're coming with us," Charlie tells her. "Pack a bag."

I let out the breath I was holding, opening my eyes when her words come out in a rush.

"What?!" she panics. "No, I'm not! I can't."

"Pack a bag," I grit out, watching as she grips her daughter tighter.

She swallows thickly, looking at the window and back to us.

She wants to leave.

"What are you afraid of?" I finally ask her, trying to smooth my tone.

"He will follow me," she admits, her voice barely audible.

Charlie looks at me, and I nod in understanding. She's a victim, as we thought. "He won't find you." I frown, wondering what the hell I'm doing.

"I can't." She shakes her head.

"But you want to?" Charlie asks.

She shakes her head, but tears fall and then she shrugs. "I'm…"

"Pack a bag. Before I change my mind."

SHE'S JUMPY, looking around us as we load the car. The street is quiet, but a few people are watching from their balconies in curiosity. It's a bad idea—terrible even, and I have no plan to speak of, but I know I can't leave her here. A child. A baby. I can't leave a minor in this hellhole; Charlie couldn't either.

"Has she had her injections, health checks?" I ask, looking at her through the rearview mirror once in the car.

She nods her head, not meeting my eyes. "My friend is a midwife. She helped me deliver."

Charlie scrubs at his face, his frustration starting to creep into his calm façade. He already knows this is now damage control, especially if she had help.

"Do you have a child?" she asks, her voice shaking.

"Why?"

She looks anywhere but at me. "The baby seat, I just presumed."

Everything becomes real in that moment.

What the fuck am I doing?

This woman fucked me over and I've just pulled her from her home.

"YOU'RE GOING to hand Betty over to the authorities."

She stands from her spot on my sofa and starts rushing to grab all her things, Betty grasped tight in her arms. "No way. She can't be without me."

"Charlie's looked into every other option. There's no way they'd let you keep her in your current situation."

"Bullshit!" she spits out, panic washing over her pale face. "You can't take her. Please. I'm sorry," she cries.

"This isn't about what you did, Jasmine. You said you wanted to get your children back. This is the first step if you want to get them back for good."

"No. I can do it myself. I don't need your help."

"We both know that's not true. Not like this." I gesture towards Betty, feeling like the worst person in the world. I don't want to take them away from each other, but this really is the only option.

"Fuck you!" she snaps, getting worked up, tears streaming down her face.

"Jasmine, you need to listen to Mason. I know this is hard, but it's an opportunity for you to get better and back on your feet. He's offering you something not many would, given the circumstances."

She looks at me, swallowing thickly, then shakes her head no.

"I will put you up and give you a job. Keep your head down and stay away from the shit littered in your apartment—"

"That wasn't mine."

"And you will get your children back. All of them."

She thinks on it, and I see the moment she gives in, her lip trembling as she bounces Betty in her arms, her chin resting on her head as she looks to the ceiling. "What do you gain from all of this?" she croaks.

Me? Nothing.

Nina? Eventually... a sister.

3

Nina

My hand palms my forehead as I try to attach the booking form to the email for the one hundredth time. Why is this so difficult?

Ashley disappeared.

She went to assist a lady in the pool and hasn't been back since. Guaranteed she's stuck talking to Hadley. He's a charmer, and she's putty in his hands.

"Nina." My eyes shoot wide as my manager, Rochelle, calls to me from the elevators.

Balls. Where the hell is Ashley?

I force a smile onto my face. "Hi."

"Did you process the payment for the gentleman in 156?" she questions with a frown.

"Uhhh." Did I? I might have. "I think so."

"You think so?" she repeats in a condescending tone. "Nina, he had a tab of nearly two thousand pounds. How was this missed?"

"I'm still learning the system, I'm sorry." God, I suck at this. How mortifying.

"You'll need to call him. Ask for payment and apologise profusely for the mistake."

"Of course," I tell her, annoyed. As if he didn't know he missed a two-grand tab. He's the one who should be apologising. Cheeky bastard.

Rochelle's eyes survey the reception until they land back on me. I swallow as I watch her, wondering what else I could've screwed up.

"Where's Ashley?"

"Helping a lady in the pool." Why is she so scary? She's only a couple years older than me, but she's disarming in her authority.

Without a word, she shakes her head and walks towards the back offices.

I drop to my seat, puffing out a breath. That could have gone worse. Although, I need to scrub up on this system before I really screw something up. I can't afford to lose this job, and Rochelle doesn't tolerate *lackadaisical staff*. Those are the exact words she used during my interview.

I wonder how I ever got the job at all.

The rest of the day goes by without a hitch. I called the guy from 156 and had him pay the tab. Ashley had to show me how to add it to the invoice for future reference and then we fixed the issue with the email.

Glancing at the clock, I notice I still have two hours left of my shift. They always seem to drag. Ashley leaves at six, and the reception always quietens down around five, so it doesn't bother me being left on my own. I usually practice on the training system to help master the bookings, but today I'm staring into space, trying to figure out how I can approach Mason. I don't necessarily feel ready to have him come to the apartment, but I know I need to let it happen.

Rip off the Band-Aid.

Lucy would speak to him for me, but maybe it's something I need to do? I know before I face him again, I need to speak to him. A text or something to find the dynamic. It's currently nonexistent.

Pulling up his name, I click the message icon and start to write.

Nina: Hi.

Ugh. No. That's not right.

Nina: Mason, I have been thinking. I think it would be better for everyone (but me)

Bitter Nina, you are bitter!
I delete the message and try again.

Nina: I think you should go with Scarlet to my apartment this evening. It might help having you there for bedtime. Nina.

I hit send and stare at the message.
I did it.
I texted him.
My palms sweat as I stare at the words.
This is huge progress, it's been seven months.

Three dots begin to bounce on the screen and I lock and toss my phone onto the desk as if it burns me, my body flushing with heat. I can't deal with this communication thing. It's too much. I don't think I'm ready for his words.

If I'm being honest, the reason I've kept myself from him is because I'm weak. Mason Lowell has the ability to bring me to my knees. He did it time and time again in the months I was with him. And I let him. Blinded by lust, and his perfect fucking face. Asshole. The thought of seeing him and having him explain himself, or try to win me back, scares me. He killed my dreams in more ways than one, even if that did give me the greatest gift in return. I don't think I will ever forgive him.

I busy myself with the computer, doing nothing in particular and trying to keep my mind off my phone. It's useless. Picking it up and flipping it over, I spot his name.

Swiping my thumb over the notification, I open the text.

Mason: Ok.

That's it?!

Ok!

I reach out after nearly seven months, allow him access into my home, and all he has to say is OK! Is he kidding me?

Squeezing my eyes tight, I stand and smooth my hands down my skirt. I'm at work, I need to keep my cool. I can't let him get to me. Not anymore, that ship has sailed. He's the father of my child and not a single thing more.

Fucking *ok*! Who does he think he is?

THE AUDI IS IDLING at the curb as I cross the road. Climbing in, I smile at Vinny and do up my seat belt.

"Hey!"

"Good day?" he asks.

"No. I'm terrible at everything, Vinny. I did well in school! I don't know what's wrong with me."

"You aren't in there enough to get to grips with it yet. It's been a month—eight shifts? It'll come."

"I hope so," I mumble, my head dropping back to the seat.

"You will." A smile pulls at his lips. "So, Mason left with Scarlet this afternoon. That was a surprise," he tells me, looking at me knowingly.

"He went to mine?" I wasn't sure if he would.

Will he still be there?

"I'm proud of you, love."

"Have I done the right thing, Vin?" I ask, scrubbing at my face, completely drained.

Checking his mirrors, he pulls out onto the quiet road. "You did the right thing, and you didn't do it for you. You're remarkable." He pats my leg. "I hope you know that."

"Is he still there? At the apartment?"

He nods. "Should I have him leave first before you go up?"

"Is Scar there too?"

"Yes, she stayed. I will come up with you if you want?"

I roll my lips, unsure. "Yeah, okay."

Am I ready for this? I don't want to see him.

"I know it's been a while, but nothing has changed with him. He's still the same Mason as before."

I think that's what I'm most afraid of.

IT'S after eight when we get to my apartment. Vinny follows me to the elevator, and we ride it in silence to my floor. I pause when I reach the door, looking up at him. He simply nods his head in encouragement, urging me forward. Here goes nothing.

I take my time, shimmying into the apartment and placing my bag on the side table, then, slipping my shoes off, I bend and place them off to the side.

I don't want to look up.

I can hear the TV and I know he is here.

I can feel his eyes on me.

My heart pounds in my ears as I turn towards the living room, looking anywhere but at the man who sits on my sofa. I can see him in my peripheral, but I can't bring myself to look him in the eye. Still, my body flushes hot.

"Hi," I say to Scarlet, spotting her in the kitchen. I walk to her instead. "Did he go down okay?"

We stare at one another as if I haven't just asked a question. She flicks her head between me and Mason, clearly unsure what to say.

I need her to be the chatty one here. She could talk the ear off a donkey. Why is she not saying anything?!

I frown at her, willing her to talk.

Mason lets out a huff from behind me, and subconsciously I turn, my eyes finally finding him.

Everything inside me liquifies as our gazes lock. His low brows, dark eyes and strong jaw. His lips, full and parted. I feel my brow crease. It's painful to look at him. My chest aches with a warmth so intense, it sears me from the inside out.

What even is that feeling?

His hair is longer, much longer as if he hasn't cut it in months. It curls around his ears, brushing his collar. His body is strong, his shoulders set wide, and his arms stretch the fabric of his dress shirt.

Everything is as I remember it.

Is that why this hurts so much? The knowing. How he felt when I was in his arms, or how he smelt. God, I miss the sensory overload that would floor me whenever he held me.

He breaks the connection first, bending to pick up his keys. "He went down fine. Had a bottle at seven." Everything about him is cold and detached. The polar opposite of the feelings he evokes in me. "Scar, you ready?"

"We're leaving?" she asks, confused.

"Yeah." His eyes eat me up again. Every. Inch. Of. Me. "We're leaving."

I don't know what I was expecting after all this time, but this wasn't it. It's as if he can't stand to look at me.

Scarlet gives me a tight smile as she steps past me. I can only imagine how awkward this must be for her. "I'll text you when I'm home."

"Okay." I nod.

Mason turns, striding towards the door. The air is electric between us, so much that hasn't been said. So much that will never be said.

My eyes well unexpectedly and I dip my head, biting my cheek as I try to get my emotions under control.

"Do you want me to stay for a while?" Vinny asks, stepping up and blocking me from view.

I stare at his chest, unable to speak past the lump in my throat.

"I will be here tomorrow. Five fifteen," Mason states from the door.

Vinny turns when I don't say anything, nodding his head.

The door slams shut, making me flinch.

"He hates me, doesn't he?" I run my hands through my hair.

"He could never hate you, Nina."

"You go." I wave him off. "I'm gonna have an early night."

I turn and walk to the kitchen, setting up the steriliser and filling it with bottles. My mind drifts back to my message to Mason earlier and his short reply.

"He doesn't hate you, Nina."

"No, it's okay, Vinny. I think it's easier if this is how it is. I don't think I'd survive a conversation with the man. I'm just being silly." I turn on the steriliser and turn towards him. "You go, I'm fine." I smile, swallowing the lump in my throat.

He's hesitant as he steps up to me, wrapping his arms around me and pulling me into him. "It's okay, love," he tells me, eventually leaning back and wiping a stray tear from my cheek with his thumb. "The first time was always going to be the hardest."

I nod my head, because I knew it would be hard. It's why I've put it off for so long.

"Go get your boy and get some sleep. You need Ellis cuddles."

I smile into his shirt. "I do. Ellis cuddles are exactly what I need right now."

Vinny leaves and I finish cleaning up the kitchen.

Somehow, I manage to hold it together, trying hardest to not let thoughts of Mason in. I'm halfway down the hallway when my legs begin to sway, my shoulders falling as I lift my hand, trying to quieten the sob that escapes me.

My back hits the door and I slide down it, knowing I will wake Ellis if I go inside.

My heart seems to break all over again as the memories flood in.

Ellis Anthony Lowell
Tuesday 5th March 2019
Boy
6lb12oz
20:32pm

Pain radiates across my abdomen, crippling me until I find a breath of air. In through my nose and out through my mouth. My nostrils burn as I inhale deeply. It's been seven hours of active labour. Unexplainable pain.

"You're doing incredible, darling."

I don't speak. I can't.

Maggie's hand finds my back and I drop my head to the bed as the contraction begins to subside. My shoulders drop as I relax.

"Nina, I need you to get up onto the bed so I can examine you," Kelly, my midwife, tells me.

"I can't." I shake my head, panicking. I don't want to move, this position works.

"Come on, love, you can do it," Maggie whispers, kissing the side of my head.

I look at her and nod, letting her take my hand as I step up and lie myself down on the bed.

"This will be uncomfortable, Nina. I'm sorry, my lovely," Kelly tells me from the end of the hospital bed.

"Not long now," Maggie says, stroking my hair back from my face.

My stomach starts to ache and I know another contraction is only moments away. "Oh god! I have a contraction."

"Don't panic, you've done so well, Nina. Deep breath in... Out."

I manage the breath in but lose it mid-exhale. "I can't!" I shout. "Ahhhhhh! Fuck, no!"

"Would you prefer to be on your knees, Nina?"

"I don't know!"

"Just keep breathing and I will get you checked as soon as this one passes."

"I need to push. Please, Maggie, I can't." I turn into her, searching for comfort.

"I know, darling," she cries.

"Is that one subsiding, Nina?"

I breathe deeply as the last of the contraction racks through me, and my body slowly sinks into the bed as I relax. I can't take much more; this is killing me.

Kelly begins examining me and I wince as she stretches me. "Nina, you are seven centimetres we aren't quite there—"

"No!" I panic, throwing myself forward and standing from the bed in a rush. "I need to push." My stomach starts to contract instantly, and I bear down, my body telling me I need to push. "Uggghhhhh!" A rush of warm liquid rushes down my legs. "Uh uh uh—"

"Don't panic, it's just your waters. Do you feel like you need to push, Nina?"

"Yes! Ugghhhhh!" I scream as the pain intensifies.

"Nina, I need to get Mason." Maggie panics.

"Ugghhhhhhhhh. No! Not yet." I'm not ready. It's been five months, but I still can't bear to face him.

I start to pant as I lean back down on the bed on my forearms —the most comfortable position I've found in the seven hours we've been here. The contraction starts to subside again, and I stand, my body wet with sweat.

"I need you on the bed, Nina. You aren't steady enough on your feet."

"I'm fine," I pant. "I'm fine."

"Try and get on the bed, darling, please," Maggie pleads, her voice thick with emotion.

"I'm... Oh, no! No, no!"

"Nina, you're panicking, you need to breathe."

I shake my head as my body tenses all over and the pain takes me completely, taking control of my ability to do anything but focus on it. "Ugggggghhhhhhhhh!" I make a feral sound that ripples from deep in my throat.

"I need her on the bed now!" Kelly calls out.

Maggie strokes my hair and uses a damp flannel to blot my forehead. "Nina, we need you on the bed now. Please, try for me," her worried voice coos.

I shake my head, my throat catching as I try to hold back the tears.

I can't do this.

I can't do this.

Strong hands slip around me, one under my breasts, and the other resting on my hip. "You can do this," he rasps into my ear.

I shake my head, pinching my eyes shut. His voice is like a sweet melody to my soul.

"Look at me."

"I have another..." I shake my head. "Oh god. No, no, no!"

"Look. At. Me!"

My eyes snap open as my head drops back to his shoulder.

"Mase, I can't." I shake my head, my tears slipping free.

He is just as beautiful as the day I met him.

"Yes, you can. If anyone can do this, it's you. Breathe, Nina." His hand smooths over my full, round belly. "Breathe."

I inhale him as my nose brushes his neck, breathing through the contraction until it eases.

I feel weightless as I'm lifted and placed on the bed, Mason slipping in behind me.

"Okay, with the next contraction, I want you to push, Nina. I can feel the head."

"See," he whispers against my ear. "You're nearly there. You going to give up now?"

"Shut up," I reply hoarsely.

I can feel his smile against my neck and I watch as Kelly's lip twitches. I wish I could smile but the ache starts to spread, and I tense up again.

"Relax, relax," Kelly tells me, rubbing my leg. "I need you to push for me, Nina."

"Uggghhhhhh!"

"Shhhh, no, that's not it. Push then pant, remember."

"It burns."

"Burns?" Mason repeats.

"Pant," Kelly tells me, panting with me.

Never in my life have I felt such pain.

"Okay, now push. Push! Push!"

I bear down with everything I have inside me. "Yes, baby," Mason rasps against my jaw.

"Good girl, stop there. I have the head, and so much hair," Kelly informs us.

I smile. Finally, something.

"You are incredible."

"When you feel that contraction, I want you to—"

I feel it and waste no time grasping the arms that hold me as I push, not stopping until the pain stops, and my chest is enveloped in warmth.

"A gorgeous little boy." Kelly beams at us. "Congratulations, Mummy and Daddy."

Looking down, I take him in. His small little nose, pursed lips and flailing hands. "Hello, you," I tell him as he looks up at me.

Mason's hand reaches around me and smooths down his cheek. I look back at him over my shoulder and catch his tear-lined face, mere inches from my own.

"Thank you, Angel," he tells me, closing the distance and kissing me.

My chest constricts as I will myself to pull away, but I can't. Not when it feels so right, not when I've been starved of him for so long, and not until I taste the saltiness of our tears between us.

I rip myself away.

"Is Dad cutting the cord?"

"Can I?" He turns to me, and I nod, my heart physically hurting in my chest.

"Does he have a name?" Kelly asks.

I look at Mason as he leans in with the scissors, his eyes lifting to mine. We haven't discussed it, but I've known since the day I found out I was pregnant what he would be called.

"Ellis. If that's okay? Ellis Anthony Lowell."

Mason only nods, as if that's all he can manage.

THE HOURS that followed my labour are a blur. I remember Elliot, Lance, Charlie, Vinny, and the girls all sneaking in and causing a commotion late in the evening—just to get a look at him. Not that Mason allowed the fuss.

It wasn't until one o'clock in the morning, when the nurse told Mason to go home to get some sleep that reality sunk back in, obliterating the post-birth haze. I knew I couldn't let him back in. Not even an inch. He would be Ellis's father but that was all I could allow.

Swiping the tears from my face, I stand, roll my shoulders, and walk into my bedroom. I always knew today would come around, and now that it has, I feel him, his presence, and his aura. That pull we have—it never left.

But I'll never let it drag me under again.

Mase

"Who's Nina?" Jasmine asks as I walk to the edge of the balcony. "Charlie mentioned her earlier. I heard the two of you in the kitchen. Why would she need to know that I'm here? And why don't you want her to know?"

Who is Nina? There's definitely not an easy answer to that question. How do I explain something unexplainable to a woman I can barely stand to look at?

"You ask a lot of questions, you know that?"

She dips her head, her face growing red.

"Nina is your sister," I tell her with little ease, turning to face the skyline as my brow creases. I wait.

"What?" she finally stutters.

"Your sister. Nina Anderson. She's twenty-nine years old

—a dancer. Your father had her and then you eighteen months later."

"You know my father?"

I scoff. "I know enough to judge his lousy ass."

I stand with my hands in my pockets not looking back at the girl on my terrace. She's quiet behind me, and I know I've shocked her. I've shocked myself. When Nina didn't believe me, I swore I'd never forgive her for it—and I won't. Which is why me having Jasmine here makes no sense.

"And Nina, you know her?"

I shake my head on a laugh and something inside of me snaps. This is stupid. "You need to pack up your things, I can't have you here. I'm sorry."

Regardless of who Jasmine is and her situation, I can't have her here. I should've known that last night.

"Where will I go? I have no money."

I turn and look at her. She's too skinny, her bones visible around her cheeks and jaw, and not in a healthy way. Her skin is spotty and pale, and she hides behind a baggy jumper.

"I'll find you a hotel. And Charlie phoned the social worker today. They will be coming in the morning; we will put you up somewhere until you're back on your feet. Okay?" I nod at her even though I can sense she's struggling. I can't get in too deep.

"Are you helping me because of Nina?" Her eyes pinch in at the corners—accusing, knowing—and I turn, hating that they have the same eyes.

"The why doesn't matter. What matters is how you behave between now and getting your children back."

"Behave? I'm not a child," she says, her voice rising in annoyance.

"Maybe so, but Betty deserves more than the life you've given her this far." I point in the direction of the terrace door. "And if you can't see that, then you should leave now."

"Not everyone is born with a silver spoon in their mouth, you know. I did what I had to do in life to get by."

She has no idea. I walk to her with my hands in my pockets, my teeth clenched so tight they ache. I'm an asshole for judging her—for taking my frustration out on her, but I also know that in life there's always a choice, and Jasmine has made some shitty ones. "I know someone just like you, someone who could have let their fate ruin them." I shake my head. "She didn't. She never let it. She soared so damn high." I look down my nose at her. "Be better. For you. For your kids." I walk past her and roll open the door.

"So, she doesn't know about me?" she calls, halting me in my steps. "Nina. She doesn't know I'm her sister?"

"No."

"THIS IS A FUCKING TERRIBLE IDEA," Elliot tells me, staring wide-eyed at me from the other side of my desk.

"She was in Stratford?" Lance asks, surprised. "I thought Vinny said she wasn't in the country?"

We're in my office. Lance and Charlie sit on the sofas, while Elliot stands, still staring at me.

"She doesn't have much in the way of identification. It's why she wasn't easily traced," Charlie tells them, looking up from his laptop.

"She has a kid?" Elliot asks.

I nod.

"Why the fuck are you helping her, Lowell?" Lance questions, rolling his lips and smoothing his hand over his moustache.

"I don't know." I drag my hand down my face. "She needs it. She doesn't know who set me up. She said she was told what to do that night, and my bets are on it having something to do with her boyfriend."

"I'd have fucking left her." Lance shakes his head, sitting back onto the sofa.

"Maybe I should have left her but it's Nina's sister, Sullivan."

"You think her bloke is dodgy?" Elliot asks.

"Yeah, the place was a fucking tip, drugs, the lot."

"So, what now? You chuck her in The Earl Marks and expect her to sort her shit out?" Lance chuckles.

Elliot frowns instantly. "Wait a second—"

"You put her up in The Earl Marks?" Charlie's voice booms as he stands, letting his laptop fall to the sofa.

"Yeah."

"What are the chances." Elliot grimaces as he looks at Charlie.

"What?" I question, frowning between them when none of them speak.

4

Mase

"SOMEONE TELL ME WHAT THE FUCK IS GOING ON?" I DEMAND.

Charlie turns, picking up his jacket and sliding it on. "Nina works at The Earl Marks."

"What?" I frown, trying to decipher what he's saying. "No, she fucking doesn't."

"Yes, she does." Elliot runs his hand across his face as he watches me. "She needed a job that would cover the bills."

"The dance lessons do cover the bills."

"No, they don't. There are no lessons." Charlie's jaw tics at that confession. "She asked us not to tell you. You just presumed."

"Are you fucking kidding me?" I yell, making them all wince. "When does she teach?"

"She doesn't. She hasn't danced since she had Ellis," Lance voices. "Fuck, I'm sorry mate. I didn't think when you told me this morning."

My nostrils flare as I clench my fists. "What the fuck!"

"Calm down. She doesn't work Fridays. We can get Jasmine out of there before her next shift." Elliot tries to reassure me, but it does nothing to ease the rage I feel inside.

"Jesus Christ."

I've put the woman who technically split us up in the hotel Nina works at?

And Nina fucking loves to dance. It was the only thing that ever meant something to her. How can she just give up on that? I think back to the night before, and what she was wearing. Her top and skirt hugged her slender body. I couldn't look at her without feeling every fucked-up emotion possible. Why did I not notice the skirt? Nina doesn't wear fucking skirts.

Lance stands. "I'll go get Jasmine. Don't stress on this, mate. Where's Vin?"

"Fuck off, Sullivan, I'll sort it myself." I don't need Vinny involved in this. I knew if I told him about putting Jasmine up and making her give up Betty, that he would meddle. Maybe if I had told him, then this wouldn't have happened.

I pick up my suit jacket from the back of my chair and throw it over my arm, then grab my keys from the drawer. "Next time you fuckers think about lying to me, consider what that might mean for the person you think you're protecting. Fucking interfering pricks."

"She trusts us, Lowell," Elliot says to my back. "You can't blame us for trying to keep that."

Without looking back, I continue through the door, pissed that he's right.

Nina

FRIDAYS AT THE EARL MARKS—WHAT an eye-opener. I thought I had it tough on my Monday shift, but this is next level busy. When Rochelle called and asked me to cover today, I knew I had to do it. I at least need to be available for the first couple months to cover extra shifts. She said she needed someone who is flexible, and I'm only able to offer her two days a week. How I got this job is beyond me. *Money, Nina. Think of the money.*

With renewed determination, I heave up the sheets from the floor and place them onto the trolley, wiping my forehead with the back of my hand. Damn, it's hot up here.

"Nina, you can stop for lunch now, lovely. Karen and the girls have already gone down," Emily, I think her name is, tells me, poking her head in the door.

Everyone is so much nicer in housekeeping. That's one thing I haven't missed today. Rochelle.

"I'm just finishing up in here and I will come down." I smile.

She checks out my trolley then comes into the room. "Well, two hands will get the job done quicker," she says, rounding the bed.

"Thanks," I tell her as she grasps the other side of the sheet I was fitting.

"You've taken to this quickly today; you normally work down on reception?"

"Yeah, although I hate it down there." Crap, should I say that. "Not hate, hate is a strong word. It's a lot some days." God Nina, you work two days a week.

"It's fine, everyone hates front of house, and there's a

quick turnaround down there. Other than Ash—she's been here for years now."

"I think that has more to do with—" I pause, *would Ash mind me talking about this?* I don't even know Emily.

"Hadley?" She laughs. "'Cause you're right if that's what you were about to say."

I relax, feeling like she is safe to rant to. "She is a saint!" I chuckle. "Rochelle is scary, Ashley puts up with A LOT."

"Yeah, not many people click with her."

"I get it. She's the manager, but Jesus. Why be so mean? We call her the she-devil."

"Nina—"

"It wouldn't shock me if she grew actual horns."

A throat clears behind me. I bring my eyes up to Emily, who is staring at me with wide eyes, giving me a barely noticeable shake of the head.

"She-devil?" Rochelle snaps.

I clench my teeth, cringing as my shoulders tense. Fuck.

"Please, at least get creative." She looks me up and down as if I'm the filth on the bottom of her shoe. "You're lucky to have the friends that you do. I've fired people for a lot less."

"I'm really sorry, Roch—"

"No, you're not." She rolls her eyes and leaves the room.

"Oh my god!" Emily whispers, falling to the bed in laughter.

I can feel my cheeks burning, they must be bright red. "Stop! This is mortifying."

She rolls to her belly and looks up at me in question. "Are you sleeping with one of the boys?"

"Who?"

"The boys? One of the sons?"

I lift the corner of the mattress and fold the sheet under. "I have no idea who you're talking about."

"The notorious Arlelly brothers. You must have some pull here to not be out on your ass."

"No! I'm not sleeping with anyone! You think she should have fired me?"

"No, of course not. But she would have normally. She said, 'you're lucky you know the people you do'," she mimics.

No, she said I was lucky to have the friends I do... I instantly think about Elliot and how he told me about the job.

Fuckers.

"Come on, get this done and we can grab lunch. Before the she-devil comes back." She chuckles.

"Shhh." I giggle. "We'll be out on our arses in a minute."

We finish up the room and are halfway down the corridor with our trolley when a flash of blonde catches my eye. A woman squeezes herself past us as she rushes to her room. I push forward on the metal handles, but something in my gut gnaws at me to turn around.

She is swiping her key card, and I can only see the side of her face, but she looks upset.

I think I recognise her.

As if she knows she's being watched, she looks straight at me, her bloodshot eyes pinching in at the corners as they drop down my frame. I give a small smile, being polite. I can see she's been crying. She isn't like the other guests we have at The Earl Marks. She looks... a bit of a mess. She turns away, swiping her card again, and then disappears into the room.

"Come on, there will be nothing left in the kitchen in a

minute." Emily smiles, pulling on the trolley to urge me along.

I'M WALKING towards the lifts on my way back from lunch when I spot Mason. He's climbing from his Bentley, his powerful legs eating up the asphalt as he makes his way to the entrance of The Earl Marks.

"Mason? Is everything okay?" I ask, concerned as I push out through the main doors. Lucy would have called me if something was wrong with Ellis.

His eyes go wide when he spots me.

"Nina, you don't normally work today?"

"I'm covering, is something wrong? Ellis is with Lucy." Mason shouldn't even know I work here, which means Lucy, or someone has told him. Panic fills me. I pull my phone from my pocket to check for missed calls.

"Uh, no. No, Ellis is fine," he tells me, rubbing his thumb over his jaw. "I could've had Ellis today. You should've called."

"I know you work Fridays." I shrug, feeling awkward. "Luce had holiday to use, it's fine." If Ellis isn't the reason he's here... "Why are you here?"

He stuffs his hands in his pockets, looking at the cars buzzing around us before bringing his eyes back to me. And he has me, just like that, locked in a stare so intense I'm bolted to the concrete beneath my feet. I wish I could see deeper into those eyes. I swear the depths of their darkness matches my soul. They feel like home, weirdly. "I have a meeting with a client." His jaw flexes.

"Here?" I question, swallowing past the lump that sets my voice wavering.

He continues to stare at me, unrelenting. "Yes."

"Oh." I realise this is probably the most we have said to each other since Ellis was born, and the majority of the conversation is being spoken with our eyes. The thought makes my face flush. "I'll let you get on then."

I thought I'd hate him. I expected to hate him. But I don't. The anger is still there in my gut, but it doesn't burn as fiercely as it once did. I could never trust nor love him again, not willingly anyway. But if I can, I want to be amicable. For our son.

"I'm still picking Ellis up tonight. Five fifteen." His gaze drops down the length of me, making the hairs on the back of my neck stand on end.

Is he doing this on purpose?

"Umm, yeah." I nod. "Actually..." I consider asking him to come later. I won't see Ellis until Sunday, and I've been at work since his nap this morning. But this is Mason's time, and I can't take that from him. It wouldn't be fair. "No, never mind."

"What is it?" he asks, tipping his chin up, and I can't help but focus on the movement.

Why is he so fucking hot? It's not fair. He has more than a day's worth of stubble lining his angular jaw. He seems fitter, sharper. *More.* I'm completely transfixed on him. *Shit.* I snap out of it.

I need to get away from him. *Now!*

"It's fine, honest, five fifteen is great," I rush out, turning and jogging back inside without saying goodbye. Rochelle spots me hurrying through the door and gives me an evil eye.

Not now Satan.

———

Mase

I WAIT until Nina is inside then turn around and walk back towards my car.

Of course, she's fucking working today.

Pulling out my phone, I pull up Jasmine's number. I haven't checked on her today, and I know she will be upset. The social worker was there as promised this morning. Seeing Jasmine break down wasn't high on my list of ways to start a Friday morning, but I know it was the right thing to do.

I dial her number and wait for her to answer but get nothing.

I call Vinny.

———

LUCY GREETS me at the door when I arrive at Nina's apartment. I take in the décor, noticing more than the last time I was here. It's minimalistic, the walls plain white and pictureless. Nina isn't a materialistic person, but I would prefer to see the place slightly more homely for them. Apart from the photos in her bedroom, you wouldn't know who lived here.

"Look who it is, Ell." Lucy smiles, bouncing Ellis in her arms.

"Stop calling him that," I tell her. "Uncle Elliot's going to grow an even bigger head."

"True." She snorts.

"How's he been? You could've called me. You didn't need to take the day off."

She gives me a look, as if what I've said is stupid. "I'm pretty sure it was more imperative that you were at work than me today. I make a pittance compared to you."

"Ellis comes first, always." I take him from her arms, kissing his full cheek. "How come Nina had to work?"

"Just picking up an extra shift. She's saving for a break-away with Ellis. She wants to show him the world. Doesn't she, puds."

Not without me, they're not.

"When?"

She frowns, walking to the lounge to collect her things. "I don't know."

"She hasn't said when she wants to go?"

"No! She's a girl. We do this. We just need a goal to work towards sometimes." She looks at me and her eyes soften. "Don't stress about it. She would've told you first."

I doubt that. Before Thursday, it had been radio silence for the past seven months.

"Has she seen Joey this week?" I ask shamelessly.

It still fucks with me that they grew so close.

"Do you actually want to know that? You know they're friends, Mase."

"Like you and Elliot are friends," I challenge.

She rolls her eyes. "Exactly like me and Elliot. What's with you people? You do realise Elliot and I have never so much as kissed."

"What about his birthday last year?"

"We didn't kiss." She pops a brow.

I smile wide as she leans in and kisses Ellis's head. "I need to get going, Nina will be home in about half an hour. You okay to wait? I think she wanted to see Ellis before you go."

"Yeah, I can wait."

"I'll see you later."

"Bye, Luce."

My eyes scan the apartment once she's gone. Toys clutter the lounge and pillows are strewn around the floor. "How did the two of you make so much mess?" I ask Ellis, tickling his ribs and making him giggle.

"Da Da Da." He claps.

"Good boy." I place him on the floor, put on the football, then pick up some of the mess in the lounge.

IT'S NEARLY an hour later when Nina gets home. She rushes through the door looking a hot mess. Emphasis on the hot. She has her own clothes on now. Something I've missed. Her yoga pants hug her round hips, and her vest showcases more of her tits than I can stand to look at right now. I meet her eyes and see she has caught me staring.

"Hi," I tell her, turning and placing the last of Ellis's baby vests on the airer.

"What are you doing?" she asks, placing her bag on the kitchen island.

I walk to the lounge, bending and picking up Ellis. I feel like an ass for using my son as a shield, but right now I need him.

"You had some washing. I had time."

"You don't need to—"

"Well, I did."

She nods her head, as if she doesn't know what to say. "Sorry, I was later back than planned."

"It's fine. Did you want—" I move forward holding Ellis out for her to take him, but he grips hold of my shirt and starts to fuss.

"Ellis, baby, come here," she coos.

"Say goodbye to Mummy, mate." I turn him and place him into her arms, but he continues to fuss, leaning his little body towards me.

"I'm going to go get his things, give us a minute." She takes off down the hall, Ellis crying for me the whole time.

All I want to do is reach out and take him.

I tell myself to give it a minute, let her calm him down. She won't see him for the whole of tomorrow and then the best part of Sunday. They need a second alone.

It goes quiet, and then the sound of laughter floats from the hall.

My feet follow the sound.

"Do you? Does Ellis need Mummy snuffles?" I round the corner and stand in the doorway, watching as Nina runs her nose up Ellis's belly and neck. He tries to wriggle away, but the sound of his gasping laugh tells me he loves it.

"You give Mummy kisses, you little monster."

He laughs again, holding her face when she hovers above him.

"Da Da Da Da."

"Yeah, I know." She leans in and brushes her nose with his.

Ellis keeps her face held in his small hands as if he's studying her face, a happy smile stretching his cheeks and exposing his dimples. He pulls her in and gives her a kiss with his mouth wide open.

"I love you, baby boy. So much."

She watches him, her hair thrown over her shoulder as she rests her arms around his body. "I'll miss you this weekend. Super snuggles in Mummy's bed on Sunday, okay?" She kisses his head one last time and stands, lifting him from the bed.

She freezes when she spots me in the doorway. "Mason. Sorry, I was coming, I just—"

"It's fine," I cut her off. "I'm in no rush." I swallow the lump that has formed in my throat.

She gives me a tight smile then passes Ellis off to me. "I'll grab his things."

I leave her to pack his bag and wait in the kitchen. Seeing her with Ellis makes something inside of me burn.

My son and his mother.

Nina and her son. The way she is with him—it makes me proud. She's everything I knew she would be as a mother.

"I don't usually pack clothes. Lucy said you have everything he needs." She passes me the bag, then starts busying herself in the kitchen without looking at me once. She knows I have everything I need for Ellis; it's been the same routine for months.

Is she nervous?

"Yeah, we've got everything he'll need. I'll drop him back Sunday if that's okay."

"Okay." She doesn't turn and I frown as I look at Ellis who is watching me from his spot in my arms.

Is she not going to say goodbye?

"We're going to head out," I tell her, feeling awkward.

"Bye."

Do I just leave?

"Nina?"

"Please, just go, Mason," she croaks out.

Is she crying? "What's the matter?" I ask, stepping into the kitchen.

"Nothing, I'm okay. It's the long weekend. I struggle with this bit; you just need to leave." She swipes at her cheek and I stand frozen, wanting to reach out and wipe her tears away.

God, is this how it always is? How did I not know this?

"Please, Mason, just go," she begs, turning away from me and wiping down the worktop I only just cleaned.

I go to turn but stop short. Fuck. How do I leave now?

"Nina."

"Mason, go!" She spins towards us, her eyes red. "I need you to go!" Her lip trembles.

"Ellis can stay, I don't have to take him," I offer, not thinking what that means for myself.

"Stop!" she cries. "Stop being..." Her shoulders slump, her eyes filling even more. "Sorry." She walks to the door and slips out, leaving her apartment, and me. Again. How has she walked out on me again, and in her own fucking apartment?

Nina

MY KNUCKLES RAP on the door once, and then I walk in, knowing Joey won't mind me being here. I wish I was stronger than this, but every time Ellis leaves me for the weekend, it splits my heart open until he comes home again. I struggle not having him with me.

Joey lives two buildings away from my apartment in a small flat. He moved to be closer for work, but it also allows him to be closer to me. Times like now when I need someone to escape to. I can't stand to be home alone—which is odd considering I spent so much of my childhood alone.

"Joe?"

"Yo. In here," he calls from his room.

He's sitting up in bed with his laptop resting on his legs, but he looks up when I step through the doorway. His arm comes out as if he knew I'd be coming, and I go willingly, needing the comfort.

I curl up under his arm, resting my head on his chest.

He doesn't say a word.

He knows how much it hurts for me to be away from Ellis. He has had his fair share of hardship in his own life.

"Sunday will be here before you know it." He kisses my hair. "Wanna order in or do you have plans with the girls?"

I shrug, catching a tear on my lips as it rolls over them.

"I hate this."

"I know you do." He pauses, adjusting the lighting on the photo he's working on. "I wish it could be different for you. I really do."

***

"Nina. Nina."

My eyes slowly part as Joey wakes me from a deep sleep. The room is blanketed in darkness.

"I left you as long as I could, but I thought you'd want food."

"What time is it?" I ask.

I can see his smile even in the dark. "Just gone nine. You slept for three hours."

"Crap." I sit up and rub my eyes. "Sorry."

"Don't be. I'll plate up."

I slide my phone from the nightstand and check the screen. How did I sleep for three hours? Once I've freshened up in the bathroom, I make my way to the kitchen.

"Mason texted and called you."

"He did?" I frown, stopping short in the doorway.

"I didn't answer but after the fifth message I just wanted to make sure it wasn't to do with Ellis." He looks at me apologetically.

"Joey, it's fine. Was everything okay?"

"Yeah, but I'm presuming he was at your apartment tonight?" he questions.

"I told him to pick up and drop off from now on. It wasn't fair on Ellis being passed from pillar to post." I start to fill my plate with the Chinese food.

"I agree." Joey nods, pulling out some cutlery for us both. "I texted him back and told him there's a spare key here. He was worried you wouldn't be able to get back into your place."

"You texted him?" I panic. "Did you say it was you?"

"Yes."

I close my eyes and begin counting to five.

"Is that a problem?" he asks, crossing his arms over his chest.

"No. But it won't make my life any easier."

"Why? I thought you said things were done between you two?"

"It is. We are. Things are just... Fucked. And hard. Really freaking hard."

"Did he say something?"

I snigger. "No." He's barely said a word to me. "I left him, and I vowed I'd never let him back in." I take a deep breath, not wanting to share this much with Joey. I need my girls. "I just didn't expect to feel so much after all this time. That's all."

"Nina, you have a history with him. It's okay to be confused." He lifts his plate and goes to the sofa, sitting down and turning on the TV.

Joey has been a rock for me recently, and I've found myself telling him everything. But I don't voice that he's wrong, because I'm not confused. I know exactly what I feel when I look at Mason Lowell. It's the same feeling I felt the first night I met him, the same feeling I felt standing on the Palais Garnier stage, the same feeling I know I will live with for the rest of my life.

5

Mase

Silence fills the car. I should get out, but I wait, dialling Nina one more time. She left without her key and the thought that she won't be able to get back in is messing with my head. I shouldn't care. Ellis is here with me and is safe. He drifted off before we made it to the end of Nina's street, and instead of taking him inside and putting him to bed, I'm sitting here, staring into the parking garage.

My knee bounces as I spin my phone between my fingers. I've called five times already with no luck. I contemplate calling Lucy, but she deals with enough of our shit as it is.

What if she goes home and can't get inside?

Unlocking my phone, I try once more.

Nothing.

"For fuck's sake!"

I run my hand down my face, annoyed that I'm even letting it bother me. She can sort herself out. She needs to grow up.

I pull open the door and go to stand when my phone lights up with a text.

Nina: Nina's asleep. Stop calling. I have a spare key to hers. I'll have her call tomorrow. Joey.

Joey? She went to fucking Joey! My rage is boiling to the surface as I get out of the car and slam my door.

Ellis wakes, crying instantly.

Fuck!

I move quickly to his side of the car. "Hey, it's okay, mate. Come here." I lift him from his car seat and pull him into my jacket, trying to calm him.

He nuzzles into my shirt, his eyes slowly drifting closed. *Thank god!* Everything inside me calms. Nothing really matters when he's in my arms.

I carry him into the lift and up to the penthouse. It's dark and cold and everything I always hated about it—before *her* anyway. Ellis is the only thing that makes it home anymore.

His bedroom is next to my own. I had the wall knocked through to create a door between the two rooms. I don't like being away from him. I place him in his cot then plant a soft kiss to his head, watching him for a moment as he roots around and settles onto his tummy.

"I love you, son," I tell him.

He's hard to look at some days. With his brown eyes and deep-set dimples. Everything about him is Nina, and I love him. But I find it impossible to love her.

THE SHOWER SPRAY hits my back, running down over my shoulders. I wash my body on autopilot, then rest my arms against the cool tile. Why the fuck is she with him? She should be with the girls, or Maggie. Where are the fucking girls?

I knew they'd been growing close. Lucy doesn't think anything has happened, but I know she doesn't let anyone in easily. To think Joey is someone she chooses to run to... It speaks fucking volumes.

When Elliot told me Nina had let Joey meet Ellis, something inside of me broke. The idea that he would be around my son, and I'd have no idea what they'd be doing. It's almost too much to bear.

Knowing Nina is the mother that she is, is the only thing keeping me from putting a stop to it. Because I fucking could. But she wouldn't allow anything to happen to Ellis, she trusts Joey and I have to trust that.

I just don't like it.

Nina

MY LUNGS BURN as I come to a stop at the edge of the green, my hands on my knees as I bend and try to catch my breath.

"Jesus, woman, slow down. You won't make it home."

I lift my head and watch Joey as he stretches and prepares to go again. I've pushed hard this morning. Harder than normal. Joey is always out in front, telling me to keep up, but not today. Today I left him and every one of my thoughts behind me.

Running has become my new form of release. It's what I used to do when things got too much at home. I would run around our neighbourhood until I was sure my mum would have passed out or be gone for the night.

It didn't take a lot to get me back into it again. Joey and I go whenever Ellis is with Mason and sometimes, Joey will watch him for me so I can go alone. It works to fill the void my dancing used to.

For now.

"That's the idea," I force out. "You go on without me. I'm good to go at my own pace."

"You can come back to mine, you know. You don't have to worry about being at the apartment alone." He drops to the bench and starts to tie his shoe. "We could get takeout?"

"You have work to do." I plant my hands on my hips. I know he's busy.

"Get the girls over then or go out. You haven't been out in months. You need to find a way to relax on the days you have off."

"I don't want a day off!" I snap.

His face drops. A sad smile forms on his lips. "I know that, and I get you can't turn the emotions off, that's not what I'm suggesting. I just think maybe you should be finding an outlet for some of this." He gestures to me.

"This?"

"You know what I mean. Jesus, you're extra snappy today."

"What do you mean, this?"

His eyes close briefly as he mulls over his words. "Nina, you haven't danced in—"

"Goodbye, Joey!" I spin on my heel and take off in the opposite direction to home.

"Nina!"

I don't need him telling me what I should be doing. He knows this. My entire life, I have made my own choices. I'm not about to have Joey tell me I should be dancing. He has no idea why I stopped. I don't know why I stopped. All I know is it won't be forever; I just need some time.

"You know, I'm starting to see the whole issue Mason had with you running off all the time."

Joey wants to die today.

"Stop talking, please."

He chuckles, his shoulder bumping mine as he matches my every step. "That's shit banter, I'm sorry."

"I want to run alone," I puff out, trying to control my erratic breathing.

"No, you don't."

I peek up at him. He's looking straight ahead, knowingly giving me the privacy I need after calling me out. He's right. I don't want to run alone. I don't want to go home alone, because when I do, I go home to silence. I used to find peace in my music—my dancing. Then I found it in Mason, but at some point, the line became blurred, and when Mason left, so did the music.

"I'll be here until Sunday. Just let me know when you need me, okay?"

I don't answer him.

I know he knows how grateful I am to have him.

"Is anyone going to eat that?" Megan asks, leaning in and taking the last taco before we can answer.

"Do we have a choice?" Scarlet laughs as Megan bites into it.

"Nope."

We're sitting on the lounge floor, with the food we made laid out on the table. Saturday nights almost always consist of this. Just me and the girls and the best food and wine we can afford.

"I am so full," Lucy moans, unbuttoning her jeans and dropping back to the sofa. "Why do I always do it?"

"You'd think we would get fed up," Megan replies, taking another bite.

"I'll be asleep by nine at this rate. I think I'm in a food coma," I groan, my eyes feeling heavy.

"God, you guys! This is pathetic. We're all nearly thirty years old; we should be out." Scarlet stands. "Let's go out!"

Lucy, Megan, and I all sit prone in our spots, not moving a muscle. "No." I laugh. "I need a month's notice for a night out these days."

"Oh, man up. We're going out. I'm calling Vinny."

"No! Scar, not tonight we can plan it for the weekend after next," I tell her.

"Nope, you'll blow us off for flipping Joey or something," she jokes.

"I saw him today by the way." Lucy looks pointedly at me. "Joey. He said to check on you because you were struggling." She rolls her eyes; the standard look I get whenever Joey Wilson is the topic of conversation.

Mason may have hurt me, but Ellis ties him to all our lives, and the girls seem to hold the torch for him even if I don't. "You know I can be here whenever, Nina? Please stop going to him. He literally only wants into your pants."

"That's not fair, Luce. Joey's had a shitty year. So have I. It's nice to have someone who understands that."

"We understand!" she exclaims.

They don't. They're here for me, they help me, and they do everything they can to make my life that little bit easier. But they don't understand what it feels like to be truly alone. "Joey hasn't ever tried anything with me. Not once. He isn't interested in me in that way."

"You're crazy if you believe that, and it pisses me off a little. You're not stupid, Nina."

"Alright girls, let's agree to disagree. Megan, make some cocktails. I'm going to call Vinny and you two." Scarlet points between me and Lucy. "Go braid each other's hair or something. We're going out."

───────

WE'RE AT MELDERS. Not my first choice of club, but it's raining tonight so Scarlet wanted to go somewhere we wouldn't have to wait.

Memories of the last time we were here smother me the moment we enter. The wingback chairs I sat on with Mason are now filled with other waiting suits. I wonder if he still comes here. When he doesn't have Ellis, does he go out? I've never allowed my thoughts to wander to him as much as I have over the past week. It's always been easy to keep my mind off him, but now that I've seen him again. I feel... off.

"Drinks, then dancing," Megan shouts. "Girl, you look hot!" She flicks my hair back from my shoulder and beams at me.

"She does, doesn't she," Lucy says proudly, eyeing up her handiwork.

The girls went to town on me. I have on a white shirt that doubles as a dress, a pair of thigh-high nude boots, and a belt pulled around my waist to give the shirt some shape. My hair is poker straight. It took Lucy a good hour to get it under control.

"Too good. We'll have to keep an eye on you tonight, girl!" Scarlet smiles.

"Drinks!" Megan pulls Lucy deeper into the club and we all follow.

We order and then make our way down the steps to the dance floor. It is packed tonight, which is standard for a Saturday, but the DJ is some hotshot and it seems like everyone had the same idea.

"Stay together tonight, girls!" Lucy calls over her shoulder as she uses her body to push through the crowd.

We dance for what feels like hours, occasionally popping to the bar to get refills. We have ignored every bit of attention given to us and just had fun together, and honestly, I think it's the girls' way of easing me back into the partying scene.

"I'm going to get a drink," I shout.

Lucy shakes her head. "Nuh-huh. We'll come with you," she mouths over the music.

"I'm fine!"

Megan grabs her around the neck and spins her onto the dance floor and I slip off before she can stop me. I laugh at them as I walk backwards and towards the bar.

Just as I turn, I bump into a solid chest, completely losing my balance. Big hands catch my waist taking my weight and pulling me into him as I sway. My face catches his white shirt and I cringe as my foundation marks it. "I'm so sorry." I apologise, lifting my face from the shirt to his face.

Okay. He's hot.

"Hi." He smiles a swoon-worthy smile, sliding his hands slowly from my body and leaving a trail of fire in their wake. "You good, baby girl?"

"Yeah. Sorry, I wasn't looking where I was going, and..." I wipe over the mark on his right pec and it flexes under my fingers.

"I'm Pax."

"Pax?" I question, taking his outstretched hand.

"Yeh, Paxo. My mum's a dickhead."

My eyes bug out and then I laugh, unable to help it. "Oh no, I'm sorry. I'm not laughing at your name, I just..." Oh god, Nina. "I'm Nina." I mentally slap myself for being so rude.

His eyes roam my body and then he smiles down at me. "You want to dance?"

"No, sorry. I was on my way to the bar."

"Let me buy it."

I roll my lips. Should I let him buy me a drink? "Okay," I answer quickly, not thinking too much on it.

"I've not seen you here before—"

"Do I come here often? Really?" I smile, feeling my dimples pop on my cheeks.

"Can't blame a guy for trying. I knew you'd be hard work." His lip twitches as he leans on the bar, biting his lip as he watches me. He is too much. The type of man to suck you in with his charm and then spit you out Sunday morning. He's too beautiful to be single and not be a player. But I'd be lying if I said his charm wasn't working.

"Sorry." I chuckle.

He steps closer to me. "I like that laugh," he rasps out.

I swallow, watching as his eyes flick between my own and then drop to my lips.

"How about that dance?" I ask.

"Yeah?" He grins.

I nod, taking his outstretched hand as he leads me to the dance floor. It's busy, and bodies push us together as we find a free spot. Instantly his hands find me, roaming my body expertly. As if he knows me.

I'd be lying if I said it didn't feel good.

To be touched—held.

"Your body is phenomenal," he rasps into my ear.

I close my eyes, putting my back to his front. I roll my hips into him. My body thrums with arousal, a taste of something I've not truly felt in so long, begging to be let out and explored.

His hands smooth up my ribs, his palms large and strong. He's always been so strong. Always known how to touch me in the right places. Always known how to get me right where he wants me, right on the edge of insanity. Our lips brush and the taste of something sweet has my eyes snapping open.

What the fuck am I doing?

I pull back, searching the room until I spot the door I'm looking for. "I'm so sorry."

Pushing off from his chest, I stalk towards the office, thankful to find it's unlocked when I get there. Stepping inside, I drop back against the door, pinching my eyes closed and taking a moment to find my *peace*.

Mase

"WHAT THE FUCK are you doing, Pix?"

I watch on the monitor as Nina stumbles into the back office, pushing the door closed and leaning against it. I can see her chest heaving, and although I know I can't connect the sound from my home office, I still fiddle with the volume, trying to hear her.

Her hand comes up and grips her throat.

"What's wrong?" I murmur.

Her hand slides down her body, and my eyes follow their trail. What is she wearing? Is that even an outfit? Why would Vinny allow her out of the damn car? I frown as she slides her hand up the inside of her thigh, subconsciously ducking my head lower as if it will miraculously allow me a better view.

"Fuck!"

What is she doing?!

She fiddles for a second, allowing my imagination to drift. My dick is instantly hard.

I should stop watching, she'd have my ass if she knew I could see her. I shouldn't want to even watch this.

I pull out my phone and text Benny.

Mase: Lock the office door

Benny: Nina went in five minutes ago

I shake my head. Fucking idiot.

Mase: I know. Wait at the bar and watch your phone

Her hand moves over herself slowly. The slightest movement in the material of her shirt is the only indicator of what she's doing to herself.

I palm my cock through my gym shorts, trying to ease the throbbing ache, but it only makes me grow harder.

Fuck.

Her eyes are tightly closed, and I wonder what she's thinking about, because all I can picture in my mind is me on my knees with my head buried between her legs—just like the first time she was up against that door.

Sliding my shorts over my hips, I release my cock. It stands to attention, precum already coating the tip. It's been too long. Wrapping my hand around the base, I fist it slowly, with just the right amount of pressure to make it feel like *her*.

As if she knew what I needed, she lifts the material of her shirt, sliding her other hand down to work herself.

"Good girl."

Her head hits the door and I watch as a smile creeps onto her face. It's euphoric and like a fucking spear to my heart.

My balls grow tight as her hand goes tense, her hips moving against her fingers in slow circles. I can tell she's close.

I start to work myself faster, stroking myself relentlessly as I watch Nina come undone against my office door. I can see her panting. I can see her chest as it rises and falls, her release tethering only a fingertip away.

Mase: Get her out of there. Knock

Hot cum leaks out and over my fingers, and my eyes fight to stay open, but I keep them glued to her.

She jumps away from the door, her hand instantly falling from her pussy. She smooths out the creases in her shirt and then palms her hand over her perfectly straight hair.

"Sorry, baby. Not on my watch." Not if it's not my orgasm.

I grab a tissue from my desk to clean myself up and then pull my shorts back over my hips and wait.

Benny walks in and I see them talk for a moment, but then he leaves, closing the door and leaving her in the room.

I dial his number.

"What the fuck are you doing?"

"She needed a minute."

"I told you to get her out."

She places herself back in front of the door and I think she is going to carry on, but then she slides to the ground and holds her face.

What the hell.

"Shall I go back inside?"

"No." I hang up.

She looks to the ceiling and wipes at her cheek, and I instantly want to go to her.

What's wrong with her? She was about to come twenty seconds ago.

I don't know how long she sits there for, on the cold floor of my office, staring at the same spot on the ceiling. But I sit with her, hoping she doesn't feel as alone as she looks. I sit long after she gets up and puts on her brave face. And I sit long after she leaves.

She always leaves.

6

Nina

THANKFULLY, THE GIRLS WERE READY TO LEAVE WHEN I WENT and found them. Vinny arrived not long after and now we are on our way home. I'm desperate to crawl into bed and forget the evening.

We drop the girls off at their apartment and they both try and get me to go in with them, but I decline, wanting to be home for when Ellis gets back in the morning.

Scarlet is staying at Mason's so that Vinny won't have to drive all the way out to Lowerwick this late.

The tree-lined road that houses Mason's building comes into view and my stomach knots. I don't know what happened tonight, but I knew I couldn't kiss Pax when it was Mason on my mind. And then when I got to the office, the need to feel him... It was overwhelming. I don't know if seeing him again is a good idea. Not when there's clearly still so much between us.

"Thanks, Vinny," Scarlet says as she unclips her seat belt.

"Will you need a lift home tomorrow, love?" Vinny asks.

"Uh, yeah, I probably will actually." She pulls me in for a hug. "You sure you wanna go home alone? Don't want to come inside and give me some moral support with my brother."

I shake my head. "I can't, Scar." I know things have been strained between Mason and Scarlet. The only thing that keeps them in contact is Ellis these days and that upsets me. They both deserve more.

"Okay, see you and my little monster in the week."

She gets out of the Audi and walks to the elevator, just like I've done myself so many times before.

My entire world lives behind those steel doors, lying asleep mere metres away.

I miss my home.

"You sure you don't want to go to the girls' apartment?" Vinny asks, watching me in the mirror.

"I want to be at home—"

"For Ellis. I know." He smiles softly as he pulls out of the parking garage and onto the busy street.

VINNY WALKS me inside my building and to my door. As always, he stands waiting for me to be inside before he turns to leave.

"Vin." I stop him, toying with the door handle as I try and articulate my words in a way that will make sense.

He turns in question.

My eyes prickle and I grit my teeth. "Did you ever... do

you think Mason..." I frown, my throat growing tight. I can't even say it.

"Do I think Mason cheated on you?" He steps closer, showing me the no nonsense side of him that I don't always get.

I nod, heat rising in my gut.

"No, Nina. No, I don't." I close my eyes as pain slices through me. "Get to bed, love. Tomorrow is a new day."

He squeezes my shoulder, giving me a warm smile before leaving.

The apartment door shuts behind me with a thwack and I'm instantly crippled by the silence that greets me. Not even the ticking of a clock can be heard. No leaky tap, no heater whirling, just silence.

I go through the motions, locking up then getting myself a glass of water and going to my bedroom. My eyes flick to Ellis's cot and then to my empty bed, and I can't help but think of Mason and Ellis at the penthouse. Where does he sleep? Does he sleep in *our* bed?

I clean my teeth and undress, then crawl under the covers, pulling them tight around my chin.

I always wondered about the photos. The way they were left at reception, and the fact the boys couldn't find Mason that night.

I'm not stupid and something always told me it was odd how the night unfolded. But once you see something that can hurt you so deeply, a physical copy of something placed in your hand that sears itself into your mind... I think I always knew Mason was set up, but I never thought I could get over the fact he'd had his lips on another woman. It will always be too much to think about. I just don't know how to be okay in this world alone anymore.

Throwing back my covers, I pull on my leggings and hoodie and take off out of my bedroom.

No matter how strong I want to be sometimes, loneliness wins.

I jog down the street to Joey's building, my heart feeling heavier than it has in months as it pounds in my chest. Flipping through my key chain, I find the right one and unlock the door.

"Joe." I shake his shoulder once in his bedroom. "Joe."

"Hmmm," he muses.

"Joe."

"Nina?" He sits up, blinking at me until he can focus. "What's up?"

"I just..." I pause, looking around the room as if it holds all the answers.

He pulls back the covers and climbs on top, creating a barrier. "Here."

I slide under, putting my back to his front. He wraps me in his arms, but I don't sleep. Joey isn't my home, and I destroyed mine over something that might not have been true.

Mase

MY HEAD IS heavy when I wake. Ellis is still sleeping soundly in his cot, so I go to the kitchen and make myself a coffee, taking his monitor with me. I couldn't sleep last night. Nina sat on my office floor crying, haunted me till the early hours.

Why was she crying?

I knew seeing her after all this time would bring back feelings from before and it has, but I also feel angrier than ever. I came to terms with the fact that she would never come back to me the minute I left the hospital, and I didn't want her back. Too many people have left me in my life. Too many important people. I can't give her any more chances to fuck me up.

At first, I tried to shut Scar and the boys out, finding it easier to keep my distance and turn my feelings off.

You can't hurt if you don't feel.

Scarlet pulled my ass in line when I was at my lowest and thank fuck she did. Ellis didn't need a deadbeat dad. I cleaned up my shit, stopped the drinking and meaningless fucking I'd been hiding behind, and made sure I was there for his birth and the days that followed.

Becoming a dad is my proudest moment to date. I'm a different man to who I was twelve months ago.

I drink my coffee and wake Ellis, dressing him and packing up his things. It's only eight thirty, so we lie on my bed for a while. I let him babble, absorbing his every sound and committing them to memory.

I know little moments like these are special.

"Yeah... then what happened?" I ask him.

He continues to chatter, grabbing my stubble and pulling my head down to his.

"Well, I'd have to agree."

He grins up at me and I smooth my thumb over his dimple before placing a kiss there.

"We have to go home soon, buddy," I tell him. "You'll be good for Mummy, won't you? She needs extra cuddles today."

"Da Da Da Da."

"I'll miss you, little dude. Wednesday will be here before we know it."

I MAKE sure we get to Nina's by ten o'clock on the dot. She throws open the door and smiles wide when she sees Ellis.

"Hey, baby!" Leaning in, she takes him from my arms. He clings to her, bouncing in excitement. "Mummy has missed you."

My eyes drop down her body, taking in her yoga pants and baggy tee. It's not sexy, or it's not supposed to be. But Nina, natural and in her comfy clothes, it does something to me. My mind goes back to the night before and the way she touched herself.

"Was he okay? Sleep okay?" she asks, looking up at me.

"Yeah, he was great. We took him to the park yesterday." I shake off my wayward thoughts. "Me and the guys."

"You went to the park?" she asks Ellis playfully. She looks back up at me again, biting on her full bottom lip as she openly stares.

"Did you want to come in, Mason?" she eventually asks, uncertainty lacing her voice.

I pause for absolutely no reason. I already know what I'm going to say. "No—"

"Nina!" I turn to find Joey walking up the steps behind me, making his way towards the door. "You left your bag." He waves it in the air. "I worried until I saw you had your keys."

Nina looks to me and then back to Joey. Ellis sits watching us on her hip. "Oh, yeah. Thanks, Joe."

Is she for fucking real?

"Mason." Joey holds his hand out for me to shake.

I place a foot in front of him, leaning across and kissing Ellis. I don't say anything else. I don't tell her I'll be back Wednesday, because I can't promise that I will be.

I leave and don't look back.

"Mase?"

———

Nina

"AND THEN HE JUST LEFT?" Ashley asks, licking her finger as she pries the paper apart.

"It was so awkward, Ash. I think he hates me. He definitely thinks something is going on between me and Joey. He's asked Lucy in the past."

She pops a brow at me. "Sounds like you care."

I close my eyes, completely confused with the way I feel. "Of course, I care. He is Ellis's dad."

"But you said you could never be with him again. After..."

"I couldn't." Could I?

"You need to get laid."

I roll my eyes and give her the finger. "Fuck—"

"Nina!!!" Rochelle hisses. "My office. Now!"

"I'm so sorry," Ashley mouths as she cringes.

I close my eyes and shake my head, not shocked that the universe is fucking with me this hard. My eyes burn into the back of Rochelle's head as I follow her into her office. I drop down into the chair and wait for her to round the table, but she stands. It makes me feel small.

"This is your second warning. The first was verbal. I will have it in writing by the end of the day. You will have some damn grace when you are working on the reception. We don't go flipping people off in front of guests."

"There wasn't any g—"

"Let's make one thing clear!" she speaks over me. "I don't like you, Nina, and you don't like me. Do your job and do it well, and you won't have any issues with me. Got it?!"

I nod my head once, running my tongue across my teeth.

"Get out."

So fucking rude. She makes me want to quit but I can't. I need the money more than her manners right now.

I shake my head at Ashley, telling her with my eyes not to say a word. I know Rochelle will be able to hear us still. Rolling myself up to the computer I get my head down and start to process bookings, not letting anything else penetrate my headspace.

ELLIOT IS SITTING on my sofa when I get home later that evening. He stands when he sees me.

"Where's Mason?" I ask, my shoulders dropping.

"He had to work this evening."

Mason never worked on the days he had Ellis. I wonder if it has anything to do with Sunday. If I'm being honest, this suits me better. Last week was an emotional roller coaster.

"Did Ellis go down okay?"

"Yeah, he did actually." He smiles proudly. "How was work?"

"Same old." I shrug, then remember Rochelle's comment. "Hey! Did you have anything to do with getting me a job at the hotel? My manager seems to think I'm there as a favour."

A devilish smirk takes over his face. "What a favour that was."

"Eww! That's gross, Ell. She's catty! She actually told me she hates me today."

"She always did use her claws. Rochelle's alright, you just have to learn how to tame her." He waggles his brows.

"Oh god," I snort. "I'm disappointed. You don't still go there, do you?"

"Only when I have to, and you're welcome by the way."

I shake my head, leaving him in the lounge and going to the kitchen. Elliot follows, taking an apple from the fruit bowl.

"Did Mason mention anything about Joey today? He turned up when he dropped Ellis off on Sunday and then he just left. I think he was pissed."

"Nah, Lowell's had his hands full in the office this week, that's all. Don't take it personally."

"Hands full with what?"

He takes a bite of his apple, not answering me, when his eyes meet mine, he raises them in question. "What's he been busy with?" I ask again.

"Nothing you need to worry your pretty head about." He leans over the edge of the breakfast bar and kisses my forehead. "Have Maggie booked in for next weekend. I want everyone out for my birthday."

"Will Mason be there?" I ask to his back as he walks away, as if he didn't just drop that bombshell.

"Of course he will be."

"Well, I won't be."

"Yes, you will, Pix—"

"Ell!"

"Sorry, I forget."

I roll my eyes, moving around the island and walking him to the door. "I'll see if Maggie's free, but I'm not making any promises. I don't think Mason, alcohol, and me, is a good idea."

"Could be a great idea." He grins.

"Stop it."

"Hey!" He throws his hands up in defence. "You guys made it through last week without killing each other. I have every bit of faith in you."

"Well, that makes one of us."

Mase

"MASON. Who is this girl? She just answered the phone! We cannot have her answering the phone. Have you heard her phone voice? It's her regular voice but worse! Please tell you have a plan here?"

George waltzes into my office, his finger running across the inside of his collar as if his bow tie is too tight. He's become a solid fixture around here, and he gets shit done. The fact he has to deal with Jasmine makes me feel kind of shitty, but I don't have the time.

"Did she leave yet?"

"No! She was late this morning. I made her stay on." He shakes his head and I laugh.

"George, you can let her get home. Yourself too. You don't need to be in this late."

"She needs to be taught some discipline, Mason. Why are you being nice?"

George is right, Jasmine probably does need some discipline, but I also know this week has been hard for her.

"Let her get home now." I nod, letting him know it's not up for discussion.

"Okay." He rolls his eyes, placing his hands on his hips and cursing under his breath. I lean back in my chair, waiting.

"Look, if she's going to be staying and I'm going to be training her, it's far more responsibility. I mean, I probably needed an assistant six months ago, and—"

"I will run it by Elliot, but I'm in agreement that you should be on a higher wage."

"Really?"

"Yes, really. You have more potential than some of the staff higher than you. You're smart, George. Too smart for reception—"

"I love the reception."

"I know, and we appreciate you."

"Thank you, Mason."

I tip my chin and focus back on my screen.

"How was Ellis today?" He walks over to my desk, picking up the photo of me and Ellis from the day he was born.

"Fussy. He has teeth coming."

"You don't normally come in on the days you have him. Is everything okay?"

"Yes, George. Thank you." I tear my eyes from the screen and look at him. "Is that all?"

"Yeah, sorry." He places the frame back on my desk and slips out of the office quietly.

I reach for the photo George had just been holding.

Ellis is wrapped up in his blanket, holding tightly onto my finger. Nina took the photo; she took so many photos. They're all I have of her from the past year.

Pulling out my phone, I scroll back to the day he was born. Torturing myself as I look through the images of the three of us.

IT'S LATE when I finally leave the office, and instead of going home, I opt to go to the twenty-four-hour gym that's down the street from The Montwell. When Ellis isn't with me, I try to spend as little time as possible at the penthouse. I prefer it that way.

I'm just pulling into the gym's car park when Scarlet's name lights up my screen.

"Hey, Scar."

"Hi," she says, sounding sad.

"What's up?" I frown.

"Dad's headstone," she sniffs into the phone.

"Scar."

"They called, said that the soil is settled enough. We can have it put on now."

I swallow the lump in my throat. It's been over twelve

months and we've been putting it off due to the soil and the insane amount of rain we've been having. I never remember waiting so long for my mother's headstone to be placed, but time flies when you're a kid. "That's good," I tell her.

"Yeah... God, this place is lonely sometimes." She laughs, but I can tell she is crying.

"Do you want to come to mine tonight? You could come for the weekend?"

"I can't, I've had a bottle of wine already." She sniffs, but there's still light in her voice. "Could you come here?"

I scrub my hand over my face, gritting my teeth. "Scar, I..."

"I know, you can't."

"I want to." I do.

"One day," she deadpans. "I need to go, Mase. Speak to you soon, okay?"

"Scar."

She hangs up. I chuck my phone into the footwell, punching my steering wheel and making the horn blare.

"FUCK!"

7

Nina

"LET ME GET THAT FOR YOU," VINNY TELLS ME AS HE JUMPS from the driver's side of the car and meets me at the boot. "You take the bags and I'll get Ellis."

"Thanks." I start up the steps with our bags, turning to call over my shoulder. "His bear is next to the car seat."

"Got it." He holds it up, smiling.

I push open the large door, noting that the entire house is lit up like Christmas. "Scar?" I call out.

"Nina?" Scarlet's head pops around the kitchen door, her hair piled on her head and her dungarees only done up on one side. "You came," she says, sounding surprised.

"Of course I came!" I drop our bags and walk to her. "Come here."

I pull her petite frame into a tight hug, wishing I could take away all the hurt. "I'm going to go settle Ellis in his cot and I'll be back down. Get Vin a coffee for the road? He's beat today."

She nods, already turning back towards the kitchen. "Okay."

Ellis is still fast asleep when Vinny brings him in from the car. I take him from his arms and carry him up the stairs to his bedroom. At first, Scarlet wanted his nursery to be on the east side of the house, but then she showed me his bedroom which sits in the west wing, and we both knew it was perfect. His bedroom has the perfect view overlooking the garden. His grandparents watch upon him whenever he is here, and it feels like the most special thing in the world.

Vinny is already gone when I get downstairs, which doesn't surprise me—it's gone eleven.

"I'm so sorry I called so late. I didn't know who else to call, and you know how Freya can be," Scarlet rants over the rim of her wine glass, clearly worked up.

"You can always call me, Scar. You know that."

"I called Mase." She drops her eyes, pulling in a deep breath and letting it out again.

I frown, pinching the stem of my wine glass between two fingers. "You told him about the headstone?"

She nods. "And asked him to come out here." She lifts her eyes to mine. "Am I stupid to hold on to hope of him coming around?"

I walk around the island and wrap her in a hug. "No. You're a good sister. He'll do it one day, Scar. He just needs more time."

"What about me? I don't get the luxury of more time. It's me who lays the flowers. It's me who tends to the weeds. Sometimes it feels like he doesn't even care." Her jaw clenches and I know she doesn't believe her words.

"I know, and it isn't fair. But you're strong. You make the

people around you stronger. It's not that Mason doesn't care, it's because he cares too much." I roll my eyes. "I have a little faith in him, still, you know."

She smiles as she swipes at her cheek. "Mum's head-stone is beautiful, but it's such a reminder. The date—the loving words of the woman she was. I don't want to look at the date Dad died. I don't want to read how wonderful he was."

"I'm sorry." I drop my head to hers, not knowing what to say. "It might not mean anything to you, but I'd give anything to be able to have such wonderful words written on my parents' headstones. God, if my mother died, I'd have no clue what I'd say. Is that terrible?"

"No." She laughs, and it makes me grin. "It's very you."

"It only hurts because of the memories, Scar. Try and focus on the good and not the words carved in the stone."

"Thank you, Nina."

"Of course." I smile, knowing that she will be okay.

"You're sure you'll be okay?"

"Yes! If I knew you were going to linger all weekend, I wouldn't have called you," Scarlet tells me, smiling playfully down at Ellis who is wrapped up in her arms.

She has to be one of the strongest people I have ever met, and I know she would've gotten through the weekend without me, but she shouldn't have to. I hoped Mason would come around and show up on Saturday, but that never happened.

We had Anthony's headstone placed and then sat out in

the garden for the afternoon whilst Ellis crawled amongst the wildflowers.

"I'm glad you called. Ellis had a great weekend. We really should come out more often."

"It's so far for you both that I never want to ask."

I shake my head, smiling. "I want Ellis to know this place. It's important to me that he has somewhere other than the apartment." Not that I'd turn my nose up at what we have now, but I always wanted a little house on the outskirts of the city. Somewhere homely.

"He doesn't know any different" —she waves me off— "and he has this place and Maggie and John's, and I know the Montgomerys think of him as one of their own." She places her finger on the end of his nose. "You, little man, are more loved than you'll ever know."

"He really is," I snigger.

"Car's loaded. Do you want me to take him?" Vinny asks from behind me, speaking to Scarlet.

"No! He's mine for another five minutes." She walks past us and out onto the front terrace.

I can see the annoyance on Vinny's face. He's been itching for a cuddle since he got here. "You can stay for tea tonight, Vin. If you want to."

"That's okay, I don't want to intrude."

He's always been too polite for his own good. "I have Maggie and John coming over, I know they'd love to see you."

He grins, perking up instantly. "John's coming across? It's the champions league final."

"Yep."

The two of them hit it off the minute John discovered Vinny to be a Tottenham fan. Vinny drove me out to the house one Sunday, and once he was invited in, that was it, he became my companion to all Sunday lunches at the Morgan's.

I shake my head, helping to put the last of the bags into the boot. "Scar, we need to get back, I need to stop for supplies!" I call to her, feeling bad but knowing I have plenty to catch up on at home.

I'M LEANT across the kitchen island watching as the boys sit on the edge of their seats. As always, my week hosting Sunday lunch for Maggie and John turned into feeding the five thousand. First Vinny, who I welcomed in, but then the hungover trio rock up, Lucy, Elliot and Lance.

I love them all, but they turn up, eat my food and leave. Which leaves me and Maggie in the kitchen to clean up the mess.

"Pass it!!!" John yells, red-faced. "Fucking shit—"

"John!" Maggie hisses from her spot next to me at the kitchen island. She nods towards Ellis who is watching John in wonder as he sits on the floor, happily chewing his fist.

"He doesn't pass it, Mags!" he explains to her, as if it will make it okay.

"Yes! Yes! Yaaasssss! Get in there, you beauties!" Elliot jumps up, getting in John and Vinny's faces in celebration.

"Stop shouting, please," Lucy groans from the sofa, where she's curled up with a blanket feeling sorry for herself.

"Sit down, you fool. You're still losing," Vinny tells Elliot.

"Just wait, old man."

"How's it been leaving Ellis? You seem to be settling into

work well?" Maggie asks me, passing me the stack of dishes she's finished drying.

"Good. It's nice to have the independence and be able to pay for this place. I can't say I love it at the hotel though."

She nods in understanding; she knows it's not the job I want. "And Mason, it still works for him to have the time off work?"

I smile to myself as I carefully place the plates in the cupboard. The thing with Maggie is she cares, probably more than anyone else, and she wants to be a part of our lives. But she isn't pushy. She'll let us know she's here, and that she will help us, but she won't force it. It's what I love about her.

"I think it works. It gives them more time together in the week too."

"That's good." She picks up a tray from the drainer.

"But I could ask Mason if he needs any help at all, maybe you could have him a day a week if he is ever too busy?"

"Whenever! I told the office I'm more than ready to drop down to three days now. I don't want you ever having to pay for childcare."

"I can't see that ever being a problem." I laugh, looking over at the people I call my family. "Do you think you can have Ellis next weekend, Mags? It would be overnight, which I know we haven't tried before, but it's Elliot's birthday and Mason will be out with him. I might go too but if not, I'll have him instead."

"It's Mason's weekend?" she questions.

"Yeah, and he hasn't asked me to ask, but he can have an extra night during the week or something."

She puts her hand on her chest and beams at me. "His first sleepover? If Mason doesn't mind, I'd love to."

I watch her as she spins and picks up the sieve, her happiness making me smile. I shouldn't feel sad, but I can't help the hurt that swamps me. I have so much love around me, and Maggie is the mother and grandmother I always wished Ellis and myself to have. But she isn't my mother. My mother hasn't contacted me in months, and even then, it was me calling to tell her she had a new grandchild on the way. I've heard nothing since that day.

"What's that look?" Maggie asks.

I scrunch up my nose in thought. "I think I made a mistake when I left Mason." A lump forms in my throat.

Did I just say that out loud?

Maggie's eyes go wide, and she recoils. "Nina. I—"

"I know." I drop my head, waving it off. "It's by the by now. I just wish I'd taken more time. I saw the photos and couldn't see anything *but* that image when I made the decisions I did. Seeing him again this last week... It's been odd. He hates me now."

"I don't believe that man could ever hate you."

"I'm nearly thirty. I have Ellis now, and I live mostly off the money I get from his father. I feel like I'm in this weird middle zone of motherhood and trying to find... me again. I don't know." I huff. "What if I don't find someone else?" I bite the inside of my cheek. "Being alone, it scares me."

"You'll never be alone, darling," she soothes, pulling me into her side. "And someone will snap you up. You just have to learn to let them in." She gives me a pointed look. "And dance, you need to dance again, Nina."

Maybe she's right, maybe dancing is the distraction I need to ease the chaos that Mason brings.

EVERY WEEK I tell myself that I will step out of my comfort zone and get the tube, go into Oxford Circus, and do my shopping. I hate relying on Vinny and Joey to take me everywhere; I know they're both busy. But right now, as I look down at Ellis and watch as he goes red-faced and grunts his way through his ten a.m. poo, I know I should've asked someone for a lift.

Do I get off at an earlier stop? It's busy and people are starting to stare.

"Ellis, what did you do?" I groan as he sits, smiling at me triumphantly.

STUPIDLY, I thought we'd be okay. I didn't get off early and by the time we arrived, it had started to come out of the sides of the nappy.

I roll the pushchair through Mothercare and into their baby changing unit to clean him up.

As I leave the shop, I can smell the stench from the clothes that I placed in a nappy bag, and I know I will have to ditch them. I can't walk around London with that smell getting under my nose.

Looking up and down the street, I search for a bin, finally spotting one on the opposite side. "Thank god." I push forward with his stroller at the same time a woman steps past me. She kicks the wheel, causing her to trip, her phone falling to the floor.

"Oh, I'm so sorr—" I cut myself off when she turns, and

my eyes zero in on her familiar face.

It's the girl from the hotel. The one who had been crying. She's made up now though and is wearing an expensive business dress.

She goes to speak but then stops, dropping her eyes to Ellis in the stroller. Her gaze lifts instantly, darting all over my face, her lips tight as if refraining from saying something. She bends and picks up her phone, then looks down at Ellis again. She pauses for a moment, her throat bobbing. "I'm sorry, I wasn't looking where I was going." She takes off quickly and all I can do is stand, frozen in place, watching as her back gets swallowed up in the crowd.

"It's her."

"Da Da Da Da." Ellis claps.

I look down at him and then to the bag of soiled clothes in my hand. Moving quickly across the street, I toss the clothes into the bin and sit down on a nearby bench.

Needing to calm myself, I pull Ellis from his stroller and then reach for my phone and dial Lucy's number.

"Hey! I'm on my way to a fitting, babe. Everything okay?"

"No. Luce, I just saw the stripper."

"The stripper?" she asks. "Oh my god! The stripper?"

"Yes! She walked into me. I was about to cross the street."

"Did you say anything? Jesus, Nina, did you hurt her?"

"What? No! I've seen her before though. In the hotel. She was going into a room when I was cleaning. I remember she was crying, and I just knew I'd seen her face before."

She looked ten times better today than she did in the hotel, with her hair washed and her roots fixed. And her dress was smart—expensive even.

"At The Earl Marks?" she questions. "Shit, Nina, I have to

go, me and Jean are just pulling up. I will call you after, okay?"

"Yeah. Sorry to call when you're working. Speak later."

I stare at the ground, completely lost in my own mind. It never bothered me to know who she was. She was a nobody to me. But now that I've seen her... I want to know more. Who is this girl, and how did she end up with Mason that night?

"I'M COMING, BABY BOY!" I call into the lounge to a crying Ellis. "Just a second. Mummy is going as quick as she can."

Since Mason has been coming to the apartment, Lucy has taken a step back in helping me in the mornings. It's what I wanted, but it means on the days I have work and Mason picks up, I have to get us up and ready for seven thirty when Mason comes to get him. It's a mad rush, especially when Ellis likes to nap so late into the morning.

He crawls into the kitchen and starts to climb up my legs until he's standing clinging to me, swaying on his chunky legs.

"Come here." I lift him into my arms and wipe away his tears. "Mummy was only getting your things ready, little man."

I hear the door and then Vinny walks in. My brows crease. "You beat Mason this morning Vin, you okay?"

"'Morning, love. Mason needs to go into the office this morning. He asked if I could have Ellis for a couple hours after I dropped you in."

"He didn't say anything about it. You have time?"

"It's not for long. And I don't mind." He smiles.

I know Vinny adores Ellis, but I sometimes worry he feels obliged to say yes. "If you're sure."

"Come on, what needs doing? You're going to be late."

ROCHELLE IS WAITING at reception when I get into work. Skirting past her, I slip into the staff office and hang up my coat. If you ask me, she's making the place look untidy.

"Oh, hello, Nina. You decided you'd come in today then?"

"My son—" I snap my mouth closed, because explaining myself to this woman is pointless. She doesn't have a compassionate bone in her body.

"You can stay on tonight, or your wages will be docked. Remember when you aren't here, it's everyone else having to pull the weight for your tardiness."

"I know. I'm sorry." I smooth out my skirt and try to step past her, but she blocks my exit.

"I hope so, because if you're late again you will be fired, and I'll make sure you never get a job in hospitality again." She side-eyes me as I walk from the room, a glare plastered on her stony face.

The she-devil lingers until lunchtime, before finally retreating back to her office, giving me and Ashley some breathing room.

"You sure know how to piss that woman off, girl." Her lip twitches, but she doesn't take her eyes off the screen.

"I barely slept, then Ellis was fussing." I drop my head into my hands, thinking about my shopping trip the day before. It's the main reason I couldn't sleep. "I saw the woman from the photos with Mason."

"No way! Where?"

"On the street. She walked into Ellis's stroller. It was kind of my fault, but she just picked up her phone and kept going." The entire interaction has been messing with me all night. "If I wanted to look someone up—"

"Oh wow, are you going to hire a PI?"

"No!" I look over the top of the desk, making sure it's clear. "I mean here, at the hotel."

"Like a guest?"

I nod. "She's been here before. I saw her."

"Well yeah, you'd need her name or room number."

"She was staying in a room opposite one of the ones I was cleaning. I saw her go inside. She was crying on the phone; I'd probably remember the door if I was up there again."

She nods her head, then looks back to her computer, typing for a moment. "Did you do odds or evens that day?"

Shit, I don't know... "Odds."

"Hmm, do you know what time it was? You checked out each room which is helpful. And Emily helped you on two-thirteen, was it before or after Emily helped you?"

"It was straight after!"

"Well, then... two-fourteen!" She bounces in her seat as she finds the information I need.

That was too easy. "What's her name? How much info is there?" I can't sit in my seat any longer. I need the information and Ashley's gone mute on me. Rochelle can kiss my ass.

Leaning over, I scan the invoice on the screen, searching for a name.

Ashley looks up at me over her shoulder. "Vinny Dukes? Is that?"

"Vinny."

What the fuck?

Ignorance is bliss.

What you don't know can't hurt you.

What the eyes don't see, the heart doesn't grieve over.

They're all sayings for a reason. Sometimes we think we have to know something; we think it's for the best or that it will bring us peace of mind.

But my mind doesn't feel peaceful right now.

It didn't take me long to work out what Vinny paying for her hotel room meant, and yet the naive girl in me still hoped I was wrong. For the best part of a week, I've doubted my decisions and blamed myself for our situation. I feel stupid to have let him get to me so easily.

His fingers rap at the door and I take my time to get up and open it, making sure my head is clear before I do.

Fuck him.

Fuck him.

Fuck him.

I swing open the door.

"Hi." His eyes eat me up, just like they always do.

"Hi," I reply.

So many feelings suffocate me as I lean in and take Ellis from his arms. Has he been with her today? Does he have Ellis around her?

"He napped around four, sorry. I think it's his teeth." He runs his hand through his hair, messing it up. He looks tired.

I drop my eyes to Ellis, not being able to answer him.

"Hey." He places a hand on my arm, and I recoil. "What's

the matter?"

So much sits on the tip of my tongue. So many words I want to unleash on him. The damage is already done, though. There's no going back. There was never any going back. For once my head and heart are in agreement.

I can't seem to pull my eyes from Ellis. He's the only safe territory here.

"Everything's fine, Mason. We'll see you on Thursday."

He crosses his arms in front of his broad chest. "Something's wrong, what is it?" he asks, his tone demanding.

"Do you think you deserve to know what's the matter with me?" I snap.

He frowns, then drops his arms to his side with a thwack. "You know what, right now, I don't care. I came to drop my son off, which by the way was what *you* suggested, but if that isn't working, we can come up with a new arrangement. Your hostility is getting old."

"What?!"

"I don't care," he repeats, hammering the knife even deeper into my chest. "I'll see you in the week."

His lips brush Ellis's head, and then he leaves.

―――――――

ROCHELLE CALLED this morning and asked me to work an extra shift, which is why I'm currently stripping beds. I should ask if there are any jobs going in housekeeping. I much prefer it up here.

I didn't want to leave Ellis this morning, but I knew I needed the distraction and Maggie has been desperate to have him. She was over the moon when I called.

Lucy came over last night and helped me find the bottom of the wine bottle while I bitched and moaned about Mason. She agreed with me that if Mason thinks he can have that woman around my son, he is deranged. I wonder if he plans on speaking to me about it first. The fact he uses somewhere to screw her proves the fact he wanted to hide her.

Pushing my trolley into the lift, I hit the button for the ground floor.

I already knew that Mason could hurt me easily. I'm used to it. The asshole sold my little studio, once upon a time. But what I didn't expect or anticipate was Vinny. I never thought he'd hurt me, not intentionally. The last time he thought he would, he left. So why is he telling me he doesn't believe anything happened when he knows full well what's going on?

The doors slide open to the reception area, and lo and behold, Mason stands at the front desk, his hands in his pockets as he waits.

I watch as he turns and walks down the corridor and into a back room. My adrenaline starts pumping until it's all I can hear.

All I can think about.

I see red.

The steel doors begin to close, and I shoot my hand out to stop them. Does Mason come here when I'm not working?

He comes here on my days off.

That bastard.

I leave my trolley in the lift and follow him, feeling completely unhinged as I push through the door, slamming it back against the plaster.

"What the fuck is going on?!" I rage, ready to unleash the pent-up anger I've kept at bay for the best part of a year.

8

Nina

"Nina?" Rochelle's eyes are sharp and zeroed in on me. She's standing over Mason with a jug of water clenched in her hand.

Mason stands and buttons his jacket, a deep frown marring his handsome face. "Nina, I didn't know you were working today."

My nostrils flare as my body flushes hot. "I bet you didn't."

"Excuse me a moment, gentleman."

My eyes flick around the room, noting the three men and a young girl in the corner who looks to be taking minutes. Unease suffocates me, but I'm too angry to allow my mind to catch up and put all the pieces together.

"Mr Lowell, I'm so very sorry for this interruption." Rochelle's lip curls as she looks at me. "*She's* new. I'm sure we can offer some kind of compensation to you and your team, and rest assured she will be dealt with." Her eyes scan me up and down in a judgemental stare and I snap.

"Oh, will you just fuck off!"

Mason's head snaps to me, and Rochelle's face drops, quickly losing all its colour.

"I beg your pardon?" she stammers.

"You heard me! This whole month you've been coming at me, telling me how much you hate me, how I could lose my job, and how tardy I am. Well, fuck you! You can shove your job up your arse." I step up to her, knowing I should stop but not being able to. "You're a piece of work, Rochelle. You must have a magic vagina or something to bed a man like Elliot. Good luck with that now."

"Nina—"

Her hand connects with my face moments before Mason steps between us. I chuckle as I welcome the sting. I needed that.

"Nina." She instantly panics.

"What the fuck do you think you are doing!" Mason's voice is like thunder, vibrating through the entire room. My eyes drift closed as I turn and leave them. "You do not lay your hands on her!"

The hair on the back of my neck stands on end as I round the threshold. If I didn't know Mason, I'd be afraid of him right now. His voice is deadly yet controlled.

"Mr Lowell, I'm..." Rochelle's voice falls quieter and quieter the farther away I get from the room.

"Nina!" Mason snaps, and I turn, his tone leaving no room for me to do anything but submit. He steps up to me, taking my face in his hands, and I melt under his dark stare. I hate being so open and easy to him. My body doesn't care though.

Like it doesn't know any better, it craves something inside of him.

Our eyes lock and find the perfect focus, as if we are looking through the same lens. He's all I see—feel—breathe in the moment. Why can't I take him back, why can't I unlearn that look. Unlearn him.

My voice is hoarse as I lift my chin. "If I could make you a stranger to me I would. I'd go back to that first night and I'd —" My mind drifts to Ellis and I close my eyes, regretting my words immediately.

His hands fall from my face as I step back and out of his reach.

"Nina," he warns, as my feet lead me backwards three steps. "Nina."

I shake my head, clenching my hands at my side. "Not now, Mason." Not ever. "I'm not doing this today," I tell him.

Anger steals his features, his jaw tightening into a sharp line as he watches me. He knows I'm going to go. It's the way it's always been.

I make my way into the back office and get my things, grabbing everything I can that's mine. Rushing through the reception and out onto the street, I spot the Audi parked at the curb.

Vinny spots me, smiling wide as he slides down the window. "Nina, I didn't know you were working today."

My eyes fill with tears before I can stop them. Vinny has become more than a friend to me over this past year. "Of all the people, I never believed you'd lie to me, Vin."

"Nina!" Mason shouts from the hotel entrance.

I move quickly, stepping into a waiting taxi. "Please just drive," I tell the driver.

He turns in his seat, looking me up and down before casually righting himself again. "I have a client."

"Please!" I plead, not bothering to wipe my tears, knowing I must look ridiculous.

He huffs and pulls out onto the road. I twist in the seat to find the Audi following right behind us.

"Where to?" the driver asks me, bored.

I swipe at my cheeks, feeling like the vilest human on earth for using it against him. "Lowerwick Estate."

THERE's something so peaceful about the dead. Maybe it's the quiet that surrounds me as I sit between the two headstones amongst Ellis's garden. Or maybe it's the unknown of what awaits us all. It could be anything really—we'll never know until it's our turn. But from my spot right now, with the sun on my face and the smell of fresh lavender blanketing me in the breeze, it seems like the most tranquil place on earth. I only ever come out here with Scarlet or Ellis, but today, when I realised that Scarlet was working and wouldn't be home for a while, I knew this is where I'd wait.

There's safety in silence.

Mason Lowell is so damn loud. A man of many words—yes. Yet his presence, his ability to consume my thoughts and drive my fears, smothers me. My anger towards him in the hotel was raging, so pent up from seven months of no contact, that when I rushed through the door and asked what he was doing, I said it with so much conviction, you'd think he was mine.

I feel stupid.

He isn't mine.

And yet he stood in front of me. He stood up for me, held my face in his hands and told me with his eyes that it was okay.

"Why can't this be easy?" I say aloud, looking up at the cloudless sky, then back to Ellis's grave on my left. "He's so difficult but so perfect. It's impossible." I sigh, dropping back to the grass so I'm lying flat. "It's not that I don't want anyone else to have him. He deserves to have someone. It's just... I don't know—"

"This is super weird."

I startle and sit up, coming face-to-face with Elliot. "Ell, hey!"

He dips his head to the side, reading me as if he can see every page that plagues me. "You okay?"

The girls are good for a lot of things, but I've grown close to Elliot this past year. His love for my son and the way he's stuck by me through everything isn't something I will ever forget.

I nod my head, taking his outstretched hand and slipping into his open arms as he pulls me up.

"Mase called me. Said you lost your job," he says into my hair. "What happened?"

"I thought he was meeting the stripper. The one from the photos. I walked in on his meeting."

"What?" Elliot retorts. "You mean Jasmine?"

I want to be sick. "Her name's Jasmine?"

"It's not what you think. He's helping her."

"Helping himself more like." I pop a brow, stepping away from him and walking towards the house.

"Mason's never been with her. It really isn't what you think.

You two need to talk it out. It's time," Elliot tells me as he falls into step beside me, making our way through the iron gate.

"Don't defend him, Ell, please."

"He's mad at you still. He doesn't admit it, but he is."

"I know."

"And you know he never slept with her—"

"I thought that was the truth, but then I saw the invoice with Vinny's name on it. I had photos delivered to me with her in his lap. You think it's easy for me to believe that nothing has happened when all I get is reasons not to?"

"You had photos delivered to you, Nina." He looks down at me, knowingly. "It's bullshit. He was set up and—"

"I know," I snap, cutting him off.

"I know you know." He smiles, flashing me his teeth.

"You're an idiot." I lean into him as he throws his arm around my shoulders and chuckles. "I don't know what to do anymore, Ell. What do you do when you want something you can't have?" Because as much as I miss Mason, I know we aren't going to be together again. Too much has happened. It would take a lifetime to repair the mess we made.

"Honestly? I go out and get laid."

Rolling my eyes, I push out from under him and jog up the steps to the front door. "How come you came here anyway?"

"Mase was worried."

I tut, fighting another eye roll.

"Luce is going to bring Ellis out here. Thought you might want to stay now you've come out."

I nod. "Yeah, I will stay. Thank you," I tell him sincerely.

"You just have to wait, Pix."

My brows furrow as I turn to face him. "Huh?"

"One day you'll have the answers you're looking for. You just have to trust me when I tell you nothing's going on, okay?"

ELLIS IS SLUMPED in my arms as I carry him through the house and up the stairs to his cot. I stand and watch him as he nestles around in his sleeping bag for nearly twenty minutes before I leave him to sleep. I'd never take him back. I'd never wish for a different life. The fact I threw that in Mason's face tonight disgusts me.

As much as Elliot's reassurance should put me at ease, I can't seem to stop my mind from reeling. Mason once paid Cara off to keep a secret, and now he is paying for this woman's hotel stays? I don't understand what they expect me to think. Maybe Elliot is right and it's time we sat down and talked about it.

Lucy is standing waiting at the bottom of the stairs when I reach the landing. I look down at her as she looks up at me with a judgemental stare.

"What's that look?" I ask.

"We need a chat," she tells me.

I join her at the bottom and sit on the step.

"Where's your head at, Nina? Concerning Mason?" She gets straight to it, choosing to remain standing.

"I thought I made a mistake, leaving him." My gaze lifts to look at her, my eyes prickling. "I started to believe he might not have done it. I thought maybe I got it wrong."

Lucy drops down beside me, smoothing her hand over my back.

"He had a room booked, and they used it. I was cleaning opposite and saw her going inside. It was that day I told you."

Lucy recoils, frowning. "What?"

"Then today I saw him at the hotel, and I thought he was meeting her again. I made a complete fool of myself. And then I ran."

"Oh, babe." She hugs me closer, resting her head on mine.

"I love him, Luce. I love him so much and I don't know how to stop."

"You want it to stop? Because love doesn't come around often, Nina, sometimes you have to be willing to swallow your pride."

Leaning back, I take in a deep breath and close my eyes, knowing there isn't a quick fix tonight. "I need wine and a job."

"Well, I can help with the wine." She stands and grabs my hands, pulling me up. "And there's no rush to find a job."

"I don't want to dip into Ellis's money, so a job *is* priority."

"Of course, but the money is there to support him, and you need to support yourself to do that."

I know Lucy is right and I will use the money to keep us afloat, but it still kills me a little inside knowing it comes from Mason's pocket.

"Logan's mentioned the gym to you on more than one occasion, maybe it's time you looked into that."

"It's located five hundred yards from The Montwell, Luce." I give her a pointed look.

"It's also a job. And a good one at that—it's your thing." She holds her hands out, as if it's simple.

"I don't know." I shrug, not knowing what I should do.

"Worth a look, at least?"

I nod. "I'll call him."

"Everything happens for a reason. And you couldn't suck at a job any more than you did at the hotel." She snorts, pulling me into the kitchen.

"True." I laugh. "I really did suck at it."

"Who's sucking what?" Elliot asks from the kitchen island.

Lucy rolls her eyes and pulls me into a hug. "The butt slut is making a comeback, watch this space, assholes."

"Butt slut? Should I warn Mase?" Elliot grins.

"Absolutely not," Lucy tells him. "She needs to find herself again, then maybe she'll work on all that other stuff."

"Mase seems busy enough at the moment anyway," I add.

Elliot pauses with his drink midway to his mouth. "You don't honestly believe Mason would sleep with that woman, do you?"

I shrug. Feeling like a broken record for bringing it up again.

"He wouldn't, Nina. I believe him," Scarlet voices from her spot at the other side of the kitchen.

"You bet your ass he wouldn't!" Elliot snaps. "Jesus, I don't think he's slept with anyone since you pulled him out of his apartment the night before Ellis was born."

"What?"

My head snaps to Scarlet who is burning holes through Elliot's head with her eyes.

"What?!" I repeat again.

Mase

"SHE THOUGHT I was sleeping with Jasmine?" I question, falling back onto my bed with my hand clenched tight on my phone.

"Yeah, I told her you haven't though, and Luce had a chat with her, told her that she needs to find herself again. Whatever that shit means."

"Find herself?"

"And then Nina still didn't believe that you wouldn't sleep with Jasmine, and I thought I was helping."

"Elliot…"

"So, I told her you haven't slept with anyone since Ellis was born."

"What?"

"Specifically, since the night before he was born, when Scar kicked your ass into line."

"Fucking hell. What the fuck is wrong with you?!"

"At the time, before the words came out of my mouth, I thought I was helping."

"Jesus Christ." I drag my hand through my hair.

"She seemed okay when I left. They went all girly bullshit on her ass and told her they would help her get back to her inner butt slut or something."

"What?!" I bolt upright in the bed.

"No idea what that means. Oh, she's looking for a job too."

"Of course she is." Nina never was one to sit around and do nothing, even when I sold the studio, she was trying to help everyone else.

"I feel like this is progress, mate. At least she's actually talking about you now."

"She lost her job, Elliot, because she thought I was sleeping with a fucking stripper. Again!" The fact she still thinks I'd do that... it's a kick in the teeth.

Why do I care what she thinks?

"I'm now pulling into mine. That's it, that's all I've got, I'll see you in the office tomorrow."

"Yeah, thanks a bunch, mate!" I shake my head as he hangs up.

What a fucking mess.

IT's my night to have Ellis tonight and I normally pick him up once I finish work, but I couldn't stop thinking about how Nina must be feeling. If it was me and I thought she had been sleeping with someone else, I don't know how I would react.

I knock on the door and shove my hands in my pockets, waiting for her to answer.

The door swings open, and I watch as the light fades from her eyes. "Mason, you're early."

My eyes scan her body. Her yoga pants cling to her like a second skin and her cropped vest fits snuggly to her breasts. She has a sheen of sweat coating her body. My brows lift in surprise as I wonder what she was doing. "Yeah, I was hoping for a chat. Have you been dancing?" I ask.

She frowns, ignoring my question. "A chat about what?"

"Can I come in?" I look over her shoulder.

She pushes the door wide and stands off to the side to

allow me access. "Ellis is napping. He was fussing and hasn't long gone down."

"That's okay, I came to see you. We need to talk," I tell her, smiling at her despite her folded arms and less than polite welcome.

"You should've called."

"You wouldn't have agreed."

She answers me with her eyes, glaring at me. "Go on then. Say what you have to sa—"

Soft whimpers come from the hallway and her head quickly snaps in the direction before she huffs and drops her arms to her sides.

"I'll go. You can carry on." I gesture to the yoga mat that's laid out on the floor. "I've got this."

"I don—"

"It's fine, Nina." I nod, walking off towards their bedroom before she can stop me. Ellis is standing in his cot when I walk into the room, and my heart soars as his face transforms —dimples and all.

"Da, Da, Da!"

"Shhh. Sleep time now." I kiss his head and reluctantly place him on his back. "Mummy's busy, little guy." I sit in the chair that's placed beside the cot and look around at the room. It feels weird being in her space, which strangely surprises me. Maybe it's because it's so impersonal. Other than a picture of Ellis with the girls on her bedside, there's nothing here that means anything.

Once Ellis is sleeping again, I slip from the room and make my way to the living area. The sight that greets me has me stopping in my tracks. Nina has her legs spread wide, her back is arched off the ground and she groans as she stretches her arms above her head.

My eyes are glued to her. Every perfect inch—which pisses me off, because it's totally inappropriate to get hard for your kids' mum when it's three o'clock on a Thursday.

Bitch.

I clear my throat, and she instantly sits up. "He went back quickly." She flushes, her cheeks turning a deep crimson. She stands and starts to roll the mat. "Sorry, just a second."

"I thought you were dancing."

"No." She shakes her head, frowning. "I don't really get the time anymore," she says, lifting her hand to her collarbone subconsciously before realising and dropping it.

"Don't lie to me," I bite out.

She recoils, putting her hands on her hips. "Excuse me."

I take a step closer to her. "Don't lie to me. You have all the time in the world to dance, you choose not to."

She steps away, putting distance between us again as her face grows sour. "That's not true and it's none of your business."

Reaching out, I grasp her arm before she can turn, pulling her into me. I go to speak but the words die on my tongue the minute our eyes lock. We're close, too close. She wets her lips as her eyes drop to my own. This is the closest we've been since Ellis was born, nearly eight months ago.

My hand instinctively goes to her waist, resting on her hip with a tight grip. I feel like I'm physically restraining myself from kissing her.

"I shouldn't want you." I grimace, flexing my fingers against the smooth skin.

"You don't want me, Mason, trust me." She grasps my

wrist and pulls it from her waist. "What do you want? Why are you here?"

She spins and moves to the kitchen. I rearrange myself in my suit trousers, pissed at myself for being so weak to her. "Elliot, he told me about last night—"

"What about last night?" She doesn't meet my eyes and I know she knows exactly what I'm talking about.

"When you left me, Nina... It was a hard time for me. You left, and with Dad being gone, I couldn't find anything to bring me..."

"Are you trying to tell me the only thing that kept you sane in the months after you cheated on me was sleeping with an endless number of women?"

Fuck. "I—"

"Because if you are, you should stop! You have no idea what *I* went through, what I continue to go through." She steps forward, pointing her finger into her chest. "I spend my weekends in this apartment alone, and then get judged for the *friends* I keep when I choose to fill the void."

"I'm struggling to see the difference here. You think I enjoy living at the penthouse without my family. I'm sorry I wasn't there for you during your pregnancy, but that was your choice. I did what I did to keep myself fucking going. You did this. You broke us, Nina, not me!"

"Are you fucking serious!" she roars, her eyes like saucers.

"Deadly! I never fucking touched another woman and you know it. I couldn't then and I fucking can't now!"

She sniggers, looking anywhere but at me. "But there were five months where you found it really fucking easy apparently!"

She won't ever understand this, why would she? She

thinks I slept with Jasmine and now she knows I slept around after she left. "I couldn't be at the penthouse alone."

"You could've gone and lived with your sister."

I scoff at her, turning. "I shouldn't have come here."

"I don't know why you did. Did you really think you could explain yourself and convince me to feel sorry for you when you were balls deep whilst I was in labour with your fucking son? You're damn deluded, Mason."

I move quickly until I'm in her space, my eyes like fire as they burn through her. "Do you truly think I slept with another woman whilst I was with you, the day after we got home from Bora Bora, you honestly believe I cheated on you?"

Her eyes don't leave mine, her throat working on a swallow. She doesn't answer me.

I nod my head, my body losing the fight it had moments ago. "Do you know why I don't want you, Nina?"

Her eyes fill with tears, but they don't affect me like they once did. She looks to the floor, not answering me. I lift her chin with my finger, bringing her face up to mine.

My lips brush her ear. "Do you know what a whore does when she's finished?"

She says nothing, her body rigid.

"She leaves."

I step away from her, my eyes dropping down her body.

9

Nina

WHEN I WAS A CHILD, I TOLD MYSELF THAT LETTING PEOPLE IN was dangerous. Trying to protect the people around you is dangerous. Because they *will* hurt you. They find the things that will hit the hardest and use them to cause you pain.

It's why I don't let people in easily.

"If you came here to hurt me, then mission accomplished." I clench my jaw, hating how my voice cracks.

Anger is etched into every plane of his face, his body vibrating with the same fury. My eyes don't leave him as he turns and leaves the apartment.

The second the door slams shut, the tears come, and I let them. This has been brewing between us all week and it had to happen. I always knew it wouldn't be pretty, but I never expected it to end uglier than it already was.

I hoped we could find some closure.

Deep down inside, I know Mason isn't a bad person, and

he wouldn't have meant the words he just threw at me. But he intended to hurt me. A quick hit to make him feel better.

I'm not sure I'll ever get used to the way his words can cut me so easily.

"Nina," his voice startles me.

I spin, rolling my lips as my throat burns. I try to contain the sob that breaks through but it's impossible. My knees buckle as I cover my face.

"I'm sorry." He closes the distance between us, pulling me into his chest.

I fall against him, giving in to the resistance and allowing him to heal the parts of me that only being in his arms can fix. My body shakes as I let it leave me, freeing myself of the emotions I've kept bottled up since the night I left.

His lips find my hair and I feel him inhale. I close my eyes and take my own deep breath, trying to commit this moment to memory. Because the moment he lets me go, I know I won't be pulled back in again.

"We need to find a way to make this work." My heart thuds hard against his chest, a warmth soaring through me. "Ellis deserves better than this."

Ellis. Of course he's talking about Ellis.

"If we can't be civil for his sake" —he leans back, looking down at me— "then maybe it would be better to go back to the old setup, just for a while."

He doesn't want to see me. "Is that what you want?"

He watches me intently, as if I'm a mystery he can't figure out. "It doesn't matter what I want."

It's too much. He's too much. Pulling back, I wipe my face then wrap my arms around myself.

"I didn't mean what I said, Nina, I'm sorry. I know how much it hurts you and I won't do it again. I mean that."

I nod my head, wiping my face. "We both said some shitty things," I whisper, sounding dejected, and nothing like the woman that once promised to never take the type of shit he threw at me moments ago. Lucy is right, I need to find that girl again.

Cut out the waterworks, Nina.

"You think we can try this again? Start over," he asks.

"I can't have her around my son, Mason." My voice wobbles and I turn my head off to the side, angry at myself for having zero control over my emotions.

His hand smooths over my cheek, tilting my head back to him. "I never touched her. I swear to you. There are things I want to tell you but it's not the right time. Know that when it is, I *will* tell you." His eyes hold so much conviction, I can't help but think he's telling the truth.

"What does that even mean, Mase?"

"You have to trust me." His thumb skims across the underside of my lip and I pull away.

"That has to stop! You can't touch me."

He pockets his hands, running his tongue along the front of his teeth in annoyance. "Fine."

"And, no turning up here early. We have the days and times planned out. We need to stick to that."

He nods his head then stares at me, his brows pulled low and his set face hard and brooding. Goose bumps pebble along my arms and I shake my head. "Don't look at me like—"

Ellis cries, cutting me off. "Well done. You woke the baby," I accuse.

"Me?!" Mason blanches, his lip tipping up on one side.

I hurry down the corridor, briefly closing my eyes, as a soft smile pulls at my own lips. This could work. If I know that woman isn't anywhere near my son, I could deal with this setup. I could see Mason and not want to punch him in the face or jump his bones, right? Switch off my emotions.

I scoop Ellis up into my arms, then grab his overnight bag, walking back out and into the living room.

"That wasn't a nap." Mason takes him from my arms and lifts him into the air, rubbing his head on his belly and making him laugh. His hair ends up an unruly mess with strands standing on end.

I watch them, my stomach flipping as I wonder about all the moments we've missed over the last eight months. "You can take him early if you want."

"Is Mummy trying to get rid of us?" he asks Ellis in a weird dad voice that shouldn't make him hotter but does.

"No, I just—"

"I know." He smiles over at me. "We'll get going. You okay?"

His brows dip low as I nod my head, my eyes welling up. "Yeah, I think I needed to let it all out. I'm sorry I'm such a mess."

"I didn't mean what I said," he reiterates.

"I know."

"You'll be okay here? I know you hate it and…"

I wait for him to finish but he doesn't, awkwardly scratching at his neck with his free hand. "You go, I'll be fine." I don't tell him I planned to meet Joey tonight. Maybe we will both have to keep that part of our lives separate from each other.

"See you tomorrow, Mummy."

"Bye." I lean in and kiss Ellis, then stand at the door watching as they leave.

L&M fitness suite is nothing like what I imagined it to be. Logan is... well, a bit of a meathead. He lives to lift weights and drink his protein shakes. So when he told me he had a new gym, I thought he meant something inconspicuous on a side street. Not a multi-levelled, glass-fronted building in the centre of London's financial district.

I stand on the opposite side of the street and check the address one more time, just to be sure.

"Wowzers!" With a renewed spring in my step, I take off across the road and push into the building, my eyes greedily eating up every inch of the sprawling reception area. It could be a hotel. It's not like anything I've ever seen before.

"Hi, can I help?"

I recognise the voice immediately, spinning around, I smile wide at Gemma just as realisation hits her. "Nina!" She stands, moving around the desk to pull me into a hug. "You're a sight for sore eyes."

"So are you, it's been so long." Gemma was always a regular at the gym—mostly because Henry wouldn't allow her to work out anywhere else. He liked to keep her close.

"Are you joining? I'm sure Logan would cut you a deal." She gives me a wink as she squeezes my hand in hers.

"Logan really *owns* this place? Logan Morgan, the one I used to employ?"

"Boy did good, huh!"

"Damn right he did." I look around in awe, wondering how it's possible. "How's Henry?" I ask absentmindedly.

"Good, he works here too."

"He does?" I snap my attention back to Gemma.

"Yep! It's more like a family around here."

"Anderson!" Logan calls, appearing from the stairs that wrap around the back wall. "Ready to meet your boss?"

"What is this place!" I smile as he steps up to me and throws his arm over my shoulder.

"You like it?"

"Logan, it's incredible, truly. You're doing well?"

"Business is booming."

I shake my head, hardly believing it. I should've reached out sooner. I always loved working with the boys. Men naturally come with less drama—most of the time.

"Want a tour?" he asks me, clearly buzzing and proud.

"Yes! Show me."

We take the stairs to the first floor, which is a colossal open space. It has everything from weight training equipment, a rig, and all the cardio equipment you can think of. I'm blown away that he could have accomplished so much in a year. Everything is top of the line and organised in a neat layout.

"It's so busy!" I check my watch and notice it's ten-thirty. "Where were all these people when we had the studio?"

Logan chuckles and takes off towards the office at the back of the gym. I follow him inside and sit down on one of the sofas. He takes a seat at the desk, watching me.

"How?"

He smiles as if he knew that question was coming. "I saw

a gap in the market, had some help from Mum and Dad, got a business loan and made it happen."

"I'm a little jealous, Logan. This place is... it's incredible."

"Thank you." He nods his head once in agreement. "You wanna come help me run it?"

I laugh, tucking my legs up under myself on the chair. "You saw how terrible I was at running the studio, you seem to have things figured out here."

He shrugs, resting his elbows on his knees. "I'm serious, Anderson. One of my PT's just quit on me and he was my go-to guy after Henry. There's not many people I trust to leave in charge here."

"You want me to personal train?"

"It's what I need right now. It will be just like old times." He grins.

"I can't PT!"

"Of course, you can! You used to."

"No, I didn't! I stood and read out the fitness plans you'd printed out for me."

"Then we will do that," he pops back at me. He's really hell-bent on this.

"Is that the only job you have for me?" I cringe, feeling ungrateful.

He hesitates, then rubs his hands together. "For right now, but we can make anything work. Gemma could probably use some help downstairs on recep—"

"No!" I snap, sitting up a little straighter. "No, thank you, I will take the gym job."

"Yeah?" He smiles.

"If you'll have me." I cringe, hunching my shoulders.

"Of course! You'll love it here."

"I hope so."

I leave Logan's office with a spring in my step, feeling like I might've just found something that will bring me that little bit closer to me again. I've missed the buzz that comes from being in this environment.

Logan told me to stick around and to get familiar with the place, which I happily obliged. I go to the changing rooms and internally scream at the over-the-top décor.

It's more of a boutique hotel than a gym.

Cubicles with changing and shower facilities line the room, each one kitted out with the most beautiful bathroom suite. Skin and hair care products line the walls along with fresh fluffy towels. I have no doubt in my mind that Gemma played a massive part in designing this place, and when I spot the hairdryer and straighteners, it only confirms my thoughts.

I change quickly and use the lockers for my things. Jogging up the steps, I step into the gym and take my time, working on every piece of equipment until sweat is running off me and I feel the weight of the world slipping from my shoulders.

I've missed this.

"I'M NOT GOING," Lucy huffs, pulling the dress over her head and throwing it to the ground.

"Stop being a queen. There must be something here," Megan tells her.

"It's alright for you! You look like a Greek goddess with

your tanned skin and silky hair. I have roots, my skin's looking all grey, and I have nothing to wear!"

"First world problems." Scarlet chuckles, elbowing me as I put another coat of mascara on.

"Luce, you look beautiful. What was wrong with the red dress?" I ask, trying to console her in her meltdown. We've all been there.

"Too booby."

"Miller wouldn't mind." Megan grins.

"I'm not going," she reiterates.

It's Elliot's birthday tonight but Lucy has a date with Miller. We all know he isn't the one—hell, I think even Luce knows that. But she always sticks it out, giving them a fighting chance before she cuts them loose.

"Suits me." I shrug, putting my makeup back into my bag. "We could get takeaway and chill?" I ask hopefully. I've been dreading tonight all week. The idea of going out with Mason and the gang seems petrifying. It's all too much too soon.

"You're going." Megan points at me. "We are all going! Lucy, get dressed, you look incredible in whatever you wear and Nina..." She looks over at me, guilt in her eyes. "Have another drink."

I get up and pour myself another vodka, adding far more than necessary.

Here goes nothing.

Mase

"SHE'S PISSED," I bite out, draining the last of my whiskey as I lean back in my seat.

"Might just be the heels, mate," says Lance, shrugging his shoulders when I glare at him as if he doesn't really have a clue.

The girls just arrived sans Lucy–much to Elliot's annoyance. They laugh their way over to us and I don't miss Megan's arm that's wrapped tightly around Nina's waist as she wobbles on her heels.

My palms itch to take her from Megan's arms as they reach the table.

She looks around at us, scrunching her nose up and smiling. "Hey, my boys!"

"You're pissed." Lance laughs out loud, standing first to kiss her cheek.

Charlie and Elliot follow suit, while I say hi to Megan and Scarlet. I eventually turn to Nina, and she smiles shyly over at me. "Hey, Mase."

My heart thrashes against my chest at that smile, and the fact she called me Mase and not Mason. It gets me right there, deep in my gut. I take my time as I lean forward, running my lips past her cheek to her jaw, placing a soft kiss just below her ear. "You look beautiful, Nina," I whisper.

Our eyes meet and I watch as she swallows the lump in her throat. She isn't as drunk as I first thought, but her eyes are still wide and glassy.

"I need a drink," she blurts, breaking the moment. "Ell, what do you want to drink?"

She struts off to the bar and leans over the marble top, looking for someone to serve her, and I watch as her short black dress rises up her thighs. I couldn't keep my feet in place if I wanted to. I stride to the bar and stand at her back.

"I'll get these." I signal to the barman.

"What? No. I can buy my friend a drink." She frowns at me, looking over her shoulder. "What are you drinking, Ell?" she calls behind us, but Elliot doesn't seem to hear her over the music.

"Four Macallans and a bottle of Dom Perignon vintage. Three glasses."

"Two. PLEASE!" she corrects, giving me a drunken glare as she lowers her voice to a hushed whisper. "Could you be any showier?"

I drop my head to her ear, talking low and with warning. "It's Montgomery's birthday, don't make this about us."

My hand barely grazes her waist when she spins, slapping my hand away. "Exactly! Leave me alone, you giant butthead." She snots as she chuckles at herself and then slips past me, leaving me to wait for the drinks. I ask for a third flute when the barman gives me two.

The girls are gone when I get back to the table. I place the champagne down and hand the boys their drinks.

"What's going on with you two?" Charlie asks as I pass him his glass.

"Nothing."

"Didn't look like nothing," Lance pipes up. "You gonna be on her ass all night?"

"I'm not on her ass now, am I? Dick."

"I think she found someone to dance with anyway."

My head snaps to Elliot and he grins up at me, clearly trying to wind me up. "Fuck you!" I spit, stretching out my neck.

She fucking rattles me.

"Just go get her, for fuck's sake. You need to stuff her full, Lowell."

Charlie and Lance chuckle, while I shake my head. "You're a pig, you know that," I tell him in disgust.

"We're all thinking it."

"She'll come around, mate." Charlie winks, lifting his whiskey to me before taking a sip.

"You think I want her, still?" I shake my head at them all, my pointer aimed at my chest. "I couldn't give a fuck, but she's the mother of my child and I won't have her making a show of herself drunk. I'll never trust the girl again. That ship sailed the day she left me."

"Geez, you don't hold no punches, do you?"

I turn to find the girls standing at my back. Nina glowers at me, before rolling her eyes and taking off towards the bar again.

"Really, Mason!" Scarlet scolds me. "What is wrong with you?"

"For fuck's sake." I pinch the bridge of my nose and go after her.

"Go away, please. I want to enjoy my night," she tells me, her voice dripping with sarcasm as I step up next to her. "This is Elliot's night, Mase. Let's not make it about us." She smiles sweetly, then turns back to the barman. "A vodka cranberry, and two shots of tequila, please."

"You don't have to be such a child. Maybe just once we could have a conversation without you running off."

She scoffs. "Seriously, Mason, I just want to enjoy the evening. I don't want to stand around and listen to you run me into the ground, but thanks for the thought. Here." She passes me a shot. "Bottoms up, asshole!"

She tilts her head back and swallows the clear liquid down. A small drop leaks from her mouth and runs down her chin and throat. Her hand comes up to wipe her chin, then she looks at my shot. "You have a nice night." She clashes her empty glass with mine, sending the contents everywhere and all over my hand.

"Cheers," I mutter, drinking down the remnants of the shot. I watch as she takes her drinks and leaves, her hips swaying with each step she takes.

I'd be lying if I said I haven't missed her fire.

THE GIRLS HAVE BEEN on and off dancing all night, and they are nowhere to be seen when I spot Lucy making her way through the club. I check my watch and notice it's still early. Catching Elliot's eye, I nod my head in her direction. Their eyes meet across the room and Elliot stands. "Alright Luce?" he asks her as she reaches the table.

"Where's Nina?" she asks, looking past Elliot at me.

I shrug.

Elliot leans in and whispers something in her ear that I can't hear. She shakes her head, looking close to tears.

Sensing she needs a female, I go to the dance floor and search for Nina, spotting her on a podium wedged between Scarlet and Megan. Shaking my head, I step up to them and tap her leg.

"Fuck off!" She waves me off, smiling down at me. "I'm having fun and you're ruining it." She wobbles on her heels and starts to fall backwards grabbing on to the girls. They laugh amongst themselves as if it's the funniest thing in the world.

"You're going to have to get her down," the bouncer tells me, pointing up at Nina.

"Come on." I grab her at the waist and throw her over my shoulder, knowing it's the only way to get her off the podium.

"Mason!" she shouts, her fist meeting my back once in annoyance.

I slide her down my body when we reach the side of the dance floor, my hands keeping her steady as she finds her feet again.

She glances up at me through her lashes with a look in her eye that I can't quite decipher.

"Lucy just got here. Something's up," I tell her on autopilot, still stuck in our trance.

She blinks, snapping out of it as she looks off to the far side of the room where the boys are seated. Just as she goes to step away from me, I pull her back.

Her hand grips my bicep and I flex involuntary—maybe. Arousal sparks in her eyes and I watch as she fights with herself, her gaze flicking all over my face. "Not now," she tells me.

Nina

I'M DRUNK.

Beyond drunk. But I feel fantastic. That is, until Mason

pulls me from the dance floor and tells me Lucy's here, seducing me with his damn face.

Brushing him off and taking some deep breaths, I make my way to our table, finding Lucy sitting across Elliot's lap. I spy his hand resting across her legs, and my gaze tightens on them. Elliot is whispering something in her ear, and she is very clearly hanging off his every word.

"Luce," I shout over the music. "You okay?"

She nods her head, giving me a sad smile. I frown, wondering what could have happened with Miller. It's early, still. Something isn't right, and the fact she is sitting on Elliot's lap says a lot.

"Nina." Lance taps my shoulder, handing me a drink.

"Thanks."

"How many's that?" Mason asks loudly in my ear.

I lean away from him, looking up into his dark eyes. "None of your business."

He mumbles something I don't catch, and it irks me. "What was that?" I snap.

"Nothing."

"You two!" Charlie tsks. "Just don't speak to each other. It's like watching a pair of children."

"He's the child," I say, thumbing over my shoulder as I move to sit with Charlie on the wingback chair.

"You okay?" he asks, grinning at me.

Using my straw, I stir the ice in my glass far more aggressively than necessary. "He pisses me off."

"He didn't mean what he said before." He sobers as his words come out with complete sincerity.

"I'm getting fed up with hearing that. He called me a whore the other day."

"Do you think he'd be acting the way he is if he didn't care, or if he thought you were a whore?"

"This is him showing me he cares. Is that what you're saying?" I sit square and sip my drink. "How did we ever work before? It's like I can see all the bad bits now that I never saw before."

"Rose-tinted glasses are a wonderful thing," he murmurs, and I turn to look at him. Charlie is the quietest of the group, and I know that's more to do with the things in his past than his personality. But I can't help but think he has a lot more to say sometimes.

"Well, I definitely don't have them on now." I snicker out a laugh but end up snorting through my nose.

Charlie shakes his head, smiling over at Mason who is watching us both. "You wanna know what I think?" he asks with a smirk.

"Hit me with it, Charles."

"I think... not if, but *when* you and Mason get back together, you'll have gotten through so much hurt and overcome all the bullshit that it will make you untouchable, you'll be extraordinary."

My brows lift in surprise, not expecting that to come out of his mouth. "You have high hopes."

"I normally know my shit, Nina. You should listen to me." He winks, leading me to conclude that he must be drunk too.

"Hmm, I don't know, maybe. I am a sucker for a sale and those rose-tinted glasses go pretty cheap these days."

"What?" he asks, throwing his head back, laughing.

"You know what I mean." I wave him off.

Shaking his head, he leans forwards and goes to stand.

"One day, you'll find your peace. You just have to go through the shit first."

"Philosopher Aldridge." I salute him.

He stands and goes to the bar, and I make myself comfortable in the large chair. My eyes go to Lucy and Elliot, cozied up on the seat opposite me. I often wonder if they'll ever end up together. Lucy is adamant they won't, and I get it. On paper, it wouldn't work. She's all about the happy ever after and running off into the sunset—she isn't into the playboys. But the way she fits with Elliot is different. The bond they have as friends is special. Maybe that's what's more important to them. Maybe they work because they are friends. Who am I to judge them?

My gaze drifts to Mason, and I catch him watching me, although I knew that already. I can always feel when his eyes are on me.

If only *we* could be friends. We definitely couldn't work like Elliot and Luce do. I'd be too friendly. I mean, if I was sitting on Mase's lap right now and he was whispering in my ear, I'd have no doubt in my mind he'd be hard, and if he wasn't it would be my mission to make him.

His eyes narrow, as if he knows what I'm thinking.

Yeah, he would definitely be hard. The man's a sex fiend.

Taking my straw into my mouth, I sip my drink, moving my lips to draw over the tip. Mason does a little two-step, taking a gulp of whiskey as he watches me over the rim of his glass.

I smile, feeling my dimple pop on my cheek. Peeking my tongue out, I flick it across the tip, then glide it into my mouth, sucking up my drink before sliding it out slowly. I repeat the process, keeping my eyes locked on his intense dark ones.

"What the fuck are you doing?!" Megan snaps, grabbing the straw from my mouth and throwing it to the floor. Her face is screwed up in question. "Filthy whore."

I hide my grin in my glass, shrugging as she falls into the seat with me.

"What's got you over here deep throating a straw? Do we need to find you a penis?" She giggles.

The vodka burns my throat and I choke, turning to look at her with wide eyes. "No! I was just messing."

"Nina," Mason interrupts, and my back goes straight, my face heating as if I just got caught doing something I shouldn't. "A word." He steps away from us, seemingly expecting me to follow.

"Do not suck that man's penis," she warns.

"Megan!" I laugh.

"You'll only regret it."

I wouldn't. But that might be the drink talking.

"Nina." She grasps my arm. "Don't leave with him tonight, okay? Not when you're this drunk."

"I'm not stupid, Megs, I wouldn't leave with him."

She nods despite her frown and then lets me go.

Mason's standing by the entrance, talking to a bouncer when I catch up with him. I step up beside him and wait while he finishes, stealing the moment to watch him whilst he's distracted. The way his jaw works as he listens to what the bouncer is saying, and the stance he takes—there's no doubt who's in charge here. His shoulders are square and full, his shirt stretching over his chest seamlessly. My gaze drops to his hands. They are so big, his fingers long, and veins that pulsate beneath his tanned skin. What is it about big hands?

"Mase," I interrupt impatiently.

"Sorry, mate," he cuts off the bouncer, turning to look down at me. His face transforms into a frown instantly. "Don't give me that fucking look," he spits at me.

"What look?" I blink.

"You know what look." Grabbing my hand, he pulls me from the club and towards the waiting taxis. "We're leaving."

"Mase!"

"I DIDN'T WANT to leave though, Mason! You pulled me out of there because I gave you..." I hold my hands up, air quoting, "a look."

"You did, you wanted me to fuck you." He follows me into my apartment, and I don't stop him. I'm too mad at him to even acknowledge what a bad idea it is.

"Can you even hear yourself right now?! What planet are you on?"

I take off down the corridor to my room. "Damn asshole. There was no look," I mutter to myself, pulling off my heel and tossing it off to the side.

"You know what I'm talking about. You can plead ignorance, but I know that look."

His phone starts to ring, and I turn my back, wobbling in my drunken state as I try to remove my other shoe. "I took her home," he says into the phone.

"Against my will!" I add before muttering, "Asshole."

"She's fine. I'll send Vinny now."

"Send him here first." I spin, my heel still on and not coming off with ease. "Why are you even here?"

"Talk to you later, Aldridge." He hangs up the phone and watches me. Shaking his head.

"Well?" I ask.

"I—" His phone starts to ring again. "Mega—" He rolls his eyes and I smile, knowing she will give him fuck. "Yes. She is fine."

Leaning down, I manage to get the shoe off. I flex my toes and drop my head back, relishing in the relief. I don't know why we wear them.

I need a pint of water and my bed, and maybe a shower. Yes, definitely a shower. I already know I will feel like the earth's ending tomorrow. Without thinking, I grasp my dress at my waist and pull it down over my strapless bra, shimmying it over my hips.

"Uhh, yeah okay, bye." Mason reminds me of his presence, and I look up to see him shoving his phone into his pocket. His eyes are wild with something carnal, but they hold anger too.

"Why are you angry?" I ask.

"What are you doing?" His jaw clenches tight as his stare drops away and to the floor.

"Once upon a time this wouldn't have bothered you, Mason." I throw my arms out at my sides.

He shakes his head, making me rage when he doesn't lift his head to look at me. "Things are a little different now, don't you think?"

My throat burns with a deep ache. "Then why are you here?"

His eyes finally lift to me and I'm momentarily paralysed

in place.

I swallow thickly, my heart hammering in my chest. Letting my dress fall, I step out of it and then kick it to the side. Reaching around, I unhook my bra letting it fall to the floor. Mason leans against the doorframe, his legs crossed at the ankle, his muscular arms straining in his black shirt. He's everything I remember him to be, and yet I crave his touch so I can be reminded of his love. Because I miss this man's love above all else.

If we ever did anything right, it was the way we loved each other.

He doesn't move, doesn't blink. He just stands and watches me with his troubled eyes. And those brows, low and dark.

"Do I look different to you now?" I ask, popping an arched brow.

"Nina," he warns.

"What? You don't like the marks your son left me? They aren't going anywhere, Mase." I walk towards him, forcing myself to not cover my body. His eyes narrow as he looks down his nose at me.

"You have no idea," he rasps.

I lick my lips. "No?"

Something passes between us, the air in the room becoming electric.

He shakes his head, not taking his eyes from my face as he pushes off the doorframe and walks over to my chest of drawers. "It's late." He pulls out a sweatshirt and comes back to me, slipping it over my head and pulling the hem down past my thighs. "Get in the bed, Nina."

I swallow thickly as I look up at him, my chest aching

with the look in his eyes. Nodding my head, I turn and climb into bed, sliding my pillow to the centre before laying my head down. I watch as Mason settles back into the chair beside Ellis's cot, his eyes trained on me.

"Mase..." I pause, not really knowing what I want to say. "I'm—"

He shakes his head, tipping his chin up. "Go to sleep."

10

Nina

STRIPPING NAKED WASN'T MY INTENTION AND LOOKING BACK now, I wish the ground would have swallowed me up whole. So much needed to be said to Mason, but in my drunken state, I somehow believed I needed to be bare to say it.

Maggie sets a mug of hot water down in front of me. The only upside to going out last night is the Sunday dinner that Maggie has been prepping all morning. Mason was already gone when I woke up this morning, and he thankfully had already picked Ellis up from Maggie's before I arrived. It's his weekend with Mason, and I know that he will want the day with him after missing last night.

"So, tell me about this new job." Maggie lifts my legs and sits at the other end of the sofa, then places them back down on her lap.

"It's three days a week to start, which I know is more than I was doing at the hotel, but I can get Mason to help, still."

"Nina, please. I want to help. Unless you would rather

have Mason take the time off. But otherwise, let me help you. Please."

"I can't help but feel bad, like I'm putting on you."

She gives me a look that basically means shut up.

"Are you sure, Mags? Shouldn't you speak to John first too? It will be later evenings sometimes."

"Jesus Christ, just let her have the damn kid," Lucy grumbles from the opposite sofa.

"Lucy Mae Morgan! That is your nephew you are talking about," Maggie scolds.

"I have a headache, Mum. Don't pick on me today."

I shake my head and laugh. Lucy's definitely feeling it more than me. She managed to get out of bed when I arrived but hasn't moved from the sofa since.

"Go shower, you smelly child." Maggie whacks her with a cushion on her way to the kitchen, making her groan.

"I can feel your porny eyes on me," she says, muffled against the pillow.

"Porny." I chuckle.

"Yes." She leans up on her elbows and looks into the kitchen to see if Maggie's listening. "I feel honoured you've managed to keep your clothes on today."

"Funny." I give her a death stare. "How did you get home last night anyway?" I change the subject, not needing a reminder of the night before.

Lucy sighs and covers her face with her forearm. "How do you think?"

"A taxi?"

She peeks out under her arm with a frown.

"Well Ell didn't drive you that's for sure. He was just as steaming as you. What happened with Miller?"

"He wanted to film us... you know. But he didn't ask, I caught the light flashing on the sideboard while he was... doing his thing," she whispers, pointing to her crotch. "You probably would've loved it." She smirks at me.

"Oh, give it up already. I was naked for twenty seconds. Stop being judgy!" I roll my eyes. "What an ass though. What was he thinking?"

"I probably overreacted but it pissed me off, Elliot was raged."

"You told Ell?"

"I tell him everything."

"Did anything happen when he brought you home last night?"

"Umm, no."

"That doesn't sound all that convincing."

"Girls, can you lay the table? Lunch is ready in ten," Maggie calls from the kitchen.

Lucy jumps up from the sofa, moving quicker than she has all morning. I glare at her as she whips past me.

THE TABLE ISN'T AS busy as it normally is and that has a lot to do with the fact Vinny isn't here. I haven't spoken to him yet and I know I need to, and as much as it upsets me, I know that sometimes I won't be the one his loyalties lie with.

John sits at the head of the table, with Maggie to his left and Lucy at his right. I sit next to Lucy.

"Good night I gather, girls?" John asks.

"Nina had a great night." Lucy laughs, shoving a mouthful of cabbage in her mouth.

I glare at the side of her head and will her to stop talking. The Morgans can take the banter. I've grown up on it. But I don't need them knowing what I get up to after dark.

She snickers to herself, and I give her a kick.

"Ow!" she snaps.

"Not nice being the butt of the joke, is it, Nina love." John smiles warmly over at me, always defending me.

"Dad, please, will you save the butt puns for Tuesdays only!"

"Oh my god, you didn't." I choke, trying to swallow around my mouthful of food.

"I did." She chuckles.

Maggie and John laugh along with us with no clue as to why. Their joy is simple and comes from us. I want that one day.

"Come on, girls, let's not get nasty." Maggie smiles, placing her cutlery on her plate. "Elliot left some cake this morning. Who wants some? Freya is an incredible baker."

"Ell was here this morning?" I frown, looking at Lucy, who takes a large gulp of water.

"He dropped Lucy home." Maggie stands, patting down her apron before excusing herself from the table.

"Of course he did." I bring my eyes to Lucy.

"Shut up," she huffs, shovelling in more food.

"You had a sleepover?" I turn in my seat and make myself comfortable. "You didn't mention it."

"Must've slipped my mind." She doesn't look at me.

"I bet it did. You stayed at his?"

"I think I will retire to the sofa for this conversation," John says, leaving us at the table alone.

Lucy sits quiet, flipping her fork absentmindedly.

"I have all da—"

"Nothing happened," she interrupts.

I recoil. "Nothing?"

"Nope, nothing, nada."

"Why?"

She bites her lip, looking over at me. "I have no idea." She smiles sadly. "But for the first time ever, I think I wanted something to happen. It felt like the most natural thing in the world, and I'm pretty sure he felt it too."

"Well shit." I sit back in my chair, my shoulders dropping.

"Uh-huh."

ONE THING I didn't anticipate with my new job was getting there, which is why I'm out of breath jogging up Joey's apartment building steps.

I knock on the door once, then walk in.

"Joe?"

"Yo!" he calls out, poking his head out of the kitchen. "What are you doing here?"

"I need a lift! Can you give me a lift?" I say, breathless.

"Where's Ellis?"

"Maggie, she picked him up this morning. I planned to run in, but I left it too late."

"Where's Vinny?" he asks.

I sigh, getting impatient with him. Joey has to know what's going on, always. It's not something he can control, it's just him. "I know you're busy, but I really need a lift in please, Joe."

"Of course, here." He picks up his keys and tosses them to me. "I'll be down in a minute."

"Thank you!"

He climbs into the car ten minutes later and passes me a coffee cup. "Sorry, I had to get the print finished."

"It's fine. Thank you for driving me. I know you're busy."

He waves me off, pulling out onto the road. I catch the cursive writing across his palm and grasp it, turning it over.

MEDS

"You need to pick up your medication?"

His brows pop and he squints down at the faded ink. "Shit, yeah."

I don't like to delve too deep into his business, especially his mental health, but I worry so much about him that I can't help but want to check. I know his family won't. "When was the last time you took it?"

He side-eyes me. He hates that I'm questioning him. "Last night. Don't stress it, I'll go after I drop you off."

"If you don't have time I can go after work."

"I got it, Nina," he snaps, gripping the wheel tight.

Nodding my head, I turn and look out the window. I will have to check later. It will put my mind at ease to know he has taken them.

"You had a good weekend? I didn't see you," he asks, visibly relaxing into the seat again.

"Yeah, I went out for Elliot's birthday, didn't I?"

"I remember" He turns to look at me. "Mase was there?"

"Yup."

He grins wide. "How'd that go?"

I shake my head, a small smile making my dimple pop. "How do you think?"

"Humour me." He slides his hands around the steering wheel, dropping his head back to the seat.

"We bickered. He told me we were leaving—"

"And you left," he finishes for me, dropping his head to the side to look at me.

"Not willingly."

"You wanted to."

"Fuck off."

"You can deny it all you want, you've been different since you started seeing him again."

"No, I haven't," I snap.

"That right there is what I'm talking about." He nods at me. "He seems to bring the bitch out in you."

"Joe!"

He shrugs unapologetically. "Facts."

"Let me out here."

He rolls his eyes and carries on driving. "Don't be a queen."

"I know you don't like Mason—"

"Understatement—"

"But he is Ellis's dad. I have to make this work."

"I know, I know, and I want that for Ellis. But you're stressing about it and you shouldn't. He will fuck it up long before you do. I'm not holding out much hope on the bloke."

If only he knew *why* I was stressing. It's definitely not because of Ellis.

"Speak of the devil," Joey mutters.

I snap my eyes to his and he nods in the rearview mirror. I turn in my seat and spot the Bentley behind us.

"Balls."

Joey indicates and pulls into the curb. "You can't drop me here!" I watch in horror as the Bentley pulls in behind us.

"That's the gym, isn't it?" He frowns as he watches Mason park behind us. "What's he doing?"

"He works just up the road." Damn it, this is fucking perfect. Trust today of all days for him to drive himself to work. Where's Vinny?

"Why's he stopping there?" Joey asks.

"I don't know, Joey."

"He can't park there. It's short stay only."

I grab my bag and go to get out of the car. "Do you need a lift home?" he asks.

"No, I'll run back tonight. Thank you for this morning, and make sure you get your meds, yeah?"

He tuts, waiting for me to climb from his car before driving off. I lick my lips, hoping Mason is out of his car and gone already, but not daring to look over my shoulder to check. I take one step in the direction of the gym doors and a horn blares.

I close my eyes and count to five, then take another step.

It sounds again, this time over and over in short succession, as if the executor is a total prick. Reluctantly, I spin, and what would you know? He sits looking out the windscreen at me, his arm resting on his door and his pointer running over his lips.

Prick.

He crooks his finger, summoning me.

I walk to the passenger side window and wait for him to undo it. "Get in," he mouths.

"What? No."

"Get in now." I can't hear him fully, but his lips move with warning.

"Open the window, Mason!" People stare as I stand yelling at him through the glass.

He sits, waiting.

Fuming mad, I wrench open the door, dropping into the seat and then slamming it shut as hard as I can. The windows shake with the force.

"Trying to mess up my car *again?*" He glares.

Trust him to throw that in my face. My gaze flicks over him quickly, his woodsy scent making me heady and stupid for him. "What do you want?"

"Why are you here?" he asks, his eyes raking down my body.

"Seriously? That's all you wanted."

"You're going to the gym?" He tips his chin in question. "Where's Ellis?"

The nerve of this asshole. "I'm going to work. Which I planned to tell you about yesterday but you sent Elliot to drop off instead of coming yourself. Ellis is with Maggie today."

"You're working at L&M now?"

"Yes."

"Right." He looks to the building, deep in thought. "Why's dickhead driving you? The guys unhinged."

Sadness floors me. I drop my head, feeling disgusted by his words. He knows how it is with Joey. "You really are a nasty piece of work when you want to be."

I go to open the door, but he stops me with a hand to my inner thigh. "Stop."

My eyes drop to his hand. I swallow, suddenly more aware of him than I was moments before. "I said to stop doing that."

He doesn't move.

"Mase." I brush his hand off.

"Vinny drives you," he snaps, his voice final.

"Vinny works for *you*. I can't trust you and I can't trust Vinny."

He screws his face up in disagreement. "That's the most ridiculous thing that's ever come out of your mouth, and you know it."

"Hmmm, I don't know, Mase. I had you in my mouth once." I shrug, pouting as I climb from the car. "You have a good day." I smile sweetly as I walk off towards the gym, swinging my hips for good measure.

Mase

THE WOMAN FUCKING RATTLES ME, and she knows it. It's her intention to wind me up, and I'm putty in her hands. All she has to do is smile and I'm semihard in my suit pants. Jesus, I have zero fucking control when it comes to her.

I scrub my hand over my face as I stand in the elevator on the way up to my floor. *Get a grip on yourself.*

"Good morning, Mason. Good weekend?" George chimes as the elevator pings. "I did spy some snaps on the gram, so I already know it was all things fabulous."

"Not today, George. Please, mate."

"Jasmine." I give her a curt nod, walking to my office.

She mutters back a barely audible "'Morning" without looking up from the computer screen.

Although Jasmine isn't bad at her job, she also isn't great at it either. She spends the majority of her time sitting quietly behind the desk.

I should probably have a word.

"I expected this mood." George follows me. "When I spotted Nina in that strapless piece of deliciousness. She looked hot! What happened?"

"George!" I yell, turning on him. "Get out of my office."

He smiles, not flinching at my tone. "You got it, Bossman." He winks, dropping the coffee cup and stack of files on my desk then leaves.

I'm at my office window before he can close the door, staring out over my home city. The skyline is fogged, the winter morning setting the sky in a dull hue. My eyes are drawn to the building three away from my own, though. The bottom floor is a blur, and the second is crowded by the equipment and people, but the top floor—although I have to squint to see it—is still, quiet, and waiting. Empty, like it always has been.

"Jasmine." Her platinum painted head pops up from behind the desk. "A word."

I turn and walk back to my office, waiting for her to follow. Vinny is sitting at my desk, his hands steepled under his chin. "What is it?" Jasmine asks from the door, not crossing the threshold.

"Have a seat," I tell her.

Her eyes tighten as she looks between us both, as if she's figuring out if she can trust us. I nod to the chair, and she moves to sit next to Vinny. I eye him cautiously before addressing her. "We need information—"

"About what?"

"If you let me speak, I'll tell you," I snap.

My teeth gnaw at the inside of my cheek as I try to contain my annoyance. As much as I don't like what Jasmine has done, I still want to help her. I want to give Nina the chance at a real family.

Or at least a sister.

"Jasmine, we know your boyfriend Lenny has been in contact. If you're serious about getting your children back, you need to think about the people you allow in your life," I spew her the watered-down line. She probably wouldn't like what I really had to say.

"He only wanted to know about Betty."

"So you didn't agree to meet with him?" I question with a raised brow.

"What's it to you?" she asks defensively.

I want to lay into her, tell her some home truths but Vinny is concerned that she's depressed. She's been through a lot but it's all on her. She has to make this shit show better now, no one else can do it for her. Speaking to Lenny will only go against her when it comes to the children.

"We're worried, love, we come from a good place," Vinny tells her in that comforting voice that seems so fucking foreign to me. I only ever saw the man soften when Nina came into the picture. "The children will be with you much sooner if you can leave him behind."

She nods, gritting her teeth. "I know that."

Vinny looks at me and nods in encouragement. "We thought you might like to meet Nina." I clench my teeth so hard I feel my teeth crack. "Get to know her."

Jasmine frowns, looking between the two of us. "Absolutely not. I get enough judgement around here. Why would she even want to meet me? I've heard a lot from George, you know."

"Nina wouldn't judge you, and I won't lie to her about who you are. When she's ready, I would like to introduce you."

"When she's ready? Is this your way of getting her back, presenting me like a prize?" She snickers.

"No. We thought you might like some friends, but I can see you are happy to continue your social suicide mission. You can leave," I say to dismiss her.

"Mason." Vinny tries.

"No, Vin, let her be. Jasmine, the only way your children will come back to you is if you sort yourself out. Change the way you live your life, and start putting the kids first, instead of always thinking about the money."

Her chest heaves as she stands. "You know what I think? I think I'm an inconvenience and you don't like it. I don't know why you brought me here, but I'm doing this for my kids. Not for you or the long-lost sister you're trying to push at me."

"That went well," I vent as she storms out, slamming my office door behind her.

"What did you expect, really?" Vinny smiles, leaning back in his chair. "I see a lot of Nina in her you know."

"She's nothing like Nina."

"Stubborn, flighty, can get under your skin," he lists.

My head drops back against the leather of my chair, and I

huff out a breath. "I'm using L&M tonight; I brought the Bentley and will drive home."

"You think it's a good idea to be using the gym still, now that Nina is working there?" he questions.

"No." But I'm going to, anyway.

He sniggers, looking towards the windows for a moment before bringing his focus back to me. "I know you've always said you wouldn't take Nina back..." His head dips as he rubs his hand over his mouth, trying to articulate his words. "If you think there could be something between you still and you want to pursue it, I will support you, always. You know I've always rooted for the two of you." He pauses, lifting his head to look at me. His eyes hold a warning and it has me lifting my chin subconsciously. I've heard from Scott about Vinny's past, and the way he can flip the switch and become something lethal. I have a feeling I'm seeing a little bit of that right now. "If you hurt her, mess her around, and play with her feelings—"

"Vinny—"

"I will personally come for you."

"Fucking hell." I rake my hand through my hair in disbelief.

He nods, stands and buttons his jacket, his face morphing back to normal again as if he didn't just threaten me.

"Vin." I laugh. "Are you serious right now?"

"I've never been more serious in my life. That girl's been through more than you'll ever know."

My lip twitches up at the corner, but I try to keep a straight face. I stand and join him at the door. I hold out my hand.

He looks down at it, his jaw locking, but then something that looks a little bit like pride washes over his face.

"Loud and clear, old man." I wink, grasping his hand tighter than I should when he takes mine.

I should be pissed that he's just threatened my ass, but I'm not. Nina needs all the people she can get fighting in her corner. Vinny is one of the best men I know, and she deserves his protection.

I DON'T EXPECT Nina to be in the gym when I arrive—it's fucking late and she's been here all day—but she is. She stands with Megan and Lucy, both of them in their gym wear. I roll my eyes, knowing that them coming here won't last long.

"Ladies," I greet smugly as I saunter past them.

They don't say a word, all of them rendered speechless. I knew Nina would be shocked to see me here, but better she knows I use L&M now than later when she is settled and thinks it's because of her. I move to the weights and pick up the barbell. Lucy and Megan quickly disappear into the back office. Probably to chew Logan's ear off.

Nina walks to the back wall and swipes her access card, unlocking the iPad from its holder. She scans it, her eyes flicking over it furiously.

Nina

Motherfucker!

I keep scrolling, checking he isn't listed under just 'Mason' but still, I come up with nothing. Why would Gemma let him up here?

My eyes zero in on him as I stand holding the iPad with a white-knuckle force. He is so fucking hot, and it makes me even more angry. His arms strain as he lifts the weights to his chest, his pecs taut and legs bulging.

Why can't he be a dweeb? This wouldn't be this difficult if he was scrawny. Maybe with a tiny penis too.

"You can't be here," I tell him, as I step up to where he stands on the rubber mats.

"Excuse me," he groans, his veins protruding—shouldn't be hot but it is.

Everything is bigger now I'm closer. I shake my head, finding my thoughts. "You aren't a member; you need to leave!"

"I'll pay on my way out." He winks.

Ugh, please. "It doesn't work like that." I glare.

"Nina, I want to work out in peace—"

"Then go home! You have a perfectly good gym there."

"No!" He continues to pump the weight and with each rep, I get a little bit more worked up. "I always work out here."

"Liar! You do realise I can see that you've never been a member." I hold up the iPad as if it's the holy grail.

He rolls his eyes and continues lifting.

He came here intentionally on my first day to try and piss me off. The bastard. I step closer and he steps back, catching his foot and stumbling slightly. I quickly grasp the middle of the barbell as he tries to recover his footing. "What are you doing!" he shouts, frowning as I try to take it from his hands. "Shit!"

"Mason!" I panic, taking the barbell fully as he falls to the floor, clutching his thigh. The weight is heavy, too heavy for me and I feel myself wobble. "Oh, no."

"Shit, shit," I hear Mason cuss from the floor.

"I can't hold it," I squeal. My left arm gives out, and the weight upends itself, smashing to the ground and taking me with it in some kind of gravity sequence.

"Jesus, shit!" Mason snaps from my side, clearly in pain. "The fuck is wrong with you!"

I look around at the few people on the machines nearby, feeling my cheeks flush. A big burly man with a long beard and a belt wrapped around his waist comes towards me. He lifts the weight from me with ease. Then takes a knee beside me. "Are you okay? You caught your chin."

"I'm fine," I mutter, waving him off as I stand and brush myself off.

"I think it's bleeding," he says.

"What?"

He reaches out and lifts my chin. "You might need stitches there." He openly cringes.

My eyes drop to the floor where Mason is still sprawled out, holding his thigh. Only now he is deathly quiet and watching the man's hold on my face with a dangerous look in his eyes.

I pull away. "Thank you, but I'll be fine."

"You okay, big man?" he asks Mason.

I bite the inside of my cheek to stop myself from laughing. He reaches down and offers his hand and Mason takes it, putting pressure on his leg then hissing.

Everything inside me coils tight.

I've hurt him.

"Let me see." He hobbles to me, tilting my head to look at my chin. He's so close, his body brushing mine as he dips down to get a better look. God, he smells delicious.

"Bloody hell, woman."

"Logan will look at it, he had first aid training just last week. Or Scar, she will sort it. Are you okay?" I ask, shooing his hand away.

"I'm fine. I'm driving you to the hospital."

"I don't need to go to the hospital." I touch my chin and feel the sticky blood pooling. Shit.

"You're not fighting me on this, Nina. Is Logan in?"

"Yes." I thumb towards the office and breathe a sigh of relief when he stalks off in that direction.

I can't have Mason looking after me. It's the last thing I need right now. I grab my things and ask Gemma to let Logan know I had to leave, then I call Maggie and tell her I'll be late.

As I step out onto the street, I feel my chin drip and look down to see blood seeping into my tank top. I know I need to get to the hospital and have it stitched. If the girls weren't in the office, I'd have asked them to take me, but Mason is too controlling and wouldn't have allowed it.

I know Joey will be busy at the gallery, and Maggie is with Ellis.

"Vinny, I need your help," I plead into the phone.

11

Nina

SIX STITCHES. THE CUT WASN'T OVERLY DEEP BUT BECAUSE OF where it was on my chin, it wouldn't stop bleeding. Vinny picked me up and took me to the hospital. I apologised for giving him the cold shoulder this past week and I hoped he would've told me more about Mason and the situation at The Earl Marks, but he didn't. I respect him for staying loyal to his boss, but it's hard to believe nothing happened when nobody will tell me what's going on.

Mason didn't stop calling while we were in the hospital, and I still haven't called him back. Feeling guilty and more in control than I was in the gym earlier, I pick up my phone and dial his number. I don't owe him an explanation, but I know I'd want to know if the shoe was on the other foot.

It rings out the first time, so I try him again.

"What?" he snaps on the second ring.

Great, he's in a mood... I try to squash down my inner bitch. I need to keep it civil.

"Hey, I'm sorry I didn't call before now. I thought I'd let you know that I'm home and everything is okay."

"I know, Vinny called."

"Oh, okay." I pause, waiting for him to speak. "Is your leg okay?"

He huffs out a laugh and I cringe. He's so pissed off. "No, no, it isn't actually."

"I'm sorry, Mase, it was an accident. I shouldn't have been so careless." I really did let my emotions get the better of me.

"What were you thinking? You could have hurt yourself far worse than a scraped chin."

The way he belittles me makes me roll my eyes. How do you tell someone they make you want to throw punches without sounding like a bitch?

Keep it civil, Nina.

"Surely you knew I'd be annoyed when you ambushed me at work? It was my first day, Mason."

"Ambushed you? I was the one who was ambushed!"

I roll my eyes again. "Don't be so dramatic."

"You haven't seen my leg."

My phone chimes, so I switch it to speaker to look. "What the hell is that?" I stare at the screen.

"My damn leg!"

I screw up my face, trying to work out what way the phone goes.

"Oh, wow." Ouch, that does look nasty. His entire thigh is a reddish purple, the bruise still coming out.

"Yes, wow. I'll see you when I pick Ellis up on Wednesday."

"Mason." He hangs up.

I look at the picture, his gym shorts are pulled up to his groin and it looks so damn painful. Guilt eats at me.

Nina: I'm sorry Mase. Really really sorry. It was an accident.

I sit and wait until three little dots bounce across the screen.

Mason: Just forget about it.

Nina: Do you have ice?

Nina: You should ice it.

Nothing. For the longest time I don't get a thing back from him and I end up going to bed, completely knackered after a busy and chaotic first day.

My chin throbs as I lie back in my bed, and I wonder if it will scar. Why am I such an idiot? I should have left him to it, he wasn't hurting me. I managed to cause a scene and injure us both.

My phone chimes with a text and I reach for it quickly to silence it, not wanting to wake Ellis.

Mase: I have ice.

Nina: Is it painful?

What a stupid question. Of course, it's painful.

Mase: Is water wet?

I smile wide, feeling my dimple pop. If he is cracking jokes, then he forgives me.

Nina: I really am sorry.

Mase: I know you are.

Mase: Do you offer rehabilitation services at the gym?

Nina: I think Henry is trained in rehab. I can ask???

Mase: I don't want Henry.

My stomach dips.

Nina: I've heard he is very good with his hands. They call them healing hands.

Mase: Are you not good with your hands?

Is he flirting with me?

Mase: What is it you do exactly?

Linger, pretend I know what the hell I'm doing. It's been a day!

Nina: I PT.

Mase: So you could help me.

Nina: No.

Mase: Why?

Because I'd end up a puddle on the floor, or there would be a literal puddle on the floor if watching him today is anything to go by.

Nina: I don't want to mix my homelife with work.

I don't expect the words he sends back, and they gut me.

Mase: I'm not your home anymore. So that's not a problem.

My smile drops and the force of it falling snaps me out of my bubble. Holding in the side button, I shut off my phone and slide it onto my bedside table. It probably wasn't meant as a jab, but it sure feels like a punch to the gut. In just a few short minutes he had me eating out the palm of his hand, waiting on the edge for the next text.

My heart seems to want something that's obtainable, and for me to give in to that need for him, I'd have to knock through the walls I've built solidly around it.

The trouble is, I'm learning that Mason has built his just as high.

IF THERE IS anything I love more than my son, and maybe dancing—although I'm so off dancing right now—it's the buzz that lives in the four walls of the gym. It vibrates within me and follows me around like a hand to the back, propelling me to keep going.

I love it here. Although my studio was more sacred to me after months of building it up alone, L&M is everything I think I needed right now. To think I worked somewhere as stuffy as The Earl Marks, blows my mind. It just wasn't me.

My only concern right now is the man-child who has just walked up the steps and into the gym. His eyes scan the room until they find me. I wonder if I will ever tire of looking at him. He is the picture of perfection—in my eyes anyway.

Is that what love truly is?

Loving someone through their scars, the imperfections and quirks that you learn to live with because you couldn't go more than a day without seeing them, no matter how imperfect that vision is.

I've always seen the good in people, even when they have been bad to the bone.

"I didn't think you'd be back after what happened."

He stops beside me and looks out at the busy gym. "If I stop it will only make it worse." He looks down at me, then focuses on my chin. He tips his head. "Let me see."

"It's fine." I wave him off.

"Let me see," he demands, taking my face in his hand and tilting my head back.

"Vinny didn't tell me you had stitches."

"He didn't?"

"No," he grits out, his face stony and pissed off.

"It's healing well, it's just—"

His thumb brushes over the broken skin. "Sore! Owww, don't touch it!"

"I thought you said it was fine," he tuts.

"It is." Is he that stupid? "You shouldn't touch it. I don't know where your hands have been. It'll probably get infected now."

"Drama queen," he scoffs, hitting me with a panty-melting smile. He seems to be in a good mood. I like it. "Will you PT me?"

I recoil, shaking my head. "What? No!"

He rolls his eyes and strolls off, ending the conversation. As if Mason fucking Lowell needs a PT. You only have to look at the man's body to see he knows his way around a gym. He's fitter than most of the men in this place. I've not had to train anyone yet, and I sure as hell wouldn't want Mason as my first client, not when he would ridicule me on what I set for him. Because he would.

"Nina," Logan calls from the office.

I go to his office and lean against the doorframe. "Yes?"

"Lowell wants PT, asked for you specifically."

I frown over my shoulder at Mason who is now on the rower. His lip curls up on one side, making it obvious that he knows why Logan called me in here. Smug bastard. "I don't want to PT him. Find someone else."

Logan pops a brow, looking up from the sheet of paper in his hand. I never took him for the type of guy who'd end up in an office doing paperwork. "You know, it could be good for you both."

"What are you, a couple's councillor now, too?"

"Call it what you want. You have air to clear, so why not do that in a safe environment."

"Because it's not a safe environment. I'd probably end up choking him with the rowing machine cord, Logan. Do you have any idea how mad he makes me feel?" I thumb towards

Mason who's going hell to leather on the rower. "It would be completely unprofessional." And just straight-up torture.

He watches me for a moment, deep in thought.

"What?" God, he probably thinks I'm being an ungrateful cow. He gave me a job and now I'm moaning about it.

"Come with me." He stands and stalks past me.

I follow him out of the room, and to the door to the left of the office. "Where are we going?" I ask.

"You'll see."

He opens the door, and we are met with a flight of stairs that lead to another door. It's dark and dingy and I don't like it. I take the first step but pause. With a deep frown lining my brow, I turn, instantly locking eyes with Mason. He's sitting prone on the rower, watching me with an apprehensive look on his face.

"Crack on, will you, I don't have all day," Logan chides at my back.

"You go first." I step aside.

"Scaredy-cat." Logan jogs up the steps and I follow, leaving the door open so we can see. "I will get a light put in here. We didn't go past this level on the refurb."

"Good idea."

He's probably sending me to the stockroom to count water bottles or something. But then, that's probably safer than training the Adonis downstairs.

"Ready?" He grins down at me, his excitement giving me butterflies.

"No, why are you being weird?" I push his shoulder. "Stop being a creeper."

I hold the back of his T-shirt, feeling on edge as he wiggles the handle.

Logan swings open the door, temporarily blinding me. Light pores into the small stairway, lighting up his face which is wide with a smile.

He flicks his head towards the room. "Check it out."

I take the last step then stop short on the threshold, completely and utterly blown away. "Oh."

"It's been empty since I got the place." He urges me forward, then shuts the door behind us. "I haven't had a chance to clear it. As you can see, I've used it mostly for storage."

The room is huge, the same size as the gym downstairs but filled with boxes and equipment. The windows are floor to ceiling and look out at London's skyline. The floors are a light wood, scuffed and in need of some love, but the room as a whole has so much potential. "It's..." I walk farther into the room.

"It's yours to do what you want with." He takes a set of keys from his pocket and chucks them to me. I don't catch them. They hit me in the thigh then fall to the floor with a clang.

"What do you mean?"

"It's yours."

My first instinct is to laugh, it bubbles up my throat and fills the room for a couple seconds before I fall quiet again. I look around at the space. Everything needs fixing, but the bones of it are here, and with the floor-to-ceiling windows and sheer size of the room... it would make the most beautiful dance studio.

"What do you want me to do with it?"

He shakes his head. "You can do whatever you want, Anderson. I'm giving you free rein."

"Why?"

"Lowell. Dickhead." He grins. "I need you to PT him."

My shoulders drop along with my short-lived excitement. "No."

"I owe him one; help me out here. Please?"

I don't like this. At all. "Why would he even want me to personal train him? It's ridiculous."

"I've had six guys request you since your shift on Monday." He smirks as if he is loving this. "Mason was in when two of them asked, he didn't like it. At all."

"Six? Who?"

"Just some of the regulars, all of them after more than a PT session. They know not to push the boundaries so don't worry about that and I won't be putting you on with any of them."

"So, this is just yours and Mason's way of pissing on me. Making them think I'm unavailable."

"This has nothing to do with me." He holds his hands up in defence. "Although, I'd never let you date any of those assholes."

"But you'll happily push me in Mason's direction," I deadpan.

"You know he's a good guy." He bends and picks up the keys at my feet.

"He put you out of a job, Logan." I shake my head, knowing Mason only ever tried to protect me when he did what he did. "I'm pissed at you."

He just nods, as if he expected it. I hate that he has me backed into a corner, but I can hardly say no when he's given me not only a job but potentially a studio.

It's been so long since I danced.

"I'll PT him," I relent. "But surely you can see it's a farce. He doesn't need a PT."

"Yeah and I asked you to PT him, I didn't tell you how you should do it." He winks. "I'm sure you can get inventive with it. He did put us out of a job after all."

I tilt my head to the side. I think he is telling me to beast him, but I don't voice it. The more I think on it, the more I think this could be fun.

"Anything you need for this place—"

"I will pay for myself. Don't push it," I cut him off, knowing what was coming next.

"What do you think you'll do with it?" he asks, looking around with a knowing smile.

"I have an idea," I tell him, mentally calculating what needs doing and what it might cost. I don't have much in the way of savings right now, but I have a little. Especially now that Mum isn't in contact.

"It might not happen right away—"

"Take your time. There's no rush, no pressure," he assures me.

"Thank you, Logan." I take the keys from his outstretched hand, excitement buzzing in my gut.

"It's like something out of a tacky romance movie." Megan laughs into her wine glass as I conclude my week's fuckery.

She isn't far wrong. Mine and Mason's entire relationship could be one big bad romance novel. "And Logan backed him on it. Apparently, I had six people request me for PT sessions, they clearly have no idea how terrible I'd be. Me with a bunch of girls in tutus fine—I can teach but put me one on one with a raging protein-filled muscle and I'd be screwed."

"Raging protein-filled muscle." Scarlet chuckles, her cheeks flushing. "That's what she said."

"You know what I mean!" I give her an elbow to the ribs as she snorts out a laugh.

"Personally, I think Logan is right. Maybe it'll give you two the opportunity to clear the air once and for all," she tells me, dropping her head to my shoulder.

I stare thoughtfully down at my coffee table. "I thought we already had."

"The last time you saw him you got naked, actually." Lucy cringes as she corrects me.

"Eww." Scarlet lifts her head from my shoulder in disgust.

"*Actually!* The last time I saw him, I made a fool of myself in the middle of the gym and split my chin open. What if I'm just as terrible as that? I can't train him."

"I have every bit of faith in you. Stop worrying." Lucy smiles. "This will be a good thing. Imagine if you can eventually be around each other and not want to kill one another. Or get naked," she adds.

As much as I get what Lucy is saying, it feels impossible. Maybe—hopefully in time things won't be as electric with Mase. Maybe one day I won't feel the way I do about him. I don't tell them about the room above the gym, mostly because I want to take my time, make sure it's exactly what I want. It's been a long time since I danced, well over a year, and I worry it won't come to me like it used to.

"At least Mason is speaking to you," Scarlet voices from beside me. "He's been avoiding me."

"He hasn't phoned?" I ask, annoyed. I wish he would be

better for her; I know the kind of man he can be and this isn't it.

"No, but he did text last week. Asked if everything was okay. I mean, what does everything entail? The house? Me? Our parents' graves? The entire estate I manage alone whilst studying medicine?"

"Someone should have a word." Lucy peers over at me. "I could speak to Ell."

"No!" Scarlet exclaims. "I don't want him to be forced into it! If he cared, he would be there. I'm over it anyway."

"You shouldn't be left to deal with everything alone, Scarlet. Have you thought about renting the house out like he suggested?" Lucy asks.

"I could never." She shakes her head vehemently.

When Scarlet decided to return to studying, Mason thought it would be a good idea to propose renting out the estate. I get the logic. She travels daily to the hospital, and she's alone in the house at night, but I know without having to even ask her that she could never leave. He knows that too.

"I know, but with your studying do you think you can balance it all right now. What if you just offered a twelve-month tenancy?"

"I know it's not my place," I chime in, "but I wouldn't be comfortable with it either. I take Ellis out there as much as possible, and maybe it's selfish for me to want you to stay but I would hate to see someone else live there."

Scarlet smiles gratefully up at me, and I know she will appreciate me siding with her on this. "I couldn't do it anyway; I love it too much."

"Does it not get lonely?" Megan asks.

I watch as Scarlet swallows thickly, her throat bobbing. "Not really."

"You are badass, lady."

"We should come out, have a girls' night there," Lucy suggests.

"I was actually thinking of a party." Scarlet sits up on the sofa a little. "Or like a memorial ball." She shrugs.

"Fuck yes! Yes! We can go dress shopping!" Megan bounces in her seat excitedly. "Sorry, that was insensitive, the memorial part is super sweet too!" she adds. "Luce, can you get Jean to sort us dresses?"

I roll my eyes at Megan as Lucy and her buzz between themselves. I turn to Scarlet. "This sounds incredible, Scar. Do you need a hand planning?"

"I was banking on it if I'm honest. It was something I thought about a few months back but I wasn't sure, but I hoped you girls would help me."

"Of course." I grin. "Have you thought much into it since?"

"Not really, but maybe Mum and Dad's wedding anniversary would work date-wise? It's only next month but I have contacts."

I beam at her. "That sounds perfect."

"And you'll be safe from running into my asshole brother, so that's one bonus. There's no way he'd come." She swigs her wine, hiding her face in the glass.

To think Mason and Scarlet have always been so close and now they're barely speaking irks me. They should be helping each other, not avoiding contact. Mason is a big boy; he needs to be better and be there for his sister.

Oh, that asshole will be going to the ball alright. With fucking bells on.

I'M ANNOYED AT MYSELF. For the longest time, I knew I didn't need Mason. I didn't want to see him, I had our son, and lived alone as a single mother. But now I stand here with butterflies in my stomach waiting for him to arrive for his five fifteen PT session. How the times have changed.

He became the light in my dark heart for the longest time, but it burned too bright for too long and eventually he burnt me. Now he is starting to glow again, but it's not the same light as before. It's like a dull, yellow, annoying gleam that I can block out with the squint of an eye.

Five fifteen on the dot, he bounces up over the steps, ready to work out. He looks delicious this evening, but so does chocolate cake and too much of that causes diabetes. I wonder what too much Mason Lowell would cause... I go with severe vomiting and diarrhoea; it will help me get through the next hour.

He saunters over, drawing the eyes of nearly everyone in the gym.

"Hey." He smiles, and I roll my eyes, not bothering to hide my annoyance.

"Hi," I say sweetly.

I'm aware he hasn't done anything wrong and already my attitude stinks, but I told Logan I didn't want to PT him and yet here we are.

He frowns at my tone. "Everything okay?"

"Everything is perfect. Are you ready for your session?"

He licks at his lips, studying my face. Is he nervous? "Sure, can we start with—"

"Absolutely not. I have your session planned out already, silly." I wrinkle my nose and smile. "Come on, let's go get some cardio."

Call me a bitch, but I want to see this man sweat.

12

Mase

"Faster! Come on, I've seen you come quicker than this."

I don't dare look at her. Sweat drips from my forehead and down every inch of my body. She hasn't stopped, even when I told her I needed to, she pushed me to keep going. I wasn't expecting her to be such a bitch, but I should have. It's fucking Nina.

"My hour is nearly up." I look up just as one of the other men walks by the rowers, a smirk plastered across his smug face. I plead with him with my eyes to take me with him.

She crosses her arms over her body. "Shh, save your energy, big boy. Last five minutes."

I glare up at her, pulling the cord back harshly as I push my legs straight, then back in again. I can tell she is loving this. "If I can't walk on this leg tomorrow, it's on you."

She rolls her eyes. "You could always find a new PT. I know some of the other guys wanted some sessions with me.

If you're not going to take this seriously, I'm sure they'd be more than ready for me."

Her brows shoot high as if telling me to try her.

Bitch.

"If you think that will make me jealous," I say through gritted teeth my left thigh on fire, "you're wrong."

"Oh, really. Why else are you doing this, if not to stake your claim?"

I pick up the pace as she goads me. "I'm not having the mother of my son dating a meathead."

"Dating? They asked me to PT them, it's not a damn marriage proposal, Mason."

"I'm well aware of their intentions," I snap.

"And your intentions? Should I be taking this as a date now?"

"No." I focus on the numbers on the dial in front of me and nothing else. Definitely not her.

"Well then, I see no reason why I can't PT them, too."

"You won't," I scoff.

"You can't dictate what I can or can't do."

"I can," I fire back.

"You're being an ass."

I continue to row, still not looking up at her.

"You're being an ass," she repeats, and I finally shift my gaze. God, she's fucking hot when she's mad. Her cheeks are slightly flushed, and her tits are all out of sorts in her sports bra, but damn does she look like a wet fucking dream. She continues despite my lack of commitment to the conversation. "For starters, I don't even want to train them, so you've wasted your time and money going out of your way to make things awkward for us."

"I'm not feeling awkward." My thigh twinges and I falter. Her eyes drop to my leg.

"That's enough," she snaps, stepping forward. I frown and keep rowing. "Mason, stop."

"No."

"Yes!"

"I'll stop when I'm ready to stop."

"Could you be any more stubborn?" she huffs, throwing her hands up and walking away from me.

I side-eye her ass as she snakes through the gym, but the minute she is out of sight I drop the handles and stand to escape to the showers. The crazy bitch has ruined me today.

***

Nina

I KNEW he'd be difficult to train, and not because of the way he works out but because of the way he looks when he works out. And the way his mouth moves. It's not only distracting but frustrating, because Mason Lowell thinks he can have a say in what I do. But he lost that right a long time ago.

"Nina, you're heading out?" Gemma asks. She is sat at the reception desk, her hair pulled back from her face and sat high on her head.

"Yep, Logan is closing tonight."

"Oh, I must have got my days..." I wait for her to finish, but she doesn't. Instead, she nods over my shoulder in warning.

"Hello."

I flinch then spin, pushing hard on Mason's shoulder. "Do you know how creepy you are?"

"I only said hello, jeez," he says nonchalantly, completely carefree and so unlike him.

"I will see you tomorrow, Gemma." I smile over at her then push through the glass double doors, pulling my rucksack on.

"I'm driving you home," Mason tells me as he steps out behind me. "Do you need to get Ellis?"

"No, Maggie drops him to me, and I'm running back. It's part of my routine now."

"Fantastic, my car is over here." He walks off towards the Bentley and I roll my eyes at his back. "Don't be all dramatic about it. I'm not going to chase you, Nina. It's late and I want to see my son."

"Next time, I'm picking a less assholey baby daddy," I mummer to myself as I reluctantly follow him towards the Bentley.

"I heard that," he calls.

I get in the car and settle into the leather, breathing in his scent. It's like a Mason sensory overload in here. It reminds me of his penthouse, his shower, his bedroom, even silly things like his watch, the smells are all memories of times I've been somewhere and inhaled him in every sense of the word.

Goose bumps pebble along my arms and I shiver.

"You cold?"

I nod, rolling my lips. Why is everything ten times harder when it's just the two of us alone? We bounced off each other in the gym. I ripped into him and him me, so why can I barely look at him now?

Mason turns on the heating then pulls out into traffic. "I'd prefer it if you'd use Vinny, you know this."

"Why are you still pushing the driving thing? You know I like to run."

"I do." He pops a brow to make his comment hit a little harder and I snap.

"Can you stop that?" I huff.

"What?" He frowns, gripping the steering wheel tight.

"Every chance you get, you pass comment on how I always run or how *you're not my home anymore.*" I mock his deep voice. "You take a dig at every chance and it's wearing thin. Maybe I was wrong, maybe I shouldn't have left. But calling each other out over our past every time we see each other isn't going to fix a thing. You aren't perfect either, Mason."

"I'm sorry, did you just say you were wrong?" he admonishes.

I drop my head back to the seat. "That's all you took from that, huh, that I'm in the wrong."

"Nina, you do realise if you'd have stayed things would be very different now."

"Would they though?" I close my eyes, blocking out the parts I can. "When were things ever good?"

"Are you serious?" he asks, and I can tell he is frowning.

When I don't answer, he begins listing things.

"That first night at Melders" —I pop open my eyes— "*I had a great time.*" He licks his lips and I clench my thighs at the memory. "That night you danced for me. Paris. Bora Bora. I have a ton of good memories."

I smile thoughtfully. "Paris was one of the best weekends of my life."

"Where's your bangle?" he asks out of the blue as if he's

desperate to know. He flicks his eyes from the road to me.

I eye my lap in an attempt to hide my face. "It's at the apartment. I don't wear it anymore."

He nods his head but doesn't speak.

"You can have it back—"

"No," he cuts me off, shaking his head with a frown. "No."

I watch him for a moment, my mind not quite sound. "I thought you were going to propose."

He flicks his head towards me. "What?"

"In Paris, on the stage, I thought you were going to propose." I smile, biting my lip as my cheeks flush.

"You did?" Deep lines mar his forehead as his lip twitches. It's only slight but I don't miss it.

"Yep. Then you gave me the bangle back and told me about your mum. It's an incredible memory. I'll hold on to it forever. That entire evening was like something out of a dream."

"What would you have said? If I had proposed," he asks, eyes back on the road.

I swallow my pride and give him my honesty. Because what the hell. "In the moment... I'd have said yes. Without doubt or thought." My throat goes tight, and my eyes burn, but I can't look away from his face.

"You would've said yes? In fucking Paris?" His lip tips up on one side, and I can't help but smile with him. "You told me in Bora Bora that you didn't want to get married."

He looks over at me in question.

"I wasn't lying. You sold my studio." His face drops. "I understand why. I've had time to deal with it now. I mean, I forgive you, but I can't ever forget it." I shrug. "I don't dwell on it, and it was Paris, Mason. I'd probably have flown to Vegas that night and got hitched if you'd asked me." I chuckle, trying to lighten the mood that's fallen over us.

"You were pregnant in Paris," he says solemnly, dragging me right back down with him.

I nod, thinking back and wondering how I never noticed. I feel like we missed so many firsts with Ellis. There was no twelve-week scan, no tests, no plans. I stare at the windscreen. "I don't know how I missed it."

He nods. "You know, we may be terrible together—apart from when we're out of the country maybe." I chuckle at that. "But we sure make fucking cute kids."

"He's adorable, right? I feel like I'm biased when I gush about him to people." I grin.

"Nope, you're right, he's going to bring so many angry mothers to our door when he grows up."

Our door. My heart pounds, begging for the reality of his words.

We pull up outside my apartment building and he parks at the curb, then follows me inside. "Maggie won't be here yet; she normally gives me a chance to shower after getting back."

"That's okay. Do you want me to wait out here?" He thumbs to the small foyer on my floor.

"No, no, come in. I have something for you actually."

"Yeah?" he asks, sounding surprised.

"You don't have to have it, but I thought you might like it." I push open the door and let him in. "I won't be a sec, wait out here."

Leaving him in the living area, I go to my room and drop to my knees beside my bed, pulling out the box from under it. I never thought I'd give these to Mason, but I only really took them for his benefit. I suppose I always hoped that one day I'd be in a position to share them with him. I don't know why I'm giving them to him now, but for some reason I feel like he should have them.

I open the lid and riffle through the things inside, silly things I shouldn't have kept but couldn't get rid of either. The bangle being one of those things.

With the folder I was looking for grasped tight in my hand, I walk back out to the lounge. The minute I set eyes on him again, I doubt the entire idea of showing him.

"What do you have there?"

I stare through him, licking my lips as I try to find an excuse not to show him. What is wrong with me?

"Earth to Nina." He walks towards me, and I hold out the file, widening my eyes, amazed that I've even offered it to him.

He frowns and takes it. "What is it?" He must feel it's weighty and carries it to the kitchen island, sliding onto the chair and placing it down in front of him. He looks over to me before opening it. "Come show me."

"It's just some pictures." I brush him off as if they aren't important. "You probably wouldn't even want to see them, but I knew I should keep them. You don't ha—"

"Nina." He stops me. "Come here, now."

I slide onto the stool next to him and he flicks over the first page, letting it drop with a thud to the counter. "I was four months. That was the day at the hospital. We cut my head out of the picture because I was being miserable, but Elliot insisted we should take the photo."

"You had a bump?" he asks, but it comes out scratchy and he clears his throat.

"I don't know. It all seems like such a blur now. It just looks like a little bloat."

"How did I not notice? Surely I would have?"

"The girls noticed on holiday. They had their suspicions."

He snaps his head towards me, his eyes glazed and wild. "Why didn't you tell me?"

"I didn't think it was possible. I've always taken my pill."

He turns the page and stares down at the pictures on the paper. "You grew fast."

"Thanks." I laugh.

"I didn't mean—"

"I know. I wasn't looking after myself before. Once I knew I was pregnant, I made sure I fixed that. I knew I had to be better."

He looks down at me again, his brows drawn in. "You are; better. You're a wonderful mother."

"I do my best. There are far better mothers I'm sure, but I'm not the worst."

He continues to look through the photos, each one getting closer and closer to my due date.

"That one was taken just a few hours before he was born."

"Did it ever get uncomfortable?" He flicks back a couple pages, looking at the photos again.

"At night. I found myself reading a lot more. Sleep was definitely harder than normal."

"I can imagine," he says in surprise. "Christ, no wonder you didn't dance."

"Yeah, there was no way." I chuckle.

Flipping over the last page, I cringe, wondering why I even put the photo in. I had completely forgotten it was in there.

It's the only picture of the three of us, the one with Mason sitting behind me in the hospital bed. Ellis is on my chest and his small hand grips my finger. It would be normal to have the picture in the album, but Maggie caught us right as our lips brushed. It's a moment I don't quite remember fully but can't seem to forget. It makes my cheeks flame and my body tense.

I wait for his reaction, hoping he doesn't think I'm a loser for keeping the picture.

"I didn't know this was taken," he whispers.

"Maggie," I say in explanation.

He flips it closed and I jump. "Can I keep this?"

"Uh, yeah." I want him to take it, that's why I made it, but the last picture is the only photo I have of us all together. I'd have to ask Maggie for another print and that would just be weird.

"Thank you, for this." He stares at me, as if he has more to say but doesn't want to. Or maybe he doesn't know how.

"Of course!" I snap out of it. "I have more pictures of Ellis. I've tried to keep on top of printing them and putting them in the album. I will sort through and make copies." His eyes are still locked on me and it has me squirming in my seat. "Unless you don't want them, you don't have to."

"I want them."

"Cool." I drop my gaze to my lap, hoping my hands will tell me what to say because I have lost all coherent thought.

"I know everything there is to know about you all the way down to the sounds you make when you come. Yet you still get shy and can't look me in the eye?"

My cheeks flame. "You don't—"

"Yo?!"

My eyes snap closed and I roll my lips as Joey lets himself into my apartment. His smile drops when he sees me and Mason sitting at the kitchen island. I may be imagining it, but I swear I hear Mason growl.

"Hey, Joey. Everything okay?"

Stuffing his hands in his pockets, he walks towards us, nodding his head at the wild animal beside me. "Mason."

"What the fuck are you doing here?"

"Mason!" I snap.

"What?" He glares at me. "Do you always just stroll on in here?" he asks Joey.

"Always, always," Joey says smugly.

"Well don't. My son lives here, and I don't fucking like you. Nina may think she knows you, but I don't."

"We aren't doing this now. Joey, can you come back later tonight, please?"

"No. He can come back in the week when I have Ellis," Mason tells us.

"Joe," I plead, sensing the animosity in the room.

He nods, gives Mason a look that says I want to punch you in the face and then leaves.

"What is your problem?!" I blurt once the door is closed.

Mason rolls his eyes and spins around on the chair. "Don't get all irate. I can't stand the prick and I don't want him around Ellis."

"Joey is my friend! A good friend who has helped me through a lot—"

"You don't know him."

"Neither do you! You don't get to judge my friends."

"I can and I will."

My nostrils flare. "Has your little stripper met my son?"

"Here we go."

Unbelievable. The man's an idiot. "How can you not see that she is the problem here? Things wouldn't be like this if it wasn't for her." I'm deflecting the blame and I hate myself for it, but right now I have a whole load of fire inside of me that I want to unleash.

"Jasmine isn't the problem," he snaps. "You are the problem. You, and your inability to trust me! Take Jasmine out of the picture and we still wouldn't be together. You would run, every fucking time."

"You do not say her name in my home again," I grit out, my blood nearly at boiling point.

"Jasmine, Jasmine, Jasmine!" he recites.

"You're acting like a damn child. If she wasn't in the picture of course things would be different."

He stands, gathering up the folder and pointing to the door. "He doesn't come into this house again. Got it?"

"Why?! Why the fuck not!" I counter, stepping up to his chest.

He grasps my throat, pushing me back into the counter before loosening his hand where he grips me, setting my pulse racing freely again.

His head drops, bringing him far too close and his lips mere inches from my own. I can feel the heat radiating off his body as it pushes up against me. Every solid inch of him. "Don't push me, Nina. You may not be mine to fuck anymore, but you are mine in every other sense of the word. You're the mother of my son and if you think I'll watch you fuck around with that—"

A throat clears at the door and Mason all but drops me like a hot potato.

13

Nina

"Everything okay?" Maggie asks, her eyes wide and laser sharp.

I watch as Mason pales. He knows how this looks.

"Everything is fine." I step forward and take Ellis from Maggie's arms, giving her a reassuring look.

"Maggie, I'm sorry, I—"

"Will you get Ellis in the bath?" I ask Mason, needing him to stop talking and not make this any worse.

"Sure," he mutters, nodding eagerly.

I give Ellis a kiss and hand him over to Mason. They disappear into the hall, and I know Maggie is waiting for me to turn around so she can interrogate me.

"What in the world? Nina, has Mason put his hands on you before?"

"It's not like that, Maggie. Mason would never hurt me."

"I beg to differ. I always thought he was such a gentleman."

"Maggie, that man is anything but gentle."

Her eyes widen, then her cheeks flush. "Oh. Oh!" She leans into me, clearly curious. "So, he wasn't being aggressive, he was being... kinky?"

"Oh, god. We aren't doing this!" I laugh.

She smiles wide. "I have to know you are okay. Goodness gracious me." She places a hand on her chest. "I panicked when I walked in here."

"He definitely wasn't being kinky," I explain. "But it wasn't completely innocent either. He's just annoyed that Joey is pissing on his carpet. But it's not even Mason's carpet anymore."

"I don't think that's the correct analogy dear."

"You know what I mean." I wave her off.

"So, he's staking his claim," she asks, still looking extremely curious.

"Yes, and no. I don't know."

I can't exactly tell Maggie that I wanted Mason's hands on me. Or that I wanted him to squeeze just a little bit tighter.

"When me and John got together, we just talked. Like an actual conversation. It was simple. He said, 'wanna go watch a movie' and I said, 'yes' and we got married six months later."

"If only it was that simple, Mags."

"It's as simple as you make it. You're both too damn stubborn. Just have a conversation."

I puff out a breath, fed up with everyone else having an opinion on what me and Mason want. "Who said we even want it to work?"

"Well, if that boy isn't kinky or aggressive, I'd say you definitely have some things to work out. Wouldn't you?"

I grin at her, not believing I'm having this conversation with her. "Was everything okay with Ellis today?"

She purses her lips. "Good as gold, he's just perfect."

"Thank you, Maggie." She gives me a kiss on the cheek and tells me to come over Sunday for dinner, then leaves.

The sound of Ellis screeching with laughter makes me smile and I sneak off in the direction of the bathroom, wondering what's so funny. Only as I round the corner I falter, caught completely off guard by what's unfolding before me. Mason is standing beside the tub, his top is soaked and discarded on my bathroom floor, and I've caught him in the middle of pulling off his trousers.

And for the love of all that is holy I am rendered absolutely stupid.

You cannot lick him.

Mason lifts his head, sensing my presence at the door. "What was that?" He frowns.

I pop a brow, swallowing the saliva that threatens to slip out and drip down my chin like a drooling puppy. "Huh?"

"You said I can't lick him."

My cheeks flame and his face morphs into a knowing smile.

"No, I didn't." I panic. I did not say that out loud.

"Sorry." His smile is so wide I'm surprised his face doesn't split in two. He's so smug. "Ellis soaked me. I was going to jump in. We do it at home."

"Okay." I nod eagerly.

He licks his lips, concealing his grin as he continues to pull off his trousers.

Am I a complete pervert for wanting to watch this? I should leave. I should go and wait in the living room, but I'm rooted to the ground. Unable to move my feet even if I wanted to.

Keeping his boxers on, he climbs into the tub and sits opposite Ellis. He looks massive in my tiny bath, and really fucking good too.

They splash the water and Ellis chuckles. I sense they do this a lot as Ellis watches Mason's every move, waiting as if he knows what's to come. They are scooping up cups of water and pouring them over their heads. Apparently, that is hilarious. I can't help but smile.

"Do you mind putting my shirt in the dryer, Mummy?" Mason asks, winking at Ellis and snapping me out of my trance.

"Of course." I walk to the bath and reach for the T-shirt.

"Nina."

"Mum, Mum, Ma." I snap my head up in surprise when they both say my name, my shock coming from Ellis finally saying Mum for the first time. Although, I'm not met with a happy smile, and I'm not given the chance to get excited about it. No, I am met with a face full of water.

I gasp, squeezing my eyes tight.

"Oh my god, did you see that! It's like he knew I was going to get you!" I barely see but I can hear how proud Mason is of his son.

They both threw their cups over me, soaking my face and tank. "What was that for!" I wipe at my face, probably smearing my mascara.

"It's tradition. Everyone gets wet at bath time, Mummy." Mason shrugs, his face cheeky and knowing.

"Not in this house! Is that why you made me come closer? You ass."

"Language, Mummy," he says to me but looks at Ellis, his abs rippling as he chuckles. "I think Mum, Mum, Ma is feeling the cold, Ellis."

I drop my eyes from his perfect face and notice that my nipples are straining against the fabric of my tank. The water has soaked the white material and my breasts are very visible.

Covering them with my hands, I shake my head at Mason and edge out the bathroom. "You need to get out of my bath, then my apartment," I say, keeping it playful.

He bites his lip, giving me a panty-melting look. "You're not getting in?"

"No."

"Spoil sport. Mummy's a spoilsport."

"And Daddy's a moron."

"Da, Da, Da, Da," Ellis babbles.

I roll my eyes and leave the bathroom, then go to my bedroom and find a fresh top.

Mase

I DIDN'T PLAN to get in the bath, and I probably didn't think it through. Because now I'm standing in the bathroom in nothing but a towel and no spare clothes to change into. Nina disappeared after nipplegate and I'd be lying if I said I wasn't disappointed. She has the best tits.

Ellis bounces in my arms, pointing towards the door, and I make the decision to go out and find her. I need my clothes dried before I can leave and that won't happen until I get them in the dryer.

We find Nina in the kitchen. She has an oversized hoodie pulled over her, hiding herself from me.

"We thought we should apologise."

She spins, her eyes dropping down my body then snapping back to my face. "You did?"

"Yeah, we didn't mean to get you wet." I look at Ellis trying not to laugh. I'm a bastard.

"You didn't?" Her head drops to the side, her eyes flitting down the length of my body.

"Not with the water anyway." I openly smirk at her.

"Will you put some clothes on already?" She shakes her head as if her reaction to me is wrong. "Please."

"I thought this is what we did? Or are you the only one who can get naked?"

Her cheeks flame and she steps towards us, taking the clothes from my hands. "I will put these in the dryer. Ellis has clothes in the dresser in my room."

"Let's get you warmed up then, little dude." I bounce him in my arms and disappear down the hallway.

Nina's bedroom is boring, with little on the walls. I wonder why she doesn't make it more homely. Placing Ellis in his cot, I take out some pyjamas then dress him.

"This is a good one, it says 'Boss like Daddy'," I tell him, pulling the top over his head and then smoothing down his hair.

"We could do with a brush." His hair is thick and dark and seems to grow more and more every day. It's long enough to style just like mine. Taking the brush from the top of the dresser, I sit him on the bed and style it into perfection.

"You look good." I smile down at him, holding out my fist which he grabs and tries to chew.

"Let's go find Mummy, and hey!" I point at him. "You need to try that Mum, Mum thing again. I think I saw the Ice Queen melt a little."

"Da Da Da Da." He bounces in my arms, and I plant a kiss on his smooth head, inhaling the clean smell of his shampoo.

I don't see Ellis anywhere near as much as I'd like, yet we have him fifty-fifty. I don't know how other dads do it, especially every other weekend dads. I can't think of anything more important than the precious hours I get with him during the week.

Before we go back out into the lounge, I pull on my jeans, the only things I saved from Ellis's water onslaught. Nina is laying out the table when we enter the living area, and she can't help her hungry eyes from roaming my body. If there was any doubt before now that I still did it for her, after today, I know for absolute certain that I do.

I can't help but mess with her. It's been too long. "Are you dribbling?"

"Shut up." She glares. "Would you like to stay for tea?"

I can see her gnawing on the inside of her cheek, and I know it would have taken a lot for her to put aside her pride and ask me that. So instead of being smart with her, I simply tell her. "Yes. Thank you."

"Maybe I could find you a top that will fit you." She stares at my chest, and I almost feel bad. If roles were reversed, and she was standing naked in just a pair of jeans, commando, with her breasts on full display... yeah, I'm hard.

I readjust myself in my jeans, whilst Ellis looks puzzled between the two of us. He has never known us to be in the same room for so long before. This must be alien to him.

"You're unbelievable, you know that?" she snaps as if she

can't hold it in any longer, shaking her head as she starts to turn away.

"What?"

"Tea won't be long."

"Did you ring that jackass and tell—"

She turns on me, her face holding a warning. "Language."

My eyes pinch in as I watch her. "Let him know not to come back tonight."

"I already did."

"Good."

"Good," she copies.

"You going to finish cooking my tea?" My lip tips up on one side. I know I'm winding her up, and I shouldn't. But she needs to let her hair down a little. The Nina I once knew was never so uptight.

She must think better of it and doesn't come back at me, instead she leaves us in the living room muttering her reply under her breath as she disappears to the kitchen.

"Is Mummy always this grumpy?"

———

DINNER IS DELICIOUS, and I ask Nina after if she would mind me putting Ellis to bed. I'm being greedy with him, but I don't care. When he was a newborn, I had to miss out because he couldn't be away from Nina as often as he is now. It was hard, but she wasn't ready to see me. I resented her for it at the time, but I understand how important that was for them to have that bond now.

Ellis goes down quickly and then I go and help clean up the last of the dishes with Nina. We don't speak, but it isn't awkward. Surprisingly, it's been a good evening. It feels like we've turned a corner.

"I'll check your clothes."

I smile after her, watching her as she walks to the laundry room. I can hardly see her body with the oversized hoodie and leggings, but I know what's underneath, and as she pads down the hall on her bare feet, I know how taut and smooth her legs are, how pert her sweet round ass is.

"Are you fucking kidding me!"

And then there's that mouth.

"What's the matter?" I ask, walking to the laundry room after her.

"It's not on! I turned it on!"

I take my T-shirt and boxers and find that they are still damp, warm, but damp. I look down at the machine. "The water container is full. It must have stopped. Just stick them in for a bit longer."

Squeezing in beside her, I pull out the water tray and then go and empty it into the kitchen sink. She's sitting on the washing machine when I come back, looking annoyed.

"Why the sour face? I'm not that bad, am I?"

"You were only supposed to pop in, then you ended up bathing Ellis, then you ended up in my bath, and now you are strolling around topless. It's a lot of YOU!"

I try to contain my smile, but I can't help the boyish grin that slips past. "Don't give me that smile," she warns.

"Why? I know what it gets me."

"You don't play fair," she huffs, jumping down from the worktop, bringing us toe to toe. She looks up at me, her head only just reaching my chin.

"I never have played fair, Pix."

Her dainty palms spread out over my chest. "Mase—"

I lean in, my hand sliding along her jaw and lifting her lips to align with mine. "But you never played fair either."

I lower my lips to hers, not being able to help myself and not thinking past the need to feel her. Taste her. It's been too long. Our lips lightly brush before she tips her chin to meet me. I quickly deepen the kiss. She moans. Our tongues touch. She pulls away. And then we stand in a haze, my cock throbbing between us and my head a scrambled mess.

What the fuck are we doing?

She reaches past me, riffling around on the shelf behind me. She grabs what looks like a pillowcase. "Follow me," she demands.

And like a damn dog, I do.

Nina

"I am not wearing that!"

"Yes, you are."

"It's a pillowcase."

"It's an extra-wide case. I never use the pillows, they're too big."

I take the scissors from the draw and begin to cut out holes. My hands shake as I cut through the fabric, and I know it's because of what just happened. I wasn't expecting this. I wasn't expecting to want Mason as desperately as I do. I want to feel ashamed, or mad at myself, but I don't. Not when it feels so natural to want him.

He still feels like mine, like I could reach out and touch

him, as if he belongs to me and no one else. And that's why I pulled away, because Mason Lowell isn't mine anymore.

"You've lost it, you know that?"

"Maybe." I finish and turn it in the right way, then hold it out to him. "Here."

"You really can't control yourself any better? This is needed?"

"Put it on or drive home half naked. It's your choice."

Snatching the pillowcase, he curses under his breath, pulling the cotton over his head and fighting his way into the makeshift armholes.

Because of the size of the case, it fits him, and it's still loose in places.

"Well?" he asks.

My first dimple pops and then I am gone, bent over in hysterics at the beautiful specimen standing before me, wearing a pillowcase.

"Only you could make it look semi-hot."

"Ridiculous." He shakes his head, storming past me and dropping down onto my sofa.

I continue to laugh as the corners puff out at the shoulders.

"If you don't stop, I'll take it off, and then all hell will break loose. Do you want that?" he asks, completely serious.

"Are you threatening me with sex?" I laugh harder.

"I never implied sex, Nina." His face gets even more serious, and he rearranges himself again. "Jesus Christ."

"Your clothes won't be long then you can go home." I sit down on the opposite sofa—feeling like it's the safest thing to do—and try not to look at him, remaining focused on the TV.

After ten minutes, I feel his eyes on me and when I turn

to face him, he jumps straight in. "I think we should have an evening a week where we have dinner together. For Ellis."

Shit. Okay, I wasn't expecting that. The evening has been good. Ellis loved having Mason here, but do I really want to tie us to one night a week, putting us both in a position to be around each other. We rarely last five minutes without disagreeing on something.

"You could come to the penthouse, or I could come here," he suggests.

"I wouldn't come to the penthouse."

"Why?"

Because it would tear me apart to go back to the only place that ever felt like home. "Too much happened at the penthouse. I don't think I'd be comfortable there."

"That's ridiculous, you pretty much lived there for five months."

"Like you lived at Lowerwick for seventeen years but now can't go back, not even for your sister."

His face turns hard and he starts fiddling with the remote control. "Forget it."

"I'm just saying, it's how I feel."

"I know, that's fine and I understand." He brushes it off, and I try to bite my tongue, but I know I need to get it off my chest.

"Have you spoken to Scarlet recently?"

"Nina—"

"We can talk about the house, and Scar if you want."

"You aren't turning this around on me. I asked you to do one night a week, for our son. This doesn't need to become a screaming match because I don't go to the estate."

"I'm not screaming, Mason, I'm willing to compromise if you will."

"What do you mean?"

"You say it's for Ellis, having an evening where we eat together. And I agree, he seemed to love tonight."

"Right..." He studies me, unsure of where I'm going with this.

"I take Ellis to the estate every other week, sometimes more. But what if we do one week here, one week at the penthouse, and one week at the estate? With Scar."

His jaw locks and he stares down at the coffee table.

"I'd be willing to face the penthouse if you are willing to face Lowerwick."

"It's not the same thing. I lost everything at that house," he mutters, not looking at me.

My throat grows tight and I move to sit on the same sofa as him, hating the distance between us.

"Yes, you did. But they're still there—both of them. Scarlet shouldn't have to be there alone all the time, Mason. I worry about her."

"I worry about her too." He rolls his lips as if his confession pisses him off.

"I'll be there, Ellis too. It would mean the world to Scar. We don't even have to do it right away, just think about it." I give him a small smile, eyeing his fingers that are playing with a small piece of frayed cotton on the pillowcase.

He lifts his head, looking so deep into my eyes, I worry he will see the secrets I bury deep in my soul. "I'll think about it."

"Okay." I don't mention the ball. I figure baby steps are

the best tactic with him after getting him to even consider going to the estate.

"I'm going to go check your clothes. I think it's best that you wait here." I give him a wink, trying to lighten the mood.

"Nina." He stops me as I pass him, grasping my wrist.

I look down at him, wanting to laugh at the stupid pillow-case but completely caught off guard by the look in his eyes. "Thank you."

"What for?" I frown.

His thumb traces my skin, where his bangle once sat. "I haven't been able to take Ellis to the estate. I presumed you went—obviously you did that day you got fired, so I hoped you did. But to know you make the effort to take Ellis to see them. It means a lot."

I nod, my eyes blurring. "I don't just go for Ellis, Mason, although he is the main reason. I go for me too. And you. Your father was an incredible man, and I've only heard wonderful things about your mum." I pause, not knowing if I want to bare myself to him completely. Tonight has been weird. "I feel close to you when I'm at the house."

He lets me go and I figure he probably needs a minute. I get his clothes which are now dry and then place them on the arm of the chair. "I'll leave you to get changed. You can post the key back through the door on your way out."

He nods and I make myself scarce, feeling more confused than ever.

In my bedroom, I slip out of my jumper and then pull on my usual nightshirt. Needing to clean my teeth, I pull open the door and stop short, finding Mason standing on the other side, his hands gripping the frame and his head hanging as if it had been resting against the wood.

My hand goes to my heart, and his eyes drop to my top, then to my bare legs. "Nice T-shirt. I'm sure I had one like that once."

My cheeks flush.

"Thank you for dinner. I'll see you soon, Nina." He bends, placing a soft kiss to my forehead before stalking off down the hall.

14

Nina

IT'S BEEN TWO WEEKS. TWO WEEKS SINCE HE KISSED ME, AND you'd think it never happened. He comes to his PT sessions and basically does his own thing. I give him some lip and he gives it back, but then he goes home. He doesn't offer me lifts, he doesn't linger when he drops or picks up Ellis. I'd call him out on it, but truthfully, I'm just glad that we can be in the same room without going at one another.

With Ellis at Mason's for the weekend, I've found myself cleaning the apartment from top to toe. I've barely slept and when five a.m. rolls around, I climb out of my bed and slip on my sweats. I'd run alone, but I know Joey has been avoiding me and I want to get him out of his apartment. He'd be a total recluse if I let him.

"Joe!" I whisper, shaking his shoulder.

"Hmmm."

"Wake up!" I shove him harder.

He groans, rolling away from me. "Please, go away."

"No, get up, we are running. I'll get you water."

"Coffee."

"You can't run with coffee."

"I hate you."

"No, you don't." I smile, slipping off to his kitchen and filling a water bottle. "You've been avoiding me," I say loud enough so he can hear me.

"No, I haven't." Joey appears in the kitchen doorway in a sleepy state. His hair is wild and flops down onto his forehead, and he is in only a pair of black boxers. He is skinnier than he should be for his size, skinnier than when I first met him. I always worry about him. He has no family here to look out for him after his mum passed away a few years ago, and his brother lives in the states. From what I can gather, he blames Joey for his mother's death. Joey will rarely talk about it and I'm okay with that. Although I know he can look after himself, he's happy being independent and I can relate to that. But it doesn't mean it doesn't get lonely. Add in his mental health issues and it's enough to have me checking in on him.

We all need someone in life.

"You have but I forgive you. I did kick you out for Mason the last time you came over."

He smiles up at me. "You did, I was pissed about that actually," he says it as if he is only now remembering and I instantly know we are okay. "But that's not why I was avoiding you. I really have been busy."

"Are you eating enough?" I ask casually, tightening up the bottle top. "You've not been up to mine for tea in the last few weeks."

I'm smothering him and I can't help it. It's as if when Ellis isn't here I look for someone to cling onto.

"Nina, it's five forty-five. You aren't lecturing me on food right now. We're either running or sleeping."

"Sorry, I've been up for hours," I complain, turning and heading for the door. "Get dressed. I'm going to stretch."

THE BENEFIT of not being able to sleep in has to be experiencing the city before it rises. Delivery men hustle to unload the trucks, clanking and clanging in their steel toecap boots, but otherwise, in the small little side streets, the city sleeps. With the cold morning air, not many fools venture out on the gleaming, icy pavements.

"I think I have a studio," I blurt out, needing to run the idea by someone. I should speak to Lucy and Megan, but if I fail, they will smother me in their pity and I can't stand it. I know Joey deals with knock backs all the time in the photography industry, so I feel a little more comfortable telling him. He won't expect big things.

"Yeah? Where?"

"Above Logan's gym."

"Really? That's great! Are you going to start teaching again?" We stop at a fountain, catching our breaths.

"Not yet. It needs some love. There's painting to do and equipment to clear. The floors are a mess too. But it has potential."

"When was the last time you danced?"

My heart seems to wake with his words, catching up with the rest of my body and beating a little harder than it did moments ago. "It was a few days after the studio sold, at the penthouse."

"Shit. It's been what? Over a year. You need to get back into it, throw yourself in, else you never will."

"Joey, I told you about this because I trust you not to push me. Dancing is my passion, you know that, and I will dance again. I just need some time."

"I know, I'm sorry." He pulls me under his arm, walking us to the gates. "You want some help at the gym?"

"No, I need to do it myself." Working on the studio will be good for me, it will give me something to do when Mason has Ellis. I thought about going this morning, but I feel like I should check with Logan before I just turn up.

And what's the rush?

"To be honest, I couldn't find the time. It's been crazy since I sold my latest prints. I have people booking for next year already. It's mind blowing to think it's finally taking off."

I smile up at him, proud of my friend and the hard work he has poured into the last year of his business. He is a phenomenal photographer. "You'll have your pictures hung up in—"

"In The National Art gallery one day. You're an idiot, you know that?" He chuckles, releasing me from under his arm and pushing me away.

I always tell him he will make it big one day. He doesn't believe in himself like I do.

"You never know, all it takes is one image."

He looks down his nose at me, tipping his chin and smirking. "You'd be the one."

"What?" I giggle, starting to jog again.

"If I were to make it big, you'd be my masterpiece."

I laugh loudly, the pigeons scattering off as I scare them. "As if!"

"The pictures of you in the studio, they're some of the best I've ever taken. It's a damn shame you don't let me sell them." He grins down at me, letting me know he is messing with me.

Once upon a time, I'd have had no problem with Joey selling the pictures he took. But when I lost the studio, they seemed to become more personal.

The image of me looking into the camera, it reminded me of Mason. And in nearly every shot stands his mother's beloved piano. They remind me of something I don't hold on to anymore, so keeping them in my grasp and only my grasp seems important to me. "It doesn't seem right to have my face on a wall. I love the pictures and I'm glad I got you that distinction."

He rolls his eyes. "Oh, because it was all you."

"But I wouldn't want them plastered on random people's walls. It seems... weird."

"Did you know Mason offered me money for them?"

I falter but keep moving. "What?"

Joey doesn't answer me right away, and his face is a mask of indifference.

"Mason offer—"

"You know, forget it." He waves me off, picking up the pace.

"No. What you just said! Mason offered you money for the photos?"

Joey runs his hand through his hair, looking conflicted. "Yeah." He nods.

My lungs burn but I don't stop. "When?"

"God, I don't know."

"Before or after I found out I was pregnant?"

He frowns, slowing to a walk. I welcome the change of pace. My legs feel like jelly. "After, it was just before you moved into the apartment."

"What!" I feel my brows crease, my mind tripping out.

"I didn't sell them," he assures me, as if that's what's important.

"Why didn't you tell me?"

"You didn't speak about him at the time. I didn't think you'd want to know."

He's probably right. I wouldn't have wanted to know. Things were tough after I left Mason. But now I do know, and it leaves me with so many questions.

Mason made out he was angry with me. That he didn't want me after I ran out on him. But why would he try to buy my photos after I left if that was the case?

I stop dead in my tracks as a thought comes to me.

"How much?" I ask.

Joey drops his head, knowing how important the answer is to me.

"How much did he offer for them, Joe?"

"More than I will probably make in a lifetime off all my other photos."

"Son of a bitch!" I seethe. "How much? I want to know."

He rolls his eyes. "I wouldn't let him have them and he wouldn't give up. He didn't go in high at first, but every time I refused, he upped the offer."

I shake my head, waiting.

"One point two."

"One point two?" I frown, shaking my head, confused.

"Yeah."

"One point two," I repeat, willing my brain to function.

"Million, Nina. One point two million pounds."

Bile rises in my throat.

Why does he have to do it? Some women would be humbled. But me? It makes me feel sick to my stomach.

"I shouldn't have told you. I didn't want to upset you, Nina."

"Why didn't you take it?"

He stares through me, thinking about it for a second.

"The pictures meant more." He shrugs.

I nod, the irony breaking my heart in two. If only Mason could see that. He's so desensitised to his own wealth, he doesn't understand the value of the things money will never buy.

"I'm sorry, that he put you in that position, Joey."

He shrugs again. "At first, I was pulling my hair out, literally. I almost gave them up at £20K." His honesty makes me smile. "But then I felt powerful, to turn down that amount of money, especially Mason's money." He grins. "It felt good."

"I can imagine. And I bet he didn't like it much either." I smile despite my annoyance.

"Nope. I had to tell him to leave. He probably wouldn't have stopped at one point two."

"He's a damn idiot." Hearing the colossal amount of money Mason can just throw around like pocket change makes the fire in my gut burn like a raging furnace. "You should've sold them." I look up at him, knowing how much even a fraction of that money would benefit him.

"Probably." He laughs. "You're going to confront him about it aren't you."

"Yep."

It's been the longest day and as Elliot pulls up outside my apartment in his Aston Martin, I yawn wide, not feeling the evening ahead at all.

Scarlet has requested us all at the estate tonight. She wants to finalise the plans for the ball. With only a week to go before the event, she's been crazy busy working on the small details. We have helped her through every bump she has found herself at so far and I know that tonight will be no different. Elliot, Lance, and Charlie have been heavily involved and a massive help. We all agreed not to tell Mason about the ball until a few days before. He should be planning it with us, but we all know he wouldn't, and Scarlet refuses to give him the opportunity to disappoint her.

Lucy and Megan are already in the back of the car when I climb in, and I can barely see them past a sea of garment bags. "Really? Did you bring the whole shop, Luce?"

"If Elliot had listened and brought the Audi, we wouldn't have a problem. Would we *Elliot*."

"You don't get that purr in the Audi, baby. I know you love it." He revs the engine, making me and Megan chuckle.

Elliot's seat is jolted from behind, but he doesn't acknowledge it. He just looks at me with a smile and gives me a wink.

"I think we should call Mason, you know, he's been much happier in the office this week. He told me you kissed him by the way." Elliot gives me a pointed look, waiting for me to do up my seat belt, and pulls out onto the road.

"What?" Megan's head pops out from the back seat.

"You never said!" Lucy bolts forward.

"I didn't kiss him! He kissed me. And it wasn't even a proper kiss." Not by mine and Mason's normal standards anyway.

"You kissed?" Lucy asks, sounding hopeful.

"No! Barely. And it was nearly two weeks ago, so calm down."

"I heard it got pretty hot and heavy. Lowell said he had to jack off in the car after he left. Had your tits out and all in the bathroom."

"Fuck!" Megan exclaims.

"Ell!" I shout, my stomach knotting at that snippet of information. "You're winding it up and making it worse."

"What? I'm just saying what he said." He has a stupid look on his face, telling me he knows exactly what he's doing.

"Yeah, Nina, Mason doesn't hold out on his boys." Lucy glares at me over the top of the bags.

I take a deep inhale and blow it out through my nose, knowing I need to explain. "He got all over the top about Joey."

"Shock." Elliot sniggers.

"He got *himself* all worked up, I didn't do a thing. Then he stayed to bathe Ellis. Your mum turned up, Luce, she thought Mason was getting handsy with me."

"No!" she says, shocked.

"Yep. I told Mason to bathe Ellis to get him out of the situation so I could explain, and then he ended up in the bath with him. He had to dry his clothes, so he stayed for dinner."

"You're getting back together!" Lucy smiles.

"What? No!"

"When and where did the kiss happen?" Megan asks, not missing a thing.

"What does it matter?" Elliot snorts.

"It matters," Lucy tells him.

"In the laundry room."

The girls laugh in the back, and I roll my eyes at Elliot. "Thanks, asshole."

"You're welcome, Pix." He taps the steering wheel, looking over at me while the girls buzz around in the back. "He seems much happier."

"It doesn't mean anything, Ell. We're both confused and so much has happened."

"Exactly. You have been through a lot. In my time, the best relationships always do."

"Nina, I'd advise against taking relationship advice from London's most notorious manwhore." Lucy laughs, falling back into her seat.

I look at her then Elliot, noticing his jaw clenched and face red. "You didn't seem to mind this morning, babe? Hmm? Whilst you were grinding your ass on my semi."

I direct my wide eyes to Luce who has now sunk down in the seat and is hidden by the bags.

Elliot huffs, shaking his head as he looks into the rearview mirror. "Touché, Luce. Tou-fucking-ché."

***

LOWERWICK IS LIT up when we arrive, looking every bit the grand estate that it is. I've been coming here for the last year and when I arrive, it feels a little bit like home.

"This place always reminds me of Christmas. Can you

imagine living in a house like this?" Megan voices, climbing from the car.

"It's not a house, it's a mansion," Lucy says, piling up garment bags on Elliot's outstretched arms.

Inside, Scarlet has an array of cocktails laid out for us to try. We pretend it's research for the ball but we all know it's not.

Lucy has sent Lance, Charlie, and Elliot upstairs to try on the suits she brought over for them. She had one put back for Mason and will get Elliot to deliver it on Friday. Hopefully, everything works out and we pull the whole thing off. A lot has been planned in under a month and I'm so proud of Scarlet and what she has achieved, it's going to be an incredible evening.

"So, I have food to be served at seven, the band is starting at eight thirty, and the auction will begin at nine thirty in their break. I'll need you girls ready for that a little while before."

"Auction?" I blanch.

Scarlet looks up from the piece of paper she's reading from. "Yeah, Lucy didn't tell you?"

I turn to Luce who is wide-eyed with guilt and gulping her cocktail. "Luce?"

"It's for a good cause?" She dabs at her lips.

"What kind of auction?" I ask, my stomach tightening with what my intuition is telling me.

"Megan is hosting, I'm dealing with the money, so Luce said the two of you would donate a date."

"A date?" I snap, staring at Lucy.

"Sorry! It's just one night and we can get Dad to bid, and Megan will take what he offers. Won't you, Meg!"

She elbows her in the side, but Megan just smiles impishly.

"No!" Scarlet asserts. "You have to put yourself out there. Come on, girls."

"Why don't you do it then? I can deal with the money!" I beg her.

She cringes, her hands crunching the paper slightly. "Uhhh, no, sorry."

"Scar!" I cry.

"You know my brother will buy you!"

My heart sinks and my body tenses. I never stopped to consider what Mason would think of an auction. He would hate it, and he *would* buy me, there's no doubt in my mind, and with what Joey told me today, I can only imagine how much deeper he would drive the dagger.

"I don't have a lot in donations yet, it would mean so much if you could do this, Nina."

"Oh god..."

Her lips thin and she shrugs unapologetically. "Thanks, babe."

My lip tips up as she starts to chuckle. "I'll think about it. No promises."

"You are doing it—"

"What do you think, ladies?" Lance announces, sauntering into the room with Charlie and Elliot hot on his heels.

15

Nina

THE FOUR OF US SEEM TO LOSE ALL THOUGHT.

"Holy hotness hell." Scarlet pants, fanning herself.

The three of them are in varying styles of tuxes. Elliot's is navy and seems to have a slight shine to it, as if it's textured. Lance's is all black, the jacket, shirt and bow tie, and his tattoos peek out of his sleeves and collar. And Charlie's looks like velvet, a dark jade shade that does absolutely everything a woman needs it to. They look fucking delicious.

"Boys, you look—"

"Fit!" Elliot finishes for me, pulling on his lapels.

"I was going to say handsome."

"Handsome is what my granny would call me."

"It's perfect!" Scarlet bounces on the spot with excitement. "Can we go pick dresses, Luce? I'm dying to see what you picked out for us."

"Yes! Boys, go get changed then carry on with these bags.

You take one gift from each plate and add it. Charlie, you can tie the bows, I don't trust the other two," Lucy orders.

"You got it, boss," Charlie says, smirking at Elliot and Lance as he claps them both on the back.

Scarlet dashes into the kitchen on our way out of the room. "I'll get a bottle of bubbles. Will be right up."

Megan leads us up the stairs, jogging at pace as her excitement grows. "I was nervous about the dresses but after seeing how spot on you got the boys, now I'm just flipping excited to see what you've picked out for us."

"Well, that's pressure."

"I have every bit of faith in you." Megan grins down at her as we meet her at the top.

"But you didn't," Lucy snaps.

"How do you two live together, still?" I laugh.

"She brings me coffee, and breakfast in bed every day." Megan shrugs.

"I actually miss my morning coffee from you, Luce. Maybe I should move back with you girls."

"Umm, absolutely not. I love your son, but we barely have enough room for the two of us." Megan cringes.

"I was joking."

We file into the room that Scarlet sent us to in the west wing. The garment bags are hung on the back of the divider and me and Megan waste no time unzipping them.

"Wait for Scar!" Lucy scolds us.

"Snooze you lose!" Megan squeals as she unzips the first bag, revealing a gold sequin dress. "Holy fuck balls!"

"That's mine!" Lucy states, moving to stand in front of us so she can unzip them herself. "Nina, that's yours." She hands me a bag. "Megan."

Megan snatches it and kisses Lucy's cheek. "Ahhh, thank you, thank you, thank you! I hope mine is as nice as yours!"

"Of course, it is," she tuts.

I leave them to their bickering and lay the bag down on the bed.

"Oh my fucking god, yes!" Megan holds a red embellished dress up against her. It's off the shoulder and falls straight from the waist with a thigh-high slit on either side. It's seductive but classy, almost alluring, maybe. It's very Megan. She starts stripping in the middle of the room.

"Megs, you do realise that Scar had the divider put up for us to change behind?"

"Nothing you haven't seen before," she quips.

"Bloody hell. Slow down or you'll fall and rip it." Lucy grabs the dress and holds it out for her to step into.

"You didn't wait for me!" Scarlet accuses, stepping into the room with a bottle of champagne and four flutes.

"I did!" I tell her, taking the glasses and setting them down on the table.

"What happened to your hair?" I ask her, frowning at the loose tendrils.

"My hair?" She looks into the free-standing mirror. "Oh crap." She laughs, releasing the messy bun and restyling it. "I caught it on the doorknob in the kitchen."

"Scar, this is yours!" Lucy grins, thrusting the bag at her.

She takes it, swapping it for a glass of champagne. "Megan, you look unreal!" She looks at me quickly before taking a sip of champagne.

"Thanks, Scar. I feel incredible."

Megan looks genuinely choked up, and so she should.

She isn't a frilly dress kind of girl, but this dress, it's like it was made for her.

"Lucy, you're a damn genius. Girls, put yours on. I need to see!" I tell them.

"Okay, I will do mine next." Scarlet takes another sip from her flute then disappears around the back of the divider.

"You were my biggest challenge, Scar," Lucy calls to her. "I wasn't sure what you'd normally pick."

"Lucy..."

"Oh, you hate it." Lucy's eyes go wide as she looks at me in panic. "I can see what else we have in the shop."

"I fucking love it." Scarlet steps out from behind the divider. "What did you do?!"

Lucy's hands go to her face as she takes in Scarlet's silk-clad form. "What did I do!"

"It's purple," I state in awe.

"It's periwinkle," Lucy corrects, smoothing out the hem. "I knew you'd wear this well, but wow, Scar. You look beautiful."

"I love it. Thank you so much, Lucy."

She moves to the full-length mirror, smoothing her hands down her waist. It's not tight to her body, but still fitted enough to show off her slender body.

"Come on, you, it's our turn." Lucy grabs my hand and my dress, pulling me behind the divider.

"Don't be mad at me, okay? You have to give it a chance."

"What does that mean? Will I not like it?"

"Just have an open mind. Here, help me into mine and then I'll help you."

Lucy's dress is everything I'd expect it to be. Gold, covered in rhinestones and sequins, and tight to her every curve. It's high at the neck and has a gaping back. It's understated elegance at its finest, and Lucy to a T.

"You look gorgeous."

"I know." She smiles cheekily over to me. "I had my eyes on this one for fashion week but I knew I had to wear it to the ball." She reaches up and unzips my garment bag. "Your turn."

"God." I start to sweat, bouncing on the balls of my feet as she lowers the zip. "Oh... Oh."

"Try it on, okay? Give it a chance."

"It's see-through?"

"The lace detailing will hide the important parts."

"Luce."

"Put it on."

She slides it off the hanger and I start to undress. "I presume I will have to go braless."

"Yup."

I step into the black lace as she holds it open for me, then lift the thin straps over my shoulders. I look down and instantly feel my eyes bug out at the view of my chest. "Luce, I can't."

"Hurry up!" Megan yells, knocking on the wood and making it wobble.

"Yes, you are, that's all I have for you." She stands, taking in my profile. "Turn around," she tells me, biting her lip.

"Stop looking at me like you want to undress me, you weirdo."

"You have no idea, Nina Anderson! I've nailed this."

She zips me up and I have to suck in a breath with how tight the dress is. "I better be able to unzip this."

"It doesn't have much give, but we need it tight. We have

to keep these bad boys safe and steady." She flicks my nipple and I cover it with my palm.

"Oww!"

"Girls! Look at this queen!" She grins, spinning me and pushing me out from behind the divider.

"No!" Megan says in shock.

"Nina." Scarlet stills, shaking her head.

Oh good god, no. I can't stand the look on their faces. All I can think about is what everyone will think and say at the ball. "Luce, I can't wear this!"

"No!" Megan tells me. "No, in a good way no. Nina, you are wearing that dress." She points.

I move to stand in front of the mirror and instantly have to catch my breath.

Fuck.

"You're going to kill him, your tits, it's the tits," Megan states.

The entire dress is lace, thin, see-through and like a second skin, hugging my every curve with its fishtail shape. It has a plunging neckline that sits just below my sternum. My nipples are the only parts of my breasts that are covered, hidden behind the black lace flowers decorating the dress. Oddly, it isn't tacky, it's so impossibly intricate with the lace embroidered delicately into the sheer fabric, that it looks unbelievably beautiful and expensive.

"Okay, I actually don't hate it."

"Lucy, you are going places, girl. I'm in awe of your talent right now," Scarlet tells her.

"Thank you, I had the most beautiful canvases."

"Champers!" Megan orders.

We all take a flute from the dresser, shuffling around

the room, feeling like princesses. "I vote to not show the boys. I mean, I don't think Elliot will keep his mouth shut to Mase and we need the full wow factor, right?" Scarlet asks.

"Right!" Lucy agrees.

"To the girls!" I toast, holding my glass high and waiting for them to follow.

Scarlet corrects me before our glasses meet. "No. To the boys." She winks at me. "May god have mercy on their eyeballs."

"And inappropriate boners," Megan adds, making us all laugh.

"To the boys and inappropriate boners!" we say in unison, clinking the Lowells' finest crystal.

Mase

MY EYES SEEK out Jasmine sitting at the reception desk the minute the elevator doors slide open. I haven't bothered to chat to her in weeks, she seems to come in, get her job done then leave. She doesn't say much to me, she doesn't really acknowledge me to be honest, but I do know she speaks to George a lot. I wouldn't have bothered to think much of her mood had the email I received this morning not arrived in my inbox.

"Jasmine."

Her head pops up, her eyes tired and red-rimmed.

It throws me off, despite my indifference towards her.

"Can I have a word?"

"George isn't in yet," she tells me, looking around at the empty reception area.

"It's fine, pick the messages up after."

She follows me into the office and instead of sitting at my desk, I gesture to the sofas. With a frown, she lowers herself to sit down, smoothing out her skirt and sitting with her knees together and angled to the side. She looks like a different woman to the one who was photographed on my lap last year. Her skin is clear, her hair shiny and not a tacky yellow colour like it was before.

"You look well, Jasmine," I announce as the thought comes to me.

I can see the surprise my compliment has on her. I instantly think back to every interaction we have had. It's always been about Nina, or her children. I've certainly never complimented her.

"Thank you." She watches me, waiting. She knows I didn't call her in here to tell her that.

"I had an email this morning. Vinny picked it up in your inbox. Do you not check your work account?"

She frowns, then smooths her hands over the edge of the sofa in thought. "You snooped through my messages?"

"We have access to all employees' emails, Jasmine." I lean forward, resting my forearms on my knees. "You listed it with your social worker."

"Oh no." She tenses, her body jolting before she catches herself. "I haven't looked."

"Here." I pull up the email, leaning forward and passing her my phone so she can read it.

"They're giving me contact?" Her smile is instant and lights up her entire face. It's the first time I've ever seen her smile, and ironically, it reminds me of one I'm all too fond of. "I haven't seen the boys in nearly two years." Her voice cracks. "I've missed so much."

Fuck.

I rub my hands together, watching on like a jackass, not knowing what to do as she swipes at her tears. "This is good news; they obviously see that you're making an effort. The meetings are going well?"

She nods. "Yeah, I just... I gave up when they took Betty." She composes herself, taking in a breath and blowing it out harshly as she reads the message again.

She looks up once she's finished. "I hated you so much that day. I still do a little."

"Watching them take Betty from you will be something I will never feel proud about, Jasmine. No matter how many wrongs you have done, I know you don't deserve the hand you've been dealt in life. You just need to learn to help yourself."

"You think they might actually let me have them back?"

"If you carry on as you are, I don't see why they wouldn't." I swallow thickly, not wanting to feel sorry for her but not being able to control my emotions. Jasmine isn't a bad person. She just got a little lost in life. "Jasmine, I'm sorry. I believe I judged you too soon, and wrongly. I can see that Lenny was a massive part of the problem." I roll my lips, my knee bouncing. "By voluntarily stepping away from him, you took a massive step towards your children."

"I know." She nods, looking at her lap.

"Charlie's worked hard to have them kept together, and he's working his ass off to build a lifestyle you can present to the social workers. But the only way you will get them back is if you show you want them back. Show them you'd do anything to have them with you."

She looks at me with so much hope. "I can't believe I'll get to see them."

"Do you want Vinny to drive you?"

She shakes her head. "I'll get a taxi."

"Well, the offer's there if you change your mind."

"Thank you, Mason."

Somehow, we've gone from barely saying a word to each other to having an actual conversation, and a successful one at that. "You're welcome."

"Mason." George's anxious voice rings through the intercom. I stand from the sofa and round my desk.

"Yes, George."

"I have Miss Anderson in reception." He pauses. "She would like to see you. Now."

Nina? Shit, this isn't how I planned to tell her. I still don't know how she will take this situation.

I look up from the desk and into Jasmine's still watering eyes. "I'd like you to meet her."

She shakes her head, her jaw clenched. "Not yet. She will judge me and I get why, but I can't handle that on top of the boys today. It's too much." She wrings her hands in her lap, looking like she is moments away from bolting.

"Just wait in here, okay?"

I straighten my jacket in the glass double doors then push out and into reception. Nina is standing at the desk talking to George, whose eyes are darting all over me as if I'm harvesting stolen organs in my office and not an employee.

Nina is supposed to be working today, and my initial worry is Ellis. "Nina."

She spins, her eyes eating me up as her gaze fixes on me. "Hey!"

"What are you doing here?" I ask, coming to stand next to her. "Is Ellis okay?"

"Oh, yeah, sorry I probably should have called ahead."

"No, no, it's fine. How are you?"

She looks between me and George then frowns, and I know she will be wondering why I haven't already ushered her into my office like all the other times she's come here.

"Could we discuss it in private? No offence, George." She gives him a wink. "And I can imagine you'd want to, also."

I know she is going to ask about the kiss and how I haven't made a move since. The tension in the gym has been hard to ignore, but I know if I go all in before either of us is ready, it won't work. Something has to give first. "Here is fine." My voice comes out an octave higher than normal and she frowns again as I cough into my hand. "What is it, Nina? I'm busy."

She rears her head back at my tone. "Oh. Of course, I can come back another time."

She turns for the elevator, and I quickly nod my head to George and mouth *get her out.*

He shoots out from behind the desk and disappears into my office.

"Nina." I grasp her elbow, but she shrugs me off. "If you just give me a minute."

"It's fine. I should've texted before to say I was coming."

"No, it's not. Wait a second, please." I step in front of her and notice George leaving my office and round the desk again. "I have a meeting shortly but come into my office for a minute."

"It can wait." She nods her head, trying to act calm but I can tell she's annoyed.

"Don't be like that," I say, hushed. Her throat bobs and I give her a soft reassuring smile. Her eyes linger on me for a moment, then I spin her around, my hand on her back as I direct her into my office.

"Mason," George whisper-shouts as we pass.

My eyes are wild when I turn on him. "What?"

"She wasn't in there."

My brow creases. "What?"

"Jasmine, she wasn't in there!"

I rub my hand down over my face, looking into the office, then to Nina who is now sitting at my desk, and then back to George.

"Good job, mate," I hiss.

"Mason, what am I to do?"

Ignoring him, I steal a breath and stride into the office, shutting the doors behind me. I opt to sit directly in front of Nina, leant back on my desk, leaving a small space between us. It makes me feel more in control than anything else and it's a total dick move, but it gives me the viewpoint of the rest of the office.

Jasmine isn't here and I focus my attention solely on Nina as she stares me down, her eyes sharp and poised. I know whatever she came here for is no doubt going to knock another inch off of me.

"I'm mad at you," she deadpans. But to my surprise, her eyes waver, dropping down my body. I can't help but smirk.

"When are you not mad at me, Pix?"

"I'm not your Pixie, Mason."

"Why are—"

"You tried to buy my pictures," she blurts out, her eyes becoming focused and locked on mine again.

Little fuck did tell her after all. I always wondered if he had, or if he would.

"So?" I shrug.

"So, I want to know why?"

"Why?"

"Yes, Mase, why?"

Why did I try to buy them? That was simple. "Because I wanted them." And I will have them, one day.

"Exactly what I thought," she huffs.

"I don't see the issue. Did you really come here to have a go at me about trying to buy your photos?"

"No." She stares at her lap before looking up at me through her lashes. "I told myself I wouldn't get angry at you. I just find it hard to understand, that's all. Your money won't ever fix, gain or define situations, Mase. I've told you so many times not to do it." Her words are getting faster and sharper despite the control she thinks she has. "A million pounds for a couple stupid photos. It's embarrassing. It's showy, and it's ugly, and absolutely everything that I hate about you."

I scoff and look down at her, opening myself up and hoping she finally understands. "You have no fucking clue, do you? Do you really think if it were just a couple of stupid photos, I would be willing to pay what I was?" My voice rises with my annoyance. "Do you think if they were just a couple of stupid fucking photos, that Joey would have told me no!" I snap.

"We weren't even together at the time. You hated me!" She shakes her head as if she still doesn't get it. "You didn't want the photos, Mase. You wanted to prove a point. A power play over Joey. You don't want me, but no one else can have me either, right?"

I push off the desk and crowd her, placing my hands on either side of her chair. "No. I wanted them because the thought of anyone else owning those photos makes me murderous. The thought that anyone else that isn't me gets to wake up to that image kills me a little bit inside every day. It wasn't about the money; it's never been about the money with you." I heave out a breath as I right myself, my chest rising and falling as I try to control my anger.

She looks up at me, her eyes glistening. "I don't believe that."

I throw my hands out to the side and snigger. "When have you ever believed me?"

I know why she's mad; money has always been a hard limit for her. But what she fails to see is that she is my hard limit, every bit of her crazy ass.

"I didn't come here to argue, Mason. I'm sorry. I gave myself a couple days to process it and I thought I was ready to talk to you but clearly, I'm not."

I can tell she means her words. She didn't want to say the things she just did, but maybe they needed to be spoken. I place my hand on her shoulder, quickly sliding it up to palm the side of her neck and stopping her from leaving. "Don't get upset."

"I just wish..." She grits her teeth, trying to control her emotions. "Why can't you leave money out of it?"

"I've just told you." I shrug. "You'll never understand." My eyes pinch in as I watch her. "And maybe that's okay."

"No, it's not okay. You're the one who doesn't understand, Mason. It's not the money—God it's not the money." She laughs, gripping my arm that holds her. "It's the reasoning. It's the motive. It's putting a price on something that is me when you *had* me once!" Her voice wavers, tears slipping from her eyes that make my chest ache. "Jesus Christ, you could have me now and we both know it."

I do know this. We probably both knew it from the day she left me. She may have broken the trust by not believing me, but I'm learning that this woman could feed me to the wolves and my heart would still find a way to beat for her. She lives inside of me, embedded in my soul so deep that I'm no longer one. We're Mason and Nina, two halves of the same soul.

But we're not ready yet, and I think she knows that too.

"I need a tissue." She tugs my hand away, rounding my desk and walking into my bathroom.

Stupidly, between the heated words and tears... I forgot about Jasmine.

16

Nina

"WHAT THE HELL!"

Stumbling back, I bump into Mason's chest. His hands land on my shoulders, pinning me in place.

"Go and sit on the sofa, Nina. I need to explain this," he grounds out the words but they don't stick, my thoughts lost and now on the woman who stands in the open doorway.

"You think you can talk yourself out of this?" I snap my head around, stepping away from him. "Who even are you?!"

My heart aches in my chest.

He has no idea how much he hurts me. I go to leave but he reaches for me. "No! You aren't fucking running; you will hear me out this time!"

I fight in his arms, not giving a crap that she watches on. "Let me go!" I shout.

Elliot and George appear at the door, obviously hearing the commotion. They both look completely mortified. "Mason, let go of her," Elliot snaps.

"You aren't leaving me."

Mason's grip is tight, and I can feel the fear in his hold. I look at the woman standing in his bathroom with her gaze locked on me. I see the pity on her face and my eyes instantly sting with tears.

How did I end up as this woman?

"Let me go," I tell him, completely deflated.

"Mason!" Elliot says sternly.

"I did this for you," he speaks into my ear, loosening his arms and then lowering me to the ground.

I move quickly away from him. Elliot catches my hand the second I reach him. He leads me down a corridor to what I presume is his office, ushering me inside with a hand on my back. It's hard to see through the tears pooling in my eyes.

The door clicks shut and he pulls me to his chest, holding me tight. "Nina—"

"Did you know?"

"Yes," he answers honestly.

"Elliot." I push off him. "Why?" I shrug, my shoulders shaking with my tears. "Why am I still putting myself through this?"

"It's not what you think, Nina. You need to hear him out. Promise me you will let him explain this."

"No. I'm done with all these promises! Promise me I don't have to hurt at his hands anymore, Elliot. Because I am done feeling the way I do."

"I'm not asking you to promise him anything. I'm asking you to promise me." He gets eye level with me, resting his hands on my shoulders. "I'm going to be honest with you."

I snivel, wiping my face with the palms of my hands.

"That man in there" —he shifts his head towards the wall

— "is petrified that you are going to run, *again*. Not just today either, but since that first night."

"We were nothing back then, Elliot."

"I don't care. You may not have meant to, but you conditioned him to keep things from you right from the get-go. Because every time he told you something that had the potential to hurt you, you ran."

My jaw clenches tight as pain pulses through my chest and shoots right to my fingertips. "I don't want to run."

"I know you don't."

"It's always been my shield. Things get bad and I put one foot in front of the other and move. Leave before the pain hits."

He stands to his full height, pushing his hands into his pockets. "But did it work, did you manage to stop the hurt? When you were a kid? And when you left Mase?"

I frown.

"I'm not trying to be a dick, Nina. But you say you run to stop the hurt, but you seem to live by a rule that doesn't seem to protect you." He pulls me back into him and I let him, hiding my face in his chest. "Ellis left him, Nina, way before her time. Then his dad. He's just afraid you'll do the same. You need to hear him out this time."

Lifting my head, I look up at the special man who comforts me, someone who I have grown so fond of over the past year. "You're a good friend, Elliot."

"The best." He grins, letting me go. "It's not what you think, I promise."

"I want to run," I admit.

"I know."

"Will you stay with me?"

"Of course, I will."

I nod. "I will listen to what he has to say." Instantly, my head is filled with visions of the two of them together and a fresh wave of tears fall. "Try to at least."

"Like, now?"

"If I don't do it now, I won't ever. Can we stay in here?"

He nods once. "I'll go get him. Go freshen up." He points to the bathroom, then leaves.

Elliot's office is the same layout as Mason's, although it's moodier, with lower lights and a more homely vibe with the décor. He has photos around the office of his family and of him and the guys and plush cushions scattered on his sofas.

I use the bathroom, splashing water on my face and straightening out my hair, then text Logan and tell him I will be slightly later than planned. Although, the idea of going to work right now is the last thing I want to do. It's been a long weekend without Ellis, and then I had to work today.

Wringing my hands, I move and stand at the back of the sofa. I count to ten, trying to calm my nerves.

One... Two... Three... Four... The door whooshes open, stealing the air in my lungs and what feels like every bit of oxygen in the room. Elliot walks to me first, giving me a small smile.

Mason stands in the doorway, his brow cast low, shielding his dark eyes.

"I want to speak with you alone, Nina."

I shake my head, biting my lip until a metallic tang oozes on my tongue. "I have nothing to say. I promised Elliot I'd listen, and I will, but I want him to stay."

His jaw clenches, his nostrils flaring with his obvious anger.

"I'm standing here, like a damn fool, willing to hear you out. You'd do well to keep your anger in check," I snap.

I consider walking away before he can talk and make everything worse than it already is.

"Let's sit down," Elliot suggests, forcing my feet forward with a hand on my shoulder.

Mason remains standing.

I can tell he is processing his words as if he needs to get them right before he speaks them.

As if he is perfecting his lies.

"I was set up." He runs his hands through his thick hair, making it stand on end. "You know this."

I only stare at him, waiting and unwilling to agree.

When he realises I'm not going to say anything, he carries on.

"I had to know who it was. I had Vinny and Scott look into it, and I was confident that they would get me a name. There was no money trail to Jasmine, to the point that we started to think maybe the images were photoshopped. The club's security footage confirmed that she was in fact real." He swallows thickly then continues. "She turned up just over a month ago. She has two children in care and a baby who was living with her when we found her."

Bile rises in my mouth and I close my eyes, unsure if I even want to hear what he has to say.

"The children's father is an addict; he's the reason the children are no longer in her care. I made her leave her apartment, she handed her baby over to the authorities, and I gave her a job."

I grip Elliot's hand tight, petrified of what he might say next.

"She doesn't know who set me up, I'll admit that was my intention at first."

I feel my brows draw together. "Why help her then?"

"She has children. A baby the same age as Ellis. I offered her the security she needed from her ex—"

"So you offered her money... to get something you wanted, I presume? You thought you could get a name." My voice shakes.

"No. I offered her a step, one that she could build on and eventually get her children back." He puts his hands on his hips, licking his lips. "I wanted her to be better before I introduced her to you."

"You think I'd want to meet her?" I look at Elliot, who sits with a grim look on his face.

"No, but I hoped that one day you'd accept the situation for what it is."

"So help me God if you tell me you love her."

His face drops along with his shoulders. He moves to sit on the opposite sofa, dropping his head in his hands. "You have no idea how much it kills me to hear you say that fucking bullshit!" He sits with his head hung, his shoulders hunched. "She's your sister, Nina. She is your goddamn sister!"

I sit statue-still, the static air around me sending goose bumps scaling up my arms. "Sorry?"

"Your father had children after he had you," Elliot tells me. "Jasmine is one of them."

"She hasn't had it easy, but she is working to get her life back on track. I thought—"

"I'm sorry." I cover my mouth. "Please stop."

"Nina," Elliot pleads.

"What do you expect me to say? You've just told me I have a sister who last year was pictured with my boyfriend."

"I don't think—"

"I'm serious, sorry. I cannot do this right now. I need a minute."

The room spins, and my body flushes hot then cold.

"I did this for you, Nina—"

"Don't, Mason. Please." I stand, taking in several deep breaths to calm myself down. He isn't with her. He hasn't been with her. Elliot's words come back to me as I prepare to leave. "I'm not mad. But you need to let me leave. I heard you out, now you'll let me leave."

I DON'T WANT to cry, not in front of Mason and definitely not in front of her. My feet carry me to the elevator on autopilot, my mind still processing what he's just told me.

Jasmine and George are nowhere to be seen and I'm thankful for the privacy that allows me.

A sister. Or a half sister, from the man I'm yet to meet. Does she know him? Do they go for dad and daughter lunches? Does he fix her car when it breaks down?

I never considered that he might have a family. It's been twenty-nine years, of course he has a life and kids. *Jasmine is one of them*, Elliot had said.

A tear rolls down my cheek, and I couldn't tell you why. I know my mind is still stuck on the initial shock of finding Jasmine in Mason's bathroom—my hands still tremble as I reach out and call for the elevator, but it's also the fact that I have a sister.

I have a sister, and Mason was definitely set up.

I feel like it's information overload, and all I want is to cuddle my baby boy. He came home from Mason's and fell asleep straight away last night, and then I had to open the gym this morning. Maggie was at mine by seven thirty to take him for the day. I miss him so much, and the weekends are getting harder. With my working hours being more at the gym, I don't see him anywhere near enough. It all feels too much.

I feel lost in my own head with no clear path to guide me to sanity.

The doors slide open, and I slip inside, my throat aching as I hold back the sob that threatens to wrack through me.

"Nina!" Mason shouts, striding towards the elevators.

His hand shoots out just as the doors start to close. He steps inside and stands watching me with nothing but anguish on his face.

"I didn't want to tell you like this." He hits the button for the ground floor. "I'm sorry."

Reaching out, he swipes my tears away with the pads of his thumbs. But he knows it's not enough and that I'm about to break—he always knows. I'm thankful when he hits the emergency stop button and pulls me into him.

"I can't stand to see you cry, baby." He breathes into my hair.

I try to get closer, nestling myself into his chest even farther. His arms are wrapped around me, his head resting on mine. His smell, the feel of his chest beneath my head, and the warmth that surrounds me, makes everything else fade away. I'm safe here, and I don't want to leave.

I don't want to leave.

I. Don't. Want. To. Leave.

"I can't do this anymore." I swallow down the lump in my throat, feeling completely overwhelmed. Leaning back a little, I look up at him. "I can't do this."

He frowns back at me, not following.

"I love you, Mason." Another tear falls, but he doesn't reach for it this time. He just leaves it to fall down my cheek. That should be my first warning sign. "I never stopped, and I know I shouldn't have left you, but I didn't know any better. I didn't know then, but I do now, and I'm sorry. I need you. You and Ellis, you're the only things that ground me." I grasp at his lapels, craving the contact. "I need you Mase, and I can't do this anymore."

His eyes search mine, dilated and lost. His hands are spread wide on my shoulder blades where he holds me. I watch as his jaw clenches, then I lose his eyes.

"I don't trust you," he says, ashamed, stepping away from me. "I want you, more than anything on earth." He lets out a snicker. "But I don't trust you not to leave me."

"You kissed me," I croak out.

His head snaps up. "I want to kiss you all the fucking time! Right now. When I wake up in the mornings. When I get out of the shower. When I leave for work. When I get home, and when I go to bed. There's no doubt in my mind whether I want you or not, Nina. It's everything outside of the want. I can't live walking on eggshells, afraid that something I do could have you walking out the door. Just look how you reacted to me trying to buy the photos."

"If you can't trust me enough to give me the chance, why are we still doing this, the push and pull? Why make me feel when you have no intention of being with me?" I shake my head at a loss.

"Because I can't seem to let you go, Pix." His eyes seem to shine with unshed emotion, and it only makes this conversation that much more painful.

He'd rather hurt than be with me.

"I hurt you that bad?"

He works on a swallow, our eyes transfixed on each other, as his hand reaches up to push my hair behind my ear. "No more than I hurt you."

My head drops, not being able to meet his unrelenting stare.

There was a house I used to run past when I was younger. It was perfect. So perfect that I used to stop and pretend to catch my breath each time I passed. A deep sense of longing to have what was behind the white picket fencing would plague me not just in the moment, but long after I got home and climbed into my bed.

Looking at Mason is like looking at that house. The house I could never get into.

I used to tell myself to be brave. *Step up, and demand to be let inside.*

That never happened.

But this is my house now. My home. My Mase.

I just have to make him trust me again.

I step forward, closing the distance he put between us. "It's okay," I tell him. "You waited twenty-six years for Elliot to find your Pixie." I brush my lips against his, rasping out against them. "I'd wait forever for you, Bossman."

I pull on the emergency stop, and the lift starts to descend again.

I don't dare look at him as I leave him in the elevator. I let the doors close behind me but know that I've driven a wedge between them, with the hope that one day, he lets me in.

17

Mase

MY PHONE STARTS RINGING IN MY POCKET THE SECOND THE doors close. I slide it out and spot Vinny's name lighting up the screen.

"Vin?"

"Nolan just called. He went to make his visits at the clinic this morning and a discharge had been filed. Scott's on it and I'm waiting to get more information."

"She left?"

"I'm sorry, Mason."

"Fucking perfect." I drop my head back and stare blankly at the fluorescent lights.

"I'll call when I know more," he tells me, sounding busy.

"Yeah." I hang up.

My head falls back to the mirror, my eyes closing for a moment before the doors slide open. Lance is standing in the doorway.

Surprise lights up his face and then it goes slack as he takes in my slouched form.

"Lowell, you all good, my man?" He steps inside and hits the button for a couple floors up.

"You ever do something thinking you are helping but it goes to shit, and you just know when the wrong person finds out it's going to blow up in your face?" I bring my eyes to him.

"Well, yeah. We're all human right?" He shrugs.

"Right." Nina won't see it like that though. She'll call me out. Find the monetary value in my actions and miss the need I have to make her happy. It's why we can't do this yet. "Nina told me she loves me today."

He frowns, fixing his tie in the mirror. "Is this about Jasmine?"

"No." I wave him off, done with the conversation. "Forget it." I pull myself up straight and drag my hand through my hair.

"Lowell, I—"

My phone vibrates in my pocket, and I pull it out again, laughing when I see the name on the screen. "My sister." I shake my head at Lance. Could this day get any more fucked?

Lance frowns, not following.

"Sullivan, when you meet her—your girl—do yourself a favour and take your balls off at the front door. You're gonna lose them eventually anyway." I slap him on the back, pushing him forward and out onto the floor he was headed for.

Everything is happening quicker than I planned, and none of it with the result I wanted. With the day from hell still brewing and hanging over my head with Scarlet's call, I go back to my office and do something I haven't done in months. I clear up my things and I go home.

The penthouse is silent when I get in. It's still and lifeless without Ellis who seems to light everything up when he's here. I had him for the entire weekend, and it still wasn't enough. There's no doubt in my mind that he's safe and loved with Nina, but I also know that for the days he isn't with me, I'm missing things. The smiles, the giggles, and the tears when he needs me. It's all things I've grown to know and love and miss.

She told me she loves me.

She told me she couldn't do it anymore.

And I told her no.

I told her I couldn't be with her.

What a load of bullshit.

They're what this apartment needs. They're all I need.

Life.

Soul.

Laughter.

If I thought now was the right time to reel her back to me, I'd do it—in an instant. But she proved today that she still can't handle my money. I don't know how we will ever get past that when it is such a big part of my life.

I have money.

I use it.

So what?

Maybe I'm being an ass. She told me she wanted me, she all but kissed me, and damn was it hard to stop myself from pulling her lips deeper onto mine. Maybe I should give her the chance—prove that she won't run.

I expected her to leave and not let me explain about

Jasmine. I sure as shit didn't expect her to tell me she loved me.

I thought I had more time.

Nothing is ready.

Would I have tried to kiss her in the laundry room if I knew she was so close? I'd like to think not, but now she is left wondering why, and my only reasoning for her, was that I wanted her, but can't trust her.

Leaving the lights off downstairs, I take the steps two at a time and disappear into my bedroom, flicking on the lights, then heading for a shower.

The hot spray hits my back and I rest my head to the tile, welcoming the cold contrast.

I need to clear my thoughts. Work out what the hell I want.

With Vinny's phone call earlier and Scarlet, who I'm yet to deal with, I know that the next few days aren't going to get any easier.

There's something I know will help though.

And I'm a selfish bastard to ask for it.

Nina

"MUM, MUM, MA."

"Hello, my baby!" My voice cracks as I reach out to take Ellis from Lucy's arms, giving away the emotions that threaten to break through.

It's been the longest day. After I left Mason's office, I went to work and didn't give myself the chance to stop until my shift was done. If I'd stopped, I'd have cracked.

Lucy's frown is instant, and I shake my head to tell her not to ask. "I've missed you, Ellis." I hug his small body to my chest, and he drops his head there. "Have you been a good boy for Nanny Mags?"

"Mum said he was an angel as always. He had a pouch thing for his tea because they're going out. She said he ate really well, though."

"Thank you for dropping him back. Is your mum okay?"

"Yeah, Dad is taking her to the cinema tonight, so she asked if I would bring him home." She leans in, smoothing her hand over his hair and he reaches for her. "Which is perfect isn't it, mate, because we have missed Auntie Lucy cuddles!" She tickles his neck, and he falls into her. "Haven't we!"

I inch away, pouting. "Hey! Mummy gets the cuddles now. I need you tonight little man." I breathe him in, the smell of his shampoo and baby oil grounding me again.

I can feel Lucy's eyes on me. "Hmmm. Does Mummy have wine in the fridge?"

"Yes."

"Good. Get Ellis a bottle and I will get the wine."

"You don't have to stay," I tell her, but I hope she will.

"I know." She disappears to the kitchen, and I look down at Ellis with a smile. We are so flipping lucky.

"Come on." She walks past us and towards my bedroom.

"Where are you going?"

"To bed. You don't want me to leave, and I want to know what's going on in that head of yours."

Half an hour later, Ellis is curled up beside me facing my

chest and snuggling into my arm. Lucy is lying on her side with her head propped up on a pillow. I've told her pretty much everything, from Joey and the photos to Jasmine being my sister.

"So I left after he explained everything, and when I got to the elevators, he followed me in. He was holding me, and after everything I had just been told and after a weekend away from Ellis, I just needed to feel... closer."

"And so, you told him you loved him?"

I nod, sliding down the bed slightly. "And then he told me he didn't trust me."

"Didn't he try and kiss you just a few weeks ago?"

"He said he wants me, but he doesn't trust me not to run." I shrug. "I get it because I left him when he didn't do what I accused him of. But I really don't think I'd run again. If I can get over Jasmine, like I did the studio and Cara, surely we can get over anything?"

"I guess, but you're not solely to blame here. You both have things to work on."

"I know that. But I think we are at our best when we're together. Elliot told me about how badly it affected him when his mum died. Then he lost his dad, too. I think when I run from him he spirals, and that's not going to heal with us apart. I have to show him I'll stay."

"So you're willing to try again with him? Even though he does things that hurt you, maybe not intentionally, but he does."

"I love him, Luce." I shrug.

"I know, and that actually makes me incredibly proud of you. You've changed. Ellis has changed you."

"You think?" I chuckle, taking a sip from my glass.

"Okay, so you still drown your sorrows in wine." She grins. "But Nina Anderson wearing her heart on her sleeve and putting it on the line for a man? You've changed."

"Hmm, maybe. Twenty-nine years and you're finally rubbing off on me."

"Nah, you haven't reached my soppiness level yet." She rests her head back on the pillow, her hands on her stomach.

"So, what now?" she asks after a beat.

I sigh, internally cringing as I think about everything I said to him in the elevator. "I go into hiding. Never look him in the eye again."

"You waited twenty-seven years for your pixie, Mason." She mocks in a stupid voice. "I would wait forever for you."

I rip the pillow out from under her head and whack it on her face. "Piss off!"

"You're not going into hiding, although that was deep even for my standards."

"You aren't helping."

She sits up on the bed, crossing her legs. "You need a plan."

I don't move, too comfortable lying back against the pillows. "What sort of plan?"

"He can't trust you if he doesn't let you in, right?"

"Right." I nod.

"So you make him let you in."

I snicker, giving her a look. "You don't make a man like Mason Lowell do anything."

"*You* can. I've seen it. You bring that man to his knees."

"Yeah and look how that ended."

"Stop being such a negative ninny! Do you want him? You, Ellis, and Mason, as a family one day?"

More than anything. "Yes."

"You made decisions that in hindsight were rash and maybe wrong, but I get it. I understood when it happened, and I still do now—you did nothing wrong, so don't beat yourself up over it for another second. But Mason doesn't understand it, he just thinks you ran because it was easier than staying."

"So, the plan is to make him understand why I ran?"

"No, you said it yourself... you don't make a man like Mason Lowell do anything. You."

She points. "Make him want you so bad, he has no other option but to let you in. Make him want you so bad he can't tell you no. Then in time, he will see that you aren't going anywhere."

"That sounds terrible. I'm not desperate."

"No? Then let him go." She shrugs as if it's that simple.

I glare at her, knowing that the only way to show Mason I'm serious is to build the foundations again.

And that's what I will do.

Luce: Operation bring him to his MF knees is ON!!! You got this girl!!! Look hot today xo

I SMILE up at my phone, and Lucy's obvious attempt to hype me.

Do I want to pursue Mason? I know I told him I'd wait for him, which was utterly mortifying for me, and I doubted the words the minute they left my mouth. But to actively pursue him... it seems... kind of exciting.

Rolling over, I instantly panic, remembering that Ellis was in my bed last night. He isn't in my bed right now. I rip the covers off and run out of my open doorway, catching my toe on the frame and hurling myself into the bathroom door opposite my room.

Pain radiates through my head and neck, and I reach for my pinkie as I rock back and forth on the floor. "Ow, ow, ow, ow!"

"What the fuck, dude?" Megan appears in the hallway, shaking her head as she watches me, then she turns to walk away.

"Ellis?" I gasp. "Where is he?"

"Having his Weetabix!" she yells over her shoulder.

"Holy shit." I check my pinkie is still facing forward and not hanging off and then fall back to the floorboard. "My heart. I think you broke my heart."

"We're on a mission or something. Lucy woke me up last night and filled me in." Her head comes into my line of sight, Ellis on her hip and a steaming cup of coffee in her other hand. "Go shower and change into something tight."

"I don't know if I'm going in today." I pull myself up and take the cup of coffee after giving Ellis a kiss. "She actually sent you over here to get me out of bed?" I question.

"No. She sent me over here to get Ellis up and out of bed. You need to go wash and do your hair and then you're going to work. Stop throwing yourself a pity party and crack on."

She disappears into the kitchen, and I follow, placing my mug down and taking Ellis from her.

"I need some time with Ellis today."

"You have tomorrow off, don't you? And the weekend."

I nod and she smirks. "One more day and you get uninterrupted Ellis time."

Deep down I know I have to go in—I can't and wouldn't let Logan down. I just wish I didn't have to leave Ellis again.

"Now will you go and make yourself look like a hot goddess! You have a five p.m. PT session tonight and we need you looking fire."

"You do realise that by five p.m. I will be a hot sweaty mess?"

"Hot, sweaty mess sounds exactly like something Daddy would like a bite of, wouldn't you agree, Ellis?"

I give her a look and try to cover his ears. "Don't dirty talk about me to my son."

"He doesn't understand." She waves me off, taking him back from my arms. "Do you have your old dance tights? The ones we ripped you for because we could see the crack of your ass."

"Probably." I frown.

"Wear those! And a sports bra, nothing else."

"You do realise how cold it is out?"

"Yes, Grandma! And we're trying to find you a man to keep you warm at night. You're welcome. Now go!" She spins me around and slaps my butt, pushing me back into the hallway.

Reluctantly, I pull open my drawer and search for my tights and bra. I chuck them on my bed and disappear to the shower. I say reluctantly, but if I'm being honest, there is nothing reluctant about my need for Mason Lowell.

Mase

Henry is leant over the reception desk whispering something in Gemma's ear when I walk through the gym doors at five past five. Neither of them see me, but I make myself known by clearing my throat as I pass.

"Do you have to lie across the furniture, Evans?" He rears his head back, a smug smile transforming his face a second later. "What's that look?"

"Nothing." He chuckles.

I don't like the bastard. Never did and never will. Logan insisted on taking him on but if it was up to me, I never would've had him loitering around the customers.

"You have a good workout this evening, Mr Lowell." Gemma smirks, pushing on Henry's chest and busying herself on the computer.

Gemma rarely speaks to me which I'm sure is all down to her jerk-off boyfriend, but her comment has me frowning as I climb the steps to the main floor.

It doesn't last long, though, because Nina fucking Anderson.

My kryptonite.

My girl.

My Pixie.

My undoing.

And undoing she does, because right now I don't know if she is the one breaking the walls I've built between us or if I'm fighting my way out all on my own.

She's on the bike wearing nowhere near enough fucking clothes. Her top is a scrap of stretchy material that I could easily rip off her with one hand. It barely covers her tits, leaving the skin exposed at her ribs.

I itch to grasp her there.

To feel her skin beneath my hands. Feel her breathe.

She moves to stand on the pedals, as if she knows I'm standing behind her. As if she knows my cock is trying to knock the motherfucking wall down all by himself.

That ass.

That fucking ass.

As if sensing my presence, she flicks her eyes over her shoulder. A smile lights up her face and the dimple that pops on her cheek is like a sucker punch to the gut.

"Hey!"

No words leave me. I can only watch her as she pushes the pedals round on the bike, her legs and ass motioning in small circles. My thumb runs along my bottom lip, and then I pinch my cheeks between my thumb and fingers. "What are you wearing?" I ask.

She frowns, but it's all cute and nothing like her.

"It's my work clothes."

"Are you dancing?"

"Well, unless you're about to come dance with me, I'd say no." She chuckles and comes to a stop, climbing from the bike.

Is that what it would take to get her to dance again?

"I'll dance with you."

Her step falters, confusion mixed with shock washing over her face. "What?"

"If that's what you wanted, I'd dance with you."

She watches me, her eyes intense and searching.

When she doesn't say anything, I walk over to the weights where I start to stretch.

"Sorry!" she says after a minute, shaking herself off as she comes to stand in front of me. She starts to pull her hair up into a ponytail and her stupidly small top rises. I try not to look at her, knowing I won't be able to control myself if I do.

Does she see what she does to me? See what's happening in my damn gym shorts right now? I have the urges of a sixteen-year-old boy.

"Testosterone-filled teenage boys," she mutters, dipping slightly to catch my eye and smirking at me.

The gall of the girl.

She's fucking with me and enjoying it.

"Watch it," I warn.

"What?" she exclaims. She knows what she's doing.

I shake my head and drop back to the weight bench.

She steps up to my head.

"Nina—"

"I'm spotting you."

I run my hand down my face, feeling hot and frustrated. "I don't need a fucking spotter."

"Are you sure?" She bends at the waist, leaning in to shake the bar above my head and effectively shaking her tits. "You dropped one like this not that long ago. See, I have the scar to prove it." Leaning even closer, she exposes her neck to me, running the tips of her fingers from the small red scar on her chin, right down to the tip of her puckered nipple on her left breast.

I snap.

Nina

It worked.

The proof is in the way he bolts from the bench, grasping my hand in his as he pulls me from the gym. I can tell he doesn't know where he's going, but the decision is made when he takes the steps to reception.

Gemma and Henry are sitting at the computer, and both of them look up as we rush past.

I should protest, right? Act like I'm being taken against my will.

"Not a fucking word," Mason tells them, his voice like molten lava.

His face is hard as he walks through the luxury changing rooms. I already know I won't let anything happen here, but I still want to know how far I can push him. Because right now I'm betting it's pretty damn far.

He finds a cubicle tucked away in the back corner and drags me inside, then locks the door behind him.

"Mase." I grin.

"Shush a minute." He keeps his back to me.

When he doesn't turn to face me, I reach out, dragging my hand down the centre of his back and then step around and in front of him.

"You said you would dance with me." I smile up at him and it's real. I'm not messing with him.

"Apparently I'd do fucking anything for you," he rasps out.

"Yeah?" I tease my bottom lip between my teeth, trying to sound confident, but the way my stomach coils tight at his words has me faltering a little.

He reaches for me fast and I let him. Our mouths clash together in an all tongue and teeth kiss, and he instantly demands more. My back hits the door and he lifts me, lining himself up then pinning me with his hips.

Our lips remain locked. Slow, long, drawn-out kisses that make my body vibrate with a deeper need. The need to sear him into my soul for an eternity.

Never in my life has something felt so right.

I pull his bottom lip between mine and suck until he draws back. He rolls his hips into me hard and the sound that leaves him as I release the now red puffy flesh... it tells me one of two things:

1. We are moments away from him being inside me.

2. Mason. Lowell. Has. Lost. All. Control.

He pulls at his black shorts, lowering them until his cock is freed. A whimper slips past my lips as his body brushes mine. It's involuntary, but my mind's way of snapping me back to reality.

His lips slide up my neck and he sucks at the sensitive spot just below my ear. "Mason," I moan.

"I need you." His body visibly shakes as he steps back from me, lowering me so he can slide his hands into my gym tights.

"Stop," I tell him, halting his hands with my own. "It's not that I don't want you." I look up at him through my lashes. I reach out and gently run my nail down the vein in his cock, making it jolt. "But you don't trust me." I pout, trying to keep the mood light.

His head drops to the side, my name a stark warning on his red, swollen lips. "Nina."

I slide the lock I had my hand braced on and then slip from the cubicle while he tries to conceal his erection.

"Nina!" he hisses.

I smile at him as I slip back inside just as fast. "I'm just playing with you. I have to show you, right?"

His nostrils flare and I know he's as hot for it as I am. He's teetering on the edge, and it shows in every inch of his virile body.

"You wanna finish yourself off?" I nod to his hand, which is cupping him. "Then we can go back to your session."

He nods. Nods his cute little boyish head at me like an obedient puppy.

"What do you want, Mase?"

His eyes fall closed as he pulls himself once. "Touch me."

"Nuh-uh." His eyes pop wide. "I need you to trust me and that's going to take time."

"Nina—"

"But I won't leave you," I tell him. Reaching up, I palm my breast; my nipples are sensitive and pebble instantly. "My need for you, Mason." I squeeze myself over my bra. "It's like nothing I've ever felt before. It starts here." I drop my hand to my stomach, watching as he starts to work himself, his eyes fixed on my hand. "Then it spreads to here." I cup my pussy and he lets out a groan. I don't allow myself the pleasure though. This isn't about me. "Then, when I think the need has eased and I've been completely undone," I flex my fingers knowing he's watching, then slide my hand from my centre, lifting it to cover my heart, "you hit right here."

"Fuck." He pumps twice more and stills, his cum spilling out and onto his abs.

I step up to him gingerly knowing I've pushed him and

completely ambushed him during his PT session. Our gazes don't waver from one another. His eyes heavy and lust filled. "You may not trust me right now, Bossman." I swipe my finger over his abs then dip it into my mouth, not losing his eyes for a second. "But you will."

It might be backwards, and a little unorthodox but I hope I've proved a point. I push up onto the tips of my toes and kiss the corner of his mouth before I walk out of the cubicle.

18

Nina

It's Wednesday, and with just three days until the ball, I know Scarlet will be stressing out. I feel anxious to go, especially since I invited Maggie and John, which means Ellis will be coming too. Vinny offered to look after him and he will take him to bed for us when he's ready. So, with Ellis and the fact that Mason will be there, I'm feeling a little all over the place.

We have to get Mason there first, though.

I have the entire day with Ellis today, and I know Scarlet will love the company and help with final preparations. She took the week off work, but she still has to study which also means she isn't likely to be sleeping.

"Hey!" I smile into the phone when Vinny answers.

"'Morning, love. Are you okay?"

"Yes, all good. I was hoping you were free this morning. I wanted to go to Lowerwick with Ellis."

I only ever call Vinny for a lift to the estate. Joey has

offered in the past, but I always refuse out of respect to Mason—and a cab costs a bomb.

"Of course, I'm now driving Mason to the office and then I can be with you."

"Oh…" Shit, can he hear me?

"Good morning, Miss Anderson."

My stomach coils tight with the rasp in his voice and I clench my eyes shut as images of him in the cubicle last night come flooding back to me.

Goddamn it, I need a cold shower!

Or something else maybe.

"'Morning!" I squeal, palming the back of my neck when nothing else comes out.

"I won't be long, Nina love," Vinny adds after a beat of silence.

"Ok, thank you. And Mason,"

"Hmm?"

"Miss Anderson is my mother's name. It's Pixie." Earth, swallow me whole.

"Of course."

I hang up then instantly cringe. What the fuck was that? I put my phone on the island and walk away, afraid I might launch it across the room in embarrassment if I hold on to it for a second longer.

I'm not telling the girls about this one.

THE SKY IS grey and looming over the estate as we pull up to the circular drive. The trees along the boundaries of the gardens are starting to swish in the wind, and the smell of moisture in the air seems to get heavier with the impending rainfall.

Scarlet is standing at the back of a truck, her hands on her dungaree-covered hips, and her hair, now a faded pastel lavender, in a messy pile on her head.

She's definitely stressed.

"I'll take Ellis in," Vinny tells me with a smug smile. "I already had to deal with one Lowell today." He winks.

To be fair, I think he drew the short straw. I've never seen Scarlet get on Mason's level of... difficultness.

"It's raining!" Scarlet tells me the second I step up next to her. "Do you think it will be raining on Saturday?"

"No, the forecast is good for Saturday," I say optimistically.

"I can't get the marquee up in the rain, Nina. I need it to be dry now!"

Okay... "Well, it's not. There must be other things we can do." I look around at the accessories she has littered on the terrace and steps.

"Like what? The lanterns? Because they're going to get wet too," she huffs, waving her hand in the back of the truck.

"Calm down, Scar."

She scrubs her hand over her face as I climb onto the small platform to see what there is to unload.

"These need to go inside?" I ask, holding up one of the lanterns.

"They're for Mum and Dad's garden, but we will have to put them out tomorrow," she tells me.

"Okay, then let's put them in the library. Just until morning. See what the weather is like then?" I hand one of the glass domes out to her. "It's only meant to be a shower. Don't stress, okay? Everything is going to be perfect."

"What if it isn't?" She pauses with the lantern in her hand, looking up at the estate. "What if Mason doesn't even come?"

"He'll come."

He better damn well come.

"How can you be so sure, have you spoken to him about it?"

"Not yet. I didn't know if you wanted me to or if you were going to ask him. It might be better coming from you."

"No, it wouldn't. He's used to telling me no. You do realise he didn't come out here at all before he met you? He might drop things off or pick me or Dad up every now and then, but he never actually came inside."

"And you think he will listen to me now, all of a sudden? If Mason is here on Saturday night, you should know it will be for you, Scar."

"You're talking out your ass but whatever, lady."

"Scar!" I laugh, watching as she disappears around the open truck door.

She comes back a few minutes later empty-handed, and I offload another lantern from the boxes. "Are you going to bring Joey?"

"To the ball?" I frown.

"Yeah. You can, you know."

"No. I can't." I laugh. Yes, Joey has become a friend this past year, but my priority right now, it's fixing my family. "I don't think Mason would be very impressed."

"Oh, how bizarre." She feigns shock. "I thought he was coming for me."

I roll my eyes. "Shut up, idiot."

"Lucy called me. She's bringing Miller," she says nonchalantly.

My head rears back, and I stand up straight. "Umm, what? I thought she was having a time-out on him?"

"Apparently, that's over." She shrugs.

"What?!" I question again. Why wouldn't she tell me? "Elliot's going to be pissed, right?"

Closing my eyes, I draw in a deep breath. Lucy thinks that her relationship with Miller is going to come good, she always does. It's what she did with Hugh and every other boyfriend before him. She thinks he will wake up one day and be Mr Right. "Elliot doesn't really have a right to be pissed, Scar. But I see it. We will have to watch him; I don't think he likes Miller very much."

"I'm not exactly a fan. He seems a bit of a dick."

"He has a penis; it's their thing."

She laughs at that, turning and carrying the lantern into the house.

I already know Saturday night will be eventful, it's why I have a big ball of anxiety sitting low in my gut. Between Mason, Elliot, Lucy and Miller—and me, of course, not that I plan to cause any trouble. But with the history that is blurred between us all, yeah, I don't hold out much hope on it being uneventful.

We unload the truck and then head inside to have some lunch.

"So... Mason?" Scarlet eyes me from behind her cup of tea. She hasn't mentioned her brother since I first arrived and I know she wants to know when I'm going to ask him.

I can feel Vinny watching me also, but I don't look his way. I stopped trusting him to keep my secrets from Mason a long time ago. Although, he has managed to keep the ball quiet, so I should give him some credit for that.

"He has Ellis tonight and is off work tomorrow, which means he'll be in a good mood tomorrow evening when he drops Ellis back. What if I ask then?"

"That's Thursday night..." I can see her leg bouncing under the kitchen island. "It's too far away surely?"

"He's a man. How much notice do they need?"

We both look at Vinny, and he instantly holds his hands up. "I am not getting involved in this."

I send a glare his way, knowing we will have to prod him a bit to get the information we want. "What sort of mood was he in this morning?" I ask him.

He thinks for a moment then nods his head. "Good to be fair." His brows lift towards his hairline. "Better than normal actually."

Of course, he was. Orgasms make everything better.

"So maybe a text would work?" I shrug.

"Hmm, no, I think maybe face to face. Could you guys stop off at the office this afternoon?" Scarlet asks us both.

"No." Vinny is quick to answer, looking between us. "Mason has a meeting."

He's lying and it takes me a second to figure out why. "Are you worried I might run into my sister?" I bite at the inside of my cheek.

"You know?" he says, flabbergasted.

"Yes, I do." I raise my brows, looking pointedly at him. I know it was never Vinny's place to tell me, it's why I didn't bring it up to him on the ride over. But I at least thought Mason would have filled him in on the office saga.

"Sister?" Scarlet asks, adding to the list of people who are out of the loop.

An exhausted over the top huff leaves me. I really should start working through my 'family' problems. My mum, Jasmine, and the fact that Mason has known who my father is for the last year and a half, but I haven't asked for the information. Truth is, life seems complicated enough as it is. Do I really need to add to that? Jasmine isn't anything to me right now, but she is here, working in Mason's office. I don't even know how to feel about that, but I can't ignore the feelings inside that come with knowing I have a sibling. The wonder is colossal. My one and only concern is Ellis. Doesn't he deserve to know his family?

Do they deserve to know him?

"I'll fill you in properly later, but Jasmine is the woman in the pictures with Mason. And she is also my half sister."

"What?" She shakes her head. "Hold on... she set him up?"

"No. She didn't know who Mason or Nina was before. It was someone else," Vinny tells her. I watch him as he looks from her and back to me, and I wonder if he knows more than he lets on.

"She must know who?"

"Mason wanted to help her. She has children in care—"

"One who is a similar age to Ellis," Vinny adds.

"And he couldn't leave her in the situation she was in. He thought he could help her and eventually she could meet me and..."

"Jesus!" Scarlet stands, pacing on the spot.

"He had the best intentions at heart when he brought her home," Vinny tells us both.

It's not that I don't believe what Vinny is saying. It's the fact that if Mason didn't have money in this situation, he wouldn't be able to help Jasmine the way he has and plans to. It's easy for him, for her even.

And that pisses me off a little, even if I am judging her unfairly.

"This is wild," Scarlet mutters, her eyes wide as she slowly sits back down at the island.

"Yup. But the answer is still no. I don't want to go to the office."

"Yeah, sure. I get that." Scarlet gives me a look that's full of understanding.

"Excuse me, ladies." Vinny stands and leaves the room, pulling out his phone as he closes the door behind him.

"Do you think Vinny is going to invite him instead?" Scarlet whispers.

I lift my shoulders to my ears. "Maybe."

At least I hope so.

"And he would listen to Vinny, right?"

I doubt Mason would listen to anyone, but I know he respects Vinny. "I suppose."

A few minutes later my phone lights up with a message and Scarlet, unashamedly leans over to look at the screen.

"You text now?" she squeaks out.

"Barely." I frown.

"Open it!"

Mason: Would *Pixie* like to stay for dinner this evening?

"OH MY GOD! He called you Pixie?! Fuck it's happening!" She slaps my arm then falters. "But what's happening?" She frowns. "Goddamn it, who cares!" Scarlet buzzes beside me and it makes me giggle, but I also have a lead weight pulling me back down to the ground—hard. Ellis is going to Mason's this evening. At the penthouse. The only place I haven't had to face since the night I found out I was pregnant.

"Will you calm down?" I swallow, needing her to chill before she sends me deeper into my anxiety.

"You have to go! You can ask him to the ball!" She claps.

I already know I'm going. This is the next step and something I told him I'd try, and I used Lowerwick to get that.

I go to the penthouse. He comes to Lowerwick.

Vinny slips back into the room and seats himself at the island next to Scarlet.

"Mason just asked Nina to dinner!" Scarlet tells him, not being able to control her mouth.

"He did?" He looks at me with a small smile.

"Yup! She's going to ask him tonight if he will come to the ball. No! Wait! She is going to *tell* him tonight that he *is* coming to the ball." She grins, excited, and I can't help but join her in her glee. Scarlet is one of the most infectious people I've ever met.

She could get Satan smiling.

"Don't you just love it when a plan comes together?" Vinny lifts his chin to Scarlet, then turns to give me a wink.

I tilt my head a little, giving him a wary look.

The old fool is up to something.

And I bet it involves me, dinner, and the one place I've ever felt at home.

Mase

"WE'RE HEADED TO LUNCH. We get to pop Jasmine's sushi cherry today! You want anything?" George asks, poking his head into my office door. He is grinning from ear to ear, and I spot Jasmine's head from where she stands at his back.

"No, redirect calls to Elliot."

"Elliot left for the day."

My head snaps towards him. "What?" I check my watch. "It's twelve o'clock."

"He said he had a meeting," Jasmine adds, peeping under George's arm which he moves to allow her room to stand next to him.

"Is everything okay, Mase?" George asks.

Meeting my ass. He's been in and out of the office all week. Guaranteed he's fucking someone new.

"Yeah, you guys head out." I turn back to my screen but notice that they don't leave. George looks at Jasmine and she hisses something back at him.

"What is it, George?"

"All it is, sir." His head rears back. "Sir?! Gosh, I've never called you sir before. Ha."

"George," I ground out.

"Right. So, we overheard you on the phone with Vinny. And—"

"How?" I interrupt.

"How?" George's perfectly groomed brows dip low.

"How did you overhear my call from all the way out there?" I point to the reception.

"We were listening on the phone. George thought it was Nina."

George covers Jasmine's mouth with his hand. "Oh my god, are you stupid! That's not what happened," George tells me in a panic.

"Why lie? That's exactly what happened." Jasmine's lip twitches on one side.

I sit back in surprise. More at the fact Jasmine is being so relaxed in front of me.

"Just when I thought you were a classy girl," George tells her.

"There's nothing classy about listening in on people's phone conversations, George." I try to keep my own lip from twitching, moving my hand to run along my mouth. "I'm very disappointed."

He stands looking at me with confusion in his eyes. "I-I..."

"Fuck off, you two," I dismiss them, not wanting them to see my smile.

"That's it?" George frowns.

"Don't question it." Jasmine pulls on his arm and they leave my office. I shake my head, wondering when they decided they were going to become friends and also wondering why the two of them listening in on my conversation with Vinny doesn't bother me like it should.

"One more thing, it was *the* thing actually. You sort of interrupted me before."

I drop my pen, looking up at him with an impatient glare. "Yes, George?" I say, short.

"If Nina agrees to come to the penthouse this evening." He smiles. "Then flowers. Promise me you will buy her some flowers."

"She's coming over to spend time with Ellis, not for any

other benefit to me or our situation. Are you sure you were listening to my conversation, George?"

"I was, *sir*. And I'm not sure if you have been living under a rock for the past year, but I haven't seen you send any, nor have I been asked to send any arrangements. The woman birthed your child."

I snigger, slapping my hands on my armrests. "Some days I wonder what I would do without you, George. Then other days, I think of how fucking peaceful my office would be without you in it."

"I'm presuming it's a no on the flowers..." He turns his head slightly in question. "Sushi?"

"You're burying yourself here, George," Jasmine tells him, pulling him from my office and letting the door close behind them.

I've never understood the gift of flowers. Why would someone want something that is only going to die within a matter of days? Seems morbid to me.

Nina isn't a gifts sort of person. She hates me spending money on her, and I can already picture her beating me with any bunch I'd give her.

Nina: I can do tonight.

Nina: What time?

Whatever Vinny knows, he isn't telling me, but that was far too easy. It only makes me feel uneasy.

Maybe flowers would soften her up? She will be anxious coming to the house.

Mase: No thorns.

George: Do I have a budget, and does she have a favourite flower?

Mase: It's flowers?? How much do they cost?!

George: Well, your use of 'they' is very vague. There are about 400,000 different flower species in the world, so...

Mase: Jasmine, could you please get me a bouquet of flowers whilst on lunch. Something substantial and still alive.

Jasmine: Ok.

I quickly text Nina and tell her to come over at five thirty. It gives me enough time to get home and shower. I will order something in for dinner so I'm not having to cook.

I scroll till I find Elliot's name and then hit call. He doesn't skip days anymore and it pisses me off that he hasn't even bothered to tell me he's left for the day. I know I was a complete bastard for the months that followed Nina leaving me, but I always checked in with the guys. Elliot has been out of office the majority of the last two weeks.

Whoever he's fucking better be worth it.

"Hello?" he answers after the fourth ring.

"Where are you?" I snap.

"'Afternoon, sunshine."

"Where are you?" I grate out.

I hear cars roaring in the background and music playing. "I'm out."

"Out where? And why am I the only one in the office this week? It's bullshit."

"Are you seriously throwing your toys out the pram when we've all not sto—" He pauses, cursing under his breath. "I'm fucking busy, Lowell, I'll call you later."

The line cuts off and I drop my phone with a thud to the hard wood of my desk.

Damn drama queen.

He's being shady and I don't fucking like it.

19

Nina

I'm anxious as I climb from the Audi. I've barely said a word to Vinny on the drive over, although he has had plenty to say to me.

You wouldn't believe that I struggled to get a word from him when we first met. No, now I have this brute of a man, giving me advice, and trying to always steer me to the right path. I love him for it, but if he tells me everything is going to be alright one more time, I might just snap.

"You want me to come up?"

I turn to him and find Ellis already out of the car and in his arms, the changing bag on his shoulder.

"What if I want to leave?" I swallow the bile that rises in my throat, then lift my shaking hand to smooth my hair off my face.

"You won't leave, but I'll be right here, okay? I have emails to catch up on anyway."

I nod. He has told me this already. I lean in to take Ellis. "Thank you, Vin."

"You're going to be just fine, my girl." He places a kiss on my hair before I turn towards the elevators.

"Shall we go see Daddy?" I smile down at Ellis.

"Da, Da, Da, Da."

The temperature has dropped, so I move quickly to the elevators to get Ellis out of the cold. With nerves fighting their way up my throat, I take my time to key in the code that Vinny gave me. Before I step inside, I turn and call over to him, "You go home, Vinny. Don't wait out here."

He dips his head, a smile tipping his lip up. "See you a bit later, love."

I've seemed to have lost the confidence I had in the gym yesterday, and I'm pretty sure it has everything to do with the penthouse, but I know I need to do this. I want to.

The keypad flashes green and Ellis bounces in my arms.

I give myself a pep talk on the ride up. I need to do this for Scar. She wants him at the ball, and I want to fix my family.

I can do this.

The doors ping open, and Mason is standing right there, waiting.

He's wearing a fitted navy button-down shirt and suit pants. His sleeves are rolled up at the arms, but the man is anything but casual. I don't know if the sight of him puts me at ease or sends me further up the anxiety ladder.

"Hi," he says, flashing me with that killer smile.

I dip my head. "Hi."

"You look lovely this evening. I appreciate the change of attire from last night."

My head lifts at that, a smile playing on my lips. "Better than my work clothes?"

"Hmm, just a very different kind of perfect tonight." He eyes his son who sits in my arms, hugging me tight.

My wide grin seems to encourage Mason's, and the tension is momentarily gone.

"You two coming in?" he asks, flicking his head behind him.

Stepping out of the elevator, I'm instantly immersed in everything Mason. The penthouse is big—bigger than a man and his child could ever need, but it's every bit of the home I've always wanted. I don't know if that's because of the way it feels being here, or because of the fact that it's where I fell in love with Mason—the home we started to build our family in.

"Do you want a drink?"

He asked me that on my first night here. The night he brought me home. The first night I slept in his bed. He wouldn't touch me. I remember the need I felt to have his hands on me.

"A drink would be good, thank you." I let the air caught up in my lungs whoosh out of me as I will myself to calm down.

Without paying much attention to my surroundings, I follow him into the kitchen. Everything is the same in here, and Ellis instantly tries to get out of my arms.

"Do you want to put him in his chair?" Mason tips his head to the high chair at the end of the island. I place Ellis into the seat and strap him in. I can't help but notice that it's top of the range and branded. I turn and stop short, coming face-to-face with a bouquet of roses.

"I got you these." He hands me the arrangement awkwardly and I stare at them in surprise. He got me flowers. "Is wine okay?"

"Yeah. Wine's fine." The knot in my stomach seems to bound up tighter again. "Thank you so much, Mason. This is so thoughtful."

He watches me as I place the flowers on the counter and lower myself to the chair at the island. My hands twist in my lap. I wish I suggested we eat out, or maybe even at mine again. The conversation seemed to flow between us better at mine.

I wonder how long it will be before I call Vinny.

"Why are you so nervous?" he asks, pulling me from my thoughts.

"I'm not." I bring my hand up to pinch along my collar-bone, his eyes trailing my movements.

Rounding the counter, he places my wine in front of me letting his chest brush my back. "You have no reason to be nervous, Nina."

I lift my chin, looking at him over my shoulder. "I don't?"

His eyes seem to darken, and I can't help but want him to tell me to be afraid. That I should be nervous. His tongue darts out, wetting his bottom lip. "Can you feel that?"

"What?" I frown, flicking my gaze to Ellis who watches us from his high chair.

Mason follows my line of sight, his chest growing bigger —stronger at my back.

His heart pounds rapidly against me.

My eyes flutter closed, my body going lax. I haven't felt this man in so long.

"You petrify me, Pix."

He's gone before I can reply. Moving around the island again and putting distance between us.

"Dinner will be here soon. I thought we could eat and then maybe you'd like to put Ellis to bed?"

"Sure." I glance around the kitchen, noticing the baby bottles and other small additions. I wonder what else has changed.

"You want to go have a look around?"

"No," I answer quickly, puffing out a nervous laugh.

"It wouldn't be weird if you did, I know you loved it here." He says it so relaxed that you wouldn't believe his heart was racing just like mine moments ago. He's calm, controlled and confident.

"Loved. Past tense," I murmur.

Our eyes lock.

"Loved, and then a lot of shit happened." His face softens. "How about we agree to not talk about that whilst Ellis is up?" he suggests.

I nod, my eyes stupidly betraying me and getting prickly.

"Any plans for the weekend?" he asks, clearly unsure what to say and catching me off guard. I can't tell him about my plans for the weekend. Now isn't the time to ask him to the ball.

"Are we really at the awkward chitchat stage?" I smile, probably looking like a complete goof as I fight to keep my hands still in my lap.

"Well, I can't exactly bend you over the kitchen island now, can I," he deadpans.

"Umm. Oh. I..." I'm pretty sure I am a bright shade of pink because I did not expect that. We're on completely different pages right now.

Mason only shakes his head, busying himself at the sink. I'm pretty sure it's so he doesn't have to talk to me or bend me over the counter? Jesus, this man is hot and cold and sometimes fucking icy. I can't keep up.

I'm certain it's this penthouse. It's throwing me off. I need to snap out of it.

The buzzer sounds for the reception, and I jump up straight away, knowing it's our food. "I'll go!" I rush from the room, taking long strides to the elevator and telling myself internally to chill the hell out.

I pull up the girls' group chat.

Nina: I AM FREAKING OUT!! Everything is so much harder being here

Luce: Give it a chance Nina you've not been there long have you?? It's only 6!!

Nina: He told me he wanted to bend me over the kitchen island

Megan: So what's the problem?

Luce: He didn't want her last week

Nina: Exactly!

Nina: He's giving me whiplash

Megan: I need to go get me some of that whiplash

Fucking idiot.

Luce: Use Ellis it's why you're supposed to be there

Luce: A couple hours and you will be more relaxed

Luce: Have a glass of wine!!

Nina: I have wine

I look over my shoulder making sure he doesn't sneak up on me while I hide out in the foyer.

Megan: Did you ask him about Saturday yet?

Nina: Not yet! I've barely said a word

Megan: Come on my little butt slut!!! What happened to the queen who I dropped off at the gym yesterday morning?

Luce: She has a point

Nina: You think I should come back at him?

Megan: DUH

Luce: A little… maybe once Ellis is in bed?

Luce: At your own pace though. DO NOT force it

I don't have to force the connection between Mason and I that's for sure.

Megan: You're forgetting that he was your man once. Go get his balls and wear them as earrings

Luce: Pretty sound advice Megs

Megan: Right???

Nina: Are you two at home together?

Luce: Yup!

Megan: Yup

Scarlet: Sorry, girls. I just finished studying. What have I missed?

I leave the girls to fill Scarlet in and go to reception to get the food.

Mason is laying the cutlery on the table in the living area when I enter the penthouse and Ellis is sitting at the head of the table.

"He sits in your seat?"

Mason's smile is full of pride. "Of course. He's the boss around here now."

I pop a brow. "Is that so?"

"For the majority of the time, yes."

Biting my lip, I pull open the bag letting the delicious smells assault me. "Hmmm, you ordered Italian?"

"I thought Ellis would like the lasagne. I got you the meatballs."

My mouth waters and I take a seat next to Mason at the table.

"I got you another wine."

I smooth my hands over my thighs where he can't see. "Thank you."

Ellis sits quietly in his chair, and I wish for once I had a fussy baby. Simply because it would give me something to do. He sits patiently waiting for Mason to feed him another mouthful.

I don't allow the silence to stretch, nervously jumping in and blurting the first thing that comes to me.

"So, have you spoken to Scarlet recently?" I ask, taking a mouthful and then wiping at my lips with my napkin. I inwardly cringe at my topic of choice, but I need to put some feelers out to know where we stand on the ball. The sooner he knows, the better. If I had it my way we wouldn't keep it from him.

"You know I haven't," he calls me out, throwing me a smile and offering me a lifeline.

"Sorry." I take a sip of wine, trying to find anything else to talk about.

"I plan on going to see her soon."

"You do?" I lean forward in my seat, invested in his every word. "I came here tonight hoping it meant maybe you'd want to come to the estate with us the next time we go?" I force my hand to stay in my lap again, annoyed with myself that I've even lied.

Maybe I'm not lying exactly, but I know that in about an hour's time I'm going to ask him to the ball, and he will be thinking about how I prepped him for it. God, if only this was a trashy romance novel, and I could hit backspace on my stupid words.

"I'm actually looking forward to it."

"You are?" I ask, surprised.

"Yeah. I don't know how much of the estate you've shown Ellis, but I want to show him it too."

Well, this is progress!

I nod, watching as he feeds our son another mouthful. "I could never do it justice. You should definitely do that."

"I'm worried about Scarlet," he admits, running his tongue across the front of his teeth.

I give him a soft pitiful smile. "Scar's doing okay."

He looks over his shoulder at me, his concern clear in his eyes. "I appreciate you being there for her this last year. She never would have gotten through it without you."

"What about you? What got you through it?"

His jaw goes tight, and I know exactly what—or should I say who—got him through it. "A lot of shit happened, Mase." I throw his words back at him as I carry on eating, giving him an out I'm not even sure he deserves.

Mase

AFTER CLEANING up the dinner dishes, I find Nina leant against the doorframe of Ellis's room. A frown marred across her forehead as she stands deep in thought. I'm so glad I had the wall knocked out to join our rooms. It's been a godsend whilst he's been teething, and I want to keep an eye on him. It gives us our own space without being apart.

I walk up beside her and look into the room.

Sensing her thoughts, I give her an inch, hoping it's enough.

"I never brought women up here. Not even at my worst." I can feel her eyes burning through the side of my face, but I don't dare look at her. "I couldn't."

"Why are you telling me this?" she asks, her tone much softer than I expect.

Leaning against the frame opposite her, I lift my eyes to hers. She looks devastated.

"Not to hurt you."

She sniggers, shaking her head.

Taking her chin, I lift her face to mine. "I need to be honest with you."

"Not with this." Her eyes shine, and I get that feeling in my chest. The painful ache that feels like I'm breaking in two. I know we need to do this.

"I'm sorry, Nina."

"Because you did it or because I found out?"

I let my hand fall away. "You left me."

She nods, rolling her lips. "So you slept with a horde of women to what? Fix that?"

"Forget, Nina. I did it to forget."

"Did it work?"

"No." I drop my head, feeling ashamed. "But I don't regret it." Pushing off the frame, I step into her, crowding her. "I never would have survived you, Nina Anderson." I push her hair off her face. "I still worry I won't." I shrug.

"It's not about surviving, Mase."

"No?" I laugh in question.

She shakes her head vehemently. "No."

"Tell me then. What's it about?"

She lifts her chin, her eyes sure. "Reason."

I frown. "Reason?"

She dips her head in the direction of Ellis who's tucked up asleep in his cot. "A reason to be good, a reason to not hurt the people you love because you hurt, and a reason to be the best version of yourself, no matter how badly we feel like we're drowning."

"I didn't have Ellis when you left, I never had a reason."

"Ellis wasn't my reason back then, Mason, you were. I believed in you even after everything that happened."

"Nothing happened." I scrub my hand down over my face, stepping away from her.

"I didn't know that then. And I never would've been able to get the images out of my mind if I stayed. Could you?"

Could I?

Live my life with the image of another man with her.

No. No, I fucking couldn't.

"I needed time, Mason, and I'm sorry for that."

"I know." I scrub my hand over my face again, feeling agitated.

She spins around in the room that was once ours and chuckles to herself, falling back onto the bed. Her chest shakes, and I fight to keep my eyes glued to her face.

"Am I missing something?" I stand with my hands on my hips, wondering if she has lost it.

Looking up at me, she starts to laugh harder. She's infectious, and my cheek tics. "No. I don't think so. It's just funny, isn't it? Us. What a mess."

298 | JC HAWKE

She continues to chuckle to herself, so I bend down and scoop her up.

"Mase!" she whisper-shouts, jolting up in my arms.

"Shhh, you'll wake Ellis." That, and if I don't get her off my bed and into safer territory soon, I might end up completely and utterly fucked. Literally.

I carry her out onto the terrace, dropping her onto a lounger. "I'm going to go get us some drinks. Unless you wanted to leave?"

Her eyes dart around my face and I sense that she wants to go, but something keeps her here.

"No, I'll stay. But just one drink."

SHE'S STANDING at the railings when I come back out to the terrace, looking out across the city.

"My son has spent more time in this penthouse than I have," she tells me, placing one of Ellis's lost dummies on top of the wall.

"That bothers you?" I place her wine next to it, and she turns her head to look at me.

"Only that I wasn't with him too."

"You're all around us here, I made sure of it."

"Not in the way that counts." A tear rolls down her cheek and I reach out to swipe it. "I never wanted my children to grow up like I did. A broken home. The confusion and unanswered questions."

I instantly regret leaving her out here. It gave her too much room to think. "Ellis won't have that."

"Won't he? Because he might not understand right now, but one day he's going to grow up, and then what?"

"We call Auntie Luce and Uncle Elliot." I smirk, giving her a soft wink.

"You're an idiot," she chokes the words out with a smile, wiping at her eyes and pulling back her shoulders.

Brushing herself off, like she always does.

I open out the blanket I brought out and wrap her in it. "You know, if you count the days, months even, that you spent living inside my mind." I reach under her top, smoothing my hand over the soft skin of her stomach. "Then I reckon you've both spent nearly the same amount of time here."

Leaning against her, I whisper into her ear, "We all missed things we wish we didn't, Nina. We can't change the past" —I flatten my palm on her hip as my finger traces one of the thin scars at the bottom of her stomach— "but we can make right now whatever we want it to be for him."

"I want Ellis to have more—more than we both had."

"I know," I tell her, dropping my head to rest on her shoulder. "I want that too."

"Mase, there's a memorial ball for your parents on Saturday night, it's at the estate and everyone has been too afraid to ask you," she blurts out.

I tense, trying to process her words but she doesn't give me more than a second before she is firing off again.

"I'll be there, Ellis too. Vinny is going to be watching him in the house." She turns in my arms. "It would mean the world to your sister if you came." She rolls her lips. "It would mean the world to *me* if you came." She searches my face for any hint of a reaction, completely and utterly unaware that I would set the world on fire for her. "Ellis too," she adds, trying to hook me.

I step away from her, waiting for her to take the blanket from my grip and then letting it go.

"Okay." I nod.

"Okay?" She rears back.

"I'll go to the memorial thing."

She has that look on her face. Like the time I told her I was allergic to dogs.

"You will?"

20

Nina

"I SAID I WOULD MAKE THE EFFORT TO COME TO THE ESTATE."

My body vibrates as I force my feet to stay rooted to the floor and not wrap them around him. Scarlet will be so happy. I'm so happy.

"I was not expecting you to agree so easily." In fact, I thought he would be pissed at me for asking and meddling in his family business.

"No? You think that low of me." He gives me a boyish grin and I feel my dimples pop at this new easy territory we keep falling into.

I shrug, stepping past him and into the warmth of the bedroom. "Without a doubt, you would've been there. I wasn't going to give you the choice not to be." I smile at him over my shoulder. "But I didn't expect you to just say, okay." Dropping the blanket down on the bed, I go to the bathroom to pee. The door is pulled closed a second later and I sit and smile to myself.

"Luce has a tux for you, but if you need to, you can give her a ring and get it tried on! We were hoping it would fit!" I shout so he can hear me.

I've peed in front of him before, mainly after too many cocktails on our holiday.

Taking my time to wash my hands, I glance around at the familiar bathroom suite. The bathtub which I have missed sinking into after a long day, and the walk-in shower that is probably the same size as the one I have now, but it's not this shower. It's not his shower.

He got in my bath.

Maybe I'm weird (I am), and the girls will die with mortification for me, but I want to get in. I want to stand where he does every day. Wrap myself up in his soft towels, and to smell like his soap.

Reaching in, I turn on the spray then start to strip—double time—before I can change my mind.

My fingertips glide along the wall as I step into the steaming water, allowing me to feel a little bit at home again. I've missed everything about this penthouse and the man who lives inside of it. I've missed the intimacy that comes with sleeping alongside him. I've missed the meals we'd make long after the sun had gone down. I've missed his eyes, watching me as I would dance along the polished oak floors. I've missed the long showers—and the quick ones—and the ones we didn't even need but had anyway, just because. And more than anything, I've missed the love we would make in all those places.

I've missed Mason. Mind, body, and soul.

Picking up his body wash, I pour a generous amount from the decanter into my palm, and then begin to lather it between my hands. Taking my time, I wash then rinse my body, inhaling the woodsy scent that now covers me like a blanket. It's so satisfying, so real to me, that when my eyes fall closed, and I let my hand drop between my legs, it's almost as if it is him touching me.

Just with smaller hands—unfortunately.

God, I wish it was his hands. His long, thick fingers stroking through my folds and teasing my clit until I'm whimpering against him.

My body tingles all over at the mere thought of his hands on me. I push two fingers into my heat, my heart thrumming wildly in my chest. I need more.

I need him.

Shit.

I imagine his solid chest at my back, his warm breath on my neck and his arm banded around me and taking the place of my own. I slide in another finger and cry out.

"Fuck," I groan.

I've touched myself on more than one occasion since I left Mason, but never, ever, has it felt this good, this intense.

He would've touched himself too, I'm certain of it. He would have stood here, in this very spot and stroked himself.

My eyes pinch tighter together, my body coiling tight as I slide my fingers out and up to my clit. The cool tiles bite at my heated skin as my back hits the wall. I allow it to support me, pushing harder into my hand with the new resistance behind me.

A fresh wave of Mason's soap assaults me, temporarily sending me tumbling, and I quickly fall into that perfect sated bliss I've missed so much.

"YOU GOT yourself off in my shower?"

I'm startled as I pull open the bathroom door. Mason is standing on the threshold, his arm draped on the frame and an accusing look on his face.

I clutch the towel I was carrying tighter in my fist. "Umm, no?"

How does he know?

Reaching up, he runs a cool finger over my heated cheek.

Shit.

"Yes, you did. Don't lie to me."

"I didn't! I'm not! I just needed to freshen up! I was all hot and needed to... freshen up." My voice comes out high-pitched and annoying.

His lip twitches. "Did you think about me?"

"Mason!" I snap, feeling my face get impossibly hotter.

"You did, didn't you?" he says, lifting a cocky brow.

I throw my towel at him in annoyance—and embarrassment. He lets it hit his face and then it falls to the floor. "I'm going to go now."

He grasps my T-shirt as I pass him, wrapping his arm around my neck and drawing me into his chest. His nose goes to my hair, and he inhales deeply. "You smell like me."

The smile that greets me as I lift my head to look at him is so wholesome, so fulfilling to me, it makes my heart beat out of rhythm and my body heat again.

I push up onto my toes and gently kiss his jaw.

"You're actually going to go?" he murmurs, and the tone he emits tells me he doesn't want me to.

"Yeah, Mase." I smile. "Tonight has been good though."

He nods, letting me step back.

Pulling my phone from the changing bag on the bed, I notice I have six missed calls, all from Joey.

"Is Vinny driving you?"

"Uh, yeah." I shake my head, distracted, as I scroll through the missed calls. "I'll text him now."

"Is everything okay?" He looks at the phone in my hand.

"Yeah, everything is fine."

I shoot a quick text to Joey.

Nina: I'm out. Everything okay?

"I'll call Vinny," Mason tells me, his tone flat as he leaves the room.

My eyes follow him out the door and then fall back to the phone in my hand. I'm pretty sure he would have been able to see the name on the screen from over my shoulder, and I know it will piss him off. I'd ignore Joey for Mason's benefit, but he never calls me. He texts or waits until he sees me.

Mason is leant against the back of the sofa when I descend the stairs. His glare follows me as I take the last few steps. It's that glare, his furrowed brow and ticcing jaw that confirms what I already knew. He saw the name on my phone.

"Mase."

"Save it." He waves me off, then stands straight and says. "Do you not think that the reason he told you about the pictures the other day was to drive a wedge between us?" He looks to the ceiling, his hands shoving deep into his pockets. "He's manipulating you, Nina, all to get what he wants from you."

Stay calm. Stay calm. Stay fucking calm. "Which is?" I ask.

He cocks his head to the side. "What do you think?"

"Joey is my friend, Mason. He hasn't so much as looked at me in another way since *we* first got together. And, it's all well and good putting the blame for the pictures on Joey, but it was you who offered up the money. Joey only told me what *you* did."

"So I fucked up because I wanted to buy some photos of you?" he scoffs, his pointer finger touching his chest before he lifts it and scrubs at his face.

"No. But I won't cut him off because you don't like him. He's my friend."

His stare is fixed on me, his eyes dark. "I won't apologise for wanting what's mine. Joey is a prize prick, and I wouldn't trust him as far as I could throw him."

"How can you be so judgemental? You don't even know him!" I yell the words at him and internally slap myself the second they pass my lips. I don't want to do it like this. "Mason. Joey would have given them to you if you'd just asked. They're—"

"No, he wouldn't."

I tilt my head to the side, knowing he won't get it and that I have to let it go. Tonight has been too good to spoil, and I need this man more than I need my pride. "Okay, maybe you're right."

"I am," he states, so sure of himself.

I shake my head, ready to drop it. "You should know though..." I swallow thickly, meaning every word that leaves me. "You could be the poorest man on earth, and I'd still love you."

He tips his chin. "Then you're a fool."

"And you're a jackass," I counter, trying my hardest to stay calm.

Talk about prize pricks.

He pops a dark brow. "A jackass who's at the centre of all your fantasies?"

"Don't flatter yourself, pretty boy."

His laugh is scornful as he steps up to me, chest to chest. "Pretty *boy*?" he questions.

Goose bumps pebble along my arms, the air in the room quickly taking on a different vibe entirely. If I don't leave now, I know exactly where this will end up.

"I'll see you on Saturday, Mason," I say, my voice coming out throaty but final.

His burning eyes hold me in place with more force than if I glued my feet to the ground myself. My eyes are transfixed on his, and as he leans forward a fraction of an inch, my mouth parts, sucking in a shaky breath. This man shouldn't make me nervous. But he does.

Time seems to wait along with me. Slowly. So, so, slowly. He brings himself closer, letting our breath mingle before brushing his lips against the corner of my mouth. I lift my chin to meet him, seeking him out, but the moment I do, a low chuckle vibrates from deep in his chest. "See you Saturday, Pix."

He looks down his stupid crooked nose at me, pulling his bottom lip between his teeth.

Cocky jackass.

Mason follows me into the elevator, a smirk firmly in place as he stands at my back and uses the mirror to watch me. It annoys me that he can be so confident. He doesn't show any reaction to what's just happened. He just smiles and carries on.

He needs to be brought down a peg—or two.

"Ugh!" he gasps, then groans as my hand squeezes his balls. Not enough to hurt him but enough to make him squirm.

"What's the matter, Bossman? You've lost your smirk."

He exhales through his nostrils, and I have to bite my lip to stifle a laugh. But my triumph doesn't last long, his breath rushes out heating the shell of my ear as he rolls his hips, grinding his erection into my back. I tighten my hand around his balls. "You think I don't like your hands on me, baby?" His teeth pull at my earlobe and I can't help but drop my head to his shoulder. "Harder," he groans, rolling his hips as I squeeze him tighter.

His chest rumbles with a laugh as the elevator pings. Warm, wet lips smash into my dimple before he rights me.

I remove my hand just before the door slides open to Vinny.

I DON'T GO to my apartment right away. I hate being alone on any night of the week. But tonight, I'm rushing to Joey's door for an entirely different reason. He hasn't returned my text and when I tried to call him on my way home, he didn't answer. It's not unlike him, but after the six missed calls from before, it makes me worry.

Joey gave me a key when he moved into the flat, and I use it freely. But the coward in me is hesitant as I approach the door.

I knock.

"Joe?!"

When he doesn't answer, I pull out my key. Worry sits like lead in my gut, slowing down my every move. He must be home. Joey is always home.

"Joe?!"

The lock clicks and I push on the door. I'm greeted by complete darkness.

"Joey?" I call out.

Something's wrong. I can feel it.

Gingerly I reach for the light, flicking it on and bathing the small flat in a yellow glow. "Joey?" I call out, even though I'm certain he isn't here.

I let the door click closed and then cross the room to his bedroom in a rush. As I expected, I find his bedroom empty and my shoulders sag as I let out a frustrated huff. Not knowing what else to do I sit on his bed and wait, calling him three more times before giving up and going home.

MY APARTMENT IS QUIET, and I waste no time disappearing to my room to crawl into my bed. It's been the longest day, and I already know the next couple days won't be easy with the ball and now Joey. I know something is up, and it makes me anxious not being able to get hold of him.

My phone beeps with a text.

Mase: I'm thinking about you

310 | JC HAWKE

Butterflies take flight in my stomach, making it dip and bottom out.

He's thinking of me?

Nina: Thank you for this evening. I really am looking forward to Saturday

Mase: Would you believe me if I told you I am too?

I smile into the dark room.

Nina: No but you made me smile

Mase: I did…

Nina: Yep

Mase: What are you wearing?

I read the message over and over. He's horny?

God, I'm not in the right frame of mind for this. I type out a reply three times and delete it before another message comes through.

Mase: Shit. Do I need to work on my game?

I chuckle at that. I sit up in my bed and try to get into it.

Nina: You don't think you have game?

Mase: I was hoping for a sext

Oh man.

Nina: Do you think you deserve a sext?

Mase: You got yourself off in my bathroom (wet emoji) It seems only fair

Impossible man.

Nina: I think you'll find it was in your shower

Mase: My dirty girl

Mase: I want details

Details? This isn't a documentary.

Nina: Absolutely not. LOL. We're even now

Mase: I don't think so. You had a front row seat at the gym. I didn't get to watch you. I need that visual else it didn't happen.

Nina: You knew the minute I came out the bathroom what I'd done. Trust my word I came. HARD.

I cover my hand over my mouth and chuckle at my words.

Mase: I'm going to need more than that

Nina: Sorry, it's all I got

Mase: Did you imagine me grabbing your hips?

Mase: Or were you riding my face? I know you love that

Oh, shit.

Mase: Or maybe I had my thumb in your ass whilst filling you from behind?

Nina: Maybe I had my thumb in your ass?!

Mase: Baby...

I sit and laugh to myself.

Nina: Good night jackass

Mase: You owe me an orgasm, Pix!

I roll my eyes, sliding down the bed as I start to scroll back through the thread.

21

Nina

THE NEXT MORNING I WAKE EARLY LIKE I ALWAYS DO ON THE days I don't have Ellis. I don't know if Joey is going to be home this morning, but I call and text him before I leave my apartment to let him know I'm on my way over. He doesn't answer or reply, and I get to his apartment and find it empty. For an hour I linger around his flat, clearing the draining board and setting the living area straight.

When seven thirty rolls around and I haven't heard back from him, I decide to go home. Just as I pull open his front door to leave, my phone rings, Joey's name lighting up my screen, and I walk back into the apartment and quickly answer the phone.

"Joey! Where are you?"

He doesn't say a word.

Silence.

I swallow the lump in my throat. "Joe?"

"I'm in New York." His voice is cold and detached.

"New York?" I check the time on my phone. "To see Jasper?"

"Yeah. He's dead."

It feels like someone has poured ice through my veins, my body running cold. "W-what?" I utter.

"He's dead."

"Joey, I'm... I'm so sorry." What do I say? What do I do? "I missed your calls last night. God, Joe. I'm so, so, sorry!"

"It doesn't matter now," he says, lacking all emotion in his voice.

He sounds lost.

"Are you coming home again?" I ask.

"I'll be back in a couple days. It's early, you go, Nina."

"No, it's okay I can—"

The line goes dead and I start to shake. He has no one else. It's just him now.

Nina: What can I do?

Please reply! Please reply!

Joey: I need a couple days

I blow out a breath, understanding he needs space but needing to see him, hug him and know that he's going to be okay.

Nina: Call me! Whenever you need me.

Joey: Okay.

My hands run through my hair as I fall back on his sofa, my heart breaking for him. He has lost his brother. All his living relatives are gone. How does anyone deal with that?

Sometimes I wonder if life would be easier if we didn't allow people into our hearts. It would keep it safe from the heartbreak that quakes us when they eventually leave, because they do. One way or another, they always leave.

The truth is, we only hurt when we truly care about something. It's a bittersweet thing. It's brave. Loving something so much you let it consume you, knowing one day it might break you, leaving you less wholesome, but full of memories that will last a lifetime.

God, I hope he's okay.

<hr />

LOWERWICK ESTATE on any day is the vision of breathtaking tranquillity. But today as I look out over the grounds from my spot on the bedroom balcony, I wonder to myself if I have ever seen such beauty.

"Scar, you really outdid yourself. It's perfect," I tell her, smoothing my hand over the railing before sipping my champagne.

Scarlet slips up next to me, grinning wide as she looks over the grounds which are lit up with the lanterns and candles. "You really think so?"

I dip my head, smiling at her.

"I did good, didn't I," she confirms.

The sun decided to shine down on the estate for the entirety of the day, the marquee was able to dry out along with the grass, and with the team that Scarlet hired to set everything up, we were done just before two o'clock. Ellis should be arriving with Maggie and John any time now. They offered to have him so Mason could get himself ready and over to the Montgomery's with the rest of the boys.

I haven't seen Mason since Wednesday. Elliot dropped Ellis home on Thursday, because Mason had to go into the office, and when he didn't call or text, I took it that he needed the space.

Having not heard from him means I have no idea how he's feeling, or if he's even going to show up. I contemplated texting him earlier, but am I really the one he would want to hear from when he is probably already in his own head about coming out here?

"Have you heard from Mason?" I ask Scarlet, hoping she can shed some light on the situation.

"No." She purses her lips, grasping the railing and letting her perfectly curled lavender hair flow down her back. She tips her head to the sky. "Not even a text."

Scarlet has worked tirelessly on this night, but I know despite her tone, that she holds a level of understanding for her brother. Scarlet is forgiving. I don't know if that's a good thing, but I know it makes her the person she is, and she is the best kind to have in your life.

"There's Mummy!" Lucy sings, carrying Ellis out onto the balcony. "And Auntie Scar." She passes off Ellis to me and I place him on my hip. "There's a guy downstairs, says he has a fifty-kilo block of cheese?"

Scarlet's face instantly drops.

"What?" I laugh. "Why so much? The pantry is full of everything we need."

"Oh my god," Scarlet deadpans, scurrying out of the room and leaving us none the wiser on the balcony.

"You need to get changed," Lucy tells me, standing in her robe just like me.

"We have time. Tell me about Miller. What happened?"

Her frown is defensive, and I'm not certain I'm going to get the truth. "What do you mean, what happened?"

"Luce, you said you were done."

"I know." She palms her forehead but pulls her hand away when she remembers her makeup. "I don't know what I'm supposed to do, Nina."

When she doesn't elaborate, I say, "It's not about what you're supposed to do, Luce, you do what you want, what feels right."

"Nothing feels right. Nothing! Not my job, not my relationship." She throws her hands out to her sides at a loss. "I was always the one with a plan. I wanted kids young." She picks up Ellis's hand. "And that's not going to happen now. What if I don't meet someone before I'm thirty?"

"So, your plan is to what... force a relationship with someone you don't love?"

"I don't love Miller," she says in agreement. She lifts her eyes to mine and shrugs. "But I could."

"You aren't ready to make the decisions you're making right now, Luce. Trust that when the time comes you will."

"It's just hard. Seeing you with your shit so together." She smiles at me, her eyes glassy. "I'm proud of you—don't think I'm not, but I feel a million miles away from your level of contentment right now."

"What? Luce, you have no idea, or you do, and you refuse to see it. I haven't danced in over a year. I have a son with a man I can't go five minutes without arguing with. My shit is well and truly not together."

"I'd still love to have half the life you do. Your independence and confidence to be alone is inspiring."

"We're all made differently, Luce, I don't like being alone." I run my lips along Ellis's head. "It's what you get used to." I shrug.

She nods. "Sorry for the rant."

"I've been the most dramatic best friend in history this past year!" We both laugh and I take her hand. "Promise me you won't settle. You deserve more, so much more, Luce."

"I promise." Her face lights up, that angelic, alluring smile that she wears so well taking over her face. "I need to get Ellis to Vinny, then we need to get dressed and you still need your hair doing!" she tells me.

"I will go find Vinny. You take a minute," I tell her, leaving her on the balcony and wandering down to the kitchen where I find Vinny, and Scarlet stood around the biggest block of cheese I've ever seen.

Mase

EVERY SUMMER from the time my mother became sick to the day I left Lowerwick for college, was spent on the Montgomery's estate. It wasn't something that was discussed; it was just the place we went when our fathers had to work.

It took years of my own ignorance, or maybe my immaturity, before I realised that my father wasn't the man he once was. He was an alcoholic, one who managed to hide it from everyone he loved—until he didn't.

The Montgomery Estate holds better, maybe even longer-lasting memories than Lowerwick ever will. It's a home, with love and laughter and life.

Lowerwick Estate is nothing more than bricks and mortar, filled with half arse promises that were made by two people who lie six feet beneath it. Lifting the glass of amber liquid to my lips I empty the tumbler in one mouthful, welcoming the burn as it runs down my throat.

Elliot watches me over the brim of his glass, giving me a nod before lowering his eyes to check his cards.

We are lounging around a table in one of the many sitting rooms. Lance, Charlie, Elliot and George—because apparently George gets invited to family parties now too.

I give Elliot a nod, tossing an ace down which George instantly straightens on the table.

"I'm out," Lance huffs, throwing down his cards.

"Me too."

"George, you were out three hands ago. You don't have to call it every round," Lance snaps. He's been even more of an asshole than normal recently.

"This is taking forever! What time is the ball? Those girls will have you strung up if you're late, you know. That lilac haired beauty who was here earlier, God, she could organise unholy nuns! She told me to make sure we were on time. I don't want to be the one she comes for."

"You won't be." Lance rolls his eyes. "Charlie, call it."

Charlie is just as quiet as me this evening and I know he's stuck in his own head. I just don't know why. Reaching forward, he slides in three-quarters of his chips—around twenty grand—into the middle of the table.

Elliot matches him, and I follow.

Elliot sits forward, rubbing his hands together. "I'm feeling lucky tonight, assholes!"

"That's what I said," George remarks, shaking his head at me with a smile that I don't return. "Is everything okay, Mason?" he calls me out.

The boys all look at me, none of them having bothered to ask the question. They aren't fucking idiots, that's why. They know better than to ask.

Was everything okay? No. No, it fucking wasn't. But I sure as shit wasn't about to get into it with him.

"Everything is dandy, Georgey." I pat him on the shoulder. "All in." I push my chips into the middle of the table, not looking at anyone else.

"Shut up you, dick. You haven't even looked at your cards." Elliot finishes dealing then grins as he checks his. "You know what, all fucking in."

"Fuck's sake," Charlie mutters, throwing down his cards.

Elliot looks like the cat that got the cream while Charlie glares at me.

I couldn't give a shit.

I can't focus on a fucking game right now.

I HAVEN'T BEEN to the estate properly since my father's funeral, and a part of me wishes I had, just to make this moment less public. The marquee is full, and people spill out onto the manicured grounds. It looks like something out of a movie. Only in my head, it's a horror film.

Businessmen, most of which I despise, nod their heads at me in greeting. My parents were respected in the property business, and now that I sit at the helm of it I'm expected to smile and greet them with the same professionalism my father showed.

When I took over the company six years ago, I knew I wasn't going to be a pushover like mine and Elliot's fathers were. They were the nice guys, and now we are the assholes, but also the assholes that sit at the top of all the competition.

All eyes follow the five of us through the crowded marquee as we make our way to the bar. Charlie orders a round of drinks, and I scan the crowd.

"Anyone see the girls?" Elliot asks, standing a solid two inches above me.

"No," I deadpan, turning to retrieve my drink.

"I'm going to go find them," he says, disappearing back the way we just came.

Ellis will be in the house, and I want to go and see him, but I feel safer out here.

Where the fuck is everyone?

I text Nina asking her where she is.

She told me she would be here, Ellis too, and now Elliot has fucked off.

"Mr Lowell Jr."

I exhale on a deep sigh, looking to the ceiling before turning. "Mrs Mills." I smile, turning to her husband. "Fred."

"Good to see you, Mason, great evening you've put on tonight," Fredrick says, shaking my hand. "Did you see

Millerton have moved in on Berkley's territory. I knew they would but not this fast."

Fuck my ever-fucking life.

"I did. Doesn't surprise me one bit, they always have been greedy in their market."

"Well, your father would've been outraged. It was these very movements Anthony put a stop to."

"Anthony isn't here anymore, Fred."

"I know, but—"

"Excuse me, I see someone I need to speak with. You enjoy your night."

I'm almost clear of the bar and back to Lance, Charlie, and George when Rupert Hemmings intercepts me.

I shouldn't be here.

I don't want to be here.

"Mason, how are you, son?"

"Rupert." I nod, shaking his outstretched hand.

"I haven't seen you in years. I'm sorry to hear about your father."

Rupert Hemmings was one of my father's biggest competitors for over thirty years. When a scandal sent his company into bankruptcy, he decided to start asking my father for financial aid. Like I said, my father was the good guy, so he helped him. But when I took over the company, I put a stop to it and had him pay back the money he owed.

There's no place in business for family and friends.

The old man isn't doing bad for himself either, he had more than enough money to pay us back. If I remember rightly, he made the call from his yacht in the Maldives. Had his PA do the transfer. Safe to say old man Hemmings had his priorities in all the wrong places.

"No, it has been a while... I don't think I saw you at the funeral." Not that I'd know if he was there or not, but something tells me he wasn't.

"Uh, no, I was away. Business trip." He shrugs glumly.

"Ah, of course."

"Lowell!"

I turn as a hand slaps me on the back. Cooper Hemmings greets me with his signature over the top pretentious smile. The prick hates me, and I hate him.

"Cooper." I nod.

"Have you heard the news, Mason?" Rupert asks. "Cooper will be taking over the firm as of next year."

"No way?" I recoil in shock, a smile tugging at my lips.

"Yeah." Cooper glares at my obvious smirk.

"Well good luck to you, Coop." I tip my chin up. "I look forward to seeing what you've got."

He places a hand on his father's rounded shoulder, tipping his chin as his lip curls. "I have one of the best to learn from."

"Indeed." I give him a tight-lipped smile.

Cooper and I went to college together. He flunked his final year and had to stay behind to repeat. The prick never got over it.

"What's this I hear about Montgomery taking over the Savale account?" Rupert asks. "Anthony always worked with them."

My eyes flick to his, then back to Cooper and I wonder if they are intentionally trying to piss me off. My hands clench in my pockets, the need to punch the smirk off Cooper's face too strong.

"Gentlemen."

I whip around, my eyes landing on Nina.

Everything drifts the fuck away.

Every thought of my parents, my business, and the pricks who bait me, it all disappears, my world stepping up and carrying me away.

Every word I have in my brain seems to die before they can pass my lips. And it's a good thing because they wouldn't be coherent.

She's wearing a black lace dress. It's tight to her body and barely covers her tits. It's too fucking tight and leaves *nothing* to the imagination.

Fuck!

Ellis sits on Nina's hip, wearing a tux that matches my own. He throws himself at me and I gladly take him.

"Mase," she says softly, gripping my arm with her dainty hand. "Sorry we're late." To anyone watching on, it would seem like a simple apology. But to us, it's Nina placing the shield up and telling me she's here.

I fucking adore this woman.

Cooper steps forward. My eyes are trained on him from the moment he takes the first inch towards her. "Who's this delicacy?"

"Mine," I announce on a growl, wrapping my hand around Nina's waist whilst placing Ellis on my other hip.

"Oh," he muses. "Mrs Lowell, it's a pleasure."

"It's Anderson," she corrects, and my eyes fly to hers.

She looks up at me with an innocent look and shrugs.

"Cooper Hemmings," he introduces himself. "And this is my father, Rupert."

"Mr Hemmings." She nods to Rupert politely.

"I heard you had a kid. But nobody told me his mother

was such a fine beauty. A dance later, Miss Anderson?" His eyes rake down her body, pausing on her chest for a second too long.

"Mason, can I have a minute with you?" Nina asks with a smile. "In private."

In my head, my fist is already on the side of Hemming's jaw, but as Nina squeezes my hand and pulls me to the bar, I begin to relax a little.

"You know it would be extremely rude to beat your own guests," she tells me.

"They aren't my guests," I grit out, my anger subsiding as I look down at Ellis. "Hey, mate." I lean in and kiss his head.

"He's super tired. I'll take him to bed in a little while," Nina says, rubbing his back.

"I thought Vinny was doing it?" I signal for the barman then bring my eyes to Nina. My throat catches as I take her in fully. "You look fucking beautiful, Angel."

She tries to hide her blush from me, dropping her head then lifting it and saying, "I said I would do it so Vinny can enjoy himself. He deserves a night off and I don't mind."

"And I said you look fucking beautiful, Angel."

Her lips twist up into the sweetest smile, and my heart somersaults in my chest because I put it there. "Thank you."

"Do you want a drink?"

She nods.

"Who invited Cooper cunting Hemmings?" Elliot tsks, sliding up to the bar along with Lance, George, and Charlie.

"Elliot!" Nina scolds.

"Shit, I forgot about Baby Ell." He lifts Ellis from my arms and sits him on the bar top. "I think he looks more like you today, Lowell."

"He looks *exactly* like Mason," Nina corrects.

"Nah, he has your lighter, brown eyes. It's that frown he does with his brows that's Lowell to a T."

We all chuckle as Ellis frowns harder. Exactly like me.

"That's fucking funny."

I lean in, taking Ellis and shaking my head at Elliot. "Watch your mouth," I warn.

"Here she is!" Elliot grins, pulling Scarlet into a tight hug as she nears with Megan in tow. "The brains and beauty of the family."

"I need a drink!" Scarlet huffs. "I feel like if I stop I'm going to fall asleep at this point."

"Everything is perfect, Scarlet," Charlie tells her, leaning in and kissing her cheek.

Lance hands her a drink and then throws her a wink.

Then she turns to me, and I worry it will be awkward but it's Scarlet and she doesn't allow it, pushing her arms through mine and around my back she pulls me in for a hug.

"They would have loved this tonight," I whisper into her ear.

"Yeah?" she asks.

"Yeah. Mum was all about this kind of thing, and Dad lived to entertain."

"Thank you for coming, Mason."

"I wouldn't have missed it for the world." I squeeze the tops of her arms and let her pull away to stand beside me.

"Where's Luce?" I ask, looking around the group, feeling better now that everyone is here.

Elliot raises his glass in a toast, ignoring me altogether. "To the gang."

We raise our glasses, mine and Nina's eyes meeting across

the group. She shakes her head, telling me with her eyes that she will explain later.

IT'S HALF an hour later when Ellis starts to get fussy and I watch Vinny sweep in and offer to take him to bed himself. I roll my eyes on a laugh, knowing how much Ellis means to him.

Nina watches on at the entrance of the marquee as Vinny carries him up through the grounds until they are out of sight. She smooths out her hair and takes a moment, breathing in the night air. I stand perched at the bar, my eyes trained on her and unable to look away, as I wonder what she's thinking.

Picking up her dress, she turns and walks back into the marquee. She strides straight over to me, making my shoulders draw back and my chest expand as I tuck her into my side. "Vinny couldn't resist, huh?" I whisper against her temple.

"Nope." She laughs.

Her eyes bore into mine as she gazes up at me, her hand running up my back under my jacket. "You okay?"

"I'm fine," I tell her, taking a sip of my drink.

She grins up at me, her dimples set deep in her cheeks. "That smile," I admire.

"I'm just happy, Bossman."

"Guys!" Megan summons from the other end of the bar. "Shots!"

"Here we go," I huff out, following behind Nina as she slides out from my side and makes her way to our friends.

22

Nina

"No!" I roar, grasping Lance's forearm as I lean over in hysterics.

"Charles was stuck there for three days," Elliot tells us.

Charlie nods as if he's reliving the story as it's being told. "My mum thought I wasn't coming home, I'm surprised she ever let me back in the house."

"Charlie! I never took you as such a playboy!" Megan accuses, laughing along with us. "Those poor girls."

"Poor girls?" Scarlet asks. "What's poor about those girls?!"

"Right!" I tip my glass to her.

"It was over ten years ago, ladies," Charlie tells us, downplaying it.

"We all had our day, Charles." I wink at him, giving him a soft smile.

"It's true. I slept with a woman once," George announces with a slight slur, making Mason, who was relatively quiet, choke on his drink. "Ah, you didn't see that one coming, did you, Bossman."

"Not your cuppa tea, George?" I ask with a grin.

"No, she was great! But, Nina…" He dips his head to his shoulder in a knowing look. "Come on, surely you've been dominated by a man before?" He pops a brow at me.

I chew on my lip, giggling like an embarrassed schoolgirl. I love George. "Well." I roll my lips. "I'm not sure I have, George." I laugh, watching as Charlie clasps Mason's shoulder in a show of support.

Mason shakes his head at me, his eyes darker than the night outside. They drop to my neck, then my breasts. I'm about to go to him, needing the contact, when Lucy pops her head between me and Lance. Miller is standing at her back.

"Girls, the band finished! Scar, we have to do the auction!"

"Oh no, can we not!" I plead.

"Yes! We have to," Scarlet tells me. "I had other prizes added too. It's going to be a blast."

"Auction?" Mason asks.

"Nina, and Lucy," Elliot tells him, his eyes set on Lucy. "They're auctioning themselves for a date tonight."

"What?!" Mason snaps, already outraged.

"It's just for fun," Scarlet reassures him.

"Vinny said he will bid," I tell him. I turn to Megan. "Accept Vinny's offer, Megs, please!"

"Sure thang," she mumbles, her eyes heavy.

Megan's drunk! Good god, this won't be good.

I give Mason a wave as Scarlet pulls me through the crowd and over to the stage. The boys all take a stand at the bar, a hard look on every one of their faces.

"The boys are pissed," I tell the girls.

"They'll get over it. It's for charity." Scarlet rolls her eyes, fluffing my hair.

"Your tits are wonky," Megan tells me, her smile lazy as she stands in a daze.

"Gee, thanks Megs. Just wait till you have kids! Scar, you can't have this idiot doing the auction!"

"She'll be fine."

"I'm fine!" Megan grins.

I stand to the side with Lucy as she slowly climbs the steps onto the stage.

I'm thankful for the alcohol I've consumed tonight, otherwise, I'd never have the guts to do this.

Somehow, Megan pulls the whole thing off. Her wit and drunken charm seem to get the crowd warmed up, and as Lucy and I step up on stage they've already raised an impressive eight hundred thousand pounds.

The money in the room tonight is unbelievable.

My stomach twists into knots as I stand on the stage, Megan's voice like white noise as I struggle to focus on what she's saying. This has to be my worst nightmare. I don't know why I ever agreed to it or why the girls thought I would be able to do it.

Fucking Lucy!

My eyes seek her out and I glare at her, watching as her face drops. *Are you okay?* She mouths.

I shake my head, wondering if I should just slip off to the side of the stage quietly and hope that nobody notices.

Taking a deep breath in, I try to concentrate on Megan.

"So, which one of you gentlemen would like to take this beautiful bombshell out on a date?"

My eyes scan the crowd. The majority of the men in the

room are married off or brought dates with them tonight. What if no one bids on us. It's embarrassing.

"Five hundred," John shouts, lifting his hand and placing a bid on his own daughter.

A smile breaks past my lips even though the situation is ridiculous.

"Six!" someone shouts.

I look at Lucy who's focused on the crowd; I follow her line of sight and see she is looking at Miller. He shrugs at her, looking at a loss.

Shit.

"A grand," Elliot calls, shaking his head as he knocks back his drink, his eyes not meeting the stage.

"Hot damn, any advances on one thousand pounds?" Megan asks.

"Two," Lance calls out, a grin plastered on his face.

"Five," Vinny announces, drawing my eye to the opening of the marquee.

He throws me a wink, a silent acknowledgement to let me know that Ellis is fine.

Everything is a buzz. Lucy is giddy, laughing and blowing kisses to Vinny, and Megan is standing, breathing loudly into the microphone.

"Ten," Elliot counters, causing the room to fall silent. He spins where he's stood, placing his tumbler down and signalling for another drink.

You could hear a pin drop.

"Megs," I hiss over at her. "Wrap it up."

"Going once, twice, sold." She brings down her hammer, swallowing loudly into the microphone before turning her eyes to me.

I realise it's my turn, and the thought that people will be looking at me, placing bids on me, Vinny or not. It makes me want to run.

But I promised him I wouldn't.

My eyes meet his and everything else slips away.

"Next up, we have the gorgeous Nina. She's a fiery one, boys, so only bid if you think you can handle her bite."

Mason's eyes grow tighter at Megan's challenge.

My heart starts to pound as the bidding starts, but my eyes don't leave his.

"How about we start at—"

"Five hundred!" John shouts again, making everyone laugh.

"Five thousand!" Vinny yells, and my heart swells.

"Ten!" Charlie calls out.

"Twenty-five thousand." My eyes snap to the bidder, realising it's the man Mason was talking to when I arrived. Hemmings, he said his name was.

I flick my eyes back to Mason and instantly get lost in him again, his stare catching me on fire. He isn't concerned with Hemmings, Vinny or John, he is honed in on me. Nothing else. Me.

His eyes seem to pinch tighter together, and I frown as something passes between us.

He won't bid on me.

He won't buy me.

"Twenty-eight!" Lance grounds out.

"Twenty-eight thousand! Wow, guys! Going once..."

"Thirty!" Hemmings outbids Lance, earning a collective gasp from the crowd and myself.

Mason's lip curls and I worry I will lose his eyes, but he

doesn't look away from me, his knuckles only grow tighter against the marble top, as if he is restraining himself from going after Hemmings. His head dips slightly, and the reassurance he gives me in that one look is the only thing keeping me on the stage.

"Uh." Megan seems to have lost her voice, and I look to her, praying she doesn't wrap things up yet.

She shrugs. "Going once... twice..."

My eyes fly to Mason's.

"Sold!" Megan fans herself, shaking her head helplessly at me when I look at her in horror.

My gaze goes back to Mason, and I find him striding towards the stage. He looks lethal, his smirk promising and measured. I learn all too quickly that he wasn't restraining himself from getting to Hemmings. He was restraining himself from coming to me.

"Oh." Megan taps the microphone. "Do we have a last-minute bidder?" She grins.

"Mase," I warn as he nears.

He doesn't slow, not stopping until his shoulder is at my hip, and I'm being thrown over his shoulder.

"Oh my god! Mase!"

"Hey! You can't steal the prizes, Mr Lowell!" Megan laughs.

I don't dare look up, placing my hands on his lower back as he strolls through the cheering crowd. Mason carries me from the tent and through the grounds until we are at the back doors of the terrace that leads off of the kitchen. He slides me down his body putting us mere inches from one another.

"What was that?"

His eyes dart all over my face. "You belong to me, Pix."

"You didn't bid on me." My lips twist up into a smile.

"I didn't need to," he says, proud. "You'll love me anyway."

I feel my dimple pop as I rise onto the tips of my toes, placing a soft kiss to his lips. Chills run down my spine the second our lips touch, and I push into his body farther, grasping his tux jacket in my hands.

He groans against my lips, tearing away from me as he tries to find an opening in my dress. With no luck, he tries to lift it, but the material is too tight and doesn't budge past my thighs. "Fuck!" he hisses.

"You'll have to unzip it, Bossman."

His nose brushes mine as he meets my eyes again. "Yeah? You'd let me unzip it?"

I nod, biting my lip on a smile.

Swinging my legs up over his arms, he lifts me like a bride and breezes in through the house. We bypass Ellis's room and then go deeper into the west wing.

"So much choice, Mr Lowell," I tease as we pass multiple doors.

"Shut it." He grins, lowering his mouth to mine again and taking my lips in a deep kiss.

He drops me to my feet as we get lost in the kiss, our tongues tangling together as I pull open his tux jacket.

I need him naked.

I need us both naked.

My back hits the door hard in our haste, and I grunt slightly as the wind is knocked from my lungs.

"Shit." He pulls away.

Slipping my hand in his hair, I draw him back into me,

biting down on his lip until I taste the faint copper tang of his blood. A growl vibrates from his chest.

The bedroom door is thrown open and then I'm being lifted again. I'm placed on a cool hard surface, and I have to break our connection to see what I'm sitting on.

"Mase." I look at him, my heart wild yet pained in my chest.

It's been so long. I smooth my hands over the smooth black surface.

"Is it weird that I feel the need to fuck you on it?"

"Completely." I reach for his jacket as he pulls at the straps of my dress.

His mouth goes to my neck, his breath hot and wanting as his tongue lashes at my heated flesh. His hand palms my breast before he bends, sucking a nipple into his mouth. A moan falls from my lips. "Mason."

"Hmmm." His mouth works back up my throat quickly, locking onto my lips, and sucking them into his mouth. It drives me wild.

I start to pull his shirt from his trousers, having already undone most of the buttons. My hands smooth over his body, feeling the expanse of his strong chest and soft skin beneath my fingers.

"I've missed this." I pant between the soft kisses I rain down his throat and torso.

"Fuck." He lifts me from the piano, dropping me to my feet and spinning me to lower the zip. My dress is discarded, and his arms encase me from behind. I didn't wear a bra and my thong is a thin lace that matches the dress. His hand dips beneath the fabric, sliding through my folds with ease.

"Pix," he growls, rolling his hips against me.

I whimper as his fingers dip into my heat, then glide up over my sensitive bud.

"Oh my god!" My body flushes hot and my body shakes as a tremor racks through me. It's been so long since he's touched me like this. I start to ride his hand, applying mine on top of his and adding more pressure. "I'm... clo—"

"Already?"

My eyes roll. "Mase—"

The sound that leaves me as my orgasm rips through me is feral, unlike anything I've ever heard before, and I can feel Mason's smile against my cheek as he lets me come undone in his arms. "Fuck. How long has it been?!"

My head drops back to his shoulder, my body still shaking. "Too long." I pant.

Lifting my chin with one hand, he kisses me slowly, easing his fingers through my folds and spreading my orgasm all over me. My body quivers and ripples under his touch. He rolls his hips into me, rubbing himself deeper, harder, until the friction alone isn't enough.

"Turn around."

I spin and his mouth hungrily drops to my lips. "Mase," I beg, needing so much more.

"Patience," he rasps, his hand held in my hair as he manipulates my neck to gain better access to my throat.

He lifts me back onto the piano, removing my thong and sliding my legs over his shoulders. "Mason, no! Please!"

The heat of his mouth makes me lose all my fight. I drop back to the piano on my elbows and watch as he looks up at me from between my thighs. His tongue lashes against my sensitive folds, tracing every inch of me as if it's the only chance he'll get.

"I never forgot how good you taste."

He swirls his tongue around and over my clit.

"Sometimes." He draws it between his teeth, making my hips buck against him. "Sometimes I'd swear I could taste you. I'd wake up from a dream and would still be able to feel you on my lips."

My hands go to his hair as I ride wave after wave of pleasure that floods through me, rubbing myself over his mouth and chin as I near the edge of insanity.

He continues to suck my sensitive flesh long after I come down from my high. I'm limp when he finally lets me up, my body sated and probably not ready for what's to come.

"What did you do," I say, gingerly lowering myself to the floor.

His mouth glistens in the moonlit room and in that moment, he looks like a wild beast that's just feasted on his prey.

Licking at his lips, he starts on his belt buckle. "On the bed."

I. Am. Not. Fucking. Ready.

Crawling up the bed, I lie on my back and watch as he lowers his boxers. He moves himself up the bed and my eyes drop to his cock, heavy and thick. "It's been too fucking long, Angel." He pumps himself three times, his throat working as he swallows.

"When was the last time?" I ask, frowning.

"It doesn't matter."

It matters to me. I stop him as he climbs over me. "Mase."

"Nina," he warns. His cock brushes my stomach, leaving a trail of precum in its wake.

"How long ago—"

"I didn't," he snaps, nudging the head inside of me. He looks down at where our bodies meet, and I clench around him.

"What do you mean?" I moan.

"I haven't. Not... Jesus Christ, Nina." He pinches his eyes tight. "Are we really doing this now?"

I nod.

He pauses, his jaw ticcing as he slowly slides into me, making my walls ache as they stretch around him. "This is the only pussy I've been inside of since the night I took you in my bed." He rolls his hips, putting himself right down to the hilt and brushing my pelvis.

My eyes flutter close. "Meaning?"

"Meaning I only ever had anal sex, Nina."

My eyes snap open.

"Because the thought of being inside someone else in any other way was never going to be an option unless it was you."

He sits back on his knees, pulling out of me. "I'm sorry." He climbs from the bed and leans against the dresser, dropping his head.

Is he ashamed? Because he shouldn't be? I mean, I'm a little shocked, and it hurts, but I'm the one who should be ashamed.

I left him.

"Mase," I soothe, "come here."

When he doesn't budge, I go to him, slipping my arms around him so I can cuddle his back. "Mase, please. Turn around."

He turns in my arms and I slide a hand up into his hair, pushing it back off his face.

"I'm sorry I left you, and I promise I won't ever leave you again."

He shakes his head. "I'm weak."

"No, you're—"

"How many men did you sleep with?"

"I was heavily pregnant," I defend.

He shakes his head, looking away from me, and I regret pushing it and making him feel like this.

"Mase, I need you to make love to me." His chest deflates, his shoulders sagging. "I've needed you to make love to me since you cornered me in my laundry room. I've only ever needed you to love me and in every way that mattered you did. You always have—even when we fought it. I need you more than anything right now and I need it to be real. Us. But first." I take his hand, sliding it deep between my legs, teasing the tips of his fingers on my puckered hole. "First, I need you to take me here."

He inhales a deep breath and lets out a shaky one, his eyes turning a dangerous shade of black.

"Nina."

"Will it help?" I ask.

He swallows, his eyes shining. "Yes."

I walk to the bed, lying myself down on my stomach as I wait for him. "I need this, just as much as you do."

He walks to the edge of the bed, gliding the pads of his fingers down my back. "I don't know what I ever did to deserve you." My hips lift to meet him as he glides lower.

"You want me here, baby?"

I cry out as his finger runs over the crack of my ass and teases my hole.

"Yes!"

He flips me, placing me on my back. "Mase!"

His lips take my open mouth, his hands locking with mine and lifting them above my head. He ravishes my body, his stubble scratching at my nipples as he sucks at the flesh around them, making me squirm and beg him for more in the same breath.

Dropping his head to mine, he waits for a beat, then slides home in one smooth thrust, making us both moan in sheer pleasure.

"Fuck!" he groans, rolling his hips deep inside of me before all too soon his fingers take the place of his cock.

His hand dips lower, gliding his slick fingers through the crack of my ass. He applies the slightest pressure until I open up and he slides a finger inside.

He leans in and kisses me as I slowly adjust around him. I roll my hips and moan into his mouth.

"That feels good, baby?"

"Hmmm."

"You're so fucking sexy like this."

I lift my head from the mattress to look at him. He gives me a small smile then drops his head, drawing my clit between his lips. My body ripples moments after, my orgasm taking me fast, just like the first.

He pulls his finger out of me slowly, running his hands up my thighs to my hips. Every solid inch of him ripples and flexes as he lifts me, moving us back until he's sat against the headboard.

He places me on his lap, sinking me down onto his thick cock. His lips brush mine, but he doesn't take them like I crave. "I need you to take me. I can't lose control with you tonight."

I nod, rolling my hips over him and giving him a small smile. I lick my lips and push to my knees. I line him up, the tip of his cock braced against me.

His head drops to mine, his heart pounding under my splayed palms.

"I love you," I tell him, needing him to know.

He trembles beneath me. The entire two hundred pounds of him, quaking as he stares into my eyes. I sink down an inch and gasp. He grasps my hips instantly, holding me off from dropping any lower.

I squeeze my eyes tight. "Mase, I need you. I need more," I rasp. I open my eyes when he doesn't move, doesn't speak, and he stares up at me with so much uncertainty it makes me question myself.

I want this.

So does he.

"Mason. Fuck me. I want you to do it."

His eyes search mine, and I know he finds his reasoning somewhere in them. "Angel."

He breaks.

All restraint is gone, as he guides my hips down onto him, stretching me, filling me in the most perfect way.

I barely brush his thighs before I slide back up his length, my nails biting into his chest as he grows harder inside of me.

"Fuck, I'm going to come," he snaps, and I feel his balls draw up as his eyes squeeze tight.

"Mason," I say with a smile, waiting for him to open his eyes.

"I'm going to come, baby."

"It's okay." I chuckle, with no idea why I find it funny, but he shakes his head and laughs with me.

"Fuck. That actually works." His head drops back, and he laughs harder. I lean in and kiss him through our smiles, our teeth clashing as we share the tender moment. This is nothing like what I thought it would be, but I also know it's important.

Rocking my hips slowly, I start to really move, dropping harder and deeper onto him until his hand moves from my hip and flattens over my clit.

"Mase," I moan, my body flushing hot.

I grasp his arm as he adds more pressure to my clit at the same time as he rolls his hips into my ass, sending my world black momentarily. My body locks tight and finds its release.

"Nina, baby!" He groans, bucking into me uncontrollably before stilling deep inside me.

His entire body is wet with sweat, and the veins in his arms seem to bulge unnaturally as he rubs his hands over my trembling thighs. He forces my body flush with his and I land on his chest hard.

"I love you," I pant. "It's okay, and I love you."

23

Mase

I brush my fingers over Nina's forehead, moving the hair back from her face. She's so peaceful. The true meaning of beauty—for me.

Being here, in this house, it doesn't bring back a haul of memories. There aren't smells or sounds that creak in the night that have me reminiscing about being a child here. Instead, I feel somewhat restless. Like I shouldn't be here at all.

"Nina."

"Hmmm." Her hand reaches blindly, smoothing over my chest as her legs tangle tighter with mine.

I smile, kissing her wrist. "Nina."

She stirs again, her chest rising as she inhales deeply. "Time is it?"

"Three a.m.," I whisper into her neck as she rolls to her back.

"Masseeee," she moans, her brows drawing together.

"I owe you a dance."

Her eyes flutter open, and I instantly feel seen. "Right now?"

I nod, kissing her forehead before rising from the bed.

"Where are you going?" she asks.

"To the ball." I smile.

"I don't have my clothes," she complains, watching as I search for my shirt. I don't miss the hint of excitement in her voice.

"Wear your dress."

"It's three a.m. Do you have any idea how long it took me to get into that thing? It's tight."

I crawl over her, blanketing her body with my own. "I want to dance with you in that dress."

"And I want to sleep." She cocks her head with a smile. Leaning in and kissing my lips. "Compromise."

I glare at her, already knowing I won't fight her on it. "Fine. Wear my shirt."

She slips out from under me, bouncing on the tips of her toes as she bends to pick up my shirt. I watch her as she slides it over her shoulders and starts to button it up.

"Keep looking at me like that, Bossman, and we'll be dancing in the sheets instead."

"Maybe we should do that," I muse, lying with my hands linked behind my head on the pillow. My cock grows harder the more buttons she does up.

She shakes her head. "Nuh-uh, I wanna *dance* with you."

My heart swells in my chest. She wants to dance.

"Here." She throws me my jacket and trousers, then pulls my boxers on.

"You sure you don't want the jacket, too?" I say sarcastically.

She pulls her long hair up into a bun, then starts towards the door. "Only if it gets cold." She winks. "Come on, Bossman."

I take off after her as she slips from the room, still barefoot. I manage to get my jacket on before I reach the door but stumble into my pant leg as I try to catch up to her.

"Shhh! You'll wake Ellis!" She chuckles, watching me struggle.

Once I have my trousers buttoned, I rush her, grinning wide when she lets out a shrill squeal. Lifting her over my shoulder, I descend the stairs, letting her down when we reach the bottom. Voices carry from the kitchen; I frown as I try to make them out.

I hear Scarlet, and—

"Mase, come on." She drags me to the front door.

Nina

MY FEET PAD along the cool paving slabs as I lead the way to the marquee. Mason is right on my heels, his hands reaching for me and roaming my torso. "It's cold, you can have my jacket."

"And leave you with a pair of trousers?" She giggles. "No."

We reach the opening to the marquee, and Mason pulls out a key. I frown as he quickly unlocks the padlock and opens the door.

When did he get the key?

"I'll find the generator. Wait here."

He disappears, leaving me standing in the entrance of the moonlit tent. Pulling on his shirt sleeves, I cross to the room and duck down behind the bar, looking for the matches we used earlier in the evening to light the candles.

Ten minutes later, Mason comes back into the marquee, a hard expression on his face as he looks down at his phone then puts it to his ear.

"What's wrong, who are you calling?"

"Vinny, I can't get the generator working."

Lifting his head to look at me, he takes in the room that's now lit up in a white glow. His face morphs into a smile, and he pockets his phone.

"You were going to call Vinny to come fix the generator at three o'clock in the morning?"

"So?" he says defensively.

"He's with our son." Something about that statement makes my stomach dip. Our sweet Ellis.

"He's a heavy sleeper, like his mother." His handsome face starts to relax.

I shake my head as I approach him. "What?" He grins, running his hands over my waist and down to my behind, giving it a firm squeeze. "I pay Vinny well."

"Oh yeah, of course," I say sarcastically. "Makes it totally acceptable and okay to—"

"Nina," he whispers.

I smile. "What?"

"Shut the fuck up." He slides his lips over mine, taking his time to find a rhythm before he deepens the kiss. His arms band around my body; keeping me locked tightly to him. I struggle to think of any other place I'd rather be at this moment.

After what feels like hours he pulls away, lips swollen and glossy. "I don't have any music. But if you'll have me as I am?"

I take his outstretched hand, a grin stretching my face. "Ever the gentleman, Mr Lowell."

He lifts a brow. "Hmm, I don't know. Would a gentleman want to fuck every inch of you until you can no longer take any more of him?"

I do a little two-step, trying to keep my face straight. "I mean, I never wanted to be a lady anyway." I jump up into his arms, locking my feet behind his back. He spins me, and I drop my head back, letting my body go lax for him as we both laugh freely.

"When was the last time you danced?" he asks, pulling me upright with a hand to my back.

My legs slide to the ground and we start to sway. "It was in the penthouse. You were in the shower, and I was supposed to be warming up our dinner."

He watches me intently; his hand drawing circles on my shoulder. "What song did you play?"

I feel stupid for remembering, but he doesn't judge me for it. "The Goo Goo Dolls, 'Iris'."

His lips brush my temple, then he spins me.

I step back into him, lifting my leg and leaning into him. He moulds to me, following my lead.

I get lost in our movements, our bodies swaying to the sound of our own heartbeats. For the first time in over a year, I dance, and not in the conscious way I move around a dance floor with my girls. I dance how I always used to dance. Freely.

"You were the most beautiful woman in the room tonight."

I laugh as he dips me back, kissing my jaw. "I'm serious. Vinny said it too. You looked phenomenal in that dress. And when you came to me with Ellis." His eyes are glazed and far off, as if he's right back in the moment. "I don't know how I ever went a day without seeing you."

My throat is thick with emotion; My love for this man is boundless.

"I'm so sorry, Mason. For what I put you through. I didn't trust you when it mattered and I don't know how to fix that."

"Shh." He brushes his finger over my lip. "We'll figure it out."

We continue to float around the dance floor, his hands lingering on my body for longer than necessary at every opportunity he gets.

I don't know how long we have been dancing for when we finally slow, rocking back and forth with my head on his chest. "I'm glad you came tonight," I whisper.

He doesn't say a thing. His response delivered with a soft kiss to my head.

I frown, then think out loud. "I'm so proud of you, Mason Lowell."

After a moment, he runs his hands up my arms, pulling away from me and looking down at me pensively. Every emotion inside him is bared to me in the reflection of his eyes.

"*They* would be so proud of you."

His eyes drift to the ceiling before coming back to me, a small smile playing on his lips. "Come with me."

Taking my hand, he leads me from the marquee. But

instead of taking me to the house, we round the side of the property, and towards the fields that lead to the meadow.

"Mase, I don't have any shoes."

It's not overly cold out but the grass is getting dewy as the morning draws close, coating my feet in wet slush. "Anything to have me carry you." For what feels like the one hundredth time tonight, he lifts me into his arms. Striding through the grass, and over to the open gate. The last time we were in the meadow together was the day that Anthony died. I know this must bring back difficult memories.

I love him so much for being here, and all the more so for being here with a grin on his beautiful face.

He stops when we finally get to the top of the hill, dropping me down and looking out over the estate. We stand side by side, taking in the eerie silence.

"You haven't been out here in a while."

His throat bobs on a swallow, not taking his eyes from the estate. "Maybe not as long as you think."

What does that mean?

I'm about to ask him when he continues.

"Dad used to come sit here on the hill while we played on the lake."

He's someplace else right now; I don't say a word.

"They both did, every day from the day I was born they would walk around the grounds, until Mum got sick. I don't remember a lot, but I remember her shouting, telling me to slow down when I would race to the lake as fast as my legs would let me go." He sniggers. "Dad would tell her I was fine, but she always worried." He pauses for a moment. "It was always sunny!" He looks to me in question, a frown marring his brow, as if it's the most ridiculous thing in the world for the sun to shine. "As a kid, do you feel like it was always sunny?"

"Uh..."

"He loved the sun." He shakes his head. "Would be out here for hours every day, and long after we went to bed."

We stand looking over the estate, the view soothing something in the both of us. My eyes drift to the garden, still lit up with the lanterns. Scar must have forgotten about them, or she didn't want to turn them off. Mason's strong hand grips mine, warm but calloused.

I lick my lips, trying to decipher his thoughts and find the right thing to say. He seems lost in his own head again.

"I think in life, especially when it isn't all that fair to us, we have a habit of clinging to the good. We feed off it, making it seem better than it actually was."

Do we have a habit of making the good memories seem better than they had been, and the bad worse than it was? Because the bad always seems terrible looking back, but in the moment we always get through it, right?

"I don't feel like I cling on to anything from being here," he says. "Bad or good."

"It was always sunny," I state with a smile, squeezing his hand in mine.

When he finally turns and looks down at me, giving me a bright smile despite his saddened eyes, I know everything is going to be okay. "What now, my beautiful Pixie?"

I loved my Pixie then, Nina, and I love my Pixie now.

Feeling the need to lighten the mood, I look down at his shirt that I have on, then to the lake, letting my dimple pop as I bite my lip.

"It's fucking freezing, baby." He grins.

I take off down the hill, letting the wind whip through my hair as I run for the water's edge. Lifting the hem, I pull the shirt over my head and chuck it to the ground, then turn, finding Mason watching me as I slide off his boxers.

"You're fucking beautiful."

"Come with me." I turn and wade into the water, my eyes widening when I realise how cold it is.

"Shit," I mutter under my breath.

"Nina, you can't go in there," he chuckles as he calls out to me. "It's too cold this time of year."

"Don't be a wuss."

I turn to face him, daring him with my eyes to come to me. "Come make new memories under the moon with me, Mase!"

He eventually wades in, grabbing me the second he can reach me and tugging me to him. I search his eyes, needing to know he's okay. His nose rubs with mine as our foreheads touch.

I get the sense that tonight will be a night I'll never forget. A night that I look back on with the fondest memories, knowing without a doubt that they are as special in my memory as they were when we lived them.

"The suns gonna shine again, Bossman. I promise."

"It's freezing!" My teeth chatter as Mason crosses the path back to the house, with me held tight on his back.

"I did tell you." He chuckles. "You shouldn't have gone in."

The sun is just coming up, and as we pass his parents garden his grip tightens on my legs. I want to tell him to go in, but I know he won't, or he will and will resent me for pushing him into it. I tell myself that if he wanted to go in, he would. And he will, one day.

"I need a hot shower and sleep. God, I need so much sleep!" I moan against his bare neck as he climbs the steps to the house. He smells delicious; he smells like home.

"Shower, sex, sleep," he lists off.

"How about sex in the shower by yourself while I sleep."

He drops me, chuckling. "Shower sex by ourselves is never happening again."

His words ground me to a halt, my feet rooting to the terrace. What happens from here? He called me Pixie, but he didn't say he loved me before.

He doesn't trust me.

What now, my beautiful Pixie?

"It's not?"

"No. If you want to be fucked," He inches closer, circling my nipple through the wet shirt, "you come to—"

"Oh, I'm sorry, we were just heading out for a walk."

Mason clears his throat as Vinny appears on the terrace with a bright-eyed Ellis in his hold.

"Da Da Da Da." He claps.

"Good morning, Ellis baby." I look at Mason with a smile as I lean in and kiss his head.

Vinny looks at my soiled shirt and jacket—which Mason insisted I wore—then to Mason, a small smirk on his face. "I'll take Ellis around the grounds then come find you." He nods his head, chattering to Ellis as he walks away.

I turn back to Mason. "If I wanna be fucked I what, Mase?" I grin wide, trying to contain my laughter.

"You're gonna get it, Pix."

I laugh, running through the house and back up to our room.

———————

IT'S late afternoon when we are finally packed up and ready to go home. Lucy has a lift with Miller and me and Megan jump in with Elliot and Charlie.

Mason, to my surprise, is staying for the afternoon with Ellis and Scarlet.

They both asked me to stay, but I know that they need some time together and with me around, Mason can get a little distracted.

"Who wants to go to a pub?" Elliot asks. "I haven't been pub drunk in months."

Elliot is in an annoyingly good mood today, and Megan being the extrovert of the group, clings to his every word.

"Yes! Hair of the dog is exactly what I need right now."

Elliot smiles. "Charles?"

"You want to go out?" Charlie asks.

"It's been a while, Lance will be game."

"Where is Lance?" I frown, only now realising I didn't see him at breakfast.

"He left late last night, got in a huff about some shit and called a cab," Megan tells me.

"I will if Lance and Lowell do," Charlie says on a shrug.

"Mason has Ellis until tonight, but he can drop him back early and you guys can go out, I need to check on Joey." I wouldn't go out even if I wanted to. My stomach twists just thinking about him.

"Have you heard anything yet?" Megan asks.

I shake my head. "No."

"Lowell won't sack off Ellis time," Elliot says.

And it's true, Mason wouldn't miss another minute of his weekend with his son.

"Come on, Aldridge, I need you to wingman me. I was shit out of luck last night after I bid on Luce."

Me and Megan look at each other and raise our brows in unison.

"What was that all about?" Megan asks.

Elliot sits forward in his seat, lifting his seat belt and smoothing it over his shoulder. "I wasn't having it."

"You wasn't having what?" I ask.

He eyes me in the mirror as if it's obvious. "Vinny?"

"I'd totally jump Vinny." Megan laughs.

"Ewww, Megs!" I push her into the door.

"I'm kidding, he's like a dad to us."

"Exactly," Elliot says. "I wasn't having it be a joke on her." His face hardens. "That prick she is with needs some sense knocked into him."

Me and Megan look at each other at the same time again, then break out into giggles.

"I get it, Ell," Charlie tells him.

"You shouldn't laugh, Nina. Have you thought about the shit show that will go down when Hemmings comes for his date?"

Cooper. Fuck! I forgot about the auction.

"Surely he won't ask for a date? I think Mason made it perfectly clear she wasn't for sale."

"You haven't met Hemmings," Elliot tells Megan.

Charlie twists in his seat so he can see me. "Mase won't have you go anywhere without him, Nina. And I agree with

Megan, he'd have to be looking for a death wish to come asking for anything from you."

"You wanna bet on that?"

I roll my eyes as Charlie smiles over at Elliot, lifting his chin in challenge. "How much?"

"Fifty. It'll round up the pot for what you owe me from last night."

"Done. There's no way he'd be so fucking stupid."

"We shall see my friend."

"I'd appreciate it if you didn't bet on my odds, thank you very much!" I feign annoyance.

"Not you, little Pixie. Just dickhead Hemmings. You going to come for a drink or are we dropping you home?" he asks.

"Drop me home please, Ell."

I FEEL exhausted as I lug my overnight bag out the back of Elliot's car. I fell asleep on the ride home and now all I want to do is climb into my bed. Mason will have Ellis until a little later and I feel for him, he'll be just as tired as I am.

I go to my apartment to drop my bags off then shower and change, then I make my way to Joey's, hoping he is home.

Before I knock, I try the door but it's locked, which isn't out of the blue for Joey. Pulling out my keys, I unlock the door and enter his apartment.

I instantly know he's home.

The smell of something smoky assaults my senses, and the darkness from the closed curtains make it hard to see into the room.

"Joey?"

He doesn't answer me, and I huff as I step inside and turn on the light. Joey isn't in the lounge and apart from his discarded hoodie, everything is how I left it on Thursday. Trickling water sounds from the bathroom, and I frown as I move in that direction, pushing open the slightly ajar door.

"Joey?!" I panic.

I run to him, pushing on his shoulder as his head snaps up out of the water.

"What the fuck, Nina!" His eyes are wide and red-rimmed, his body jolting up in the bathtub.

"You were fucking asleep, Joe!" My heart is erratic in my chest, my hands shaking. "Your face was all but under."

"It wasn't."

"Yes, it was!" I snap. "Jesus! Do you know how dangerous it is! You could have..."

I cut myself off, feeling awful for what I was about to say.

"Say it," he spits, rubbing at the end of his nose with his palm.

"I'm sorry."

"Died." He chuckles. "I could have died."

I roll my lips. "When did you get back?"

"Last night." He looks up at me and then drops his eyes quickly. "Good night?"

My shoulders drop as the guilt sinks in. "Yeah, it was amazing."

He nods his head, water dripping from his hair onto his chest.

"I know you are hurting, and I can go, but—"

"I'd prefer it if you did."

"Joey, don't speak to me like that."

He pinches the bridge of his nose. "I don't want you here."

I stand wide-eyed, not knowing what the right thing to do is. Do I leave him?

"GET OUT!" he yells, making me jump. I turn and leave the bathroom quickly and pull the door shut behind me.

My eyes sting with tears as his words embed themselves, even though I know he doesn't mean them. Joey is good at being alone, it's the way it's been for a long time for him. I go to his kitchen and pour a glass of water, then pull down his medication box. He can yell at me all he likes.

I place the water on his dresser in his room and leave the pills beside the glass. The packet was half empty and I have no idea if he would have taken them when he was away. It was only a few days, but I don't know how much it would affect him.

Twenty minutes later, he pushes open the door. He doesn't enter the room, he just stands on the threshold with a towel wrapped around his hips.

"You okay?" I ask.

He chews on his bottom lip, his hands clenching twice before he steps into the room and over to his drawers. I watch him out of the corner of my eye as he picks out some joggers, pulling them on under his towel. He stuffs the two tablets into his mouth, swallowing them down dry.

I breathe a sigh of relief.

Without a word, he leaves the room, coming back a few minutes later with his hoodie pulled over him.

"I told you to leave." He walks to the small window and opens it.

"Joey—"

"You shouldn't be here."

"Are you okay?"

He sniggers then shakes his head. "No, Nina, I'm not okay. Is that alright with you?"

I step closer and place a hand on his back. "I will go. I'm sorry, I was only worried. You'll call me?"

When he doesn't say anything, I turn and walk towards his bedroom door.

"Nina," he says, sounding agitated.

I stop. "Yeah?"

He walks to where I stand and palms my cheek, taking me by surprise. I try not to flinch, but I can't help my reaction to his touch.

His eyes shine. "I'm sorry."

The second his head dips, I pull away. "Joey, what are you doing?"

He stares through me for a moment before his eyes find focus on mine. "Kiss me. Just once." He reaches for me again, this time grasping my neck. I turn my head to the side and his lips brush my cheek.

"Joey, stop!" I push on his chest and he stumbles back. "What are you thinking?!"

Tears fill my eyes and I stare at him, not understanding.

I turn and run from the apartment.

24

Nina

I PUSH OUT THROUGH THE APARTMENT DOORS OF JOEY'S building and hurry towards the taxi that's idling at the curb. I step back so the gentleman that is climbing from it can retrieve his coat then pull open the passenger door.

"Can I get in? I only have Apple pay."

"Sure."

Feeling relieved, I climb into the front seat and quickly close my eyes. Mason will be bringing Ellis home soon, but I don't want Joey coming after me.

"Rough morning?"

My eyes open and I turn to look at the driver. He gives me a smile that doesn't quite meet his eyes, then looks back to the road. "Yeah. It's been a day already."

Joey tried to kiss me.

Tears fill my eyes and I try to blink them away. I feel so stupid for all the times I defended him. I know he's hurting and he never would've done this if he wasn't, but Mason doesn't deserve it. Not when he's always believed Joey's intentions weren't pure. Maybe they weren't. But I trusted him to be my friend. I know this will hurt Mason. He'll be furious.

I text Mason and tell him that I'll meet him at his.

I know I have to tell him. After the weekend we've had together, I know we need to be honest with one another going forward. This has to work out. There's no one else I want to do this with.

I get to the penthouse and make my way to the elevator, using the code Vinny gave me last week. My phone rings just as the doors start to close. It's Mason.

"Hey."

"Hey, you're at mine?" he asks, sounding surprised.

"Yeah, I just got here." I roll my lips. "Could I stay tonight?" My voice cracks and I look to the ceiling.

"What's wrong?" I hear wood scraping across tile. He's still at the estate.

"I'm fine. I just needed to be close to you... after last night. Don't rush back, okay? I'm just being silly."

"Nina."

"Mase, I'm fine." I soften my voice and chuckle to try and persuade him that I'm okay. "I'll see you when you get back."

"We won't be long."

"Okay, love you." I hang up and drop my head back. Why does this have to be so difficult?

What was Joey thinking?

He wasn't thinking, I know that, and I already know that I can't expect Mason to understand. Because I wouldn't. I didn't. I just have to be straight with him.

The elevator pings and the doors slide open. Every muscle in my body relaxes as I take a step into the familiar space, but it's short lived. I stop short at the realisation that the lights are on. I walk to the edge of the wall that divides the foyer from the living area, then peek around it.

"Lance?" He lifts his head that was buried in his hands in a rush, and I know I've startled him as much as he has me.

"Nina. Where's Mase?"

"At the estate." I tilt my head to the side, frowning at the folder on the coffee table and the USB stick that sits on top of it. "What are you doing here?"

"I came to see Mase."

I nod, my eyes flicking to the coffee table again. "What's that?"

He steeples his hands in front of his mouth as he rocks on his bouncing knees. He doesn't look at me, his eyes focused on the folder. My stomach seems to freeze, turning my blood cold as I step closer.

"I fucked up—"

"Lance—"

"I watched it happen with Cara and I thought you were going to do it too. I-I—"

"Lance." I stop him, moving to sit next to him on the sofa. "Stop."

He turns his head, his hands falling from his face.

My body mirrors his on the sofa, but where his eyes burn into the side of my head, mine stay locked on the file. "You set him up, didn't you," I say in disbelief. "It was you."

"You'd been together a couple of months. I didn't think he was so deep and if I knew you were pregnant, Nina."

I turn my head towards him, his eyes wide and unfocused. "Lance."

"I'm so sorry, Nina. I couldn't keep it from you and Mase anymore, it's not right. I can't live with it."

I frown, shaking my head. "Did you plan it before hand? Did you plan it before Bora Bora?"

"I was off my face that night. It's no excuse but Lowell was fucking all over the place for months. Everything came out about Marcus and Cara, and I felt like everything I spent the year burying was being dug up."

"So after?" I ask, filling in the missing pieces. "You planned it after the holiday?"

"It was after you spoke to your mum on the phone. At the lodge. You told her you'd send her money and I read it all wrong. I read you so wrong, Nina, I'm so sorry."

A tear rolls down my cheek as I look at him. Lance has been in my home, he's spent hours and hours with my son, with me.

"You're in love with Scarlet," I say absentmindedly, my lip trembling. "What will she say? What will she do, Lance?"

He drops his head again, running his hands through his hair as he shakes his head no. "She told you about us?"

"No." I snigger, wiping the tears from my face. "It's painfully obvious though. It has been since Anthony passed away. I knew she wasn't alone."

"Does Mason know?" he questions.

"No. But it wouldn't've been long. He heard you last night in the kitchen."

He scrubs at his face, his body vibrating with pent-up energy. Mason will be home soon, and I have to tell him that Joey tried to kiss me. I have to tell him that the one thing I swore wouldn't happen, that I called him out on, happened. I have to hurt him a little bit, knowing it's the right thing to do so that we can take another step. A step towards our family.

"I'm so sorry. I'm so so sorry," Lance repeats, swiping at the corner of his eye. My gaze catches on the tattoo that peeks out from his rolled-up sleeves. Lavender branches wrap around his forearm in a spiral, disappearing under his shirt. "I have it all here, every copy of everything that was sent to me. I will stay away from you, from Scarlet too, I won't be around."

"He's your best friend."

"I know."

"She won't forgive you."

He grits his teeth as tears fall down his face that he refuses to wipe away. "I know."

I run my hands through my hair then stand, gathering up the USB and file. "Go home, Lance."

"I can't," he huffs. "It has to come from me."

"No. Go home, Lance."

"Nina."

"GO HOME, LANCE!" I yell, my own tears prickling my eyes. "You've caused so much unnecessary pain. You've kept me from my family," I cry. "But telling Mason that you did this won't lessen it. It won't change anything and it will break him. The boys too." My tears fall, and my stomach dips. Do I really want to keep this from him? Will it protect him like I need it to? "I want my family back now. I want to stop hurting him. I want to see him happy. I need to see him happy."

His face screws up almost painfully. "You want to keep it from him?"

"Not just him." My head tilts. "Mason would never forgive

you, and that would hurt both of you enough, but Scarlet wouldn't forgive you either."

He starts to openly cry, breaking down where he stands as his secrets marinate between us. It has my brows drawing in as I fight to keep myself from going to him. "Nina, I don't deserve her."

I shrug. "Maybe not, but Scar's the only person who gets to decide that. Telling them won't change this, Lance. It only brings it all back, for us all."

"I don't know what to do."

"Go home," I tell him, layering it with all the conviction I can scrape from the depths of me. "You've made a lot of mistakes. We all have. But don't let her be one of them."

His nostrils flare as he steps up to me. His head shakes with fear, gratitude, reluctance—I don't know, but I let him pull me into him. Amongst the anger, pain and uncertainty I feel inside of me, I know that this man loves the very same people I do. He wouldn't act out of malice—not towards them. It's a fierce thing, love. It's dangerous. I've hurt Mason so many times. Every time I've run, every time I've found annoyance in his giving, and each and every time I didn't believe him. I don't deserve his love any more than Lance because I left him. I made a mistake far more detrimental than Lance's. I did what I never dreamed I'd do. I walked away from my family.

Maybe I don't deserve his love at all.

"You're more than he could ever wish for. You came along right when he needed you and I'm sorry I didn't see that."

Lance leaves and I dispose of the files, burning them out on the balcony and washing the remnants away once I'm finished. Then I do all I can to damage the USB before putting it in the bin.

───────

MASON WALKS through the door not an hour after our phone call, yet it feels like days—a lifetime. I smile despite the unease I feel and stand from the sofa to take the changing bag from him. Ellis is asleep in his arms, and he whispers with a frown, "I'm going to take him up."

I nod my head, watching as he disappears up the stairs.

I have to do this.

It's better for everyone.

Mason finds me in the kitchen once he has Ellis settled in his bed. His face is full of concern as he walks towards me. "What is it, Angel?" I wrap myself in him the second I can reach him, and he holds me, his hands slipping under my T-shirt so he can run his hands up my back. "Nina."

"I'm sorry," I tell him.

"Sorry for what?" he says defensively, pulling away from me.

"I need you to promise me something—"

"Nina," he grits out.

"Promise me that you will trust me enough to let this go. I know I don't deserve it and I've not given you enough reason to... but I need you to know that I will let *him* go. Because I need this to work. You and Ellis are my only priority, and we have to make this work." I rush out the words. My gaze locked on his.

"Who? Who will you let go?" he snaps, clearly confused.

"Joey." I draw in a deep breath. "Promise me, Mase."

He scowls down at me, his brows furrowing as his spine straightens. "What did he do?"

"He tried to kiss me."

He doesn't move. Doesn't flinch. Doesn't do anything. But inside I get the feeling that he's at boiling point. "Mase, I would never have gone to his apartment if I knew he was in the state he was in, if I knew he'd come at me." I grab his hand as I try to make him understand. "His brother died just a few days ago and I wanted to check in, that's it. I won't see him for a while. I'm telling you because this—we—mean so much more than what he did and I won't let it set us back, not when I feel so damn close to having you again."

"You said he tried to kiss you."

I nod. "I'm so sorry for putting you in this position."

He swallows thickly again, taking a rough breath in then scrubbing a hand over his mouth. "I'll fucking kill him."

"Mase." I panic.

"I know!" he snaps, turning away from me and leaning against the kitchen island.

"I pushed him away. Nothing happened, and I left right away. I won't go back to his again."

"Did he hurt you?" His voice is sharp, deadly even.

"No." I watch his back, wanting to reach out and touch him but not knowing how he'd react. "What are you going to do?" I ask.

He lifts his head, eying me over his shoulder. "Nothing." He sniggers. "Not a damn thing." There's an instant relief that comes with his words, but also huge shock. I stand in wonder as to whether I've heard him correctly. "I've never doubted your faithfulness, Nina. I don't like this, but I won't let it come between us. We're going to make this work this time. Me, you, Ellis."

My chin wobbles and I try to stop it, covering my face with my hands. "I'm sorry."

My tears break as his arms wrap around me. "Shh," he soothes, rubbing a hand over my back. "It's okay."

I breathe in a lungful of air, hoping it will stop the emotion that's bubbling in my throat. I need my family, and if that means carrying Lance's betrayal and taking a step away from Joey then that's the price I pay.

"I didn't know what you'd say. I thought you'd push me away."

When he doesn't say a word, I pull back so I can see him. After last night, I hate the thought of him not being himself with me.

"Mase."

"Hmmm." He stares down at me, his face hard and his body strung tight.

My hands smooth over his shoulders in the hope that it will relax him. "Thank you," I tell him. "For not making this what it could have been. You have every right to be mad."

"I'm not mad, at least not at you." His eyes pinch in as he squeezes my hips. "I'm trying here, Nina."

"I know, I can see that." I smile gingerly up at him, my love for him growing to impossible levels as the seconds pass.

"Don't," he rasps out, dropping his forehead to mine.

"Don't what?"

"That fucking smile." His thumb dusts over my cheek.

"I love you, Mason Lowell," I tell him, not blinking as I lean in and peck at his lips. He shuffles closer, his jaw clenching as if he's fighting to keep his words to himself. "What is it?" I ask.

My body heats as his nostrils flare. His hand comes up to grip my chin, our lips all but touching. "I want to hurt him. I want to cause him pain." I frown, hating myself for caring so much. "But more than that, I want to fuck you. I want the world to see me take you so that they know you're mine, and that nobody else can have you."

"You could just fuck me here so that I know," I suggest, even though he has my pulse racing with his words.

He shakes his head no. "I'm mad at myself," he states. "We aren't doing this again."

"Doing what?" I ask, concern lacing my voice as he steps away. His cheeks are flushed and I can very clearly see his erection straining behind his trousers.

"I'm serious about getting this right, Nina." Reaching out, he smooths his hand over my cheek, then wraps it around my neck. His hands on me, possessing me in a way only he ever has. It brings me right back down to where I need to be. "I won't sleep with you. It's the only thing we're good at. We need to learn to do everything else. I want to do this properly."

"You. Mason Lowell... Do not want to have sex." I blink. "Have I got that correct?"

"We are going to date instead." He frowns as he says it as if the idea is only now coming to him. "No sex."

"What?" I snap, a smile tugging on my lips. "Mase..." I reach out, palming his straining length through his trousers. "Have we not deprived ourselves for long enough?"

He growls deep in his throat, grinding his hips into my hand. The sound calls out to my wicked soul.

I squeeze him.

"Nina, I'm serious. I want to try it my way." He steps away from me, his eyes heavy-lidded and tired. Probably due to the lack of sleep last night.

"But sex is your way. You think I couldn't go without it?" I smile up at him. "You forget I went over a year!" I step back, biting my lip to suppress my laugh. "I'll date you. No sex."

"Good." He nods.

"Good?" I question.

He's gone mad. I can't wait to see how long this will last.

"Yes, good. Now come to bed with me." He pulls me by the hand and out of the kitchen.

"We can't sleep together, people who date don't sleep together."

Leaning in, he kisses me. It's deep and loving and everything that I needed. "Get up those stairs and into my bed. Now," he groans against my lips.

Backing me up the stairs, he places light kisses to my lips, pausing every now and then, letting our lips linger. We walk through the bedroom door and my legs hit the back of the bed. Then I'm falling to the mattress with him on top of me.

He looks down at me, running his hand down my tank, exposing my bra. "Promise me when I—"

I cut him off with a shake of the head. "Nope!" I grin. "I can't promise you that."

He wets his lips, smiling lazily. "Good girl." Climbing from the bed, he goes to his draw and fishes out a T-shirt, then tosses it to me. I watch as he pulls back the covers and then starts to unbuckle his belt.

His gaze meets mine. "Go get changed."

This man has seen every inch of me, discovered every

inch of me. Yet he expects me to go hide away to change. I smile as I slip into the bathroom, pulling the tee over my head and letting it fall to my thighs.

Tonight has been bittersweet. I feel sad about lying to Mason by not telling him about Lance, and I still don't know how I will fully forgive him for what he's done. But if I can't forgive Lance, how can I ever expect Mason to forgive me? And he's going to try, despite his lack of trust in me he wants to try this. He wants to date me. I smile and look into the mirror, cringing when I see my red blotchy eyes. It will be hard not seeing Joey, and I feel like I'm betraying him by not being there when he probably needs me most, but I also know that this will be a new beginning for me and Mason. Ellis too. I can't let anything else get in our way.

I leave the bathroom and round the bed, feeling his eyes on me the entire time. Crawling under the sheets, I roll to my side to face him. His arm reaches out, curling around my waist and pulling me into him. Our legs entwine, slotting us together like a perfect jigsaw puzzle—creased corners and all.

It's been too long since I've been here, in this bed and in his arms. Tears flood my eyes, but I don't let them show.

"Mase," I whisper against his warm chest, his woodsy scent making me heady.

"Hmmm," he mutters, already sounding sated.

"I love you."

25

Nina

"Hey." I smile as I drop onto the sofa next to Megan at the Elm. I pluck out the menu and open it.

"Hey," Lucy says sceptically. "You've got a spring in your step this morning. Everything okay? You didn't call me back last night and then missed our chat."

"I turned off my phone once Mason and Ellis came home. I had nearly four hundred WhatsApp messages this morning." I eye them all with a look that tells them I think they're idiots. Or at least that's what I'm trying to portray.

Scarlet looks at me with a soft smile. "Are you okay, though? Mason was worried when he left last night."

This morning in the shower I broke down in tears to Mason. I don't know why he accepted my reasoning, but he did. I don't feel good about cutting off Joey. Simple. I don't want to care, but I do. His brother has just died and I feel like the worst friend in the world turning my back on him.

"Something happened with Joey when I went to check on him yesterday."

"Like what?" Megan asks.

I swallow, feeling stupid. Like Mason, the girls all warned me that Joey had feelings for me, which I wasn't blind to. I just didn't ever expect him to cross the line. "He tried to kiss me."

"Wow," Lucy mutters.

"What the fuck, Nina," Megan snaps. "Were you going to tell us? Does Mason know?" she gasps.

"Mason knows. That's why I went to his last night. I knew I had to tell him."

"Are you okay?" Lucy asks.

I shrug, biting my cheek to stop my eyes from welling. "Yes and no. Mason was amazing, and I couldn't ask for the situation to be better with him right now."

"Oh, I love this." Lucy grins. "I feel proud of you both already. Tell me more."

"I'm not going to see Joey for a while."

She rolls her lips, tucking her hair behind her ear. "I actually think that's a good idea. He's been at the centre of some of your arguments with Mason these last couple months."

"I know. And it was my choice, but I worry so much about him, girls."

"Because of his brother?" Lucy asks.

I nod. "He isn't right. It scares me to think he's in that apartment on his own at the best of times but now that this has happened it scares me. I found him in the bath on Sunday. He was asleep, and I had to wake him. He's always been Joey, you know. I've never seen how his illness affects him when it's bad, but he isn't acting himself and I don't know if that's because of his brother or because he isn't taking his medication."

"He has bipolar, right?"

"Schizophrenia," I correct her.

"He'll be okay, babe," Lucy tells me, placing a hand on mine.

"I hope so."

"I know this is hurting you, Nina," Megan says, sipping her coffee, "but I think this will be a good thing. You and Mason made big steps this past month. You have a chance to get your family back here."

"I know."

"And maybe it will mean Joey makes new friendships. He seems stuck on you."

"I think Joey cares. Maybe too much at times but he isn't a bad person."

"So you and Mason are okay?"

"Yes, but he wants to take things slow." I smile down at my lap. "We're going to date."

"Slow?" Megan laughs. "Mate, you can't fuck him yesterday then be like... Oh, we're taking it slow today."

The girls all chuckle in agreement with her.

"You know what I mean. I already know he won't last five minutes." I laugh. "We're just not going as fast as last time."

"Definitely... like condoms this time, right?" Scarlet jokes and I chuck a salt packet at her head. "But, Nina, if you want me to, I can check in on Joey? Maybe send over some bereavement leaflets or something? Just to check in so you don't have to stress."

"You'd do that?" I ask.

374 | JC HAWKE

"Of course! I get what it's like to lose someone you love. Maybe it will be good coming from me?"

"If you could, that would be amazing, Scarlet. Thank you."

I relax in my seat and look over at Lucy who is watching me in thought. She gives me a soft wink and smile. *It's going to be okay.* For the first time in a long time, things seem to be falling into place.

Mase

AFTER THE DAY I've had, I almost forgo my evening workout. But knowing Nina is working, and after her leaving me before the sun was even up, I drag myself up the steps of L&M at ten past five for my evening PT session. She's working with a client when I reach the top step, so I go to the treadmill and start with a jog. I watch her as she helps the lady with her weights, taking off the larger one and dropping down a size. She is reassuring her; I can tell by the way she's looking at her.

Sometimes I wonder how she is as caring and selfless as she is. It pisses me off and makes me love her all in one big eye roll. The way she has to be there for her friends, up and leaving if one of them needs her. Like Joey yesterday. Or the way she used to help her mother, when she spent her life never helping herself. Another thing I need to fix.

Nina has the same support from her friends that she gives out, but she doesn't have the family. After my weekend with

Scarlet, it makes me angry that she hasn't ever had what I have. All because of her parents.

"Hey, you!" Nina bounces up next to me, a smile playing on her sexy lips. "You look wrecked." She frowns, placing her hands on her hips.

I shake my head, smiling down at her. "I have this wench that kept me up all Saturday night."

"Hmm, is she hot?" She waggles her brows at me.

"She's alright." A bright smile spreads across her face, making my heart somersault in my chest. "Are you okay now, after this morning?"

She nods her head, her lip turning up on one side. "Can I show you something?"

The excitement in her eyes makes me grin, and I come to a stop on the treadmill. "Of course."

Nina

I HAVEN'T HAD a lot of time to think about my dancing recently, but after the weekend and the way things are going with Mase, I'd like to think it's something I could go back to soon. The girls from my old studio have all moved onto other companies, so I wouldn't have it for classes. Or I wouldn't expect it to take off right away anyway—it's been too long. But to just dance again, feel the music like I used to—for the first time in a long time I feel excited about it.

Linking my fingers through Mason's, I walk us through the gym and over to the door that leads to the room above the gym. I haven't told anyone but Joey about the space yet, and other than Logan, no one else knows about it.

"What's up there?" Mason asks, looking up the steps in wonder.

"It's a surprise!" I jog up the steps, not feeling afraid of the small dark space with Mason at my back. "Logan told me I could do what I want with it." I push open the door, letting the light hit my face. I smile wide as he steps past me. I don't tell him what it is. He'll know what's in my head. If anything, he'll already be plotting how he can make it everything I want it to be—and I have to be okay with that.

I walk to the window to look out across the city, giving Mason a minute to take in the room.

"You have plans for it?" he asks, sliding his hands around my waist as he stands behind me, his nose brushing my temple.

A smile pulls at my lips. I continue to look out the floor-to-ceiling window. "Eventually, maybe when Ellis is a little older." I run my hands over his where they rest over my stomach. "I already feel like I'm away from him too often. I miss him so much after the weekend."

"It was just one weekend, and it was well worth it." His lips nip at my jaw, his hand dusting the underside of my breast. "We won't be spending weekends apart anymore, angel."

I twist my head to look at him. "We won't?" I ask hopefully.

Pulling me back into him, he buries his face in my neck, sucking on the skin there. "You smell edible." I can feel his erection in his gym shorts, and I instinctively push back against him.

His hand dips into my leggings, sliding his fingers through my heat. "I need you. I need you so fucking much."

"Mase," my hoarse whimper pulls me back to the now and I grasp his arm. "What are you doing?" I pull on his arm, removing his hand from my underwear as I spin to face him.

He groans, dropping his mouth back to my neck once I'm facing him.

"Mason!" I laugh. "You said no sex."

His beautiful, confused face pops back up. "Come on, Pix." He looks down at his gym shorts then back to me.

My smile is instant. Leaning in he places a kiss on my dimple. "*You* said we had to date. No more sex until we get this right between us."

"And you choose this point in our relationship to actually take heed?" he sniggers, licking at his full lips.

"This will be good for us. They were your words."

"I got it wrong." He pinches my nipple.

"Well, it makes sense. I think we should try."

"Nina." He takes hold of my hips.

"Mason." I smile, brushing his lips with my own.

"Baby," he pleads.

Our kiss is messy and broken from our smiles. "It may be a silly rule, Mr Lowell." I breathe out against his open mouth. "But... I think we should stick to it."

His hands slide into the back of my tights, and he palms my ass. I giggle to myself as a deep sigh leaves him. "Fine. But our first date is tonight."

"I can't tonight. I need to speak to Joey." I run my fingers through the hair at the base of his neck. "I need to explain things to him. I just left yesterday, and I need to tell him not to come to mine again. I need to get my key."

Mason's jaw clenches, his body growing tighter.

"Mase, he was my friend. I need him to know why I'm doing this."

"You'll come over after?"

I watch him, his face still hard. I love this man. So damn much. "I will."

He nods, looking down his nose at me. "I need you to consider something for me... about Jasmine."

"What's that?" I ask.

"We will speak about it tonight—"

"On our date." I grin, excited.

"Yeah, on our date." He places a soft kiss on my lips. "Are you going to PT me or should I find something else for you to work on?" He grasps my hand and covers his still hard cock.

I chuckle into his chest. "You're quite simply the most impossible man I've ever met."

I'VE BEEN TRYING to think of the right thing to say to Joey all day. Nothing seems to sound right, or fair, yet he tried to kiss me. He crossed the line and now I have to fix that before our friendship is completely ruined.

When he doesn't answer, I pull out my set of keys and unlock the door.

"Joey?" I call.

The wheels of his desk chair grate across the wood floor, sliding until he appears at his bedroom door.

"Hi," he mutters, running his hand through his hair and twisting his neck.

I'm surprised to find him so bright eyed. Especially after

how I found him yesterday. "Hi... how are you today?" I ask, not going any farther into the room and putting off bringing up the real reason for being here. "You seem better."

"Fine," he says, quickly. "Working."

I nod. "Of course, you have prints going out soon, right?"

"No. I cancelled them. I have something else I'm working on."

I openly frown. Because what the hell? "You cancelled them?"

"Yeah. Do you want a drink?" His eyes blink rapidly and he shakes his head in frustration.

Joey stands from his chair, crossing to the kitchen and getting a drink.

"No." I swallow the lump in my throat. Why is he acting like nothing happened? "I need to talk to you, Joey."

"Yeah?"

I stand next to him at the sink, trying to figure out what to say. "I need to take a step back from our friendship." My eyes burn with the words. "I need to focus on my family for a while."

"Family?" he asks, nodding.

He thinks I'm being insensitive. "Just for a while, I'll still be around. I just won't be dropping in."

"I don't need you dropping in." He gives me an awkward look that makes me frown. "Did you want something else?" He looks past me, flexing his fists before pointing past me. I follow his line of sight to his bedroom. "I got work."

There's a calm that comes over him. It's as if he hasn't even heard me. He was so upset yesterday and now he's like this. "Yeah, that was it. I should have texted before coming, sorry."

He slips past me, disappearing into his room.

I go to the door and open it, but something stops me from leaving.

Backtracking, I go to his room and walk to his computer chair. He's working on an image on the screen. It isn't clear what it is, but it holds every colour you could think of. "Joey."

"Hmm."

"I'm going to go now." I pull the card with Vinny's number that he gave me last year from my purse and slide it onto the desktop. "Will you call this number if you need anything?"

He looks at it, then to me. His eyes are emotionless, piercing straight through me. "Okay."

Turning away from me, he starts working on the image again, as if I'm not here. My eyes blur with tears and I quickly lean down and wrap my arms around his body, resting my head on his. This doesn't feel right. But I don't say anything more. Standing straight and wiping my eyes, I leave his apartment, knowing I won't be back for a while.

VINNY ARRIVES SHORTLY after seven to pick me and Ellis up. When I got back from Joey's, Maggie was waiting at mine and I ended up telling her everything. She thinks I've made the right decision, which coming from Maggie means a lot to me. She agrees that Scarlet should go and check in with him in a couple days. It will make me feel better and I really do think it will be good for him to get help and support after the news about his brother.

"Hello, love," Vinny says, rounding the bonnet and taking

the two bags I had packed for me and Ellis. "You're both staying at the penthouse tonight?" he observes.

I nod, taking a deep breath in. I need to try and push my emotions aside regarding Joey. I have my own life to fix. "Yeah, I'm going to stay in the spare room. But I think it's a good step." I bounce on the balls of my feet. "This is progress, Vin."

He chuckles, placing a hand on my back and guiding me towards the car. "The spare room." He shakes his head.

"Yes, the spare room."

He gives me an amused look. Is it so hard to believe that we can stay away from each other? We did it for over a year.

"Come on, Mason will be waiting for you."

We are in the car and on the way to the penthouse when a thought comes to me. "Vinny, you must have my father's name, right?"

I watch as his hands tighten on the steering wheel. "Yes."

"I would like it if possible, and his address if you have it?" I know he does.

He pauses for a second and I narrow my gaze on him. "I think you should speak to Mason—"

"No," I tell him. "I'm asking you for a reason. I want you to come with me."

His brows shoot up as he turns to look at me. "Come with you?"

"To meet him. Mason won't have me go alone, and I don't want him to come. I'll tell him that I'm going and that you'll take me."

"What's brought this on, love?" he asks.

I look at my hands and contemplate lying before thinking better of it. "Everything with Jasmine..."

Vinny nods his head. "She doesn't know him."

I flick my eyes to him. That surprises me.

"She doesn't have contact with her mother either. Hasn't since she left school. She doesn't even know who her father is."

Why did I think it would've been different for her? "What is she like?"

"A lot like you."

My eyes lift to his face, a wide smile stretched across it. "You have a new favourite now?" I say, messing with him.

"That's impossible." He winks.

I rest my head back on the seat. My eyes close momentarily, giving myself a minute to think about what I want. "Do you think I should meet him?"

"Your father?"

"Hmm," I mumble.

When he doesn't answer right away, I open my eyes and search his face. It's hard and I get a feeling that he knows a lot more than necessary about the man.

"That's up to you, Nina."

26

Nina

THE MOMENT WE ENTER THE PENTHOUSE, I'M FLOORED BY THE sheer effort Mason has gone to for the evening.

"Where is your daddy, baby?" I whisper to Ellis, placing a kiss on his head.

Stepping into the room, I take in the dinner table that's set for the three of us. A large bouquet of red roses adorns the centre of the table and candles sit on either side. The lights are dipped low, and everything feels warm, special. Reaching out I pinch a petal between my thumb and forefinger.

"Hello," his deep voice purrs from behind me.

I turn. "Hi."

"Dadee," Ellis sings.

Mason's gaze holds mine for a moment with an intensity that makes me blush. All I can do is stare back, completely lost in his eyes. Stepping forward he takes Ellis from me, sitting him on his arm and then reaches out to push my hair behind my ear. Leaning in, he kisses my cheek. "You okay?"

I nod, knowing he's talking about Joey. "I didn't think to dress up." I look down at my leggings and baggy tee, then back up at his navy shirt and trousers. His hair is a tousled mess, but with obvious effort. He looks delicious.

"You're perfect," he tells me.

I smile, rocking back on my heels as I try to control my breathing. "Something smells good."

"I ordered in. Has Ellis ate?"

"Yeah. He ate with Maggie."

"Perfect." He smiles, and it's full of mischief. "Come with me."

He starts towards the stairs with Ellis in his arms.

"Where are you going?" I ask.

I follow him when he doesn't answer me, only muttering something to Ellis that I can't hear. It's surprising how normal it feels being here. It's been so long since I've felt at home. I get the same grounding feeling when we sleep at the estate, but my apartment feels like four walls. There's no comfort in it.

Mason walks into his bedroom and through to Ellis's. "Mummy, can you get the changing mat? It's in the bottom of the walk-in wardrobe."

My brows rise in surprise as I walk to the door on the other side of the room. I try to contain my gasp when I open it, but it's no use. What almost one-year-old needs this many clothes? He will never wear it all. I spot the changing mat on top of the dresser and quickly grab it for Mason.

"Here." I place it on the floor next to where he's stripping Ellis of his clothes. "Does he wear all that stuff?" I ask, nodding over my shoulder.

"Some of it," he says without looking up.

I nod, not passing comment on what a waste of money it is. If this is ever going to work between us, I need to get over the fact that Mason has money. He knows not to buy me expensive things and I know to get the hell on with it when he does it anyway.

Mason dresses Ellis into his pyjamas then spends well over five minutes raining kisses all over his small torso, making Ellis wriggle and giggle until he gets the hiccups.

"Oh man! Not the hiccups!" Mason says, looking down at Ellis with a wide smile on his face. Ellis continues to giggle while I watch on.

"Well done, Daddy," I tut, kneeing Mason in the ribs. He grunts and falls to the side—I barely touched him. "Come here, baby." I kneel to lift Ellis from the changing mat.

Just as I slide my hands under his armpits, Mason grabs me around the waist and pulls me to the ground, tickling my ribs.

"Mason! No!"

Ellis seems to find it hilarious, crawling over and bouncing on his knees beside my head.

I laugh uncontrollably in Mason's arms, trying to catch my breath so I can tell him to stop. "Mase!" I cry out. "Please!"

He finally lets up, leaving both of us breathless. His body is spread behind me, and his hand brushes my hip as he leans across to tap Ellis's nose. "See. It worked."

Ellis pats his knees as he bounces in excitement, his dimples set deeper than I've ever seen them before. If I could wish for anything, it would be to have my son feel this glee every day for the rest of his life.

"Mummy" —Mason leans in, kissing my cheek again—

"is going to get in the bath. Daddy will put Ellis to bed and then warm up dinner."

I pull my lip into my mouth, looking up at him with so much love and adoration. "Do I smell or something?"

His scruff rubs along my neck as he whispers in my ear. "Fucking edible, angel."

I stand and give Ellis a kiss good night, then as ordered I go to Mason's en suite. The bath is still steaming, bubbles filling it to the top. There's a robe lying across the chair, a rose placed on top of it along with a bottle of champagne and chocolates left on the steps leading to the bath.

The happiness coursing through me is everything I've wanted—needed for the last year and a half. Yet there's a guilt eating away at me, reminding me of the selfish thing I did to get here.

***

Mase

NINA TAKES her time in the bath which doesn't surprise me. It's been a while since she's been here and I can't imagine the bath at the apartment is quite the same as the one here. She used to spend hours in the tub after a day in the studio.

I'm pouring myself a beer when her arms slink around my waist. "I was waiting for you to join me, Bossman," she purrs.

I can't help the smile that splits my face. "You wouldn't have let me in."

"Hmm, we all know what happens when you give a girl champagne."

I turn, smoothing my hands down the back of her robe. "Had I known you'd have let me in." I kiss her, meaning to make it a quick peck, but losing all train of thought when she deepens the kiss. I grasp her jaw in my hand as I take over, pushing her back to the island as my tongue licks through her mouth.

"Mase," she breathes breathlessly against my lips.

Lifting her at the waist, I place her on the island, sliding myself between her smooth legs as her hands work on pulling my shirt free from my trousers. I let her do her thing, my eyes on her dainty fingers that work my buttons.

"Mase," she purrs. "We should have dinner, right?"

I lift my gaze to hers, my cock growing stiffer behind my zipper with the look in her eyes.

We're both fucked.

Slowly, I loosen the tie at her waist, keeping my eyes locked on hers as I use my finger to nudge open one side of her robe. "Oops," I mutter.

Her full round breast is exposed to me, and I drop my eyes to her hip noticing she's completely bare. Pushing her hair over her shoulder, I give her a long, wet kiss, then run my lips down her neck to her chest, taking her stiff nipple into my mouth. I bite down.

"Ouch!" she cries.

I continue down her side, running my mouth over her exposed hip and thigh. Flicking my eyes up, I watch her head drop back, rolling to the side then falling back to me.

I don't ask if she wants more, it's clear to my own eyes what she needs. My hand slides into the other side of her robe. I push it aside, letting it fall off her shoulder and onto the counter.

"Jesus Christ," I groan, dropping my head to her stomach before I come in my pants just from looking at her.

I feel her stomach jiggle against my stubble as she laughs lightly, running her hands through my scalp. I place a kiss on her stomach then lift my head. Closing my eyes and leaning into her touch.

"What have you done to me?" I sigh.

"I've made your ass mine, Bossman. That's what I've done to you."

I take her nipple again, biting down on the hard nub. "That cockiness will get you fucked, angel."

"Fucked? I don't think I've ever been fucked before."

I arch a brow at her. "No?"

She shrugs a shoulder, her chocolate eyes fixed on me. "Not that I remember, I've had some good sex."

"Good sex." I nod, licking my lips.

She giggles, pulling my head up and demanding my lips. I place my hand to the base of her throat and guide her back to the counter. The very tips of my fingers trail down the centre of her chest until I meet her pussy. I bring my other hand up and then grip each of her legs, bringing them up and placing them on the counter. "Are you going to fuck me now?" Her lip twitches despite her best efforts to control it.

"No, Pix. I'm going to have my dinner."

She chuckles as I slide my hands under her thighs and up to grip her full hips. I lift her at the ass and onto my waiting mouth.

A sigh falls from her parted lips, her head dropping back to the marble with a thud. Her hips lift voluntarily as I flatten my tongue, slowly licking up through her slickened folds. "I could live off of the taste of you." I bite down on her swollen clit and her hips jolt under my hold. I grip her tighter, my tongue swirling over her as I nip and suck until she's trembling beneath me. Lifting my thumb to her mouth, I slide it past her lips, her teeth scraping along the skin. "Suck."

She does as I ask, hollowing her cheeks and drawing my thumb deep into her mouth. I pull back, letting it pop and place it on her now pulsing clit.

"Oh god," she moans.

I apply the slightest of pressure, sliding my thumb down to trace her slick pussy until I reach her opening. I dip my thumb inside and suck her clit into my mouth. She tenses around me, her legs locking my head in place. "So fucking tight," I groan.

She whimpers as I pull away from her, lifting herself up onto her elbows to look at me.

"Do you know how good you taste?" I ask, licking up the side of my thumb then offering her a taste with my hand stretched out to her.

She gives me a devilish smirk then leans forward, grasping my wrist. She pulls my hand to her mouth. Starting at my pinkie, she starts to suck each of my fingers into her mouth. I watch her in fucking awe.

When she reaches my slickened thumb, she stops. Leaning in, she bites the pad, then places a kiss on my palm. "This is for you," she whispers, directing my thumb to my own mouth.

I suck every inch of her off my skin, then take her lips in mine again in a rushed frenzy.

With our mouths still locked, she blindly reaches for my trousers, finding the button easily and shoving them down my legs.

My mouth drops to her neck, her hands roaming over my head, holding me in place when I reach her nipple. "Don't stop," she begs.

"Hmmm, I need inside." Grasping my cock, I glide it through her folds before pushing the tip inside.

"Condom!" she shouts. "We have to use a condom!"

"What? We didn't on Saturday."

"We are now!"

"No," I snap, sliding into her to the hilt.

"Mason," she murmurs, her teeth scraping my shoulder.

"There's never been anything between us, Nina. I'm not about to start now."

She groans into my neck, and I lift her from the island, letting her legs drop and her pussy slides deeper onto me. I squeeze my eyes tight as I fight for control.

Her hot tongue traces my lips. "Are you going to fuck me now?"

I pop open an eye and find her smiling up at me. Her cheeks are flushed, her eyes dazed and heavy. "You're already fucked, Pixie."

I roll my hips, and her smile drops. "But if you really want it... I can have you," I thrust hard into her, wrapping an arm around her back and forcing her down onto me, "completely." Another thrust. "And utterly." Thrust. "Fucked!"

My balls draw up as Nina claws at my skin, trying to get even closer as she wraps herself around me.

"Fuck," I groan, pounding harder, faster.

"Yes!" Nina cries out into my neck, her pussy clenching like a vice around me.

I pump into her three more times, then I'm coming right along with her.

"I REALLY DIDN'T THINK I'd cave so easily."

I chuckle at Nina's admission, smiling up at the ceiling as I lie sprawled out on my sofa with her on top of me. "Nah, I knew we wouldn't last a day."

She lifts up onto her arm to look at me, her warm hand smoothing over my chest. "You? Sure. Me? Nope. Didn't think I'd cave."

"This is *all* on you," I tell her. "I didn't seduce you in the kitchen with my tits."

"Uh, thankfully you didn't, no. But you did seduce me with the whole daddy, mummy, Ellis vibe, and 'go get naked in my tub' tactic." She arches her sharp brow at me. "I'm not stupid, Mr Lowell."

I pull her back down so she's flush against me. "I wanted to cheer you up. I knew you'd be sad when you came here."

She doesn't say anything for a minute, her finger tracing circles on my chest. "He didn't get mad. He didn't really do or say anything."

Probably because he's a fucking psycho. "He probably saw it coming."

"Hmm," she hums, not delving any deeper into it. "What did you want to tell me about Jasmine?" she asks.

My hand falls to her hair, sliding the silky strands between my fingers. "I told you she's going through social services to get her children back."

"Yeah," she sighs.

"She's not a bad person, you know. She's working to get her life straight again. It's the only reason I gave her the job and a place to stay."

"I'm glad you did," she murmurs, barely audible.

"You are?"

She props herself up on her arms so she can see my face. "She would've been pregnant, right? If she has a child the same age as Ellis. I don't know why she did it, but I can only imagine the situation she must have been in for that to ever become a scenario. I don't know. It just seems awful to think about."

"From what we saw, I'd say her boyfriend had a lot to do with the why. She was afraid of us."

"Us?"

"Me and Charlie. We went to her flat. There were drugs, it was damp and mouldy, and she had Betty, her baby, living amongst it all." I grimace just thinking about it.

She purses her lips, a sad expression on her face. "Do you think you took her in because of Ellis?"

"Maybe. I knew I couldn't leave her there though." I roll to face her, wanting her to understand my reasoning. "But I also wanted something—someone for you. Family, Nina, real family."

She watches her own hand as it runs through my hair again. "I know, and I love you for it."

"Would you consider meeting her, properly?" I ask, hopeful.

She doesn't say anything right away, her brow creasing as her beautiful mind works. I give her a moment, not trying to push her into anything.

"One day. I think I could one day." Her gaze meets mine again. "But right now, it seems a little soon. I feel like we're only now finding our new dynamic as a family and there's so much room to fuck it up. I'm sure I will fuck it—"

"Shut up with that," I cut her off, squeezing her hip.

"But it's not a no, and I want to know more about her." She shrugs. "I'm intrigued."

"Of course, you are." I give her a soft smile as I smooth a hand over her back.

"I want to meet my dad too." My heart seems to jolt in my chest at her words, my body running hot with unease. "I haven't heard from Mum since before Ellis was born. I've reached out but haven't heard a thing back. I don't think I can do any more than that, but I could try my dad." She looks up at me again sheepishly and I try to relax my features. "I spoke to Vinny about it today."

How do I tell her, her father is a fucking oxygen thief? How do I tell her that I know exactly why her mother hasn't been in touch? Keeping things from Nina now will only come back and kick me in the ass. But it's been a day, and I don't necessarily want her to kick me in the ass now either.

I don't want to disappoint her.

Not when things are so good.

"I can see if I can get hold of your mum." (Not a lie.)

"I wouldn't bother. I've lost all hope for the woman," she says it with disdain, but I know she hurts. She only ever wanted her mother to care.

"I'm sorry." I kiss her head.

"It's not your fault," she hums, wrapping her arms around my back and snuggling close. "Thank you for tonight, Mase. It's been the perfect first date."

"This isn't a date." I smile into her hair.

"No?" she asks, sounding surprised.

I chuckle as I tell her, "No. This was just foreplay."

"Date foreplay? I don't think that's a thing."

"Is now."

"If this was foreplay." I feel her smile against my bare chest.

"We won't fucking survive it," I deadpan. Her laugh that follows flows through me like silk, making my eyes close as I absorb every bit of it. I've missed this. Her.

"RIP me."

I frown. "You did not just say that." I laugh, throwing my head back. "RIP me," I mimic in an eerily girly voice.

"Shut up!" She giggles, biting down on my nipple.

"Ouch!" I grasp my pec, pushing on her shoulder and away from me.

"Don't dish out what you can't take, Bossman."

I manoeuvre myself so I'm above her and between her legs, kneeing them far apart. I sink my growing cock deep inside of her. "Let's see just how much you can take, smart girl."

27

Nina

WAKING UP TO AN EMPTY BED ISN'T HIGH ON THE LIST OF HOW I like to start my day but waking up in Mason Lowell's bed—empty or not empty—seems to make it suck a little less this morning. Rolling over, I snap up the piece of paper that's laying on his pillow.

YOU TASTE FAR BETTER THAN THIS SHIT COFFEE.

My chest warms as a soft laugh slips from my throat. "So romantic, Mase."

"Dadiee," Ellis's sleepy voice drifts through his open door, and I quickly stand to go to him. It's been a busy weekend and couple days in the gym. I've been looking forward to my time with him. Poking my head around the doorframe, I wait, watching as he traces circles on his mattress. "Dadieee," he coos, almost perfectly. He doesn't look up, and I wonder how their morning routine normally goes.

"Not Daddy, baby boy."

His small body jolts at the sound of my voice, his head popping up as he stands in a rush, grasping the cot's railings. A smile quickly spreads his cheeks wide when he sees it's me, his hands slapping together as he wobbles on his chunky legs.

"Come here." I lift him from the cot and snuggle him close to my body. My toes flex in the fluffy rug that covers a large portion of the room, and I stand rocking him, feeling more content than I have in months. "You have a special daddy, Ellis." I lean back to look at him. "I'm sorry I kept you from this. I'm sorry, baby, Mummy won't let us be apart again. I promise."

Reaching out, he grasps my hand, curling his fingers around my pinkie and shaking it. "What are you doing?" I chuckle, ruffling his hair before placing a kiss on his head. "Let's get some breakfast, then you can show me your super cool clothes."

After breakfast and over an hour of being continuously shocked by my son's impressive wardrobe, I put him in his pushchair and walk back to my apartment. By the time we get there, Ellis is flat out. I do a load of laundry and clean up the couple dishes that were left in the sink on Friday night before we headed to Lowerick. Then I take my exhausted body and plant it on my sofa. I feel tired. It's like Mason is on catch up for the last year that he hasn't had me—not that I'm complaining.

Pulling out my phone, I scroll through my contacts. I want to try Mum again but I know she won't answer. She hasn't in months. There was no way I could afford to keep helping her each month after I had Ellis, but if I knew cutting her off financially meant losing all contact, no matter how selfish she can be I still hate that I don't get to hear her voice. She's my mum and for the longest time, she was all I knew and loved.

It might be a stupid idea, and one that she probably won't even appreciate, but I've seen pictures of me as a baby. My mum held me proudly once and I want her to feel that again —maybe it will work. I slip into my bedroom and slide out my box, then pick out a picture of Ellis and take it back to the living room.

I let the ink guide me without too much thought.

Hello, Nanny.

I presume Nanny is okay? I can't imagine you'd like to be called a granny just yet.

My name is Ellis Anthony Lowell and I am 9 months old. Mummy has told me about you. She tells me you're super good at cuddles, and that your cupcakes are some of the best in the world. I hope I can try one, one day. She also says I have your smile, but mostly I look like my daddy. He's an amazing man and I think you'd like him too. Mummy and I would love to hear from you. Here's our address in case you'd like to write back to me, or you can call any time. I hope I can meet you one day. I know it would mean the world to Mummy and I think with the way she smiles every day, that my cuddles could be just as good as yours.

Love Ellis xx

There's nothing that can't be fixed in life if you have love in your heart x

I find an envelope in the kitchen drawer and write out my childhood address on the front. I'm unsure if she even lives there anymore, but I want to try. I have so many unanswered questions yet what I want more than anything is solely for Ellis. I want him to have every bit of the love he deserves in life. I slip the photo into the envelope and add my address on a piece of paper. It's in her hands now. She can make the choice.

The rain starts to pour around the same time that Ellis wakes up and I almost put off going out, but I want to post my letter and I want to go and see Mason at the office. I call Vinny and have him come pick us up.

"Sorry for calling you out in this weather," I tell him, smoothing out my hair that's now rain soaked in the flip-down mirror. Vinny told me to get in the car when he arrived, but I didn't listen and insisted I would get Ellis strapped in. Now I look like a drowned rat.

"Don't be, it's better than being stuck in the office."

"Could we stop off at Starbucks?" I ask, already anticipating the frown he gives me.

"Of course. There's a post box close to The Montwell, too. I can pull over for you?" He nods his head to the envelope I placed in the centre console when I got in.

"Thanks, Vin."

We stop close to the office so I can post the photo and Vinny doesn't ask questions. There's a possibility he will tell Mason I'm trying to contact my mum and that's okay, I know he doesn't understand, but I would tell him about it anyway. I wait for Vinny to get the umbrella then we rush towards the doors with Ellis held tight to my chest. Once inside The Montwell, Vinny hands me the coffee.

"Are you okay to go up from here? I need to run some things through security before I go back up."

"Yeah, of course," I tell him, waving him off as I walk to the elevators. The guard gives me a welcoming nod and gets the button for me. "Ellis and Frey?" he asks, seeing I have my hands full.

"Yes. Thank you."

He dips his head in reply and presses the appropriate button. The doors slide closed and I take in a deep breath, absorbing the feeling of being carried closer to him as the smell of the coffee in my hand assaults me.

"Nina!" George sings at me, being his usual cheery self as the doors open. He's leant over the reception desk and stands when he spots me. "Oh, let me take this edible little poppet!" He leans in and takes Ellis from my arms. "How are you?"

"Good!" I tell him, gripping the coffee with two hands when I spot Jasmine rising to her feet from behind the desk. A small ball of energy knots my stomach, but I knew she'd be here.

"You look it!" George agrees.

I nod, smiling awkwardly as I try to think of what to say next. Jasmine is standing just as unsure on the other side of the room. She doesn't look anything like the girl who passed me in tears at the hotel all those months ago. Her black dress is simple but looks thick and expensive, fitting her slim frame like a glove. I try to figure out if we share any resemblance. I don't particularly see it from a first glance, but she does have a full face of makeup on. As if she doesn't know what to do, she reaches up and fingers a wayward strand of blonde hair from her face.

I'm certain she feels just as uncomfortable as I do.

"Hello, Jasmine." I nod, cursing myself internally when the words come out barely loud enough for my own ears.

"Hi," she replies, quickly losing her frown and replacing it with a softer look.

"Ellis, should we go see if Daddy is finished in Uncle Elliot's office?" Ellis watches George intently, slowly reaching up to stroke his navy and white bow tie. "Won't be a minute, girls."

"He's about as subtle as a brick through a window," Jasmine mutters as they disappear, making me dip my head as my lip curls at her comment. George really is as subtle as a brick through a window.

For five solid seconds, we just look at each other, waiting for the other to say something.

I jump in. "So—"

"I—"

"Oh god." I chuckle. "Sorry."

"You go first," she tells me, nodding her head as if it's what she wants.

"So, I guess you're going to be around here—the office, for a while..."

"Yeah, I like it here. It's... good."

"That's good." God, this is too much. "Look, Jasmine, I'm going to be super honest here. I have a lot going on in my own life right now, and I know from what Mason has told me you do too. I don't feel ready to explore this." I gesture between us in a weird unnecessary way and quickly grasp the coffee with both hands to stop myself from looking any more of an idiot. "Sister thing," I add, hoping I don't sound like a complete bitch. It hasn't come across well at all, I can tell by the drop of her shoulders.

"Me too! I can't... like it's not that I don't want to know you but..."

"No, I get it!" I smile at her, instantly relieved that we're on the same page. "Maybe we could grab a coffee at some point, once things aren't so…"

"Sure." She nods, pursing her lips so as to stop her smile from widening.

"Nina." My head turns at the sound of Mason's voice. He has a wide grin lighting up his beautiful face as he stalks towards me.

"Hey!"

He wraps an arm around my waist and kisses my temple. "This is a nice surprise." He eyes the coffee cup in my hands then flicks his eyes back to mine with a wicked look on his face. "For me I presume?"

"I thought I'd bring you some more shit coffee."

"You couldn't get me some of the other that I like?" My eyes bug out at him. I look at Jasmine who thankfully thinks we are talking about coffee. At least she doesn't let on if she knows her boss is a sex fiend. "Excuse us," he tells her, taking my hand and leading me into his office.

"Where's Ellis?" I ask, taking a step towards his desk before his hands snake around me and I'm dragged back into his solid body.

"With Elliot," he hums, his lips running up the length of my neck. "You really do taste delicious, angel."

I tap his arm playfully and step out of his hold. "That's not why I came here! You're obsessed."

"I am."

"Go get our son, Mason. We came here to give you your coffee."

"Fuck the coffee." He tries to pull me back to him, but I push him away.

402 | JC HAWKE

"Mase, go and get him!" I laugh.

"Fine." He rolls his eyes and leaves the room, returning a few minutes later with Ellis who now has a perfectly positioned bow tie around his neck. "Look at this champ, Mummy!"

"What's George done to you?" I follow Mason around the desk and stand leant against his office chair when he sits down with Ellis on his lap. The second I'm close enough, his hand slips down to glide up my inner leg, grasping me just above the knee.

"You came to see me," he says, looking up at me with a boyish look on his face.

"We missed you. You left without saying goodbye this morning."

"I didn't want to wake you both."

"Always wake me," I tell him, smoothing my fingers through his ruffled hair. "It was odd waking up at the penthouse."

"Odd how?"

"I don't know... It felt like I'd never left."

"Good. I like that." He smiles, beckoning my lips with the twist of his.

I lean down and give him a deep kiss, keeping it short for Ellis's benefit. Mason's eyes are heavy and full of lust as I pull away. "Come to mine tonight. I don't want to be alone," he admits.

"We're supposed to be taking things slow," I remind him. I should have known he'd have no restraint. But his honesty has me conflicted, and I already know I won't deny him.

"I can go slow." He winks.

"Get away you sex maniac." I push on his chair and step back.

"I'm serious. Come to mine tonight. We can keep it PG." He gently slides a hand down Ellis's back, looking up at me with so much adoration in his eyes it floors me. "I want you both with me. Always."

My heart sings with his words. Is there anything I want more than to be with this man—always? I don't think so.

"Will you pick us up on your way home?"

"Of course I will."

I SPEND the rest of my day giving Ellis one hundred percent of my time. The last few months have been nonstop. I started working at the gym, then Mason—he gets his own category all to himself, and then all the preparation for the ball. For the last year I've thrived off of routine–even though I've struggled being alone. But the idea that everything is changing again and so quickly, despite how much I've wanted all these things, it still scares me.

Leaning down, I kiss Ellis's smooth hair, inhaling his sweet shampoo. Something deep inside of me tells me things are about to change for us again. Mason doesn't want us apart anymore, and I get it. I hate being alone too. But my concerns are that we will move faster than our hearts can handle. I'd like to think I know Mason, that I can deal with the curve balls that come our way now. But am I foolish to think that after only a couple months we can find our happy again?

Right now, I want to spend my time with my son, snuggling on the sofa and listening to the rain fall outside.

I look down at his little face which is resting against the crook of my arm. "You're so tired today, baby."

His wide eyes don't leave the TV screen and I smile as his small hand clenches my vest, holding me tight. "Daddy will be here soon."

———

THE SOUND of my phone vibrating has my eyes snapping open. Ellis is asleep in his cot. He drifted off whilst we were lying on the sofa, and I felt so drained after yesterday and this morning that I decided to have a lie down.

Searching my bed, I find my phone.

"Hey, Scar," I whisper, pushing back the covers and slipping from the room.

"Hey!" She sounds happy and cheerful, and it instantly lifts my mood. "I just got back from work. I stopped in to see Joey today..."

"You did? Was he okay? What happened?"

She sighs through the phone. "I did pop over to yours after but you weren't home."

"I went to the office with Ellis. We took Mason coffee. How was Joey?"

"He let me in. Well, not in, but he opened the door, eventually. He's definitely struggling, but I think he's okay. I gave him my number and told him I would pop back in the week which he seemed to be okay about."

"He was?"

"Yeah. Did he sleep much before all this with his brother?" she asks.

Did he sleep? I would say yes, he never looked tired, but

he was a workaholic when it came to his photography. "Most of the time."

"Well, he isn't sleeping. But I think that's normal given the circumstances. I didn't ask about his medication; it isn't really my place. Is there a neighbour or anyone you know who could check in each day?"

Me. I'm the only one. I know this. "No."

"Okay, don't stress over this, Nina. I'll do my best to go over as much as possible around work."

"I'm so sorry, Scar. I just wanted to wait a couple days, give Mason time to chill out about Sunday."

"I get it," she tells me. "From what you've told me, Joey has been through a lot. He probably needs time."

"Thank you, Scarlet, I appreciate you doing this."

"You don't have to thank me. I feel for him, and I want to help."

She has no idea how much peace of mind it gives me knowing that someone is checking in. "Will you be at Elliot's on Saturday?" I ask her. "He said he wants us all there."

"I have work, but I'll pop in after," she promises.

"Good, we can catch up properly then."

"Yes! I'm dying to get the scoop on Lucy and Miller. Things did not sound good at the café on Monday! Have you spoken to her?"

"Not since our coffee date." Shit! I forgot about Miller. I'm the worst friend.

I hear keys rattling in the door. "I have to go, your brother is here." I smile as Mason steps into my apartment, he's still in his suit and looks just as edible as usual.

"Hmmm."

"Did you just 'hmmm' at him," Scarlet exclaims.

I chuckle down the phone. "Goodbye, Scarlet."

Mason's eyes are heavy and locked on me as I hang up the phone. His hands are relaxed at his sides, and he stands and waits, unmoving as he watches me.

"Hello." I grin, flipping the phone between my fingers.

"Hi."

I close the distance between us, not being able to help myself. "How was your day?"

His arms wrap around my back, and I stare up at his handsome face. "It was going great... until you showed up, gave me a raging hard-on and left."

"Umm, I did no such thing. You need to control your urges."

"You need to take responsibility for your actions." His boyish grin makes my stomach flip.

"I didn't do anything." I chuckle.

"You're doing it right now." He grinds his hips into me, his cock hard against my stomach. "Where's my boy?"

"In his bed," I whisper, loving the feel of his hands on me.

"He's a good kid. We need more just like him."

"If I had a penis, it would be getting soft over that comment."

His head falls back on a laugh, then he says, "You want me to talk dirty to you, angel?"

"Always." I grin.

His eyes darken within a millisecond. My Mase—my favourite Mase—is here. "Turn around."

I spin instantly, a giggle falling from my lips.

"She's obedient. Who'd have thought?" he tsks.

"What are you going to do to me?" I ask innocently.

His breath fans across the shell of my ear. "What do you want me to do to you?"

I decide to play a little. "I don't know... I've never..." I look down to the ground, hiding my face. "I'm a virgin."

He handles it well, and I expect him to be laughing when he speaks. What I don't expect is what actually happens. Sliding his hand into my hair, he tugs my head back. "Well, that just won't do," he rasps against my cheek. His breath is ragged as his chest vibrates at my back. Pushing me forward, he bends me at the waist, rolling his erection into my ass. "You'll take me here," he states.

"I cannot. It's not a Tuesday."

His hand connects with my left cheek. "Holy fuck, Mase!" I yelp, shooting forward.

"Watch that mouth. Unless you want me to gag you."

I giggle again, loving this all a little too much. "I'm not sorry," I mutter.

"What was that?" He pulls me upright, turning me to face him. "Did you say something?"

His eyes are wild and dark, but I can still see the light in them. He's more turned on than maybe ever before. "No."

A sharp brow pops. "Oh, but she lies."

I shake my head, lowering my eyes to the ground as a small smile pulls at my lips. "No, I swear. I didn't say a thing."

"Get on your knees."

I subtly shake my head, dying a little inside knowing he's taking this so seriously. I'd be lying if I said I wasn't completely turned on. I fall to the hardwood and onto my knees, licking my lips... because they are dry...

He unbuttons and shrugs out of his shirt, then starts on his belt. His eyes stay trained on me, but my eyes roam his body. "You're so perfect, Mase," I tell him, not being able to help myself.

He falters, pausing with his hands on his suit pants. "Are you trying to make me forget your filthy mouth, Pixie?"

I shake my head no.

"Good. 'Cause it's about to be fucked."

"I've not done that before. Will you teach me?"

"Of course, I will." He slides his boxers off, his body flexing as he kicks them to the side.

"You have a really big penis."

His façade cracks and he breaks out into a breathtaking smile. "Fucking hell." He chuckles.

Licking his bottom lip, he mouths, "*open*" before pushing the head of his cock into my mouth.

I slide him a little way in, not doing anything fancy. "Is this okay?"

"Perfect," he tells me.

But I know my man, and I know this is far from his perfect. I look up at him, giving him my best innocent eyes. "Really? 'Cause my parents will be home soon." I dart my eyes in the direction of Ellis's room. "And I was kinda expecting more." I flick my tongue over the tip. "But... it's okay if you are... a bit vanilla."

"You little shit."

I bare my teeth and run them down his shaft. "Show me what you got, Bossman."

Sometimes, we think we want the kink. We ask for it—entice it even. But then we get it, and the next thing we know we have tears rolling down our cheeks, and our hair being ripped from our scalps—let's not forget the urging from the perpetual cock that's being thrust down our throats. But, honestly, is there anything hotter than watching a six-foot-two deity come undone because of your mouth and your mouth alone? Right now, staring up at this man as he drips down my throat, there's absolutely no place I'd rather be than on my knees swallowing around Mason Lowell's cock.

"Jesus fuck, Nina," he says, his voice strained. I pull away, letting him fall from my mouth with a loud pop as his hips still pump ferociously.

"I thought you wanted to come inside of me?" I twiddle my hair between my fingers.

"Angel, I was this close to blowing in your mouth." He sighs.

"But you promised. You could be the first to ever get inside of me." I bite my bottom lip and his eyes zero in on the movement. "I've never even used my fingers."

"Strip. Now."

I pull my clothes from my body double time, noting that my T-shirt and joggers really aren't a turn on.

Mason rounds me, his breath tickling my ear. "You'd make a shoddy virgin."

I don't expect his words and instantly turn to face him with a grin on my face. "What?"

"You look like a woman that's been well fucked, angel."

"Oh really?" I laugh.

His hand connects with my ass again, only this time it's bare, and the sting takes longer to soothe. "I'm going to tell you what I want and you're going to do it. Only you will do it with that potty mouth shut. Do you understand?"

I nod.

"Good girl."

Ugh. If I wasn't wet before—I was—I sure as hell am now.

"Your body is perfect." He kisses my shoulder, smoothing his lips over the skin. "Follow me."

With not a care in the world, he stalks in all his naked glory to the lounge. Sitting himself down on the sofa, he widens his legs, then looks up at me expectantly. "Turn around," he tells me.

Turning, I plant my feet between his, waiting. Anticipation runs up my spine, making a shiver roll through me. "Mase?" I ask.

His hands take my hips, pulling me back and down onto him. He lines us up perfectly and I sink down on him to the hilt. "Yes!" I hum, my mouth dropping open as I roll my hips onto him.

Caressing my waist gently, he groans into my ear, "Bring your knees up."

I lift them one by one, sliding my feet along his thighs. The new position has me dropping deeper. "Ready?" he asks.

What a stupid question. Of course I'm ready. I roll my eyes, getting ready for the moment he takes over my movements and shows me his talents. "Catch yourself, angel," he warns.

I frown, not understanding until my head is being flung towards the ground. I gasp in horror. "Mase!" I place my hands on the hardwood, my hair fanning all around me and blocking my vision. My ass is in the air, and I can only imagine the view he has right now.

His warm breath tickles my clit. "I might put this in a fucking frame one day."

"Oh my god," I groan, a mixture of mortification and pleasure making my head spin.

Taking my ass cheeks in his large hands, he squeezes

them together before stretching them apart. "Do you ache here" —he runs a finger through my pussy— "as much as my cock aches for you? Because the way your clit's throbbing between my fingers" —he squeezes my pulsing nub— "tells me that you do." Gripping me at the hips, he directs me onto his waiting mouth, unhinged as he ravishes my entire lower body. His nails bite into the flesh on my thighs and I buck into him. It's as if he can't get enough, crazed to taste every inch of me.

My body goes rigid as his thumb slips into my ass. I feel him suck at my centre, the sound of his lips smacking together making me heady.

"Fuck," he hisses, pulling his hands away and gripping my hips to pull me upright again. He thrusts up and into me right as my orgasm rips through me, sucking him deeper and tighter to my walls.

He bounces me on his lap, our skin slapping and our moans filling the silence in the apartment. Curling one hand around my shoulder and one around my hip, he takes complete control, thrusting into my body until he finds his own release.

I fall back, panting to his chest. My legs are tucked up under me still, and I can feel his cum sliding down his softening cock.

"Well, thank god I'm not a virgin."

His light chuckle has goose bumps pebbling over my skin. Soft lips graze my cheek. "I said you'd make a shoddy virgin. You're too much of a butt slut."

My mouth drops open into a deep O. "I am not!"

"You go wild when I go near your asshole, Pix."

"Stop talking. You're ruining it."

His chest vibrates against my back. *Somebody thinks they're hilarious tonight.* "Shower, wake the boy, dinner, and then, I'm going to take you home and show you all the ways I love you."

"Better."

"I'll even put it in your arse."

"Mase!"

28

Mase

Two weeks later.

NINA ANDERSON IS THE FLIGHTIEST WOMAN I HAVE EVER HAD
the pleasure of knowing. I'm at one with the fact that I will
spend the rest of my life fighting against the tide to keep her
with me. Because I love her.

"You're making a big deal out of this," Charlie tells me
from his spot on the weight bench. "She's been at your place
every night since Lowerwick."

"Are you still pussyfooting around this? Just ask her
already," Elliot says, grunting as he does another bicep curl.
His eyes follow the brunette who coincidentally needed to
walk around the rigs to get to the treadmills.

"Shut up, dick." I whip him in the gut with my towel. "You
have no idea what it took to get her to move in the first time."

"What did it take?" Elliot asks, dropping the weight to the
rack and smirking as if he already knows.

I wish it was as easy as sex. "I took her to Paris."

"Oh," Elliot says, disappointed.

"Charlie's right, Lowell. I don't think you have anything to worry about," Lance tells me, stepping up to us and swiping his brow with a towel.

"Is it too soon?" I ponder. "It doesn't feel too soon, and we've never been good at going slow."

"You have a kid together, of course it's not too soon," Elliot mutters, running his fingers through his blond hair. "It's Nina, mate. You're not moving on, are you? So just get on with it already."

Nina

I'm ALMOST FINISHED WASHING up when Lucy and Megan come bouncing into my apartment. Their faces are bright and excited, and I frown as they approach me. "Why do you look like that?" I ask, placing a saucepan into the cupboard.

"Look like what?" Megan smirks.

"Like you have a secret up your ass."

They look at each other. "Maybe we do." Lucy's grin is so wide, I'm surprised it doesn't crack her face.

Lucy's wearing white jeans and a powder blue silk shirt, her heeled ankle boots making her a good foot taller than me. My eyes flick to Megan, noting her suede skirt and polo. "Where are you going?" I ask, trying to figure out if I've missed something.

"Megs, go get Ellis." Lucy bounces on the spot, pulling an envelope from her clutch.

"What's this?" I ask, watching as Megan skirts off down the corridor. "Megs, don't wake him up!"

"Shh! Open it," Lucy fusses.

I shake my head, pulling open the seal.

Angel.
I need you to bear with me here.
I ask that you follow the clues to each location.
I'll make it worth your while.
M

My forehead creases as I look up at Lucy. "What's this all about?"

She shrugs, but the look on her face tells me she knows exactly what it's about. Megan rushes up next to her, eagerly looking over at the note in my hand.

"You opened it already?!" she complains, readjusting a sleepy Ellis on her hip. He looks around at us, confused.

"Turn it over!" Lucy tells me.

I flip the paper.

Where lay the keys is where she found her passion.

"Eh?" Megan wrinkles her nose, not understanding.

I look at Lucy, unsure. "My old studio?" I guess.

A smile takes over her face. "Come on, Vin is waiting, and you need to get changed."

Lucy dresses me in what she considers the perfect outfit —yoga pants and tank. The thought of going to the studio has my stomach twisting. I have no idea what Mason has planned, but I presume this is all part of his elaborate 'date' he is yet to give me. I'm excited but extremely apprehensive as I slide into the Audi.

"Hey, Vin. You going to tell me what's going on?" I ask, leaning in and kissing his cheek.

"Nope."

I roll my eyes and pull on my seat belt. Megan has taken Ellis back to hers. Apparently, it's all a part of the orders she was given. "Well, I hate this. I don't want to be a brat but it's the worst kind of a date." I wring my hands in my lap, hating not knowing what's going on.

Lucy and Vinny both laugh, eyeing each other in the mirror. "Go with it, love."

We pull up to my old studio minutes later, and instantly I feel a pang of sadness as I look up at the new signage. Lucy jumps out of the car, her excitement not slowing her down. I look over my shoulder at Vinny when he places a hand on my shoulder.

"I know he wanted this to be a surprise, but he doesn't always think things through before he does them—"

"Vin." I sigh, my nerves ramping up with his admission.

"Just remember that he only does what he does to make you happy, that's his only driving force. Do one thing for me today, please?"

"What?" My stomach twists at the idea of what he might've done.

"Remember that you deserve everything that comes to you. You've worked hard, you've endured more than you ever should have—the both of you." He gives me a reassuring smile. "And you're entitled to what he wants to give you."

My eyes well as Vinny's words sink in, and I twist in my seat to pull him into a tight hug. "God, Vin, I'm scared."

"You shouldn't be. I'm thrilled for you." His eyes hold so much sincerity and pride it makes a warmth spread through my entire chest, giving me all the confidence I'd need to take on the world.

"Thank you," I mumble into his shoulder. "For everything."

"You don't ever have to thank me." He nods to Lucy who is waving her hands at me through the car window. "Go on."

I step from the car and walk to the gym doors, frowning when I see that the inside is under construction.

"It's going to be a bakery! It was a printing house for most of last year but then it sold. If it has a café, we'll have to check it out!" Lucy pulls out a set of keys, unlocking the door.

"You have a key?" I ask, looking around, feeling like a criminal for no reason.

She grins at me over her shoulder as she rattles the key in the door. "You have a man who knows how to get what he wants," she tells me, grasping me by the hand and pulling me through the door.

I swallow past the lump that seems to be lodged in my throat as I follow her up the steps at the back of the room. I should be excited—it's my studio. But something in my gut makes me hesitant. It feels tainted. Everything about the studio was a twisted lie, and I never had a chance to come back here. It was ripped out from under me.

"You're sweating!" Lucy frowns, swiping her thumb over my brow and wiping it on her jeans. "Trust me, okay?"

I nod. My teeth ache as I clamp them together. I peek around the door as she starts to open it.

"It's exactly how I left it," I murmur, walking past her and into the studio.

"Here." She holds out another envelope. "I'm not allowed in. I'll wait downstairs, okay?"

She leaves the room and I chuckle as I take it all in, my eyes not knowing where to look. *What on earth?* My gaze falls on the bay that once housed Ellis's piano. It feels cold and empty without it. I miss the days—and the nights—I spent here.

I tear open the envelope with shaking hands, unsure where this is going.

> *With so much regret came new beginnings.*
> *A new space to find her passion.*
> *But first, she deserved one last dance.*

A tear slides down my cheek. I always knew Mason was sorry about the studio. It wasn't ever his fault; he just didn't handle the situation right in the moment. So much happened here, so much I will never ever forget. I'm proud of what I achieved in these four walls. Everything I built for me.

Looking around the room, I spot a speaker in the corner. Dropping my head back, I inhale a deep breath, trying to stop the emotions from spilling out of me. Sliding out of my shoes, I pick a song and let it drift into me. I take the closure I never knew I needed as tears pour down my face, hope and excitement driving me to move not only around the studio, but forward, towards a *new beginning*.

I FEEL LIGHTER when we step out the doors and onto the street. I let the fresh air blow through my hair, whipping away the last of my ties to the building at my back.

"Do you know where you have to go next?" Lucy asks, looking over at me.

I squint my eyes as I think, then check the note again. "A new space to find her passion." I look at Lucy, her brows popping as if it's obvious.

"Come on." She grabs my arm and tugs me towards the Audi. "You can figure it out on the way."

Five minutes later, we're pulling up outside of the gym. "Here?" I smile.

"Yep. Here." Lucy snorts, climbing from the car.

Vinny chuckles in his seat, not looking at me. "What?" I ask.

He looks at me then away again, focusing on the windscreen. "I've said enough."

I'm not as slow with my steps as I head towards L&M, linking my arm with Lucy's and pushing into the reception.

"Hello, ladies!" Gemma greets us with a face-splitting grin.

"Hey!" I go to stop and chat, but Lucy forces me past her. "We can catch up after. Sorry, Gem!" I yell around the staircase. "Luce! What's the rush?"

"I'm excited," she admits, quite literally buzzing at my side.

I shake my head, following her through the gym and over to Logan's office. "Ahh, here she is." Henry's smirk is arrogant and knowing.

"You're in on this too, aren't you?" Is there anyone who doesn't know what's going on besides me?

420 | JC HAWKE

"Maybe." He chuckles.

"Is it safe yet?" Lucy asks Logan who's leant back in his office chair.

"Sure is!" He nods to me, a pleased look on his face.

"You ready?" Lucy asks, her shoulders bunched.

"No," I say, honestly. We're going upstairs, and the thought of what he's done terrifies me. Lucy guides me from the room and lines me up in front of the stairs that lead to the room above the gym.

"Go for it," she tells me.

I pull open the door and instantly notice the light that shines in the stairwell. "Lights!"

"Lights?" She laughs all goofily, and it sparks so much excitement inside of me. "Oh girl, you just wait."

Not wanting to wait a minute longer, I run up the steps, throwing open the door. "What the fuck?" I stop on the top step.

My stomach bottoms out, tears springing to my eyes and falling quickly.

"Why are you crying?" Lucy panics.

"Are you serious?" I splutter. I'm pretty sure I now have snot on my face.

"You hate it?"

I shake my head.

"You love it?"

I nod.

"These are happy tears!"

I nod again.

"Well, thank god!" She chuckles, placing a hand on her chest.

"Oh my god, Luce." I walk deeper into the room, inhaling

the fresh pine that seems to smother my heart and set my chest aflame.

Everything is done. Finished and brand new. The floors have been replaced, a dark solid wood, smooth and polished. Mirrors line the entire back wall with a barre running the length of it, and a bunch of red roses lie on a grand black piano that's set back in the corner of the room. It's not Ellis's —I know that without needing to inspect it—but it's perfect. It's thought out, and special, and even better than I could ever envision it myself. "When did he do this?"

"Over the last few days. He had someone in to do most of the work, but the boys did a lot too."

"It's perfect," I whisper.

"He bought this place for you, Nina. The whole building."

My brows crease together, and I swear I can feel every one of my bones ache right down to my toes. "What?"

"He sold your studio and wanted to make up for it. I didn't know," she reassures me. "But when you left, he offered downstairs to Logan at a fraction of the price. He kept this level for you."

My eyes drift closed as I absorb her words. I should've known. He seemed to hold out so much hope even when I lost it all.

I don't deserve this man.

"L&M fitness. Lowell and Morgan, or Logan and Mason—depends on who you ask." I try to make out her facial expression through my tears but it's useless. They aren't stopping. "This is all the business mumbo jumbo you'll need. Like I said, Logan has downstairs, and this is yours." She hands me the folder and I flick it open. "So, it's in your name but there's a clause where you pay a sum

—a percentage, I think, to Alcohol Change UK each month, which is peanuts if you ask me." She chuckles. "You also have all the start-ups to pay back—which if you moan about, I will hurt you. You asked for this, you crazy girl."

I laugh as I grip the documents to my chest, not even trying to dry my face.

"Logan knows that you'll be working up here from now on, and you can start whenever you want."

My dimples ache from the smile that stretches my face. Could he be any more perfect? "I love it." I spin on the spot, then walk to the floor-to-ceiling windows, looking past the three other buildings to The Montwell. It sits taller than the rest, proud and dominant. "I love it so, so much, Luce."

"Almost there..." She holds out another envelope.

"There's more?" I gush, my hands shaking as I take it from her.

I rip open the envelope.

They'll grow an empire, fit for future kings.

I giggle, looking at Luce. "Elliot wrote this with him, didn't he?"

"Yup." She laughs.

"Ellis and Frey?" I frown, looking up at The Montwell again.

"Oooo, you're getting good at this. Come on, this is the last one!"

I pick up the bouquet of roses, glancing around one last time before leaving the studio. This whole afternoon has been insane.

Vinny is watching me closely as I climb into the car, clearly gauging my reaction.

"I love it, Vin," I say, bunching up my nose and letting him pull me under his arm.

"I knew you would. You'll be fantastic, love."

"Thanks." I turn to look back at Lucy. "Thank you both."

"Not necessary," she snaps, getting back into beast mode. "To the office, Vinny!" She slaps the back of his seat.

———

GEORGE IS on the reception when we enter the front area, and he stands as we approach the desk. "Well, hello. You're only half an hour late." He looks at Lucy accusingly.

"Sorry, she took her sweet ass time getting ready. Then we had tears."

"Tears?" he asks, genuine concern etched across his face.

I hand him the notes I've received so far.

"Mason writes in third person?" He fans his face. "You need to teach me your tricks on how to tame him."

I chuckle, taking them back from him. "Trust me, George, if anyone is good at taming that man, it's you."

"Hi." Jasmine walks out from behind us, a stack of papers in her hands. "Sorry I can't stop, super busy today."

"That's okay." I smile.

"Yes," George says. "The Bossman took the day off. Something more important to be doing apparently." He rolls his eyes jokingly at us.

"Mason isn't here?" I ask, turning and frowning at Lucy.

"Nope! The last clue's in his office," she tells me, pushing me in the back and steering me to the double doors.

I enter the office and instantly get lost in all things Mason Lowell. His smell, woodsy and just him, it smothers me—it always has. Everything about the office has him branded on it, from the chair rolled up to the desk to the cushions scattered on the sofas. Such irrelevant things yet so personal to him, and to me. I spot a photo frame on his desk, a note tacked to the front of it. I slide down into his desk chair and peel it off.

The frame holds three photos. The first is of the two of us in Paris, standing under the Eiffel tower. The second is of me, my stomach stretched and full. "I was around seven months along when this photo was taken," I say absentmindedly. "He must have taken it from the binder I gave him." The third picture has me gasping through more tears. Sunlight beams through the floor-to-ceiling window, momentarily reflecting off the frame and setting a glare around the room. It has goose bumps rippling up my arms and neck. It's a picture of Mason, Ellis, and me at Lowerwick Estate. Vinny took the photo at the ball. He asked that we stand on the steps in front of the house. Mason is standing to my left, his arm proudly around his son in his arms, and his other arm is wrapped around my waist.

I sniffle, trying to compose myself as I steal a moment. I stare at the photo.

"Open the envelope, Nina," Lucy tells me softly from somewhere in the room.

One day she will go to the meadow, sit on the hill, and watch her family grow.
One day, but not yet.
For now, he asks that she comes home.

Please, Angel. Come home.

"Home?" I ask, darting my eyes up and searching for Lucy's blue ones.

Lucy nods from her spot on the sofa. Her face is more serious now. "The penthouse."

I bite my bottom lip, looking back to the picture. Is he saying he wants to be at Lowerwick one day? Would he really leave the city and go back there?

"I want to go home," I say, staring at the note.

"Course you do."

"Am I rushing into this?"

She shakes her head no. "I think this is exactly what you, Ellis, and Mason need."

"I'm scared. What if it goes wrong again?"

"Then we round up the girls and go dancing." She winks, making me smile. "It is going to go wrong at times, Nina. You'd be naive to believe it won't." She stands, sighing as she walks to the desk in thought. "But I know for a fact that you and Mason can overcome anything that's thrown at you. Just look at what this past year has brought to your door. You fought back, said a big fuck you, and got through it. Trust that you'll always get through it."

"You promise you'll always be available for dancing—no matter the time of day?"

She grins wide. "You know it."

"Okay. Let's go home."

29

Nina

THE SOUND OF THE ELEVATOR WHIRLING AS IT CARRIES ME TO
the penthouse is the only sound audible over the beating
drum that seems to pound against my chest. I don't know
why I'm so nervous. It's the penthouse. And Mase. And home.
There was always something about the penthouse that I
loved; it was almost instant. And then I fell in love with him
here. Amongst stolen moments and stupid fights, it all led me
deeper into *us*. Not a relationship or another person but a
promise.

I flinch, despite anticipating the ping that sounds. I calm
my breathing and look up into a sea of candlelight. The living
area is littered with candles, just like that night all those
months ago. It was one of our first nights together, and we
were supposed to be going out on our first date. I shake my
head at the memory, a smile forcing its way to my face. I
freaked out over his money, sulked in the bath, we had sex
and then woke hours later to find the downstairs in puddles

of candle wax. God, if I could go back... would I change things?

Tentatively, I step out of the elevator, making my way through the foyer, and deeper into the lounge. I stop and take in the view, never tiring of the visual sensation that is the City of London. It's a rush of cars, people and flashing lights, yet so peaceful from up here.

"You're late." His voice is deep and instantly pulls me from my trance.

I spin in place, finding him watching me from the middle of the dining area. "I was sent on a wild-goose chase."

"You didn't like it?" he questions.

I start towards him. "I loved it."

"Yes!" I hear someone hiss from the kitchen. I frown at Mason, and he shakes his head.

"The studio—"

"It's perfect. It's all perfect, Mase." I slide my arms around his neck, smoothing my hands over his navy fitted shirt that hugs his strong shoulders perfectly.

His nostrils flare as he fights to control his emotions, and I smile, my tears seem to have dried up thankfully. He takes a step away from me, holding my hands in his.

"I know I said we would take things slow, and this is probably all happening quicker than you want it to, but I can't think of one good reason why we would spend another second apart. I love you, Nina. Even the ugly parts that should make us impossible, I love. If I had things my way, I'd call in a vicar and marry you right here, right now." I draw in a sharp breath, my heart thudding in my chest as my stomach bottoms out. "But I also know that you would run a million miles from me if I did that." He smiles, and I see the nerves that flutter deep within his eyes. "What *you* should know, is that I will spend the rest of my life climbing over every hurdle we create—and Angel, we'll create them." I laugh, stealing a hand away to wipe a stray tear from my face. "You could run to earth's end and I would still find you. In this life, and the next, you will always be my one. My Pixie. So, I ask that you *consider* being my wife. You don't have to answer me now, you can take all the time in the world to decide–I don't even have a ring." He smiles, patting his pockets. *So perfect.* "But come live with me, with our son, as a family, and then when you are ready, know that I will be too. I'd be your husband today, tomorrow, and forever."

What in the world did I do to deserve this man? I'm in awe of him—of his love.

"Of course," I splutter, trying to control my voice as my throat burns.

"Of course, you'll move in?" His shoulders drop in relief.

"Mase," I cry, struggling to speak. Does he really believe I wouldn't want to marry him? "You have no idea how much I love you, do you?"

His eyes look lost, searching mine for the answers I've always had but not always shared. "I want to be with you, Mason. Even though it terrifies me that it could ruin us again. That it could hurt like it did before. But I'd do it a thousand times over. There's nobody else. There never will be anyone else. If that means I have to get off my high horse and accept all the aspects of your love—even the parts that I don't always like—then know that I will. I'll bend until I break every time, if it means I get to spend the rest of my life with you."

He rolls his eyes playfully. "You just had to bring up all the ways I hurt you. Couldn't just say yes."

"Mase." I swat his arm, laughing through my tears.

He lifts his chin. "You'd marry me, Pix?"

"In a heartbeat."

He shakes his head as he looks to the ceiling, laughing. I watch as he steps around me, his hand outstretched. Vinny is at my back, Lucy stood by his side, her face red and blotchy from her own tears. *When did they sneak in?*

I laugh as my eyes meet Lucy again. "You could've warned me, bitch!"

"As if," she sniffs.

Vinny steps forward and places something in Mason's hand, giving me a soft wink before moving back to stand with Lucy.

"I swear to God if you don't say the word yes this time."

Laughter fills the room but Mason's eyes take a hold of my soul. One look and he has me. Completely.

He drops to one knee, staring up at me with so much love.

"Will you marry me, Angel?"

I nod through my tears as I look down at the beautiful ring he holds between his fingers. "Yes!" I whisper. "Yes! Yes! Yes!" I proclaim, getting louder by the second.

His smile, so full and perfect, lights up his entire face. Scooping me up from behind the knees he thrusts me up into the air. "She said yes!" His chest rumbles with laughter beneath my thighs.

I look down at him, my hands linked in his hair. "I love you," I promise him.

"I love you too." It feels like forever as we stand looking into each other's eyes, and I know that a piece of paper could never compare to the vow we make there and then. I want to be *Mrs Lowell*, that alone makes me crave the words that will bind us together one day, but the actual words—our vows, they are branded in our love, in a look, unspoken.

Cheers fill the entire penthouse as Elliot, Charlie, Megan, Ellis, Scarlet, and Lance all spill from the kitchen. "Congratulations!" Elliot grins, kissing Mason's head first and then mine, wrapping his arms around the both of us.

Scarlet and Megan are just as emotional as me and Lucy, and we steal a moment as Scarlet hands me Ellis. "God, I cannot believe you're engaged, Nina," Lucy's voice wobbles as she inspects the ring on my finger. "It's phenomenal."

"It's Mum's." Scarlet tells me, hugging my waist. "It's perfect."

"It is." I look down at Ellis as my throat burns, getting thicker and thicker with emotion by the second. Everyone fusses around us. Champagne is poured and more hugs and kisses are shared than I have ever seen shared between a group of grown men.

It's late into the evening when everyone has left that I crawl into bed and completely bawl my eyes out. Mason pulls me to him the second I rest my head on the pillow.

"I'm sorry," I cry.

"Shhh, it's okay," he whispers into my hair, holding me tight in his arms.

"I... I—"

He sits up in the bed and pulls me to straddle his waist. His thumbs swipe at my tears as he holds my face. "Talk to me, Angel."

"I don't think I ever allowed myself to believe in all of this." I spin the diamond-encrusted band around my finger. "Growing up, none of this was real to me. It was a dream that I didn't think I wanted. I danced a lot, and it became my only focus. It became my dream." I take a breath and try to calm my breathing. "When I saw the studio today, I was so happy. It's truly incredible and I will dance again—I know that." Mason looks at me intently, his eyes narrowed and dark. "But when I came here, saw you, and then our family, the boys and girls, Ellis and Vin." I roll my lips, needing him to hold me closer, for longer—forever. "Mase, it made me realise that dancing was just something I did whilst I waited for you. It felt real. And for the first time in my life, it was as if all my dreams came true."

His eyes shine. Our lips brush. And then he rolls us, telling me everything he can't with his words.

30

Nina

"AFTER ALL THESE MONTHS YOU'RE FINALLY GOING HOME," Scarlet says, lifting an empty box and placing it on the kitchen counter. "How does it feel?"

I smile over at her as I bite down on my lip. "Exciting."

It's Saturday, and today I'm moving back to the penthouse. I didn't get a lot of time to think on the decision, but with everything that Mason did for me yesterday, and the fact that I won't ever love like I love him, I know without a shadow of a doubt that this is the right move.

"I knew you'd get here. I just didn't think it would be yet. I'm so happy for you guys."

"Thank you, Scar. And thank you for helping me today. Hopefully the girls will show their faces this afternoon." I chuckle, thinking back to the night before.

"Hmm, Megan was blind drunk! I don't expect to see her at all."

"True." I smile, sealing the full box with tape and placing

it on the floor. "How's everything going at the hospital? Are you still enjoying it?"

"Yeah, it's great actually. I have big plans for the future which I never considered possible when I started."

"Like what?" I ask with a frown.

"Well, I've been thinking, and I think I'm going to go into paediatrics."

"With kids? That's amazing, Scar!"

"I need to choose a speciality, and I love children. I do worry it will be tough sometimes, but I think I could handle it."

"You could! I know so, you're stronger than you think."

She shrugs excitedly. "We shall see! What about you, do you think you'll start up less—"

The rapping of knuckles against the door cuts Scarlet off. "Just a sec!" I call, placing down the curtains I'd been folding and walking to the door. I pull it open and am caught off guard when I see Joey standing on the other side.

"Joey, hi."

"Hey, how are you?" He gives me a smile then walks in past me. I stand at the door for a moment watching him as he disappears into my lounge. "I brought you these." He places a box on the coffee table and then picks it up again. "Do you want them? I presumed you did. You don't have to."

I chance a glance at Scarlet who looks just as perplexed as I do. "Is it..."

"Your photos," he finishes for me. "Scarlet told me you were back with Mason."

I nod. "Yeah. Yeah, I am."

"Did you catch that session yesterday, Joey?" Scarlet asks casually from the kitchen. I turn and look at her and she gives me a small shrug, but I know she is seeing what I am. He seems off.

"No." He scratches at his arm, then rubs at his neck. "I didn't sleep then I slept through it."

"Ahh. I see." Scarlet side-eyes me then comes farther into the lounge. "How are you feeling?"

"Fine. Why?" He tips his chin at her, his gaze narrowed, then he looks over at me.

"I'm just asking, Joey. I haven't been over in a couple days, that's all."

He flicks his eyes between us, then picks up the box of photos. "What was that?" he snaps.

My eyes widen, and I look at Scarlet. "What was what?"

"What did you say?" he asks me, placing down the box again.

"I didn't say anything, Joey."

He frowns, and I can see that he believes me. His eyes drift to Scarlet again and soften.

"Thank you for bringing these over, Joey. I really appreciate it."

"Of course." He nods. "You haven't been over."

"No, I'm taking some time. I came and told you that already."

He stares through me, his eyes assessing and full of questions. "Joey, are you okay?" I ask, taking a tentative step towards him.

"You asked me that already." He continues to stare at me, even when I avert my gaze to Scarlet, I feel his eyes on me. Never have I been so awkward and uncomfortable with someone I know. A friend at that.

"Sorry, Joey, I think—"

The door clicking shut has me pivoting on the spot. I'm momentarily relieved for the interruption, and I expect to see Mason, or one of the girls, walking through my front door. What I don't expect is my mother.

"Well, haven't you done well for yourself." My mother's voice is like ice in my veins, shooting right through me and sending every hair on my body standing on end.

"Mum?" It's been years since I've seen her, and from the lines around her eyes and slick roots that pass her cheekbones I can tell she hasn't been looking after herself. "You got my letter?"

Hope blooms in my chest at the thought of her coming all the way to my apartment. I knew it would work. The picture, the letter.

"I got your letter, but there wasn't my money," she slurs.

Feeling embarrassed, I flick my eyes to Scarlet. I know she wouldn't judge me; she went through equally tough times with her dad, but it doesn't make this moment any easier. "What do you mean your money, Mum? You haven't asked for money in months."

"Because you cut me off!" she yells, gripping her bag with trembling fingers. "Is this him?!" she sneers at Joey, taking a step farther into the lounge.

I blink three times, shaking my head and wondering how my day can go so backwards so fast. I contemplate asking Joey to leave but I'm just as worried about him as I am about my drunk mum. "By him, I presume you mean Mason. And no, this is Joey—my friend. And Scarlet, Mason's sister."

"Don't get smart with me!" She pulls her bag off her shoulder and grips the straps with a white-knuckle grip. Her wild eyes snap from Joey to Scarlet, then back to me. "Where is he?"

"Are you serious right now?!" I rage. "How dare you come into my home and speak to me like this!"

Before I can think, before I can process what is happening, my mother pulls a gun from her bag. She points it at Scarlet. I feel the blood leave my body, the panic taking its place and demanding more from me than I know what to do with.

"Mum?" I question, my voice deathly quiet as I try to stop my body from trembling. I chance a glance at Scarlet and close my eyes when I see a tear slip free. "Mum, please calm down. I will get you money, okay?"

She snaps her head around to look at me, tears brimming her own eyes. "I want my money, all of it. What he promised."

I don't know what she's talking about and it makes my throat grow tight, because I don't know if I've ever seen her like this. She's on something, that much I'm sure of, but what? And why is she doing this? When did things get this bad? "Okay, I will get all of it." I swallow thickly, willing my words to not fail me. "What did he promise?"

"A new life. A fresh start. A lot of money, and then he took it all away."

"Mason?" I frown. "Mason promised you that?"

"Yes!" she hisses. "I went to rehab; I did the time and then when I came for my money he told me no."

"You went to rehab?"

"Yes!" She shakes her arm as she shouts and I step forward, making her freeze up, her finger flinching on the trigger.

"I'm going to go and get my phone, okay, and then I will call Mason. Mum, please put the gun down."

"GET ME THE MONEY!" I watch as her entire face reddens, her eyes watering from anger or maybe sadness. I don't know because I don't know the woman standing in front of me.

My tears slip free, and I roll my lips as I look back at Scarlet. *I'm so sorry,* I mouth.

She nods her head, and I know that she doesn't blame me. But I also know that she is just as petrified as I am.

"Joey. Go to my bag at the kitchen island and get my phone, okay?" I nod at my mum, trying to reassure her. "I'm going to call Mason and get him to send me your money, Mum."

When I don't hear any movement behind me, I turn to face him. Joey is standing with a vacant expression on his face. He doesn't blink, his eyes zeroed in on Scarlet and nothing else. "Joey."

He doesn't flinch. "Joe!" I demand, needing him to help me. "Go to the kitchen and get my phone so that I can call Mason!" The grit in my voice brings his gaze to me. I nod my head. "Please." I widen my eyes at him, hoping he understands that I won't leave Scarlet and my mum alone.

He brings his hands to his face and pinches his cheeks, and I notice scratches lining his arms. "Okay," he tells me, and I breathe out a sigh of relief and he walks around the sofa and out towards the kitchen.

I turn back to my mum, and she frowns in disgust at me. I shake my head and watch her, feeling none of the things I thought I would after so many years. "Mum, please put the gun down. I will get the money. You're scaring us all."

438 | JC HAWKE

"He should have just done as I asked."

"He was going to give you money to go to rehab?" I ask again, looking at Scarlet and hoping talking to her is the best tactic to keep her occupied.

"You knew!" she spits. "He said it was for YOU! So that I could be there *for you*! Poor, poor, Nina. Always needing to be babied. You couldn't ever go a day fending for yourself. Now look! What are you going to do now?"

I don't want to make her angry, but the need to put her straight, it niggles.

"You couldn't do it yourself could you, you had to weed out a hotshot billionaire to fund your dreams. Then you got yourself knocked up. Stupid girl."

"You don't know me," I tell her.

"Oh, but I do. You think you're any different from me?" I watch out of the corner of my eye as Joey walks back into the room. The blade of a kitchen knife is poised in his grip and his focus is solely on my mum.

Her focus is solely on me.

Scarlet's on the gun.

And me, I don't know what to do. But I know I have to do something.

"Mum, please put that away," I beg.

"I want my money!" she seethes, getting angrier by the second.

"Nina," Scarlet whispers, her voice panicked.

I cut my eyes to Joey, watching as he takes three steps before my mother turns. I grab her arm and try to aim the gun at the ground, but she holds it strong. I hear Scarlet shouting out to Joey. I see Joey coming at us. I see the knife drop to the ground and then I drop too.

My mother puts a stop to the chaos.

She puts a stop to everything.

"NO!!! God, please, no!!!" Scarlet cries, falling to her knees at my side.

Pain shoots through my side, rendering me unable to speak and unable to breathe.

Scarlet is right there when I find focus, rolling my body so I'm on my back. She pushes down on my stomach and I heave in a half breath. "Scar," I cry.

She doesn't say a word, her eyes closed as she mumbles something incoherent to herself.

"Scarlet," I beg, my chest heaving as I fight to pull air into my lungs. Flicking my eyes over my head, I see Joey on his knees and pulling at his hair. My mother stands motionless just a few feet away, her eyes fixed on the ground. "Mum," I rasp, the taste of blood coating my tongue.

Her neck twists, venom lacing her words as she spits out, "You always did mess everything up." She throws the gun in her hand at the drywall with so much force the bullets scatter to the ground.

Scarlet doesn't flinch.

Joey starts to rock.

My mother leaves.

She leaves me as I gasp for breath.

She leaves me in my last breath.

Mase

"MASON, WAKE UP!" Lance's panicked voice pulls me from sleep.

I snap open my eyes and sit up in the bed. "What?"

He grasps my arm and heaves me out of bed. "We have to go! Now!"

THE WORLD SHOOTS past us as Lance drives us to Nina's apartment. No one is answering their phones, and I'm about to lose all my remaining sanity with the lack of information I'm getting from Lance.

"What did the message say!" I repeat.

"It was vague, Mase. But I know something isn't right. Scarlet's been going to see Joey because Nina wasn't. She didn't answer when I called."

"What did the message say?!" I yell.

"It wasn't from Scarlet, it was Joey. It didn't make sense, but he said he had a gun."

"Why the fuck is Joey texting you from Scarlet's phone." I pull at my hair. "Why aren't they answering their fucking phones!" My fist crashes into the dash in frustration.

"Call Vinny," Lance tells me.

WE DITCH the car at the entrance and run through the apartment building until we reach the fourth floor. The door is cracked open and instantly I hear a distressed cry.

My body sways on the spot. Lance pushes past me and runs into the apartment.

"What the fuck!"

I follow him in, my world halting to a grounding stop the moment I see Nina's lifeless body on the ground, and Scarlet hunched over, giving her chest compressions.

"No." I shake my head, stepping towards her.

This can't be happening.

"What the fuck did you do!" Lance questions incredulously, picking up a gun from the ground. "WHAT THE FUCK HAVE YOU DONE!" he roars.

My blurred eyes fly to Joey who is standing off to the side of the kitchen island grasping a knife in his bloodied hands. "I. I. I. They," he wails, not making any sense as he trembles on the spot.

I turn my back on him, blocking him out.

I fall to my knees at Nina's side, hitting the ground with a thud. "Scar," I say, not recognising my own voice as it breaks. "Scarlet," I repeat, frowning up at her when she doesn't acknowledge me.

I shake my head. "Tell me she's going to be okay."

"Scar!" I snap, clenching my jaw tight when she only squeezes her eyes tight and continues to push on Nina's chest.

How is this happening?

I take Nina's face in my hand, my chin quivering as I try to understand. "Angel, you can't leave me. You promised me forever." I drop my lips to her forehead, her body jolting beneath me. Tears line my face, dripping from my chin and onto her pale face. I gently swipe them away. "Don't be afraid, baby. You aren't alone, I'm here. I won't ever leave you."

Please don't leave me.

I look up, spotting a paramedic entering behind Lance, and I stand to rush them. "Help me, please!"

"We can take it from here," they tell Scarlet, but she doesn't move. Her lips are moving but nothing is coming out. She's completely checked out.

I move on autopilot and pull her away, even though my head tells me to let her carry on. She stands off to the side, looking down at where Nina bleeds.

I place my hands on the back of my head, praying to the gods that she will be okay. She has to be okay. She promised me.

"Sc-car-let."

"Stay fucking still!" Lance shouts at Joey from behind me.

"Put the gun down!" I hear the paramedic shout, forming a shield around Nina and getting low to the ground.

I turn to see Joey barrelling towards Scarlet with the knife still clenched to his chest. "Nina! Oh god, N-nina. I-I'm so sorry!" Joey shrieks.

I turn as Lance's voice shakes with warning. "Stop!"

"Sc-ar-l-let. I-I didn't mean to, I—"

My body jolts as the gun fires. I blink slowly, my heart thudding faster than any rhythm that's healthy as Joey's body crumbles to the ground with a sickening thump.

31

Mase

SIX HOURS. SIX AGONISING HOURS OF WAITING. NINA WASN'T breathing when we arrived at the hospital. What I witnessed in the ambulance isn't something I'll ever forget. The way the paramedics worked on her relentlessly shook me to my core. I'm surrounded by our families now, every one of them completely shattered as we sit in the waiting room.

Elliot drops down in the seat next to me, his hands running through his hair as he pulls at it. "I can't take much more of this," he mutters.

I don't answer him, not having the words to ease the pain that's embedded itself inside of me and probably him too. Lucy is lying with her eyes closed on the row of waiting chairs opposite us. She's been the calmest of us all, eerily so. It's almost like she isn't here, and I wonder as I sit watching her if there's a way to follow her to wherever she is right now.

Megan hasn't stopped crying since she arrived. She's sat

with Vinny who I can barely make eye contact with. Charlie's on his phone out in the hallway, already in work mode and prepared to fight for our best friend. I have no idea what Lance was thinking, and I don't have the mental energy to process his actions right now. Then there's Scarlet. She sits resting her head on her hand as she stares at the ground, her eyes wild and agitated.

"I'm going to go find someone," I snap, shrugging off Elliot's hand when he grabs my shoulder.

"Lowell, they're going to kick you out."

"I can't just sit here!" I take a deep breath, my chest tight.

Scarlet comes to stand at my side. She looks up at me with understanding in her eyes. "I'll go check with the nurses, see what I can find out."

"I'm coming with you," I tell her.

She nods, her face pale, drained of its usual spark.

We leave the waiting room and make our way to the nurse's station where they all gaze at us with pity-filled looks. "Mr Lowell, I'm sorry but there's still no news."

"Ah, actually." I spin around as I hear the deep voice at my back. A man in scrubs is exiting the elevator, his lips pulled tight into a hard line. "Are you Miss Anderson's next of kin?" he asks.

I shake my head, anger lacing my voice. "She's my fiancée, please, just tell me."

He clasps a hand on my shoulder and stares down at me, before nodding politely at Scarlet. "Hello." He starts to walk me down the corridor. "Let's talk somewhere a little more private, okay?"

I'm about ready to brawl, needing to know how and where Nina is, when Scarlet's hand takes mine. She squeezes tight but doesn't look up at me. Is it bad? Does she know?

We're led into a room with a horseshoe of seats and nothing else. It's like the waiting room we were ushered into by the nurses down the hall but smaller. None of us sit down. My entire body trembles, my stomach churning as it readies itself for what's about to come.

"Nina is stable—"

"Fuck," I hiss out, clearing my throat and covering my face as I drop back to the chair.

"She isn't completely out of the woods yet. She lost a lot of blood and will need to be monitored over the next forty-eight hours. We aren't sure yet as to the extent of the damage it will cause her long term, but, and it's not a but I give out often, she is extremely strong. I feel positive with the situation we are in at this point."

I stand. "I want to see her."

"You can't. Not yet," Scarlet tells me sadly.

The doctor watches Scarlet for a moment, then looks at me. "Nina's in recovery. She won't be able to have visitors until she wakes up. And then I'd like her to have at least an hour's rest before anyone but my team goes in."

"I'm not waiting that long." I shake my head. There's no way I can go that long.

"Right now, Mr Lowell—"

"It's Mason," I snap.

"My only concern is for Nina. Her recovery will be very dependent on the next twelve hours, and I will not, under any circumstances, put her at risk." He nods his head, an apology of sorts. "The minute I have more news, I will have them call down to you. You should get home and get some rest."

Lifting my hands, I scrub at my face, completely drained from the emotions that have left me half the man I was yesterday. How can things go so wrong?

"Thank you," Scarlet says, following him to the door and shutting it behind him. I watch her with my hands linked behind my head as she turns around. My eyes burn, and no matter how hard I try to stop the lump in my throat from breaking the dam, I can't. Everything blurs.

"We were so damn close, Scar."

"Mase." She comes to me, wrapping me in her arms.

"I can't do this without her."

"It's going to be okay," she soothes. "It's going to be okay."

We go back to the waiting room where Scarlet tells the others what the doctor said. "We should go home, get some rest and be ready for their call." Scarlet looks to me, knowing I won't leave. "Or at least take it in turns."

I shake my head and then go to stand at the window. It's as if everything is at a standstill. The world outside and everything inside of me. Nothing is right, and it's all I can think about. I just need everything to be okay.

"Mase, you're going to stay?"

I look down at Megan as she slides a hand around my bicep. She looks as ruined as I feel. "Yeah."

"I'm going to check in with Maggie and John, make sure Ellis is alright. Is there anything you need from home?"

My eyes burn at the mention of Ellis's name. Jesus, why can't I get a handle on my emotions. I rub at my eyes. "No, thank you, though." I want to tell her to give him a kiss from me, to tell him Mummy will be home soon, but I don't trust myself to voice it. I pull Megan into my side and tell her everything I can in my embrace, hoping she will go hold my son until his mummy can.

"She'll be okay, Mase. I can feel it in my bones."

I nod, squeezing her shoulder and catching Charlie's eye behind her. Charlie Aldridge has to be one of the strongest men I've ever met. He is sensitive, intuitive yet can stand here and take control; he doesn't have room for the emotions that I know will be killing him inside. Instead, he acts as a pillar holding up the dark that threatens to fall on us. Today would have been much different without him.

"I'll drive the girls back," he tells me, his voice strong. "Call me if anything changes."

"Yeah."

He pulls me into a hug and then guides Megan out of the room. Elliot is crouched down in front of Lucy who is still lying across the seats.

"I'm going to go home and shower," Scarlet tells me. She has Elliot's jumper thrown over her, but I know she has blood on her top beneath it. A mixture of Nina's and Joey's. "Unless you want me to stay?"

"No, you go Scar. Is Vinny driving you?"

"Yeah."

"Elliot," I call. He looks over his shoulder at me. "I've got her." I nod to Lucy.

He straightens, his eyes falling back to her. "I'm going to stay too. I'm going to get us some food. You guys need to eat."

I roll my lips and nod my head even though he doesn't see. I can't think about food. I can't imagine anything I eat staying in my stomach if I wanted to eat.

Vinny doesn't speak as he walks by me, and I know everything that's happened will be weighing heavy on him. He'll blame himself for not pinning down Sarah sooner, but I already know it's all on me. I never should have meddled.

I stand looking out the window as the room empties, quietness falling heavy when it's just me and Lucy left. She hasn't said more than a couple words since she turned up. I know her silence comes from a place of pain. She's hurting, needing something only her best friend can give her.

Like Elliot, I crouch down in front of her, waiting. I place a hand on the side of her face and her icy blue eyes drift open and land on mine. I give her a small smile, telling her I get it. *I feel the same.*

She lifts her neck from the seat and I slide in under her, letting her rest her head on my thigh.

"I've sat in so many waiting rooms impatient for the doctor to come back so he can tell us what's wrong with her." She sniggers under her breath, her tears seeping through my jeans. "Always ready to go get ice cream with Mum or have her come home to us for the weekend." I sit quiet as her voice struggles to fill the room. "She's the best person I know, Mason. How does this happen to someone so good? There are so many bad people in this world. Why her?"

"I don't have the answers. I wish I did, but I don't," I say in a pained daze, imagining Nina as a child.

"She would know. She always has the answers."

My head drops back to the wall, my eyes drifting closed.

Wake up, Angel.

"MASE."

I jolt awake, my eyes flicking open to find Elliot standing in front of me. A nurse is hovering at his side, smiling softly at me. I sit up in a rush, my neck jolting in pain from the unnatural way I'd been sitting. I remember Lucy on my lap and slow my movements, grasping her upper arm to steady myself.

"What is it?" I rush out. My heart is pounding. Adrenaline has my eyes flicking wildly between them.

"It's Nina." A grin stretches wide across his face. "She's awake."

"You said she was awake!" I whisper-shout at Elliot as we stand outside of Nina's hospital room. The doctor arrived at the same time we did and the nurse informed us all that Nina had gone back to sleep. They're in her room now, doing an assessment on her.

"She was! I spoke to her," Elliot says.

"What?" I snap. "What did she say?!"

"She told me I was beautiful," he tells me proudly, a smirk on his face.

"Fuck off!"

"Straight up. She said, 'You're so beautiful, Ell.' Then I ran to get you."

Fuck! I just need to see her. "Why won't they let me see her?!"

Lucy gives me a hopeful look. "It won't be long now. Try and stay calm."

"Never in the history of life has someone stayed calm after being told to stay calm, Lucy!"

The back of Elliot's hand meets my chest. "Don't speak to her like that."

Not being able to wait any longer, I walk to the door and push it open. I try to calm my movements, not wanting to rush into the room like the maniac I feel, but my entire body vibrates as I stand on the threshold.

All eyes in the room flick to me. *All* the eyes. But my gaze is stuck on the most perfect—captivating of them all. Nina is lying back in the bed, her head turned to the side as she looks towards me in the doorway.

She smiles.

She fucking smiles, and it's just about all my heart can take.

"Hey, Bossman," she whispers, her lips barely moving.

Raising my hand, I rub across the ache that threatens to crack my chest in two. She's okay. My shoulders drop, relief pouring out of me with every step I take towards her. I crouch at her bedside, my forehead dropping to hers. Tears fall from her eyes, but still, she smiles. It might not be the big dimple popping smile I crave on the daily, but to think no more than twelve hours ago she was sprawled on her apartment floor dying and now she is here, eyes open and fucking smiling at me.

"Jesus Christ, Angel."

Nina

MASON'S HAND is clutched in mine, his eyes locked tight. I search his face, not being able to take my eyes off him.

"Mase," I whisper, a tear sliding into the line of my mouth. I roll my lips, sniffling as he takes a sharp breath in. "Mase, look at me."

I remember when I first met my Mase. Leant against the top of his flashy car, staring up through that low brow at me—cocky smirk in place. His eyes were so clear and sure. A man who knew exactly what he wanted. Smoothing my finger over his dark, looming brow, I glide it down to skim his cheek and swipe a tear away from his jaw. His eyes aren't clear, nor sure. His eyes are sad, scared, and broken, and I want nothing more than for him to say something filthy and give me that cocky smile that I so desperately love.

"It's okay, baby. I'm okay," I promise him.

His mouth opens, another tear sliding down his face as he looks at me helplessly. It's as if he's afraid to speak in the fear that he will break. I can see him breaking.

"Can we have a minute?" I croak out, looking down at the nurse who is speaking with a doctor at the end of my bed. I wince when I get a stabbing pain in my side.

"You need to rest now, Nina. Just a few more minutes and then we are going to need you to leave, Mr Lowell. I'm sorry."

Mason's eyes are wild as he looks up at the doctor. Knelt at my bedside. He looks rabid and teetering on the edge of losing all control.

"He isn't going anywhere." I clench my teeth, the pain getting stronger by the second. "I don't want to be alone, and if you won't allow it, then I'm sure I can be taken somewhere that will take the both of us." I look at Mason, and he nods with a deep frown, confirming that it's possible. I sigh as I relax back down onto my pillow. "I'm in pain. Please, will you help me?" I roll my lips, tears leaking from the corners of my eyes. Mason is here. I'm okay.

"I can get you something for the pain," the doctor tells me softly. "You are going to be in a lot of pain over the next couple days, Nina, and you will need to make sure you're getting adequate rest. If you have any questions or concerns you should let the nurses or doctors know, okay?"

I nod, watching as the nurse comes closer and fiddles with the cannula in my hand.

"What happens now? You told me earlier that the next forty-eight hours are important," Mason asks, rising to his feet. He seems to have found his voice, slipping back into the unruffled man I know. "Will she need more surgery?"

The doctor finishes writing on the clipboard, then slides it into the slot at the end of my bed. "No. No more surgery. However, I'm very serious about the next forty-eight hours being critical. I will not hesitate to have you removed if I feel like Nina's recovery will be compromised with your presence. I understand emotions run high in situations like this, but while Nina is under my care her health becomes my responsibility and priority." He bows his head a little, trying to show that he means well with what he's saying. I see that. But I know the man at my side—who would tear down skyscrapers, and the cities that house them to keep me safe—is all but ready to clear the bed that separates them.

"Thank you," I rasp out, lacing my fingers through Mason's and pulling his hand to my side. He leans in and kisses my forehead.

It's not enough, though.

It will never be enough.

The nurse finishes then says, "This is a morphine drip. If

you find you're in pain, you can press this button and it will top you up. It won't allow you to overdo it so you can press it as and when needed. It's very normal to rely on it in the early days of your recovery, so don't be afraid to use it. It will make you sleepy, but that's very normal." She looks up and over to Mason, her cheeks fanning red as she smiles sheepishly. "I'll fetch you a recliner."

"Thank you," Mason tells her, dipping his head.

And then finally, we're alone. Mason rests himself on the edge of the bed, staring down at me deep in thought. "I thought I was going to die." I smile awkwardly, trying to stop my lip from trembling.

"Baby—"

"Did she come back? Did Mum come back?"

He shakes his head no as his eyes drift closed, and for a moment the pain in my side is gone, my heart instead exposed to the repercussions of my mother's actions once again.

"You sent her to rehab?" I ask, my eyes feeling heavier than they did a few moments ago.

"I only ever wanted you to have a family, Nina. Your mum. Jasmine. I thought if I could fix the things that led us here, then maybe we'd be okay. If I knew she'd—" His head bows, his voice cracking, and I screw my own face up in pain. "I'm so sorry."

His head drops to my chest, and I cradle him there. "Mason, this isn't your fault." I exhale a long breath, my arms getting heavy. "It's nobody's fault."

"I should've been there." His tear-smothered voice wavers as he gently smooths a hand over my side. I can feel myself starting to drift to sleep, but I try to fight it. "Scarlet. Is she okay?"

He nods.

"Ellis. Where's Ellis?" I lazily open my eyes.

"He's with Maggie and John."

I smile, starting to give in to the darkness. "And Joey?"

When he doesn't answer and I don't feel his head move against me, I frown, but I can't open my eyes.

"Mase?" I try to say.

My body is weightless, the pain gone.

"Mason?"

MY BODY TELLS me to wake up, but my eyes are unmoving. I can smell pancakes, I'm sure of it.

"It's syrup. Gotta be." I frown, Elliot's voice drifting into my semi-state of consciousness.

Open your eyes, Nina.

"Yeah, if you want your teeth to fall out! You need to try my pancakes. Game changer." Warmth spreads through me at the sound of Lucy's voice. It's the best feeling.

"You wanna feed me pancakes, princess?"

Everything goes quiet. Then there's the sound of creaking leather. Then silence. I frown, wondering what's going on.

"Tastes good, doesn't it?" Elliot's voice is full of want, the throaty sound making my own stomach flip.

Slowly, my eyelids start to flutter. The room is a blur as it comes into focus, and I'm surprised when I realise I am partially sat up. I squint, trying to clear my vision. Lucy is standing in the corner, her back rested against the window. Elliot is standing in front of her.

I feel like a third wheel. "Hi," I croak out, and my throat burns as I swallow.

Lucy flinches, rushing out from behind Elliot. "Nina! Oh my god, finally!" She drops her head to my shoulder, hugging me gently. "How are you feeling?"

For a minute I consider lying, but I know she'll see right through it. "Crappy."

Elliot hands me a cup of water. "Here."

"Thank you," I tell him, giving him a small smile.

"I'm going to get Mase," he tells us, quickly leaving the room.

The hour that follows turns out to be more manic than I expect, and I'm surprised when I manage to stay awake for it. Lucy and Elliot left and then Megan and Charlie slipped in. Then George arrived with flowers from himself, his boyfriend, Liam, and Jasmine. As the time passes on, I can see Mason getting more and more agitated, and see him watching me, his face hardening at my every wince.

It's as the room clears and he turns to me, ready to have some alone time together when my eyes fall heavy.

"Mase."

"Shh," he tells me, climbing onto the bed and resting my head on his chest. "Sleep. I'll be here when you wake up, Angel."

Mase

Three days later

Something soft tickles my brow.

I frown, then open my eyes and am instantly captured in beautiful brown ones.

"Hey, Bossman," she whispers softly.

Nina is lying on her good side, her body mirroring mine in the small bed. She has one hand curled under her head, while the other smooths over my forehead. I waste no time, leaning in and taking her lips in a deep kiss.

"Are you in pain?" I ask.

She gazes at me, looking content. "A bit." She sighs. "I just want a little longer before I fall asleep again."

I press the button that lies between us to give her more morphine.

"I have no idea what time it is." I stretch over her to pick up my phone on the hospital tray. "Are you hungry?"

"I want to get married." My brows pop in surprise and I drop back an inch to look at her. "The minute I'm allowed to leave and it's safe for me to do it. I want you to be my husband." Her eyes are wide and glossy, focused, as if she has been thinking about it for hours.

"There's nothing I want more, Angel." I kiss her, careful not to be too rough with her.

"You can plan it, else it will be small and crappy." She smiles. "The girls will help you."

I rest back on the pillow, bringing us nose to nose. "Why the rush?"

She shakes her head as if it's obvious. "I'm not wasting another second, Mase. If this year has taught me anything, it's that you have to live. I don't want to look back with regrets because I waited for things to be right. What we have is far from perfect, but it's completely perfect for me. Please."

I take her face in my hands, gliding my thumbs over her cheekbones as I gaze into her eyes. "Baby, you don't need to beg me for this."

"No?" She frowns up at me, and I see a hint of a smile trace the corner of her mouth. "You don't like it?" She gently palms my growing, insanely inappropriate erection through my sweats. I squeeze my eyes shut.

"Nina."

"What? Did you think I wouldn't notice?"

"Not now."

"When then?" She smiles, her dimple popping.

"Don't give me that smile," I snap, shaking my head no.

"When, Bossman?"

"When you're home."

She slips her hand inside, her warm palm wrapping around my now hard length. "It's only been four days, but I'd give anything to taste you right now."

Shit.

Block her out.

She works me up and down, her hand pumping me in a perfect rhythm.

I should stop her. She shouldn't be doing this in her condition.

She continues to lazily pump me. One, two, three. "God, that's good," I huff out.

My balls start to draw up. Her warm breath fans my face. I push my hips up, needing her to grasp me tighter. "Nina," I groan.

My cock slaps me in the stomach, and I look down to find her eyes closed.

I still then gently nudge her shoulder. "Nina?"

Nothing.

"Fuck. Off." I groan again.

She's asleep?

Fucking shitting morphine!

32

Nina

Twelve weeks later.

BENDING AT THE KNEE, I WATCH THE TEAR THAT FALLS FROM MY eye, as it seeps down into the rain-soaked grass. So many people in this world don't deserve the lives they live, yet good people can have their lives cut short in a single second. The only crime Joey Wilson ever committed was caring for me and my son, and just as he started to let me go, his life was ended.

I haven't told Mason about Lance and what he did. And I won't. Not now and not ever. Mason has been hurt more than any of us, and if I can hold on to some of the pain myself, carry it for him so that it doesn't take him down again, I will let it fester within me for an eternity. What's worse than knowing I have to keep something from him, though, is we now have to watch as Scarlet tends to a broken heart as Lance faces sentencing. I lie awake every night hoping he gets the time he deserves for taking an innocent life, yet my tears fall in hope that he can come home and make everything right for her.

Setting down the garland of flowers I had made, I place my pale hand on top. "I hope you're okay, Joe." My voice wavers as more tears start to fall. "I miss you. I miss our runs —although I'm still not allowed to do that. I miss you always knowing where Ellis's dummy is when I can't find it." I laugh, pursing my lips. "I miss having you to talk to about every-thing and nothing. I want to hear about the picture you're working on and the random facts you'd tell me about some hotshot photographer I've never heard of. I want to chew your ear off whilst you pretend to listen to me." I inhale a lungful of air. "I'm sorry this happened to you, Joey. You didn't deserve it." I run my hand through the damp soil, swal-lowing thickly as I fight to gather my words. "I hope you're at peace. With your mum and Jasper." I bow my head, feeling so much remorse and regret over how everything unfolded. "Thank you. Thank you so much for being there when I needed you. It wasn't long enough but I won't ever forget it, or you."

Vinny steps forward as I rise to my feet, grasping my elbow as I step back from the grave. I wasn't able to go to Joey's funeral, but the girls, Mason and the boys all went, which I'm grateful for. I've been home from hospital for four weeks, and it wasn't until Mason told me we were going away this morning that I knew I had to come out here. I'd been putting it off, but I couldn't leave the country before I did this.

"I'm okay, Vin," I tell him, pulling my arm away and smiling up at him. He holds out the umbrella and I step under it.

"You ready, love?"

I nod my head with a smile, walking with him back to the car. "Where are we going?"

"You can ask me as many times as you want. I'm not going to tell you."

I slide into the car and strap myself in, looking at Vinny when he gets into the driver's seat. "Where did everyone go this morning?"

"They're exactly where they need to be."

My eyes follow the graveyard until it's out of sight, and I smile to myself as I stare out the window at the rolling hills. Joey would love it here.

"I'm not stupid, Vinny," I say, righting myself in my seat. "Mason was more than obvious last night—"

"Whoa! I don't want to know, thank you."

I chuckle. "I didn't mean..." I shake my head. "He brought me flowers, told me he couldn't see me and that he had to go sleep in the spare room."

His eyebrows lift in surprise. "He did?"

"Yep." I grin, excitement swirling low in my stomach. "I'm nervous, Vinny. I'm the sort to fall flat on my face."

"Mason won't let that happen." He looks over at me. "I won't let that happen."

I swallow, trying not to get emotional again. "I know I told you back along that I wanted to meet my dad. I asked you for the information you had." I roll my lips, watching him thoughtfully. "I don't want it anymore. I don't want to know him."

He flicks his eyes over at me before looking back to the road.

"I don't have a good enough reason, but I know that he

isn't a man I want nor need in my life. He hasn't been here when it mattered, so why let him be here now?"

"I can understand that." He nods.

"Will you tell me about him, though?"

I watch as he tightens his grip on the steering wheel. "What do you want to know?"

"Is he a good man?" I ask, simply.

He hesitates for a second too long, telling me exactly what I thought I already knew. "Yes, he's a good man," he tells me.

"Okay." I turn and look back out the window with a small smile. "I still don't want to know him."

I drop the conversation and pull out my phone, allowing Vinny a moment to process the lie he's told me. And it only makes me love him all the more for it.

It's late evening when we arrive in Paris. It was just me and Vinny on the flight, and I feel like my feet haven't hit the ground from the moment we stepped off the plane. Everything from my hair to my makeup and dress is perfect. All picked and left in my room, courtesy of my beautiful fiancé.

The girls were waiting for me at the hotel and whisked me away the minute I arrived.

And now, I stand at the side of the steps in a building I could only dream about being in again. My hand reaches blindly as I try to find something to steady me, my nerves completely shot. I grip the cool marble under my fingertips and take in a deep breath.

Breathe, Nina.

I glance up and catch Vinny's eye, a wide smile taking

over my face as I watch him across the two staircases. He dips his head in silent encouragement.

Stepping out from behind the pillar, I take the eighteen steps to the middle of the Grand Escalier, where Vinny meets me. Pushing up onto the tip of my toes, I kiss his warm cheek.

"You look breathtaking, love."

My dimples ache from the smile that dances across my face. "Thanks, Vin."

There hasn't ever been a lot of thought when it came to the man who would give me away. Lucy told me that John would be honoured to walk me down the aisle, but I knew that was something for them to do one day. I couldn't take that away from her. I may not have known Vinny my whole life, but his eyes shone with the same pride that he's wearing now when I asked him to give me away, and I know in this moment, right here, that I made the right decision.

It takes me back to something Mason once told me.

If you ever need to trust a man, you'd be wise to pick him.

We turn and link arms, and I instantly lock eyes with my Mase. He's standing at the bottom of the sprawling steps, looking up at me. His tux is immaculate, his hair styled in my kind of messy perfection.

We take the first step, the etched marble tapping under my strappy heels.

The string quartet starts to play, the sound reaching the very top of the magnificent vaulted ceiling, then drifting back down to wrap around me in a warm veil. It calms me. I'm not sure I've ever felt so sure of my next step.

I dip my head to the side when I spot Charlie, Ellis, George, Liam, and Jasmine standing at the right of the staircase. Jasmine beams at me, then reaches up to blot the corners of her eyes with a tissue. I have to look away, blinking rapidly to stop myself from slipping a tear. Our families are all here, spread out at the bottom of the steps, smiling happily up at me, and although so many people are missing from the image before me, I feel them. I know they're watching us today, and there's no doubt in my mind that they're proud of the man who awaits me.

Mason takes my hand as I reach the bottom step, linking our fingers and then nodding his head once to Vinny. His eyes shine with so much emotion, I struggle to look away from his beautiful face. Lucy steps up and takes my bouquet, and I catch Megan's eye as she gives me a cheeky wink. I smile and wait for Scarlet to look up. She looks beautifully broken, standing off to the side, yet as she lifts her head and returns my smile, her tears rolling free, I know she's truly happy for us. And I know that I'd be lost without my beautiful girls.

In the very opera house Mason told me he loved me, we stand again today, to take our vows. Devoting our entire lives to one another with our words and rings. I never would've picked it, yet there's no better way to become Mrs Lowell, and I'm floored and in awe of the man at my side for the sheer level of love and devotion he shows me time and time again.

He takes my hand in his as the vicar steps towards us.

Elliot clears his throat, leaning in to whisper in Mason's ear. "Who gets married on a fucking Tuesday?"

Mason looks at me and it's the dirtiest, most soul destroying, yet beautiful look I've ever seen.

My favourite kind of look.

My Mase. Today. Tomorrow. Forever.

EPILOGUE

Nina

Two years later.

I WALK DOWN THE CORRIDOR, FOLLOWING THE NURSE AS SHE leads me into the hospital room.

My mother was admitted late last night and I had the phone call in the early hours of this morning to say she'd been taken unwell at the prison and was in accident and emergency. I rolled my eyes at the time. We'd just started to find our new normal at the house, and I really didn't want her bringing back everything we vowed to leave behind us.

And then the lady on the phone told me she was on life support. My world all but stood still, although I had Mason at my side to keep me moving.

I don't know why my mother ran, or why she left me dying on the ground. But I know that I made a promise to myself years ago that I would be with her when the time came.

And I will be.

My stubborn husband didn't support my decision, refusing to come with me, and I respect him for it. He won't ever forgive her for what she did to me.

Stepping into the room, the nurse places a hand on my back. "Take your time, and if you need anything you just ask, okay?"

"Thank you," I tell her.

She leaves the room, shutting the door gently on her way out. I walk attentively to my mother's bedside and look down at her, my eyes spaced and fixed on her rising chest.

I stand in silence for the longest time, just watching her.

"You once told me that I needed you more than you needed me." I lower to the chair, letting my gaze move up to her gaunt face. She's barely the woman I once knew. "I never believed you. You would've let me go all those times social services got involved if that was the case. You wanted me to stay. You fought for me—lied to keep me." I run my tongue over my teeth. "I don't know what happened to make you the way that you are, Mum, but what I do know is that nobody is born bad. I'm sorry that life wasn't always fair to you, and I'm sorry I don't have more forgiveness, that I don't feel the things I probably should right now." I swallow, rolling my lips as I take another breath in, hoping it gives me the strength I need. "But I won't leave you like you left me, because that's not who I am." I quickly grasp her hand in mine before I can change my mind. "I'm not you."

I will never be you.

A little while later, I call for the nurse and ask her to turn off the life support machine. My mother drifts away, *peace-*

fully, moments later and I allow the pain that wracks through me to hit.

Then I leave.

We're taught from such a young age to deal with pain. From the griping pain in our stomachs as babies to dusting off our knees as toddlers. Growing up, I ran whenever life got hard. I never dealt with the hurt.

Over time, I've learnt to let the pain in. Because the quicker I let it hit, the quicker it fades.

Pain is a part of life. We will grow with our pain. So, we have to let it in. Let it bring the darkness and fear, and then when it's too tired to live within us anymore, let it go— quietly. Refuse to give it the voice it wants by enabling it to stay with us for longer than it deserves. Because when we do let it go, coming up from the pits of darkness to find the bad not really as bad as we first thought, we realise that all the pain wasn't actually pain, it was a lesson that needed to be lived, so that we can move on and be better in the now.

THE HOUSE IS empty when I arrive home, but it doesn't take me long to find them. I look out from the terrace, smiling at the small figures I see out on the hilltop. Being in the condition I'm in, I round the house and go to the garage, sliding into Anthony's golf buggy with a wide grin on my face.

I don't spoil the flowers like he did, choosing to slowly walk my way through the meadow once I reach the gates. Ellis runs to me as I approach, and I scoop him up and place him on my hip. He's almost three now and growing into a mini-Mason by the day. "Mummy is home!"

"Hey, Ellis baby."

"I not a baby. I a big boy."

Mason pulls me by the waist and into him, placing a long deep kiss on my lips. "Hello, my beautiful wife."

"Hi."

He squints his eyes at me, asking me if I'm okay without saying the words.

I nod, looking down as his hand sprawls out across my growing stomach. A sharp kick has it jolting, and Mason's eyes shoot wide at the same time I ask, "Did you feel that?!"

"Fuck yes!"

"Daddy!" Ellis scolds.

"Ellis, give me your hand a second." Mason takes his hand when he holds it up and then places it on my bump. He watches Ellis's serious face until I get another kick and it transforms into one of pure glee.

"I felt it!" He shakes his hand out as he rips it away, pulling his shoulders up to his ears in excitement.

"Incredible," Mason whispers, leaning in and kissing me again, lingering longer and drawing my lips even deeper this time. His hands slide over my stomach again which has Ellis making a disgusted sound as he turns and runs off towards the lake where Scarlet is swaying back and forth on the restored rope swing.

I break the kiss, squinting up at him as a ray of light beams down, catching the sides of our faces. "The sun's shining," he says, looking out on the grand estate.

I wrap my arms around his back, nestling into his chest as I look down on our family. Our home. Our future.

"The sun's shining, Bossman." I smile.

I said it would.

THE END

ALSO BY JC HAWKE

THE GRAND PACT

Elliot & Lucy's story

We all have a dream.
But I think I preferred holding mine at arm's length...
It's not that I don't want to go to New York.
It's that it's *all* I've ever wanted.
So when a dream internship lands in my lap, the last thing I
should be doing is hesitating.
Elliot thinks I should take it — he's always believed in me.
Smirking, smouldering Elliot Montgomery.
Playboy-about-town.
Notorious womaniser.
And...dearest friend?
It was Elliot's arms I'd innocently fallen asleep between on
lonely nights.
And those same arms that promised all kinds of unspeakable
things when I found myself writhing between them...

But even as he threw me out of my comfort zone, Elliot promised me something *immeasurable*.

So now I'm here, living my fashion design dreams in the trustiest outfit I own — indecision. But the longer I stay in New York, the further I feel myself drift from everything I thought I wanted.

And somehow, absence is making the heat grow stronger...

If Elliot Montgomery is no Prince Charming, why does he feel like happily ever after?

Available at Amazon.

AFTERWORD

Thank you so much for reading.
If you enjoyed Grand Love, please consider leaving a review on Amazon!

Want to be notified about future book releases of mine?
Sign up to my Newsletter via my website
www.jchawkeauthor.com

Come join my Facebook reader group for a first look at sneak peeks and teasers. This is a PRIVATE group and only people in the group can see posts and comments!
Hawkes Hangout - JC Hawke's Reader Group

ACKNOWLEDGMENTS

To my betas, D, Jo, Lindsay, Annie, Lauren & Jessica. Thank you for everything!! From the good to the bad you've all been here for it. We got there in the end, though, and Nina and Mase are all the more perfect because of you all.

To Laura, for being my 'maps'. God you must be fed up with me by now. Haha! Thank you for always being so giving with your knowledge. This book makes sense because of you, and that's pretty cool. You're wonderful.

To The Fourway, there is nothing, NOTHING, more exciting than working along side you all, watching our growth daily and hitting our milestones. My co-workers, confidents, friends. How fortunate we are to have found one another. I'll love you till the death!

To my sisters, Gem, Rach, and Dani. I suppose I should thank you for putting up with me above all else. You may not always get around to reading every sentence I write, but you should know you inspire me everyday. How to write a kick ass best friend like Lucy and Megan. How to write a beautiful, hard working mother like Nina. And, above all, how to love unconditionally as a sister like Scarlet. I don't base my characters off of anyone, but they definitely wouldn't be who they are without you. I love you always.

To Mum and Dad, thank you for all you've done. I could write a novel on all the ways you've enabled me to do this (and life). You're the most incredibly supportive, loving, slightly cool, inspiring parents I could ask for. There's so much I want in life, but if I can ask for anything it would be to one day find myself as content and happy as the two of you. I love you.

To Shelley, thank you for always being right there. Whatever the time, question (even the weird shit I ask), or need you always show up. I know without doubt you will be on this ride with me for life, because that's what we do. I love you.

To my Jessica Jones, *I've said it once and I'll say it again. If I never sell a single copy of this book, it would be okay. Why? Because I met you.* Dude, I sold copies and got to keep you. LOL. What a year. Firstly, the time you spend working with me and my words, asking questions that make me better and bring me growth, and laughing with me over stupid typos, words, sentences—it's selfless, and comes from your love of not only my beautiful Nina and Mase, but your love for me. My girl, you have so much love in your heart—so much soul. I adore every part of you. I cannot wait to see where life takes us next.

To Chalk, thank you for loving me. You don't read my books and that's okay. I mean, when would you find the time. We work four jobs between us now. FOUR! Babe, you work so hard, and I couldn't ask for a more supportive team mate. We have so much to look forward to. So much planned! I ask one thing from you... It's not to read a book of mine (calm down). It's to always love me. In the little free time you do get, love me. That's all I'll ever ask.

To my girls, stay wild. I love you.

And of course, YOU, my reader. Thank you for reading Nina and Mase's conclusion. It means the world to me that you've picked my books up out of millions of others. You make this possible for me and I am forever indebted to you.

Stay wonderful xo

ABOUT THE AUTHOR

JC Hawke is an author of contemporary romance. She lives in the South-West of the United Kingdom with her husband, two curly haired daughters, and beagle woofer.

Printed in Great Britain
by Amazon